THE
CURVE OF THE
EARTH

SIMON MORDEN

orbit

www.orbitbooks.net

Orbit
Hachette Book Group
237 Park Avenue, New York, NY 10017
HachetteBookGroup.com

First U.S. Edition: March 2013

Orbit is an imprint of Hachette Book Group, Inc. The Orbit name and logo are trademarks of Little, Brown Book Group Limited.

The Hachette Speakers Bureau provides a wide range of authors for speaking events. To find out more, go to www.hachettespeakersbureau.com or call (866) 376-6591.

The publisher is not responsible for websites (or their content) that are not owned by the publisher.

Library of Congress Control Number: 2012951501
ISBN: 978-0-316-22006-4
10 9 8 7 6 5 4 3 2 1

RRD-C

Printed in the United States of America

To Chaz and Karen

Happy anniversary

I

Petrovitch wanted to be alone, to worry and to brood, but he was part of the Freezone collective and that meant never having to be alone again. Company was built in, through the links they wore. Except for him. He didn't wear a link: he was so connected that, at times, it felt like it wore him.

So he'd taken himself off so he could pretend – not far, just to the top of the hill which overlooked the collection of different-sized domes below. The narrow strip of land before the sea looked like a collection of luminous pearls cradled in the darkness of a winter night.

He'd reached the summit, as determined by at least four satellites spinning overhead, and sat down on the wet, flowing grass to wait. He faced the ocean and felt the first tug of an Atlantic gale stiffen the cloak he'd thrown around him.

[Sasha?]

"*Yobany stos.*" He'd been there for what? A minute? Less. "When there's news, *vrubatsa*? Otherwise *past' zabej.*"

SIMON MORDEN

He hunched over and stared at the horizon. The last vestiges of twilight were fading into the south-west, but the moon was almost full behind the racing clouds. Enough light for him to see by, at least, even if the climb up would have been crazy for anyone else.

Somewhere over there, over the curve of the Earth, was his daughter, his Lucy, and she had been out of contact for fifty-eight hours and forty-five minutes.

These things happened. Once in a while, the link technology they all carried failed. It meant a break in what kept each individual bound together with the rest of the collective, and a quick trip to the stores for a replacement.

White plastic pressed against bare flesh. A connection restored, and the collective was complete once more.

Lucy was beyond the reach of any Freezone storeroom. She was on the other side of the world, and even he couldn't just pop over and present her with another link. There were difficulties and complications, not entirely of his own making.

The clock in the corner of his vision ticked on, counting the seconds. Relying on other people still didn't sit easily with him, though he'd had a decade to get used to the idea. Relying on the Americans and their ultra-conservative, hyper-patriotic, quasi-fascistic, crypto-theocratic Reconstructionist government?

His heart spun faster just thinking about it. They had a joint past, one that barely rose above mutual loathing, and he was certain there was something they weren't telling him. There'd been – a what? At this distance it was difficult to tell. The Freezone had only just started the laborious process of gathering the raw data and trying to fashion meaning from it.

He pulled his cloak tighter around him, not for warmth but for comfort.

2

[Sasha?]

There was a figure standing next to him, dark-clothed, white-faced. It hadn't been there a moment before, and it wasn't really there now. It stared west with the same troubled hope that Petrovitch had.

[There's,] and the voice hesitated. It hardly ever hesitated. The only times it ever hesitated were when it was dealing with meat-stuff. Important meat-stuff.

"What?"

[There's been a development.]

"Tell me."

[There is no sign of Lucy.]

"Yeah. That figures." Petrovitch clenched his jaw and bared his teeth. "Where the *huy* is she?"

[The search-and-rescue team's initial findings do not indicate the actions of any outside agency.]

"They wouldn't, would they? I knew it. I knew it was a mistake to let her go. I should have—"

[Forbidden it?] said Michael, looking down on Petrovitch. [She is twenty-four years old and an autonomous citizen of the Freezone.]

"She's still my responsibility."

[Not by law or custom. Need I remind you what you were doing when you were twenty-four? Or when you were eighteen?]

Petrovitch fumed. "It's not the same."

[Sasha, we will find her.]

"Of course we will. Tell me what they're saying."

[That at eleven fifteen local time, a search-and-rescue team comprising USAF, Alaskan police and University of Alaska personnel, flying out of Eielson Air Force Base, conducted a preliminary search of the University of Alaska Fairbanks North Slope research station. The single known occupant of that research station, Dr Lucy Petrovitch, was not located despite a thorough search of all the solid structures. There was nothing to indicate that she had either left the station on an expedition, or been forced to leave against her will. A search of the immediate area has commenced, though it will be necessarily limited in scope.]

"What the *huy* does that mean?"

[It means they have four hours of daylight in any twenty-four-hour period, and the air force transport must return to base. An overland expedition is being arranged. They estimate it will arrive in a week,] and Michael paused again. [Which seems unnecessarily delayed. I will attempt to ascertain a reason for this.]

Petrovitch felt impotent rage rise like a spring tide. His skin pricked with sweat.

[Talk to me, Sasha,] said Michael. [Tell me what you're thinking.]

Lucy's link was standard Freezone issue. Satellite enabled, always on, not just reliable, but dependable: powered by the heat from her body.

"They don't go wrong. They just don't." He looked up at Michael's avatar, framed against the silver-lined clouds. "She took a spare. I made her, because I'm a good father. And neither of them are working."

To prove the point, he pinged her machine – both of them. He got nothing, and there was so rarely nothing.

"Something's happened. I want to know what. I want to know now."

[How many of our protocols are we going to break this time?]

asked Michael. "As a point of reference? More than the Baku incident?"

[More than Beirut. We're going to break them all if we have to. Assemble an ad-hoc. They can decide.]

Michael polled the Freezone collective and selected five names with the required expertise and wisdom. There was no need to wait for them to assemble, exchange pleasantries, enquire about the kids; that wasn't what an ad-hoc was about. He'd been in enough to know the score.

There were preliminaries, though: for the record.

[Welcome, Freezone ad-hoc committee number four thousand seven hundred and ninety-two, convened on February fifth, twenty thirty-four, at twenty forty-eight Universal Time to discuss the preliminary response of the Freezone to the disappearance of Lucy Petrovitch. Please state your names.]

The five people could be anywhere on the planet. They could be in the mother dome in Cork, or planting electric trees in the Sahara. It didn't matter.

"Mohammed al-Ghazi."

"Stephan Moltzman."

"Jessica Levantine."

"Gracious Mendelane."

"Tabletop."

Petrovitch blinked. "Hey," he said.

"Hey, Sam."

She shouldn't have been on the ad-hoc. Though she was one of the few North Americans they had, it was a veritable United Nations as it was. The point being, it was personal for her. She was Lucy's big sister in all but name. She wasn't going to even pretend to be impartial.

He used a backchannel to talk to Michael. "Are you sure about this?"

[You don't get to question the make-up of the ad-hoc, Sasha. That's one protocol you don't get to break.]

That was him told.

Addressing the committee, Michael gave them bald facts: shortly after midnight, three days ago, Lucy Petrovitch lost contact with the Freezone. That she had been conducting research on Alaska's frozen, dark North Slope was a complicating factor, but not the primary concern.

The point was, she'd vanished. And no one seemed to be in any particular rush to find her.

[We need to decide what assets we dedicate to the search, and how they are best deployed.]

Human minds worked differently to Michael's. There was a long gap before anyone spoke.

"I would say, we do everything, despite the Americans," said Mendelane, "but it cannot be denied that we require – at the very least – the co-operation of the relevant authorities. We must tread carefully."

"She is one of us," said al-Ghazi. Where he was, he could see the same sky as Petrovitch, the same Moon illuminating the tops of the electric trees as they cooled and clicked in the Saharan night. "There is no question of us doing nothing. Would they permit Freezone personnel in Alaska? Or our proxies?"

[I will pass on a request to the US State Department,] said Michael. [You must decide whether we ask, or whether we insist. And if we insist, how forcefully we put our demands.]

"I would be cautious," said Mendelane.

"I wouldn't," said Tabletop. "I'd threaten them with every-thing we can, and if that's not enough, we make shit up until they give in. Look, Lucy's not the sort of kid – not the sort of woman – to go wandering into the night in her slippers and dressing gown, especially when that night lasts for twenty-plus hours and it's fifteen below. If they're not interested in looking for her, we'll do it instead. We could have a team on the ground by tomorrow morning."

"The university said it would take them a week," said Moltzman. Petrovitch didn't know him personally, just his reputation score, which was a respectable eighty-something. "Why would they say that if, firstly, a military search-and-rescue could be deployed in hours, and secondly, they know we could do it faster, with most of our people half a world away?"

[That is a good question,] noted Michael, and Moltzman's pregnant rep birthed another point. [I can suggest some possible answers, but assigning probabilities to them will take time if I am to be accurate.]

"It's because she's a Petrovitch," said Tabletop. "This whole thing was a set-up from start to finish: the original invitation, which she should have refused, the fact that she was alone, in winter, in the dark, in an isolated location. I said she shouldn't go."

[An ad-hoc said she should accept.]

"They were wrong!"

[Samuil Petrovitch was on that ad-hoc,] Michael reminded her, reminded them all. [He agreed with the decision made then.]

"That's come back to bite him on the arse, hasn't it?" She lapsed into sullen silence, and the dead air that followed stretched uncomfortably.

There was another protocol surrounding the ad-hocs, that the petitioner wasn't supposed to speak on their own initiative: they could answer questions, clarify positions, discuss motivations. But not be an advocate, and certainly not grandstand. The committee members weren't a jury, and an ad-hoc wasn't a court.

Petrovitch held his nerve, and his tongue.

[It may have been that the ad-hoc was not in possession of all necessary information, although I did my best at the time.] Having slapped him down once, Michael was now taking responsibility for Petrovitch's piss-poor judgement. [That also may be the case here: however, this is the way we decided we would conduct our decision-making, and if you do not come to a consensus, I will dismiss you and convene another ad-hoc.]

"No," said al-Ghazi quickly. "We will decide." He had no way of knowing if he was in the first ad-hoc or the tenth: the Berber tribesman had embraced the nature of the Freezone's ad-hocracy with all the fervour of a convert, and he'd been called on to play his part.

[We have not heard from one of the committee. If you please, Mrs Levantine.]

"Well now," she said, and Petrovitch imagined her leaning back in her chair, knitting needles maintaining a steady click-clack rhythm. She didn't knit out of utility, but out of respect for the craft. "Lucy's the age of my eldest granddaughter, and I know she hasn't got her birth mother or father to worry about her, but she has Sam and Madeleine, and all of us instead. She never struck me as a silly girl: a little too serious for her own good, if you ask me, so I agree with Tabletop. She wouldn't walk out of a safe place for any reason except a very good reason. So either someone took her, or she was persuaded – by someone else or her own mind."

"You think she is still alive," said Mendelane, "despite what an extended break in linking usually means?"

"Oh, for certain. No one would take the trouble of going all that way just to, you know, hurt her."

"Will whoever has her look after her? Until we find her?"

"Well now," she said again. "We can hope, can't we?"

Moltzman cleared his throat. "So, what do we need to do? Demand in the strongest possible terms that the authorities treat her disappearance as a crime, not as accidental or negligent. That they put all reasonable effort into finding her . . ."

"Strike 'reasonable'," said Tabletop. "They need to prove to us they're doing everything they can. Missing persons is an FBI thing: we want nothing less than someone on the ground, up on the North Slope, directing local assets."

"One of us or one of them?" asked Moltzman.

"Both," said Tabletop emphatically. "We watch over their shoulder so we know it's being done right."

[Does everyone agree to this course of action?] Michael tabulated the votes, and reported back the result. [The committee is unanimous. The question remains, who do we send?]

"I will go," offered al-Ghazi. "I would be honoured to accept the duty."

Honoured he might be, but the Americans would eat him alive. Petrovitch jumped in, almost without thinking. That was a lie: he'd done nothing but think since Lucy had gone offline. When the moment presented itself, he was ready.

"No. That's my job," he said.

Tabletop was instantly furious. "Sam: they've got one Petrovitch already. We're not giving them another."

"Who else, then? You?"

"You know I can't . . . anybody. Anyone else but you."

"Fine. Name someone better equipped to survive Reconstruction America. Someone who'll get Lucy, and bring her home."

"This isn't meant to happen, Sam. You're not supposed to get involved again."

"Yeah, well. I am involved." A muscle in Petrovitch's face twitched, and he started to notice the cold and the wind again. "I suppose I'd better tell Maddy."

It was just him and Michael again, on the hillside, with the domes below and the sky above.

[Good luck with that,] said Michael.

"Yeah." Petrovitch scrubbed at his face and thought about getting up. "Probably best done in person. Difficult to land a punch over a link."

Michael's avatar patted him on the shoulder. Petrovitch could feel the reassuring pressure, despite it all happening somewhere on a virtual interface buried deep in his brain.

"You'd better fuck off now. Certain you've got better things to do than nursemaid me."

[You know where I am . . .] The avatar vanished, and Petrovitch levered himself up.

"You're everywhere," he said, and started back to the sea.

2

It was almost like old times. The four of them, kicking their heels and waiting for something to happen.

Petrovitch paced, cursing both the vagaries of international travel and international diplomacy. First to his left, then his right, were the arrival gates and all the paraphernalia of arriving: scanners, customs, officials in suits and paycops in armour.

Madeleine and Valentina sat at opposite ends of a row of seats: Madeleine dwarfed her chair, made it seem fragile and childlike, while Valentina was very still, upright, self-contained.

Tabletop leaned against a pillar, obscuring the moving advertising on the screen behind her. Every so often, a pair of pixelated eyes would pop up behind her shoulder, widen, then duck down again. She hadn't noticed – like Petrovitch, she was fixated on the gate.

There was a rush of people. Many of them managed to look both tired and bewildered, still adjusting their bags and pockets after the formalities of entry into the Metrozone. Some looked up, searching for the holographic signs that would tell them where to go, then drifted away. Others were met, by friends and family, and there was a moment of awkwardly public reunion that was joyous and constrained in equal measure.

Then there was Newcomen and his handler Auden, at the very end of the tail. The ever-urbane Auden had one hand at his countryman's back, his dark infoshades and black tie making him a conscious parody of what he really was: not a consular staffer as advertised, but a National Security Agency spook.

Newcomen appeared singularly discomfited. He was dragging a huge suitcase on wheels – no, worse than that, the suitcase was motorised and it was following him like a dog on a lead. He looked grey, something of an achievement for someone with his corn-fed complexion, and his G-man buzz cut had gone spiky with nervous sweat.

Petrovitch stopped his pacing, and scowled. Behind him, Madeleine and Valentina simultaneously stood. It took Madeleine much longer to reach her full height, and he could see Newcomen's eyebrows crawl up his forehead.

The two Americans stopped in front of him, and Auden deliberately pushed the other man forward into the space between them.

"Dr Petrovitch, can I introduce Agent Joseph Newcomen of the FBI?"

Petrovitch did a thing that meant that Auden had to take his abruptly opaque glasses off, revealing a pair of unnaturally deep blue eyes. They narrowed at the affront.

"I can hack your contacts too, if you like. Destroyed any good cities lately?"

"So hostile, Doctor. You really shouldn't throw accusations like that around, in public, without any evidence." He flicked his now-useless shades into a nearby bin. "I'm actually here to help."

"As opposed to what? Lead an assassination squad into the Metrozone on the back of an Outzone invasion?" Petrovitch's own eyes whirred and clicked, cycling through ultraviolet and near infrared. Auden was actually blushing. "Tabletop says you were in charge. More than good enough for me."

Auden leaned slightly to one side to catch sight of Tabletop's pink hair and cat eyes. He brought his fingers to his temple in the mockery of a salute. "Now, where were we?"

"You were attempting to introduce me to this . . ." Petrovitch glanced up momentarily at Newcomen, "this vat-bred Reconstructionista as an escort, which is nothing but a distraction to the main cause. Helping would imply doing something, instead of this. Where is she? Where's Lucy?"

Newcomen cleared his throat. "Uh, Doctor . . ."

"*Past' zabej!* I don't want to hear from you until I'm ready. Come on, Auden. You've a much better idea what's happened to her: what d'you say to taking a little walk with me? Somewhere no one's looking." Petrovitch stared pointedly at the other consulate staff dotted around the concourse, trying to remain incognito but with flashing augmented-reality arrows pasted over their heads, placed there by Michael. "Why don't we sort this out man to man?"

"We know that's not going to happen." Auden gave his fixed smile. "That's not in either of our interests."

"Or we could just take you. Right here. And you know it." Petrovitch rubbed the bridge of his nose, feeling for ancient scars.

"You agreed not to," said Auden. At least he looked nervous now.

"Yeah, well. There'll be another time. Come on, then. Let's get this over with."

Auden relaxed, just a little. "Dr Samuil Petrovitch, this is your liaison, Joseph Newcomen. I hope you'll find him as useful as they do at the Bureau."

"That's supposed to be a recommendation?" Petrovitch stepped back to examine the agent. "They've sent Joe Friday, right? Just the facts, ma'am?"

Auden intervened. "Now you're just being cruel, Doctor."

"Yeah, I can only stomach talking to one of you at a time. Auden, in words that even you can understand, fuck off back to that fortress you call an embassy. We'll take it from here."

The spook held up his hands in surrender. "Hey, I know when I'm not wanted."

"You're never wanted. You killed my friends and kidnapped my wife. It's an affront to basic humanity that your government appointed you to the Metrozone in the first place, and if I have the time and the inclination after all this is over, I will hunt you down and kill you like the dog you are."

Auden kept smiling around the edges, but he started to back away.

"That's right. Start running, little man. It won't help, but it might buy you an extra day or two." Petrovitch's lips turned thin and mean.

"Good luck, Agent Newcomen," called Auden. He twirled his finger in the air, and the people he had positioned in the hall gravitated towards him. He reached into his pocket for a new pair of infoshades and stalked off.

Petrovitch watched the man's back until it was out of sight, then finally turned to Newcomen.

The agent looked ready to turn tail and flee. If he had to cross the Atlantic on foot, so be it.

"And what the *huy* am I supposed to do with you?"

In Reconstruction America, a single swear word could cost him a twenty-dollar fine. Petrovitch had cussed more in five minutes than Newcomen had heard in the last five years.

"I, uh. I'm here to, uh."

"*Yobany stos*, stop. Just stop." Petrovitch dug his hands into his coat pockets and clenched them into fists. "I know why you're here. I know who you are, where and when you were born, who your parents are, where you live, work, drink coffee, your entire case history at the Bureau, how much you earn and what you spend it on. I know you better than you know yourself, because you tell yourself little lies, and I see through them."

Newcomen stared longingly in the direction that Auden had taken.

"That *govnosos* Auden's going to be of no help to you now, even if he pretended to be in the first place. He's the Bad Shepherd. He's thrown you to the wolves, and he doesn't care what we do to you."

The FBI agent closed his eyes for a moment, and his lips moved in a muttered mantra. When he regained his composure, he seemed to have visibly grown. He topped Petrovitch by a head anyway, and when he stood straight, he looked less like a sack of rubbish and more like a college pro footballer. Which he had been. He had the clean good looks of an advertising model — selected and spliced for, like his height, his eye and hair colour – except for the vague knot on the bridge of his nose. The perfect all-American ideal.

Petrovitch didn't know whether to pity him or despise him. After all, Newcomen hadn't chosen to be born that way.

"Dr Petrovitch. I have a job to do. An important job given to me by my government, one they trust me to do to the best of my abilities. I do not intend to make them ashamed of me."

"Yeah, okay. Maybe we've got off to a bad start. I blame Auden: seeing him enrages me in a way few others can manage. Welcome to the Metrozone, Joseph Newcomen. You've read the Fed's files on me, right?"

"I've read the briefing notes," said Newcomen. Even as he said it, Petrovitch could see him trying to put names to the three women behind him.

"*Chyort.* They've told you jack shit, haven't they? I'm guessing that out of the whole Bureau, they've picked the one guy who'd never even heard of me before." Petrovitch blinked. "Is that why you bought a copy of *Fodor's Guide to the Metrozone* two days ago?"

"I had heard of you before, sir!"

"So who's that?" He pointed at Madeleine.

"That's . . . your wife?"

Madeleine's fingers flexed in a way that appeared both casual and menacing. Petrovitch looked back at her. Two metres tall, lean in a way that a tigress was lean, hair caught up in an intricate mathematical plait that coiled over her shoulder. If she wanted to rip someone's head off, he wouldn't stand in her way. He'd even enjoy the show.

"Assuming that you're not so stupid as to walk into this situation blind, I have to believe you're willing to learn." Petrovitch stood aside. "In order, my wife, Madeleine Petrovitch,

Valentina Pavlichenko, hero of the second battle of Waterloo, and Tabletop. Whose reputation, by the look of you, precedes her."

While he was addressing Petrovitch, Newcomen had gained a small measure of confidence. He lost it all again. They weren't dressed at all how women in America dressed – demurely. They didn't seem to know how they should behave, or how they should look at a man. To Newcomen's mind, they looked like ferals. They were all ferals. Especially that last one, the one with the crazy name. The ex-CIA traitor.

"Uh, ladies."

Tabletop stalked up to Newcomen, the heels of her boots clacking against the hard floor. She stared at his shiny leather shoes and the length of his bristly blond hair, and everything in between.

In return, Newcomen tried to look away from the bright pink ponytail, the lean – almost hungry – face, and the curve of her neck where it shadowed into the collar of her flying jacket. Tried, and couldn't.

She dismissed him with a flick of her hair. "I don't trust him," she said. "Get them to find someone else."

"It's him they sent," said Petrovitch.

Tabletop turned her back on them and walked to her pillar. "So why him?"

"She's got a point, Newcomen. Why you?"

The agent didn't respond, so Petrovitch kicked him, not gently, to get his attention away from Tabletop.

"Why'd they choose you? Plenty of other people they could have picked. You've no experience of Alaska, no experience of missing persons, you're pretty junior, never had any real responsibility before. In fact, could they have picked anyone less suited for this?" Petrovitch pursed his lips. "Yeah. That'll be it, then."

"Is insult," said Valentina, whose accent came to the fore when she was angry. "Americans do not care, do not see why we should care. Bastards all." If she'd had her favourite Kalashnikov, she would probably have shot Newcomen where he stood. As it was, she put her hands on her hips and looked sour.

"I," said Newcomen, beginning to bluster, "was chosen. Selected. I'm good at my job."

"You have not done job long enough to find out if good, bad, or merely competent." Valentina sneered at him. "We ask for help, and we get you."

"Dr Petrovitch, can't you control . . ."

Madeleine's timely hand on Valentina's shoulder cooled the temperature just long enough for Petrovitch to steer Newcomen away and down the concourse.

"Yeah, look. I know how it is in the USA, but over here? Men don't control everything, and especially we don't control women. I know that's what you're used to. You've lived your whole life thinking it. But if you want to survive more than five minutes in the Metrozone, then you have to realise a woman will not defer to you just because you've a pair of *yatzja*." He pressed his fingers to his temples. "If that's too much conditioning to break, treat them all as honorary men. *Chyort*, I can't believe I'm having this conversation."

Newcomen's luggage dogged their footsteps slavishly, but the agent still glanced around.

Petrovitch realised he wasn't checking where his spare pants were. He was stealing another look at Tabletop.

"Where are we going?" asked Newcomen.

"I said I'd look in on a friend. Couple of friends, really. We can do one on the way to the other."

"Just you and me?"

"Why? My company not good enough?" Petrovitch kept his eyes on the exit, but hacked the security system and windowed an image of the three Freezone women back at the gate. They stood close together but ignored each other, full attention focused on him and the American.

"I thought . . ." said Newcomen. "I thought we'd be straight back on a plane. What with your daughter missing."

"Plane tomorrow." The rotating doors swallowed him up, spat him out on the roadside. Newcomen more-or-less successfully negotiated the same route and joined him.

"I don't understand," said Newcomen. "I'm your escort. You were waiting for me, and now we're out here."

Petrovitch ignored both him and the few taxis waiting for a fare, and walked between them to the open road. A car pulled out of the February mist and drew up alongside.

"In you get."

Newcomen opened the back door with a sigh and heaved his luggage on to the seat, then slid across next to it. He'd opened his mouth to greet the driver when he realised there was no one else with him.

Petrovitch walked around the front of the car and dropped behind the steering wheel, which was on the other side to the one he was used to.

"Close the door. And stop drooling like an idiot. I'm likely to make assumptions."

"But." Newcomen pointed back down the road.

"All the cool kids can do it. Now shut the *yebani* door and we can get going."

19

Newcomen eventually leaned out and pulled the door shut. Petrovitch frowned at him in the rear-view mirror as they pulled away. Petrovitch's hands were firmly in his lap.

"How do you do that?" blurted Newcomen.

"I am the New Machine Jihad," said Petrovitch with a lupine grin. "They made cars smart enough to drive themselves, and eventually they did. Well, I let them, and they like me, so they tend to do what I ask them to do. I know there are laws against this sort of thing, but I have diplomatic immunity pretty much everywhere I go, so I tend to ignore a lot of small stuff. And the big stuff. You'll have to get used to that."

"I thought the Jihad was that computer."

"The computer has a name. Michael. Remind me to introduce you sometime. But no, the Jihad was originally its evil twin." Petrovitch twisted in his seat to see Newcomen hunched up on the back seat, his knees almost up around his ears. European cars were usually smaller than their steroidal American counterparts. "You could have sat in the front."

"I didn't know."

"There's an awful lot you don't know, Newcomen. I need to work out whether that's deliberate, as Tina says, or just that you're ignorant. I mean that in a good way."

One thing that Newcomen hadn't remembered was they were driving on the wrong side of the road. Another car passed them on the right, and he flinched.

Petrovitch settled back in his seat, a slight smile on his face, ready to enjoy the ride.

3

Petrovitch kicked the door open again when the car had come to a halt. It was parked, two wheels up on the kerb, next to an extravagant length of corroded iron railings. Just ahead of the bonnet was a set of ornate gates hung between two blackened stone pillars, each topped with a chipped obelisk.

"Out," he said.

"What about my luggage?" said Newcomen. He'd seen enough on the journey from Heathrow to convince him it was only a matter of minutes before someone tried to mug him.

"What about it? You thought you'd be here for less than a few hours: what could you possibly have brought that justifies that size of crate?"

"Well," said Newcomen, "there's—"

"Yeah, I know about the Secret Squirrel stuff already. If you lose it, so much the better." Petrovitch climbed out of the car and used his backside to push the door closed. He started towards the gates, raising one hand and beckoning the agent.

Newcomen caught him up, puffing slightly.

"Out of shape, Newcomen? What would Coach say?"

"Do you have to bring that up?"

"Don't have to. But it used to be important to you. Sorry if it's a sore point."

Newcomen unconsciously rubbed his arm, midway between right elbow and shoulder. He looked around him for the first time.

"We're in a graveyard."

"Yeah, that'd account for all the, you know, gravestones."

Some of them were old, pre-Armageddon, the ones closest to the entrance. Most were not: some dated back to the foundation of the Metrozone, and then as they walked along the cracked tarmac paths deeper into the cemetery, the death dates got more and more recent.

Even the designs of the memorials marked an evolution of sorts: varied and effusive early on, to more uniform, utilitarian later, until almost all variation had been weeded out and a simple narrow rectangular slab became the norm. Name, date of birth, and the day they died. That was all.

They were passing by row upon row marked with May 2024. Petrovitch's eyelid twitched as he remembered.

Those ended, and after a few more serried ranks, a vast field of November dates, same year.

It took a while to get to walk by those.

Finally, Petrovitch headed down one of the rows, off the path, disturbing the ragged grasses that were growing unchecked between the upright stones. It looked more or less a random choice, but he knew exactly where he was going.

Six graves down, there was a black marker engraved in faded kanji, with the dates in Roman numerals. He stopped in front of it and worried at his lip for a few moments.

Newcomen watched from a respectful distance, hands clasped behind his back.

"You're probably thinking this is the first normal thing you've seen me do," said Petrovitch.

"I, uh, I wouldn't want to intrude, sir."

"Stop calling me sir. I'm not sure you mean it, and I really, really don't like it." He knelt down in the wet grass and pulled a long-bladed knife from inside his coat. He gripped a handful of green leaf blades and hacked at their base. "We're going to have to come to some sort of working relationship, Newcomen. Like I said, I don't know why they sent you, out of all the people they had available. Personally, I don't think you were chosen for any other quality but your ignorance. The less you know, the less information I can tear from your still-living flesh. That makes you a victim in someone else's game, but unfortunately for you, it won't stop me from ruthlessly exploiting any and every advantage that's presented to me. I'm going to apologise in advance for that."

He worked his way across the grave plot, holding and cutting the grass.

"You said he was a friend," said Newcomen, nodding at the stone.

"She. She was a friend. Body cremated, ashes interred right here, half a world away from where she was born. She was twenty-two when she died." Petrovitch straightened up, his left hand stained green. "I brought you out here deliberately, to see this almost-anonymous grave, because I wanted to show you what your countrymen are capable of. Sure, we can drive by the site of the Metrozone's very own Ground Zero, but I can make my point better out here."

He dug into his pockets again and came up with a steel lighter and a small flat candle in a foil container. He trod down the grass next to the headstone, and placed the candle in his bootprint.

"This is where Sonja Oshicora ended up. I don't know if they've told you about her, or if you've bothered to look for yourself. It was a decade and another life ago for me. You were still in high school in Columbus and probably too busy being a jock to pay any attention to what was happening here. Maybe you remember the nuke and Mackensie resigning, but not necessarily the reasons why."

Petrovitch bent down and flicked the lid of the lighter. He stroked the wheel with his thumb and fire flickered, yellow and trembling. Eventually, the candle wick caught, turned black, and glowed with its own fragile flame. He crouched down and watched the wax melt and turn clear.

"She was my friend. Accidentally so, but my friend all the same. She ran the Freezone – the first one, here – and this is where she died."

"That's, uh," said Newcomen.

"Shut up and let me talk. I'm trying to warn you. You'll probably think I'm the Antichrist by the time I've finished with you, the very embodiment of evil. The problem you have is that the worst acts against you have already happened, and I've had nothing to do with them whatsoever." Petrovitch nodded at the gravestone. "I was at the sharp end of a CIA assassination squad, and Sonja tried to save me from them. But the way she chose to do that nearly broke me. She didn't tell me about it, and she didn't give me a choice. Her plan fell apart, and she ended up putting a bullet through her own brain. While I was watching." He'd erased the recording long ago. Yet he could still see it with aching clarity. His name called, his head turned, the gunmetal-grey barrel slipped inside her pretty pink mouth.

24

Newcomen shifted his weight from one foot to the other. The bottoms of his suit trousers were wet, and were starting to cling. "I don't understand what you're saying, sir, Dr Petrovitch."

"Of course you don't. I don't expect you to. You're not going to believe that your own government, the people you work for, the people you look up to and think protect you, have not just determined that you're completely expendable, but have deliberately and explicitly marked you for termination. You're a dead man walking." Petrovitch shrugged. "Sorry for that, but it wasn't my choice."

The candle flickered in the slight breeze, then burned brighter for a moment.

"They told me to expect this. The Assistant Director briefed me. Said you'd try and get inside my head. It won't work."

"I don't give a shit what Buchannan said," said Petrovitch mildly. "But you'll remember this conversation. When the time comes and you realise I was right all along, you might suddenly discover that I'm your only hope for staying alive."

"I'll wait for you by the car," said Newcomen. He walked away, a slowly dwindling figure in amongst the gravestones.

Petrovitch scratched at his chin. "I know we're pretty much the same age, but *yobany stos.*"

[His upringing was not as cosmopolitan as yours.]

"Yeah." He looked at Newcomen's retreating back. "*Chyort,* I feel *yebani* ancient compared with vat-boy over there."

[Not being irradiated in his mother's womb might account for some of the differences between you. Not being in a womb at all for others. He was raised on an automatic farm, you in post-Armageddon St Petersburg. He was an athlete, whilst you had your failing heart. Apart from his one accident, I doubt he has ever felt pain.]

"What I meant . . ." Petrovitch rested his hand on top of Sonja's grave marker. It was cold to the touch, the stone numbing his fingers. "I feel like I'm being dragged in again. Being forced to trace the old patterns that I thought I'd left behind. It didn't end well the last time."

[We are ten years wiser, Sasha. We have a whole decade of experience to consult. We are now many.]

"It's not going to stop us making an utter *pizdets* of it, though." He moved to trace the calligraphic strokes of Sonja's name.

[It might. If nothing else, the Americans are now more scared of us than we are of them.]

"But they don't learn, do they? They keep trying to slap us down, and we have to be quick every time. I'm afraid, Michael, that when it really matters, we're going to be a fraction of a second too slow. Too slow for Lucy."

[Then we must be ready for every eventuality, no matter how unlikely. I can calculate layer on layer of possibilities.]

"And still something might come out of nowhere and knock us off course." Petrovitch stood up and put everything back in his pockets. "History's not going to repeat itself, is it, Sonja? We're too smart for that, right?"

She had no opinion to offer, one way or the other, so Petrovitch left her with the candle guttering in the fading daylight and made his way to the car, and the waiting Newcomen.

He unlocked the doors when he was still a good distance away, making the American jump. Newcomen's phone was built into his tie: tucked down beside his now-sweat-stained collar was the earpiece. If it had been put together better, it would have been a poor imitation of Freezone tech. As it was, it was just a phone.

Petrovitch tagged it and made it ring.

"Hello?"

"Get in the car. You'll catch a cold, and I'm not having you sneezing on me all the way across the Atlantic tomorrow."

Newcomen crawled in, next to his luggage. "Doctor?"

"Yeah, we're going to have to sort this out now. I only use the title when I want something, or you've pissed me off so much I won't answer to anything else. Call me Petrovitch and have done with it."

"That would be disrespectful, si . . . Doc . . . I can't call you just 'Petrovitch'. What would people think?"

"Oh, fuck off, Newcomen. Call me whatever you want. I don't care. We're going to find some dinner."

It was getting dark, and the less salubrious side of the Metrozone was asserting itself. The authorities had reverted to the municipal model of government after the years' hiatus of the Freezone. Petrovitch thought that his way of doing things was demonstrably better – an AI-administered co-operative had its own particular problems, but scaring off three desperate-looking men from robbing him wasn't one of them.

He got closer to the car as they circled it. One of them had a half-brick, which wasn't a surprise as they weren't exactly in short supply. Knives, too. Perhaps they hadn't spotted him, or maybe they had and thought that they could take this slight, short guy as well as the one crouched on the back seat. Petrovitch wasn't armed, except for his weed-cutter, and Newcomen wouldn't be allowed to carry outside his jurisdiction – unless Auden had slipped him a piece. Which would be typical of the man.

All three would-be thieves had phones. He tagged them and chased down their numbers, call histories, came up with a few houses over Wembley way where most of the calls geolocated. From there it was a short step to dragging identities off a database, bundling it all up with video footage of the current scene and posting it to the police.

They'd all be gone by the time anyone turned up, but he had an affection for the Metrozone that never went away. It was still his city, mean streets and all.

One of the men hefted the brick, circling the car with its terrified occupant.

"Don't throw that," Petrovitch called when he was within earshot. "Because then I'll get pissed with you and you wouldn't like it."

There were no street lights outside the cemetery, and he switched to active infrared. Everything became so much clearer. He could see their hot bodies swaddled in thick clothes against the cold, could see their blood run bright. Meatsacks. So easily damaged.

He kept on walking: not a moment of falter or hesitation. Even when the brick was thrown at his head. He'd calculated the entire trajectory of the missile almost before it had left the man's hand, and he didn't need to so much as duck.

Petrovitch was beside the car. He rested his palm on its dusty roof and started it up, though he deliberately kept the headlights off. It was tempting to try the "don't you know who I am?" line, but it was clear that in their in-between state of drugged joy and dragging withdrawal, they had no idea. The dull red glow coming from his eyes didn't appear to jog their memories either.

"I'm happy to run you over. I'm equally happy for you to disappear. Your call."

The one who came for him had obscured his face with a scarf

and pulled his hood tight around his head. Petrovitch knew enough about him already to know he wasn't a kid doing something stupid for the first time, but a really not-very-nice man who hurt people and made their lives a misery.

After the first missed swing and before the second milling arm could reach him, Petrovitch casually pushed out his left hand against the bigger man's sternum. He used enough force to crack ribs, momentarily stop the heart and send the body hurtling to the far side of the road.

"You can go home if you want," he said to the other two, then ignored them. He opened the door and got behind the wheel. "You okay, Newcomen?"

"How . . .?"

"This file on me the FBI gave you: what did it actually say?" The car's engine whined, and they drove off. After a while, another car passed theirs, and he remembered to put the lights on.

"I can't tell you. It's classified."

"Yeah, course it is, though to be honest, I think so little of it I haven't bothered hacking it. But judging from your reaction, I'm guessing it didn't mention either the automatic car thing, or that I've got extensive cybernetic replacements." He turned off the infrared before looking directly at Newcomen. "I can do these things because I'm a *yebani* cyborg. *Vrubatsa?*"

Newcomen wasn't confirming or denying whether he understood. He was busy trying to push himself backwards through the upholstery, intent on putting as much distance as possible between him and the aberration before him.

Petrovitch faced the windscreen again and watched the Metrozone glide by. "We've fallen right into Uncanny Valley there, haven't we? Don't worry, Newcomen. You'll get used to me."

4

Petrovitch put his shoulder to an anonymous door on Brixton High Street, and led the way up a set of bare wooden stairs. Cooking smells grew stronger the further he climbed – signature smells he recognised from earlier days when he was new in town.

"Hungry yet, Newcomen?"

"No, not really," said the agent. He looked like he was already eating some particularly sour lemons. Particularly he wasn't enjoying trying to squeeze his suitcase up the narrow staircase.

"I've ordered for both of us. It's probably safer that way." He got to the top of the stairs, where a massive slab of a man blocked entry to the dining room. Infoshades hid his oriental eyes, but the wireless earpiece was clearly visible: no hair at all on the man's shaved, scarred head. "Wong's expecting us," said Petrovitch.

The bouncer sneered down at him, and on seeing Newcomen half-hidden behind his luggage, spat on the floor.

"Yeah, I get to choose the company I keep, not some neckless *svinya.*" Petrovitch flexed his fingers. "I could throw you down the stairs and the nerve impulses won't have travelled to your walnut-sized brain by the time you hit the bottom. You can choose that, or get the *huy* out of the way."

The man started chuckling to himself, and his great belly shuddered in waves. "You're him." He had a grin of black and silver teeth. "You're Petrovitch all right. Go right in."

"Thanks." The door opened with a burst of noise and steam. "*Mudak.*"

A dozen tables were already full of diners, talking, laughing, shouting and singing. C-pop cranked tinnily through inadequate speakers in the ceiling, and the air was almost opaquely blue with burnt cooking oil.

Moving through the fug towards Petrovitch was a thin figure wearing a stained white apron. "Hey! Bad man!"

"Hey, Wong. Your sign outside still isn't working."

Wong folded his scrawny arms. "You fix it for me?"

"Kind of busy at the moment. Maybe when I get back."

Wong nodded slowly. "Pay me back for all those free cups of coffee, yes?"

"Free? From you? How is the coffee, anyway?"

Then they were hugging, slapping each other's backs and cackling like loons. "Coffee hot and strong today!" they choroused.

"Where that wife of yours?" asked Wong after they'd separated.

"Taking care of business. She sends her apologies."

"Okay. Next time, bring her, not this thing. She much prettier." Wong peered at Newcomen. "Case out back. No room in here. No room!"

"He treats it like it's got the *yebani* crown jewels inside. Let him stick it in a corner somewhere."

"Who this? Makes place look untidy."

Petrovitch peered through the chemical fog. Tidiness had never been a hallmark of Wong's establishments. Or cleanliness, for that matter.

"This is Agent Joseph Newcomen, FBI. He's going to help me find Lucy. Isn't that right, Newcomen?"

"Yessir . . . yes," he corrected himself.

"American, huh?' Wong stalked around him like he was viewing a grotesque artwork. "This one end up dead too?"

"Yeah, maybe. I seem to have a bit of a record for that."

"What? What do you mean?" Newcomen looked startled.

"First American?" Wong snorted. "Bang. Bullet in head."

"And the next?"

"Bang. Bullet in head."

"Pretty much tells you everything you need to know, Newcomen." Petrovitch scratched at his nose. "You got a table for us, or are we going to have to eat standing up?"

"This one, here?" Wong pointed to a table in the middle of the floor.

"Yeah, how about that one over there, behind the pillar, where no one will be able to overhear everything we say to each other?"

Wong's eyes narrowed. "You organising crime again?"

"No, not with Joe Friday here, anyway. I just want to sit somewhere we're not going be disturbed. We can do drunken revelry later."

"Okay." Wong persuaded the two Rastafari out of their seats and carried their half-eaten egg fu yongs to the table he'd tried to foist on Petrovitch. They grumbled about Babylon, but then saw who it was they were making space for. The men both slid their palms across Petrovitch's white hand and seemed content.

The table was cleaned with a damp rag smelling strongly of bleach. Petrovitch shrugged off his coat and threw it across the back of his chair before falling into the seat.

Newcomen hovered nervously, looking around him in wonder and fear. His shoulders finally slumped, as if he'd accepted his fate, and he dragged his suitcase into the space next to the red-hot radiator.

"You don't honestly think I'm going to eat anything here, do you?" He sat down opposite Petrovitch and leaned across to hiss at him. "What are you trying to do to me?"

"I'm trying," said Petrovitch, "to talk to you. Find out what you're like. Find out whether I can trust you to do your job or not. I know all the facts about your life: what I don't know is you: how you react, your own particular strengths and weaknesses. The files I've read don't tell me that sort of stuff. Now, do you want coffee?"

"We could talk at my hotel. Have dinner in the restaurant. With food that isn't going to poison me."

"Hmm." Petrovitch flipped open an imaginary notebook and started to write. "Freaks out when removed from comfort zone."

"I do not do that."

"Unable to cope with novelty."

"Shut up."

"Scared of absolutely everything." Petrovitch flipped the notebook shut and tossed it away over his shoulder. "That's about right, isn't it?"

"Don't make fun of me, Petrovitch."

"Or what, vat-boy?"

"That's not an insult."

"Is where I come from. Hell, at least my upgrades took."

"And what's that supposed to mean?"

"Okay. This isn't going well. Some of that is my fault." Petrovitch placed his palms on the table. "Let me ask you a question: do you actually care that my daughter's missing?"

Newcomen worked his jaw. "It's my job to help find her."

"That's not what I asked." Petrovitch stared across at the American. "Let's try another. When they tweaked your genes, did they throw out the code for your soul?"

"Are you trying to get a reaction from me? Provoke me? Get me into a fight that'll land me in front of the Assistant Director's desk on a disciplinary matter? You won't be able to do that. You want to know what was in your file? You don't need to warn me about your behaviour. I know about it already."

"Okay, okay." Petrovitch held his hands up. "I know what you care about now. Your position within the Bureau. That's what's important to you, I understand that now. Let's get a coffee each and calm down."

Right on cue, two mugs appeared. It was almost as if Wong was waiting for a gap in the conversation.

"He takes it white," said Petrovitch, dragging his own drink towards him.

Wong sniffed, and came back a moment later with a jug half-filled with something resembling milk. "Ready for food?"

"Yeah."

"We haven't even seen a menu yet," objected Newcomen.

Petrovitch pointedly ignored the interruption. "What I said earlier will be fine." After Wong had left, he said: "You know when you go round someone's house for dinner? You don't ask for a menu then, do you? No. So don't be an idiot."

"This is a public diner . . ."

"You don't know anything about Wong, and you don't get

to say what this is or isn't. Especially when your government killed most of his old customers with a cruise missile."

Newcomen chewed cud for a while, and ignored his coffee. Petrovitch didn't, and welcomed it like an old friend. Hot and strong, just how he liked it.

"Look," said Newcomen suddenly, putting his forearms on the table and crowding close. "Can we agree on a truce?"

"And why would I want something like that?" Petrovitch centred his mug down in the brown ring of liquid already on the wooden surface. "But go on, I'm listening."

"We've been thrown together by circumstances beyond our control. I don't have a choice about being sent, and you don't get to choose who escorts you around."

"Someone chose. Don't you want to know who? And why?"

"I know why they sent me. It's because they thought I was the right man for this job."

"That begs so many questions." Petrovitch held up two fingers. "Mainly, what's the job and why are you right? You see, I was expecting some high-level State Department official, not some junior G-man. What did Buchannan tell you the job was?"

"Stick with you. Show you around. Keep you up to date with the investigation. Wait until you were satisfied we'd done everything we could, and then," Newcomen sat back, "get you out of the country."

Petrovitch's eyes narrowed. "You have remembered my daughter's missing, haven't you?"

"Petrovitch. Dr Petrovitch, you have to realise that the chances of find—" His words finished in a choking sound, because Petrovitch had lunged across the table and had him by the throat.

"Finish that sentence and I'll break your neck." He squeezed a little more. "*Vrubatsa?*"

Newcomen's fingers managed to prise Petrovitch's hand away, but only because he'd let him. The American rubbed at his throat and glared across the table. "I thought we were discussing a truce."

"We will find her. This is not an article of faith, this is a statement of fact. The moment you stop looking for her is the moment I kill you." Petrovitch looked around the pillar to see if Wong was coming with their food. "That's not just hyperbole, Newcomen: I do mean it."

"Then you'll be arrested and charged with first-degree murder. You'll be executed for sure."

"And when I said the thing about diplomatic immunity, it wasn't a joke. Uncle Sam can kick me out, but not arrest me. For anything." Dinner arrived sizzling, and Petrovitch moved his mug out of the drop zone. "Even that."

"You're not going to kill me." Newcomen looked through the steam and smoke rising from his plate. "It's a steak."

"Yes. Yes it is. Well spotted. And you're right, of course. I'm not going to kill you. I'm going to rely on your fear that I will kill you to make you do pretty much everything I want. Only at the very end will you find you had a choice all along."

Wong returned with a big bowl of glistening chips and a leafy green salad that didn't look like it had been hanging around in the back of the fridge for a week.

"This actually looks edible. I owe your Mr Wong an apology."

"No you don't. Just dig in." Petrovitch twirled his knife between his fingers and started to slice into his meat.

The steak was just how Newcomen liked it: seared on the outside, still pink in the middle. He ate some fries, and moved salad to the edge of his plate. "Things will be different," he said between mouthfuls, "when we get to America."

"I know they will," said Petrovitch. "That's why it's important we do this now."

"Do what?"

"Eat, drink and be merry. We're free to fall out into the street, worse for wear from *baijiu*. We're free to say fuck and shit and call each other bastards. We're free to wear what we want, no matter how immodest. Now, I know you think that these aren't freedoms at all, that all we're doing is enslaving ourselves to our passions, but you'd be wrong."

"And why would my whole country be wrong?"

"Because you're lying to yourselves. You can think we're all foul-mouthed drunks and our women dress like whores, but you're missing the point. Underneath the veneer of Reconstruction, you're all monsters. In the Freezone, no one ever goes hungry. If they fall sick, we cure them if we can and look after them if we can't. No one's lonely, because there's always someone listening. We take care of each other, and we all have a say in the big decisions. Which is pretty much how we got to this point."

Newcomen realised he couldn't feel his fingertips any more. Nor his toes. He tried to stand, and fell hard against the bare boards of Wong's empty dining room. Everyone else had left while they were hidden behind the pillar. Even the kitchen space, all flame and spice beforehand, was silent.

"What . . ." he managed before his tongue grew thick and unworkable in his mouth.

Petrovitch scraped his chair back and went to the door. No slab-bodied bouncer, but Madeleine, Valentina and Tabletop. "Give it another minute. He's almost there."

He came back and sat cross-legged in front of Newcomen's paralysed form.

"You see, the whole point of this evening was genuinely to find out what you were like. If you weren't such a craven, self-absorbed careerist, you might have saved yourself from what happens next. But we'd already made the decision based on what we knew of you, and we've decided that the only way we can ensure your single-minded dedication to the task of finding Lucy is by planting a bomb in your chest. The irony is that we just want you to do the job you're paid to do. Do it, and you'll be fine."

Petrovitch reached out and rolled the unresisting Newcomen flat.

"The drug's very specific and quickly metabolised. No ill-effects afterwards." He knelt up and started to unbutton the agent's shirt and unknot his tie. "You won't feel a thing."

Tabletop placed a slim case on the floor next to Newcomen's head and opened it. Inside was a scalpel, and she was already wearing surgical gloves. She held the blade up to the light, then without doubt or hesitation, brought it down.

5

Petrovitch sat on a chair at the end of the bed, hunched over in the shadows thrown by the drawn curtains. Metrozone sounds leaked in, despite the triple glazing, and outside in the corridor a man and a woman laughed on their way to breakfast.

Newcomen stirred, buried his head deeper into his soft white pillow, then opened his eyes. He gasped and sat up, clutching at his bare, almost hairless chest.

"It wasn't a dream," said Petrovitch.

There was a small strip of canned skin, just left of Newcomen's sternum, no longer or wider than his thumb. The colour matching was good enough, and in time there wouldn't even be a scar.

"What have you done to me? Where am I? How did I get here?" He pulled the duvet up to his chin. It made a poor shield against Petrovitch's forensic gaze.

"You're in your hotel room, I carried you in, and we have to be at the airport in a few hours." Petrovitch levered himself upright and pulled the curtains back to reveal the north bank of the Thames. "As for the rest of it? Michael's been busy calculating the odds of not just getting Lucy back, but even getting me back. Frankly, they weren't looking good, so we've shortened them. A little. What we've done is really shitty, especially since it seems you're not actually that important in the whole scheme of things, but we have to work with what we've got."

He went to the wardrobe where he'd hung up Newcomen's suit, more or less neatly, and laid it across the bottom of the bed. There was a freshly ironed shirt, and the phone tie too, and he'd previously found spare socks and boxers in the ridiculously sized suitcase.

"You need to get up, get washed and dressed, then meet me in the restaurant downstairs. Unless you want me to call room service."

"I have a bomb? In here?" Newcomen's fingers searched where the wound should have been.

"Okay, yes. May as well fill you in on the details. We've inserted an explosive capsule into the muscle surrounding your left ventricle. It is very small, very difficult to find even if someone's looking for it, and we've made it as radio-transparent as we can so it doesn't trip any sort of scanner. Despite its size, it's more than capable of making a hole big enough that you'll bleed out in five seconds. Ten tops, but your blood pressure will fall like a stone and you'll probably be unconscious for most of that."

While Newcomen digested this, Petrovitch buffed a pair of brown leather shoes with his sleeve.

"What," said the American, "what if I don't co-operate?"

"What sort of dumb-arse question is that? I had hoped that

despite all your shortcomings, you were at least smart." Petrovitch put the shoes on the floor as a pair, toes pointing out. "This is the deal: if I die, you die. If I'm about to die, you die. If my diplomatic status is revoked and I'm imprisoned, you die. If I discover that you and your Federal colleagues have been giving me the runaround, withholding information and generally pissing me off, guess what? You die. If you try to take the bomb out, you die. If you tell anyone about the bomb, you die. Simply put, if you don't do your damnedest to get my daughter back, you die."

"She's not even your . . ." started Newcomen, then caught himself.

"She's mine. She's all of the Freezone's, too, but she is mine. Now get up: I expect you to be downstairs in ten minutes."

"Or what? You'll kill me?" It wasn't so much a rebellion from Newcomen as a flash of petulance.

"I'm not going to go around making you my *suka* because I can. I will, however, kick your sorry arse every time you act like a *peesa*. Just grow a pair, will you?" He tapped his non-existent wristwatch. "Ten."

Petrovitch walked out and down the corridor that seemed both too narrow and too low-ceilinged to be sensible. He could reach up and touch the recessed lights. There were lifts, but he ignored them and took the stairwell instead, bouncing down the steps two and three at a time.

His heart responded to the exercise by spinning up. He was tingling by the time he reached the bottom, seven floors later.

He parked himself in the restaurant by a window seat and watched the waves lap dangerously close to the top of the flood defences. By the time Newcomen arrived, looking damp and grim, he was on his second cup of coffee and pleasantly wired.

"Sit," he said, and pushed the opposite chair away from the

41

table with a foot. He continued to stare out of the window while a waitress brought Newcomen his own coffee.

Both men ignored the self-service buffet for the moment.

"You've ruined my life," said Newcomen.

"Yeah: as I've already explained, your life was ruined long before we first met, but not by me. Surprisingly enough, I want you to live. I want you to help me find Lucy. Your bosses want exactly the opposite. They don't want me to find Lucy, and they don't care if you live or die. Whatever's happened up there on the North Slope is much more important than your frankly insignificant existence." Petrovitch nodded outside. "You've been sold down a river which looks a lot like that one. Big, cold, and supremely indifferent."

"If I promise to do everything you ask, will you deactivate the bomb?"

"No, you'll have to dig it out yourself. Though I will free you of your obligations when we're done."

Newcomen raised his eyebrows along with his hopes. "No matter what the outcome is?" He didn't say, if Lucy turns up dead, and Petrovitch was grateful.

"No matter what. I'm not spiteful. I have as many revenge fantasies as the next guy, but mostly I'm a peaceable man who just want to be left alone."

"Are you going to ask me to do anything illegal?"

"Probably. At some point, there'll come a time when it becomes obvious – even to you – that our search is being blocked. You'll do what I think necessary, however distasteful it might be." Petrovitch shrugged. "Better a black mark against your name than a black line through it."

Newcomen clattered a teaspoon against the side of his cup. "Am I allowed—"

"No."

"You don't even know what I'm going to say!"

"Yeah, I do. You can't tell anyone, not even your fiancée."

"I haven't even mentioned her yet."

Images flashed into Petrovitch's vision of a slender but vital blonde-haired, green-eyed young women with a ready smile and a quick temper.

"You've got no secrets left, Newcomen. Not from me. Christine Logan, only child of Edward Logan, CEO of Logan Realties. Twenty-four, and pretty in a spliced, cheerleadery sort of way. Wedding date is set for this September twenty-second, at St Mark's Episcopal Cathedral." He regarded the man across the table. "To be honest, I'm surprised you even met, let alone were allowed to date her."

Newcomen puffed up. "What do you mean by that?"

"She's virtually Reconstruction royalty, and you're a low-ranking FBI agent." A thought occurred to Petrovitch, but he kept it to himself. "Good luck with that: you're going to need it."

"She loves me."

"I'm not questioning that. It's whether she'll still love you after this."

"Of course she will. That's a terrible thing to say. Though," Newcomen grimaced, "if I get fired, how am I supposed to support her?"

"Maybe Teddy'll give you a job. Maybe he won't. Look," said Petrovitch, "I'm not unsympathetic. I didn't have to worry about the in-laws, unless you count Maddy's mother joining the Outies and trying to kill her. I did have to worry about Sonja, but that was later." He drifted off in a reverie of his own, then snapped back. "If it'll mean a little more co-operation on your part and a little less coercion on mine, I'll hold off the black-ops stuff until absolutely necessary. Fair?"

"Fair?"

"Well, not fair. But it's the only concession you're going to get out of me, so take it or leave it. Now," Petrovitch twisted in his seat, "breakfast is calling me. What I'm going to do is fill up on fried food, and maybe a big stack of pancakes, then I'm taking us to the airport."

"You're not even a resident here. I hope you've paid the supplement." Newcomen flapped his napkin open and rested it on his place setting.

"I did try. They wouldn't let me."

"They wouldn't let you?"

"No. Look around the place. Tell me what you see." Petrovitch stood up and surveyed the scene.

"I . . ." Newcomen knew he was being tested, but couldn't work out the question. "There aren't that many guests. A hotel like this in America would be busy."

"Anything else?"

"There's not such a wide choice of food?"

"Yeah. Your eyes are sliding right past the waiters and waitresses, the cooks and the receptionists. Ten years since I last saved this city, and I still can't pay for a meal." Petrovitch headed for the food counter, weaving through the other diners.

He was already loading his plate with bacon when Newcomen came up beside him. "So what you're saying is, no one questioned you when you walked in here last night with me slung over one shoulder. And no one ever would."

"They even found me a wheelchair to put you in. There's no record of me ever being here. If you asked them direct, to a man and woman they'd deny they saw me, spoke to me, gave me any help at all. I'm like a ghost in the machine. You know, I love hotel breakfast mushrooms. They get to cook in their own juices in a way you can't manage on your own with just a frying pan." He helped himself to a large spoonful, and then a few more. "That's the way it is, Newcomen. The Metrozone is still home."

"How very tribal of you." Newcomen's plate carried a couple of pieces of brown toast, nothing more.

"Your room was bugged, by the way. I took care of it."

"Bugged."

"NSA surveillance. Pretty basic."

"The NSA?" Newcomen was reduced to merely repeating the key points.

"I expected them to try. They expected me to take them out. It's an opening gambit, just a warm-up before the main event."

"Main event?"

"Yeah, they're going to want to keep close tabs on us once we get to the States. Who we talk to, what we say, where we go, what we see. They'll use all the tricks in the book, and then a few more on top." Petrovitch shrugged again, nearly dislodging the triangles of fried bread he had balanced on his thumb. "It'll be fine. I'll feed them enough that they'll think it's working, while we get on with the important stuff."

"We're being surveilled by the NSA? I'm a Federal agent: they can't do that."

"They can if either they've cleared it with the Director, they've an executive order, or they just don't care. I do notice that you don't dismiss the idea out of hand and call me a liar, though. We might actually be able to work together." Petrovitch looked down at his plate and decided he couldn't physically fit anything else on it without inviting disaster. He headed back to his place, where with no ceremony at all, he proceeded to demolish his food, a layer at a time.

Newcomen scraped some butter across the dry surface of his toast and nibbled at it, while looking with increasing disgust at his tablemate.

"What?" said Petrovitch, struggling to keep one of his beloved mushrooms in his mouth.

"Your manners. They're disgusting."

"Yeah, well, I've got a lot of hardware to power. As fun as it is for the fuel cells to start consuming my body fat, I'd rather they digested this stuff first." He forced the errant fungus back in with a piece of crispy potato square. "Beats being plugged into the mains every night."

Newcomen put his toast down and stared longingly at it for moment, before pushing it away.

"Your loss." Petrovitch snagged the uneaten slice and chewed off one corner. "I appreciate you can't see anything beyond this, that it feels like your world's ended and everything you've spent the last few years working for is in ruins. That's not necessarily the case. Assuming you don't do something congenitally stupid, there will be an afterwards. I can't tell you what it might look like, because a lot of that's up to you. One thing I don't want happening is you fainting on me every five minutes because you're too depressed to eat. So get that *yebani* toast down you and show some backbone."

They sat more or less ignoring each other. But Petrovitch was watching Newcomen's every move, every slow grind of his jaw, every frown of his brows.

[His reaction is not what I predicted.]

"He's corruptible. In a good way, I think. I can make him care: it's just going to take a little longer, that's all."

[You will be on the continental USA later on today. If the State Department's schedule is to be believed, you are expected in Seattle by nightfall, and Alaska the day after. Time – real time – is critically short if you are going to break this man's Reconstructionist conditioning.]

"I've already planted the virus in his subconscious. Sooner or later it's going to infect his whole mind. All I have to do is find the right trigger."

[We need to identify points past which it will be necessary to kill him and for you to continue alone.]

"I think those points will become self-evident the deeper into this *pizdets* we dig."

[Even so, if we list them now, I can remind you of them when we reach them. If we are trying to induce Stockholm syndrome in him, it is also true that you might feel reluctant to follow through your previous intentions.]

Petrovitch scratched at his chin. Newcomen was choking down his last piece of toast.

"I'm already there. Doesn't mean I won't do it, though. Not if Lucy's depending on me."

[She is.]

"I'm still a bastard, aren't I? Still using people to get what I want." He growled, and such was his frustration, he vocalised it.

Newcomen looked up sharply.

"Sorry. Not directed at you." Petrovitch glanced at the clock in the corner of his vision. "We need to go."

He screwed up his napkin on to his plate, swigged the last of his coffee, and started for the exit. Newcomen was left playing catch-up.

"I need to get my case, pack my things," he puffed.

SIMON MORDEN

"Five minutes, then. When I said go, I meant it. You're checked out and your bill's been paid already, so there's no need to hang around in the foyer." They passed the lifts, and Petrovitch shooed him into the one specially held for him by the hotel's computer. "Five minutes. Outside. Go."

The doors shushed shut and the lift sent him upwards.

"What's he doing?"

[Resting his head against the wall. You may have destroyed him, Sasha. Can you put him back together again?]

"We're all about to find out." Petrovitch summoned his car to the kerbside, and kept on walking through the foyer.

6

Auden was waiting for them at Departures. He suspected something because he was a suspicious man. He knew the Freezone. He hated them.

Petrovitch hated him right back, though he doubted very much that Auden would guess what they'd done to Newcomen. Neither would he find out until it was too late. That, at least, allowed Petrovitch a moment of smugness.

If Newcomen had Auden, Petrovitch had Tabletop next to him, looking cool and efficient, and no matter how much he disliked the NSA operative, Tabletop could double that emotion and more. There was every good reason to believe Auden knew her real name, knew her whole history, and Tabletop would like nothing more than to beat that information out of the man. Preferably over the course of a few weeks.

It meant they were ridiculously polite to each other on the infrequent occasions they met.

"No Mrs Petrovitch to wave you off?" asked Auden.

"It's not required. I talked to her just now, I'll talk to her again in a moment."

"And only the charming Miss Tabletop for company."

"Hand it over." Petrovitch turned his palm upwards, and Auden placed a thin plastic rectangle on it.

Petrovitch turned it to face him. There was his image on the left, burnt in three dimensions into the hologram, and on the right, the dots of a machine-readable data matrix. The back told him it was his Department of Homeland Security visa, and remained its property.

He passed the card to Tabletop, who ran it through a portable scanner she'd pulled from her shoulder bag. She held out the card to Auden, who took it back with an audible sigh.

"That one seems to be full of spyware, Mr Auden. I wonder if you have an alternative?" She smiled.

"This was what I was given, I'm afraid, Miss Tabletop. It's either this, or Dr Petrovitch won't be allowed on the flight." He wasn't sorry at all as he re-presented the visa to Petrovitch.

"Never mind." She opened her bag again and pulled out a rectangular box with a slot in the top. She held it out for Petrovitch, who posted the card inside. "We'll clean things up for you."

The top of the box had a button and two lights. Neither was currently illuminated, but when she pressed the button with her thumb, the red light came on. There was a crack of electricity, and the green light glowed.

"There," she said brightly. "All done."

Petrovitch retrieved the card. It looked unaltered, but the microcircuitry that would keep Homeland Security informed of his whereabouts was so much molten slag.

He idly stuck it in his back pocket. "That particular charade over, Auden?"

"So it seems. Have a good journey, and Agent Newcomen? I appreciate that your duty is a difficult one, but we always try to carry ourselves with dignity and fortitude. I'll be sending a report to your superiors informing them of your exemplary conduct so far."

Even Newcomen had the sense to be diplomatic. "Uh, thank you, sir. I'm sure AD Buchannan will appreciate that."

"You're a credit to the Bureau, and to America. Dr Petrovitch will find you a valuable guide when he's in unfamiliar territory."

"*Yobany stos*, enough of the corn, Auden. We both know that Newcomen's a fall guy and I'll probably ditch him at the first opportunity, so there's no point in your *govno*. You've done your job. Take your goons and go."

Auden accepted defeat and peeled off. As before, several nondescript travellers suddenly aborted their flight plans and flanked him as he strode away.

"And just like that, I'm abandoned." Newcomen looked at his shoes.

"He's still got people here, watching what we do. There's even a couple of agents booked on the flight over, three rows back from us. Remember, if you ever think you're not under surveillance, you still are. You can be overheard at any time. I let it slide this morning, because you needed to know the score. But from now on, on the plane, in a cab, on the street, in an office, over the phone, on a computer – unless I explicitly say so – you have to assume they can read your thoughts. *Vrubatsa?*"

"You keep saying that. What does it mean?"

Petrovitch felt like he was explaining something to a child. "Do you understand?"

"Yes. I understand."

"Really?"

"I get it."

"Good. Now go and get your stupid case checked in and meet me back here." Petrovitch watched him go, the luggage trundling after him. "*Chyort*, so many things can go wrong."

Tabletop tugged at her ponytail. "Are you going to be okay?"

"I'm standing on the edge of a cliff, ready to jump, and you ask me that?" People passed around them, ignoring them, not even seeing them.

"Of course I do. We're here to catch you. But there's nothing wrong in being afraid."

"They can smell fear. Auden knows we've no real idea what's going on, and he's told Washington that." He screwed his fingers into fists and jammed them in his pockets. "It's *pizdets*."

"The data miners are hard at work. We'll have something soon." Tabletop nodded over at Newcomen. "And he may well surprise you."

"The only surprise I'm going to get from him is guessing how long he can hold it together. How the *huy* did he ever end up working for the Feds? He's scared of his own shadow. Fidelity, Bravery, Integrity my arse."

"He graduated from Quantico with decent marks."

"All that proves is that he's fit and not stupid." Petrovitch snorted. "I could pass."

"You'd fail the lie detector test five different ways," Tabletop countered. "And the psychological profiling. And you're not an American citizen."

"I could fake all those." He ground his teeth. "Why now? Why Lucy?"

"It'll be all right." She put her hand on his shoulder and squeezed. "I gave you a hard time earlier, but I know she had to go off and do her own thing."

"Yeah, well. She could have chosen Antarctica, but no. *Yebani* Alaska."

Newcomen came trailing back. "Bag's been checked."

"Still don't understand why you brought all that stuff with you." Petrovitch noticed Newcomen staring at Tabletop, and where her hand was. It was nowhere inappropriate, except it was on him. "What now?"

"I don't think your wife would approve."

"All hail the nuclear family. Newcomen, I got married while you were still throwing pigskins around in college, but if I was going to run off with a mind-wiped CIA-trained assassin? You're right: I'd choose her." He stared the American down. "You don't have any female friends because your warped social conventions don't let you. The rest of the planet think you're idiots."

"She's a traitor to my country," said Newcomen, baldly.

"Yeah. Doesn't stop you from trying to look down her top, though," said Petrovitch. "I think it's time we were going before the Reconstruction virus you're carrying infects anyone else."

He pushed Newcomen around and aimed him at the security screen. Halfway there himself, he turned to see Tabletop adjusting the strap of her bag across her body, watching his receding back plaintively. He stopped, shooed Newcomen onwards, and went back to her.

She hugged him to her, pressing the side of her head against his. He held her for a moment longer than was strictly necessary, and whispered, "Good luck" in her ear.

"And you."

He didn't look back this time, just strode through the arch of the screen without pausing. It didn't detect anything, although the operator's console should have lit up like a Christmas tree. The real-time editing of data wasn't difficult:

all it needed was enough processing power and the bandwidth to pull it off.

Newcomen was scandalised by Petrovitch's behaviour with Tabletop. Petrovitch didn't care.

"I don't expect you to understand, now or ever. Neither do I feel that I owe you an explanation. All you need to know is that she turned against you and everything you stand for when I accidentally showed her a different future. And she's in love with that future – not me – even more than she despises her past. Come on," said Petrovitch, heading off in a seemingly random direction, "we're leaving from gate thirty-four."

Newcomen dug his heels in. "I know I don't know much about international travel, but when I was at JFK, I had to wait two hours between checking in and departure."

"I'm sure you did. According to the airline's computers, we've been at the airport for two and a half hours already, and if you'd noticed the displays, we're already boarding."

"But what about my case? And I wanted to get Christine something from one of the concessions."

"Your case will be fine, and if some giant bear stitched in a sweatshop is your idea of a suitable present for the woman you're going to marry, God help you. And her. Besides, getting back from the Metrozone in one piece should be enough of a gift." Petrovitch shook his head and stood to one side to let a family of eight go by, the man in front, the bejewelled and shimmering woman behind, and six children of various sizes between. "I can delay the flight for as long as I like, but let's not waste any more time, okay?"

Newcomen tore his gaze away from the vast array of shiny baubles and reluctantly followed. Petrovitch didn't wait, but Newcomen's stride length meant he was finally caught. They fell in, side by side, walking down the connecting corridor: Petrovitch caught his reflection in one of the windows, hands in pockets, slouching gait and all. Not that different from the last time he went out to war. He looked past himself to the man next to him, tall, broad, filling his coat and tending to fat around his middle. Newcomen had the appearance of being sculpted, created – which he was.

They looked like they were from different species. He wondered how long it would be before that became true.

They'd been booked business class, but Petrovitch had upped the ante and upgraded them to first. He could have bought the airline, but he didn't normally need one. Just this time – and it wasn't like he was a frequent flyer – he decided he'd take the easy way out and give himself some leg room.

The flight attendants treated him like he was an egg, and Newcomen noticed: how they referred to him as Dr Petrovitch, showed him to his seat, asked if they could stow his luggage and to be sure to call if he needed anything.

He noticed Newcomen's sideways glance.

"It's either because they're scared of me, or because I'm as famous as a physicist is likely to get. Look out the window." Petrovitch had the window seat, and Newcomen had to lean over him to see. "Those bumps on the wing? I invented the things inside them. Remember when you were a kid on the farm, and all those planes you used to see flying overhead like little silver crosses? They're rusting in a desert somewhere in New Mexico because of me."

"Uh, sure."

"We're not sitting in cattle class, are we? Even our tame spooks have had to get bumped so they can keep tabs on us."

Newcomen looked out of the window again. "It still has wings."

"They don't do much of anything except act as something to strap the engines to." Petrovitch frowned. "You didn't honestly think something this vast could fly on those stubby little things, did you? Or did you just not think at all? You flew from Seattle to New York. Then again from there to here. *Yobany stos*, man. Didn't you notice the difference?"

"We took off and landed."

"Vertically?" Petrovitch threw himself against the back of his seat. "I'm going to throw you out mid-Atlantic. Is that all right with you?"

The fuselage filled up with passengers; not that many of them came into Petrovitch's part of the cabin. The secret service guys turned up, dark suits, infoshades, and eased into the rearmost seats. Made aware of their arrival by an alarm he'd placed on the manifest, Petrovitch half stood and gave each one in turn a good minute of his undivided attention.

They stared back at him in return. He'd rather not have had them on the flight, and it would have been straightforward for him to have made the carrier lose their tickets. But a wave of their badges and they'd have been allowed to board anyway. Only US planes could fly to the US, and the carrier depended on a permit from the government to fly. Petrovitch still had to work within the bounds of what was possible. He wasn't omnipotent enough to just wish his dreams into being. Not yet, anyway.

"Problem?" asked Newcomen when Petrovitch had sat down again. He'd been leafing through the safety information on the little handheld screen tucked in the pocket of the seat in front.

"Spooks. Back of the cabin. Don't worry about them for now. They're as trapped here as we are."

"Doesn't mention your name in any of the literature."

"Bet you it doesn't mention Frank Whittle, either."

The cabin staff toured the seats, checking all the passengers were sitting comfortably and securely. The pilot started to taxi them to the edge of the runway, nudging the jets to above idle. They rolled on their fat black wheels out away from the terminal buildings, and Petrovitch watched the cracks in the concrete slide by.

By bending lower, he could see a China Eastern flight coming in from Shanghai, the vast torpedo shape occluding the sky as it drifted overhead. Its undercarriage was down, ready to receive the ground, and its engines pushed it forward until it had a clear space to land on.

The fat, rocket-shaped body rumbled away into the distance, and it was their turn.

The pilot engaged the repulsors. The airframe creaked as the weight shifted, and when the wheels were clear of the runway, they retracted with a series of positive clunking sounds.

The ground dwindled away. With no forward power, they spun slightly, giving Petrovitch a view of the towers of the Metrozone, then the wilds of the Outzone looking towards Windsor down the Thames valley. Tangled trees held their bare arms up in amongst the sighing walls and fractured roads.

They passed through a layer of cloud. The map of the ground was obscured, and they spiralled upwards into the thinner air unsighted.

With the aircraft's nose pointing north-west and bright pillows of cumulus beneath them, the engines started with a rumble that grew into a roar. Shortly into the flight, they passed over Ireland, almost directly above the domes of the Freezone.

Petrovitch felt a pang of longing, and wondered if he'd ever see his home again.

7

Five and a half thousand kilometres later, Petrovitch landed at John F. Kennedy airport at the same time he'd left Heathrow.

It didn't feel right, like so many things. They'd come in over frozen Newfoundland, and he'd shivered at the sight of so much ice and snow. Yet he'd been brought up in a city ten degrees further north. He was out of practice, and he knew he had to get back up to speed quickly. Lives might depend on it. Lucy's. His. Even Newcomen's.

They slid down the east coast until they were poised above Long Island Sound, where they made their descent. It wasn't like at Heathrow, where the airspace outside the M25 was Outie-controlled, and on the off chance one of them had a still-working surface-to-air missile, the planes landed straight down. Here they glided in old-style, lining up with the runway while they were over Long Beach.

The plane touched down with barely a shudder, but next to him, Newcomen visibly relaxed.

"Back on home soil, yeah? Don't let it go to your head."

"The land of the free," sighed Newcomen. Even his fingers had softened from the stiff claws they'd been from the bouncing around they'd had just south of Greenland. Just in case someone had accidentally boarded the wrong flight and needed it pointing out to them where in the world they were, the tannoy started the opening bars of "The Star-Spangled Banner". A legal requirement, apparently.

"Oh, please."

Newcomen stood, along with most of the other passengers. Petrovitch stayed resolutely sitting down.

The woman in front of him noticed his unseemly rebellion and raised a perfectly sculpted eyebrow at him. Her chiffon scarf would have cost more than Petrovitch's entire ensemble, and she thought it only fair to deliver her judgement to the unbeliever.

"Communist."

"Yeah. What of it?"

The woman's husband noticed the sudden chill flowing from his spouse. He turned and frowned.

"Henry, this . . . man; he says he's a communist."

What would they have seen? A thin-faced blond-haired man, cheekbones sharp and Slavic, eyes the colour of old ice. They would have seen the fine white scar that ran from one side of his face to the other, and that he was missing an earlobe. No suit or smart casual for him, either. The last time he'd worn a jacket was on his wedding day. He had an ex-EDF combat smock, and cargo trousers with a hundred pockets.

Definitely not Reconstruction. Anti-Reconstruction: put the two together and wait for the explosion.

"Newcomen? Sort this out. I haven't got the energy."

Petrovitch pushed the agent into the aisle and levered himself across the seat. "It's not like I'm going to be leaving copies of *Das Kapital* in hotel rooms across America any time soon."

"Ma'am, I'm sure he meant no harm." Newcomen reached for his badge. "He's on his first visit, and he's not used to our ways yet."

Petrovitch, his back turned to the stuffily indignant couple, caught sight of the secret service men. Against all the rules of engagement, he stopped on his way past.

"What did you expect me to do? Parachute out over Massachusetts? Or were you just making sure I wasn't going to hijack the flight?"

They, sticking to their roles, refused to acknowledge him.

"Hey. Spooks. Talking to you." He was blocking their exit. They had no choice but to listen to him. "Where's Lucy? You know anything about that, do you? Or are you too low in the food chain?"

Newcomen, having placated the McCarthyites, found himself with a completely different level of altercation.

"Not here," he said into Petrovitch's ear, and tried to bundle him along.

Petrovitch was the immovable object, and Newcomen's force was far from irresistible.

"Not here? Then where? Maryland? And before you say I shouldn't piss these guys off, tell me why they're even here. They're just getting in my face, and I don't like that."

The whole cabin had fallen silent when Petrovitch had said the word "piss". Newcomen was gritting his teeth and had one eye closed, just so he could see fewer shocked expressions.

Petrovitch didn't bother lowering his voice. "Is this what it's going to be like? Your government have agreed that I can come and watch while you fail to find my daughter, and yet I'm treated like a criminal before I've even left neutral ground. *Yobany stos*, I've been here less than five minutes and already I want to kill someone." He eyed the nearest NSA agent. "You, specifically. If I see you on my tail again, I'll blank your bank account."

He growled and headed for the door, while Newcomen had to explain that the sweary man had diplomatic immunity and wasn't going to be hit for the usual twenty bucks profanity fine.

"Have a nice day, Dr Petrovitch," said one of the cabin staff as he passed through the outer door. "Welcome to America."

"Someone is," he muttered, "but sure as hell isn't me." He kept on going.

"Did you have any hand luggage, sir?" came the worried voice from behind him.

"No. No, I didn't. It gives them less to bug."

Once out of the transit tube and in the airport proper, he loped along the travelator, past his fellow travellers, who seemed content to let the moving walkway take them to baggage reclaim.

He was thin enough to slip through any available gap, un-encumbered and light on his feet, almost elfin against the gen-engineered body shapes of the locals. Everybody's parents had gone for height. If they'd selected a boy, they'd gone for muscle bulk; a girl meant either Midwestern natural or Californian beach. Those too old or too poor for the vats were more or less balloons, with expanding waistbands and no necks.

But of the people he could see, most of those under thirty looked the same, and it depressed him.

Somewhere back down the corridor, he could hear Newcomen struggling to catch up. He was never going to make it. Petrovitch didn't need to wait around for a suitcase to come spinning around the carousel.

He stepped off the end of the walkway to the distant sound of "Federal agent, coming through," and strode out towards customs. He had nothing to declare but his own genius, and slipped through the green channel.

It was either honesty or fear of accidentally breaking one of the arcane rules governing imports that drove most people into the red queue. The customs officers – two men, one woman – watched him pass under the brims of their peaked caps. He carried a card that meant they had to leave him alone: that message was being buzzed into their earpieces as he approached, and from the questioning tone of their responses, they didn't like that instruction at all.

He was still officially an enemy of the state. His immunity was only a temporary concession.

Immigration was next – a choice of one of three queues. US citizens could step through a screen, glancing up at the camera that read their retina and confirmed their identity from the tags on their passports, and be out in the arrivals hall without further checks. NAFTA members had to have their documents machine-read before going through a similar arch. Everyone else was herded to one side like cattle, and subjected to a laborious manual process that was going to take the best part of an hour.

"Screw that," said Petrovitch to a passing teletrooper. It heard him, and its metal feet stamped to a halt. It turned what passed for a head towards him, and light flashed out across his face from its visor. And again. It couldn't work out who he was that way, and its camera lens whirred as its vaguely humanoid metal frame leaned in for a closer look.

Petrovitch could feel its presence: not just the burnished metal skin and hydraulic pumps that marked its physicality, but its electronic self, its processors and servos. That someone in a room nearby was hooked up to a VR rig was almost immaterial. The thing itself was what was important. It reminded him of the New Machine Jihad.

He probed the protocols and routines that joined the two entities, slave and master. Not tamperproof, then. Not this model, anyhow. He mentally backed away and kept the information for later.

The teletrooper still couldn't work out who he was looking at, and repeatedly tried to scan him. Petrovitch smiled up at the camera. "Done? Good."

He turned his back on the metal giant and started for the US-only gate. He reached into one of his pockets for a bag. It contained two squash-ball-sized spheres, and he tore at the bag with his teeth, spitting out the strand of plastic when he'd done.

He selected one of the spheres and held it up at head height as he walked through the scanner. This time when the camera peered down at him, it could find a name, an address and a social security number. He strode through, following the plaid back of a man just in from Kansas.

Petrovitch was done with the visible security presence. He had no doubt that he'd been picked up already by human agents, but he didn't bother sifting through the digital chatter for code words deliberately designed to be obscure and difficult. The Freezone data miners could do that later at their leisure.

Instead, he stood and waited for Newcomen to catch up. He could see him through the high perspex barriers that separated the airside from the landside, searching the non-US line for his charge. At first he appeared merely harassed, but on his second trip along the queue of patient supplicants, he grew more agitated.

He stopped, put his hands on his hips and appeared completely bewildered. He looked around jerkily, searching every face, his head turning one way, his body another.

Petrovitch decided to put him out of his misery when the teletrooper started showing an interest in the agent's increasingly erratic behaviour.

He dialled Newcomen's number, and eventually he picked up.

"N-Newcomen."

"You're looking in the wrong place. Through the screen. I'm waving at you."

Petrovitch raised his hand and waggled his fingers, and he couldn't tell whether Newcomen was going to faint dead away or burst into tears.

Whichever, he forgot to look up as he cleared the arch, and had to be manually scanned by one of the transportation officers with a gun-like device which they pressed against Newcomen's eye socket.

He was still blinking away the after-image when he staggered up beside Petrovitch.

"How? How did you get through so quickly?" The agent's luggage trailed after him like a lost puppy and banged into the back of his legs.

Petrovitch uncurled his hand to reveal two artificial eyes, the irises staring boss-wise up from his palm. "It's not like it was difficult."

Newcomen reached for one of the eyes and Petrovitch closed his fist firmly before rebagging and pocketing the items.

"You went through the wrong channel."

"So sue me."

"You're just making a mockery of, of . . ."

"Everything? Newcomen, so much of this is beyond parody.

This whole building is dedicated to security theatre, and it plays every single hour of every single day. Very little of what goes on here actually makes you any safer, but because you all participate in this consensual illusion, you're willing to put up with all the indignities and intrusions." He snorted. "Meh. *Eto mnye do huya*. What you do in your own country to your own citizens is up to you. But you don't do it to me."

They stood while all around them people passed by. The babble of voices, the sounds of the announcements, the bright displays, the steady stream of bodies and odours: it was a world away from the near silence of ruined Dublin.

Petrovitch, the city street kid, overwhelmed by crowds now as well as awed by snowfields.

He was going to have to get a grip. He was soft.

Finally he said: "How were you planning to get us out of this mad house?"

Newcomen blinked. "Uh. What? There's the connecting flight to Seattle in," and he searched the sky for a clock when there was a perfectly serviceable one on his wrist. "Four hours. We could grab a coffee, something to eat . . ."

"Okay, Newcomen, it's like this. Firstly, four hours here is going to make me go postal. Secondly, I've changed the flights. We're going later."

"You can't do that."

"Clearly I can," said Petrovitch. "What you're saying is I shouldn't. I have things to do here in New York. And you have to come with me, whether you like it or not."

"Our travel plans were made days ago. They've been filed."

Petrovitch reached up and snagged Newcomen's neck. He tried to pull away but found he couldn't. They were touching foreheads when they spoke again.

"I'll do what's necessary to find my Lucy. Anything and everything. If that means messing last minute with someone else's schedule, I'll do it without hesitation, and if they don't like it, they can suck my *yelda*."

Newcomen recoiled, and Petrovitch increased his pull.

"At least let me tell AD Buchannan."

"You don't get it, do you? Your saintly Assistant Director already knows. For the moment, he's content to let it happen. They have to allow me the appearance of acting freely. Only at the last moment will they try and pin me down."

"You're paranoid. First you think your daughter's disappearance isn't an accident, and now you think everyone's out to get you."

"It wasn't, and they are." Petrovitch let go, and Newcomen massaged away the finger marks. "Now, are you coming?"

"I guess so."

"Taxi rank's that way. Let's find us a yellow cab."

8

There was a long queue for the taxis, but there was also a long queue of cabs waiting for a fare. It was painfully inefficient, with all except one access point roped off and the order enforced not just by public opprobrium but by a couple of uniformed cops, buttoned up against the cold. The cab driver at the front of the procession of cars would leap out, glad-hand his fares and stow their luggage, then drive off. Everyone would move up one space, and the ritual would be repeated.

If they'd allowed everyone who needed a ride just to grab one, both queues would have vanished in an instant.

"Who the *huy* designed this?" muttered Petrovitch.

"We have to wait in line. It's the way we do things here," Newcomen explained. "It's polite."

Petrovitch writhed in mock agony. "Arrgh, the stupid: it burns, it burns!"

Things were moving, though. Slowly, but moving. Seeing no easy way to subvert the system, Petrovitch seethed his way through the next five minutes and watched the aircraft drifting lazily overhead as they rose to their operating altitude. It was strangely subdued. Objects that size should have been making a thunderous noise. As it was, giant cigar shapes were hanging in the clear air, their engines ticking over, barely producing enough thrust to clear the airport. Just because he'd made that whole process possible didn't mean he was comfortable with it.

Newcomen's luggage trundled up a few more steps as they approached the head of the queue.

"Where are we going?" he asked.

"Embassy. I've a few things I need to pick up."

"Couldn't someone have met you here? It would have saved you the time, and we could have got to Seattle quicker."

Petrovitch finally got to stand on the kerbside, and he half-heartedly raised his hand. He certainly wasn't standing there for the benefit of his health. "Newcomen, we'll be back in plenty of time for your hot date."

Newcomen coloured up. "How did you . . .?"

"Because we're listening to every single conversation you have over every network and every medium you can think of. Even if you wrote Christine a letter and had it fast-couriered to her by pigeon, I can near enough guarantee we'd know what it said before she got it." Petrovitch reached up and closed Newcomen's mouth for him. "Your table's booked for half eight. You'll be there in plenty of time."

The taxi driver flung his door open and raced around to the boot of his cab. "Welcome, welcome, gentlepeoples. You have good journey so far, yes?"

"No, it's been fucking awful. Get Farm Boy's case in the trunk — if it'll fit. Otherwise we'll just leave the pile of crap here and have done with it."

There were more open mouths, and the two cops started to move towards them.

"Diplomatic immunity," said Petrovitch, opening the passenger door for himself and getting in. "Go screw yourselves."

Newcomen climbed in behind him, furious. "You are going to have to stop doing that."

"Why? It's not like I'm going to bring down Reconstruction with mild invective, am I?"

"Mild? Mild? People don't need to hear such appalling profanity anywhere, let alone on the street."

Petrovitch twisted in his seat. "Yeah. You think that's coarse? Screw up finding Lucy and you'll find out just how profane I can get."

The driver eventually managed to close the trunk on Newcomen's case, and dashed back to his position. He was surprised to see one of his fares next to him: they normally rode in the back.

"You should not say such things," he laughed. "Where to?"

Petrovitch gave him the address in the man's native language, and with a bigger grin than he'd worn all year, the driver pulled away from the pavement and out into the traffic.

"*Inch'pes yek' chanach'um?*"

"Read your licence plate, searched for your name and history. A few background checks." It was strange being in a car that wasn't driving itself and couldn't be taken over at a moment's notice. "I'm being followed by a whole alphabet soup of security agencies, despite having my own personal G-man here. I wanted to make sure you weren't a plant."

"You are wanted?"

"Yeah. No. It's complicated." He stuck out his hand. "Petrovitch."

The driver took his hand off the wheel to respond, causing Newcomen to cough loudly.

"Artak," said the driver.

"I know," said Petrovitch. "I know everything about you."

"Petrovitch. *The* Petrovitch?"

"Don't shout about it. Everybody will want one."

"I will not get into trouble for this?" Artak's fingers clamped back on the steering wheel, white-knuckle tight.

"I come with my own FBI escort. You'll be fine." Petrovitch peered out through the window.

They were driving down the Expressway through Queens, and there wasn't much to see yet. The buildings of Manhattan rose tall and slender through the gaps in the street plan, and occasionally he caught a glimpse of the Staten Island arcology, looming bulbous and organic in the distance.

"You ever been in the arco?" Petrovitch said to the back seat.

Newcomen leaned forward. "I've never been to New York before. Except for the stopover."

"One building with a hundred thousand inhabitants. Even I'm impressed by that: a serious piece of engineering."

"I could get you an invitation," said the agent.

"I'm not here as a tourist. Besides, we've stolen all the ideas we want from it already. Suggested some improvements to the architects, too, though I don't know whether they think our knowledge is dangerously tainted or not."

The car reached a bend in the road, and suddenly the commercial heart of America was right in front of them, across the East River. Towers as thin as needles rose into the sky, holographic adverts projecting around their crowns like medieval haloes. There were so many structures it looked like a forest of thorns.

The taxi slowed briefly for the toll booths. Artak chose one of the automatic lanes, his pass on the dashboard talking to the barrier on the booth. Money was deducted from his account, money he'd add to his fare on arrival.

It went dark, and the lights of the tunnel reflected off Petrovitch's eyes as he turned again to Newcomen.

"If you were wondering, we're going to the Irish consulate on the corner of Sixth Avenue and Tenth Street. I have to clean you off."

"Clean me?"

"You're lousy with microbugs, stuck to your back like burrs. Someone must have dosed you at the airport. Don't worry," he said. "We'll sort it."

Then they were out in the daylight again, no longer covered by the radio shadow of the tunnel, and Petrovitch stopped talking. He put his finger to his lips, just in case Newcomen hadn't understood properly.

The daylight didn't last long. As soon as they were clear of the tunnel, they were in amongst the buildings, which blocked out the sky. A thin slit of blue glowed overhead, but street level was lit with a gaudy mix of adverts, projections and fluorescence.

People crowded the pavements – properly sidewalks now – in a thick carpet. Like the Metrozone used to be before successive disasters had struck it, and how it would be again one day. Store windows blazed with shifting lights, many of them red and patterned in the shape of hearts.

"Valentine's Day. It's today, isn't it?" Petrovitch leant his head back against the seat. "So that's why you're in such a hurry to get back to Christine. Apart from the obvious, of course."

"What do you mean? Of course it's today. Doesn't your wife expect, I don't know, something?"

"It's not her saint's day. Oh, you mean the other thing."

"I'll put up with almost any indignity you want, but don't be crude about my fiancée. Okay?" Newcomen's tone was guarded, but it wasn't pleading.

"Yeah, okay. Got to protect the purity of young love." Petrovitch looked at Artak as he navigated the streets with exaggerated care. "*Na mi kuys.*"

"*Dzer kartsik'ov, aydpes?*"

"Yeah. Absolutely certain. I recognise the signs."

They passed a police podium at the next intersection, raised above the level of the street to allow the two officers on top to spot and stop any trouble before it started. No one seemed to be doing anything illicit: the cops were watchful, though, because they knew they were being watched as well.

The taxi nosed left, on to Sixth Avenue, and started the trek down to where Tenth Street crossed, down towards the south end of Manhattan Island, past some of the two million people who lived there and the two million who travelled there every day to work.

It made the Clapham A domik pile where he'd lived previously seem like a wilderness by comparison. So many, crammed into such a small space. It was a wonder they didn't all go mad and kill each other, just to have room to move their elbows.

It was Reconstruction that made it possible. Without it, it would never have even tried to grow so big. Petrovitch wondered what other surprises America had lined up for him.

Then they were there, outside the old Jefferson Market library. Made of municipal red brick, it looked like a church with its tall windows and arches, but the tower attached to it was more reminiscent of a Soviet-style rocket.

"*Inchkan?*"

"No charge," said Artak.

"Yeah, you're just being silly now." Petrovitch pulled out a stack of cash cards and sorted through them until he found one in the right currency. "Unless you want paying in yuan."

He grabbed the reader and peered at it for a moment, deciphering its idiosyncrasies, then slotted in the card and debited the amount on the glowing fare meter, adding a tip large enough that at least one of Artak's kids could make it through college unburdened by debt.

The driver would find out later. Petrovitch felt no need to make a song and dance about it.

"*Merci*," he said, springing the door. "*Shat hatcheli e'.*"

Newcomen scrambled out, and Artak dumped his case on the kerb.

"Thank you," the agent remembered to say. Petrovitch was already diving through the flood of pedestrians on his way to the seven stone steps leading to the consulate's wooden doors.

A little brass plate on the stonework stated the building's purpose. Petrovitch looked up and down the street and at the blank-faced building opposite. The library was an island from the nineteenth century stranded in the twenty-first.

"You know how many cameras are trained on us at the moment?" he said to Newcomen. "The NSA, the FBI, INS, CIA, ATF, Homeland Security, Treasury. Pretty much every single one. It's not like we don't tell them what we're up to."

"You do?"

"Most of the time." He smiled slyly.

The door opened, despite Petrovitch not having even knocked.

"Hey, Sam."

"Hey, Marcus. Don't touch the hired muscle: he's broadcasting."

A thin black man with puffball grey hair stood to one side and waited for Petrovitch and Newcomen, followed by his case, to come inside. He pushed the door shut behind them, and paused while some definitely un-Victorian-era locks whirred into place.

"So," said Marcus, "you made it this far."

"Relatively unscathed. If they left us alone, we'd get this done so much quicker." Petrovitch held open the door to a metal cabinet in the corner of the foyer, revealing a space just large enough for a man to stand. "Get in. Stand perfectly still."

"Uh, what is this?" Newcomen asked, even as he was drawn irresistibly towards it.

"It's a bigger version of what Tabletop used at the airport. Rather than spend an hour picking each individual bug off you, we'll just nuke the lot of them." He jerked his head at the container. "You might see some bright flashes, smell something funny or convince yourself you've seen God. Just side effects – they don't last."

Newcomen squeezed in, still uncertain. There were no windows, or even a light. He hesitated, causing Petrovitch to sigh. "What now?"

"I might be claustrophobic."

"Well, perhaps you should have worn your big girl pants when you got up this morning." He slammed the door and pressed the button. As the capacitors charged up, he retreated across the foyer to stand with Marcus.

"How's he shaping up?"

"I don't think they could have sent anyone worse." Petrovitch pursed his lips. "All I have to do is figure out whether that's bad for us, or bad for them. He grew up on an automatic farm, so he's only not quite a pampered city kid. He played college football, but gave it up after one bad accident. He was an English major, not a proper subject. He's served his two years in the army, but no one ever shot at him. He got through the FBI selection in the middle of his class. He's been a special agent for two and a half years, yet he's never made an actual arrest. He seems to be a perfectly blank slate. If he has any identifiable skills, I've yet to see them: if he holds any opinions, apart from on my vocabulary, I've yet to hear them."

Marcus stared at his shoes. "He is a Reconstructionist, though. To the core."

"Yeah. That's why I'm holding out some hope. If they're passing over the candidates who're actually qualified for this job in order to give it to party apparatchiks, the whole Bureau – hell, the whole system – might be staffed by incompetent ideologues we can have fun running rings around." Petrovitch snorted. "How very Soviet of them."

The capacitors were full. The energy they stored was dumped into a series of coils made of wire fat enough not to melt, and a high-intensity magnetic field briefly enveloped Newcomen.

Even outside the shielded box, Petrovitch felt the surge.

"If that wasn't enough, they've been hardening their spyware." He walked over and hauled on the door. "Okay. Out. Assume the position."

Petrovitch produced a wand, which he ran slowly and carefully over Newcomen, who stood, spreadeagled, with his palms on the now-warm cabinet.

"Clear," he said eventually. "Marcus'll dump your luggage in too, but right now? A decent cup of coffee, and I can show you why I think Lucy's still alive."

9

Inside the main reading room, it was warm and bright. Little light penetrated through the stained-glass windows except at midday, so most of the illumination came from elaborate chandeliers decorated with thousands of crystal prisms. Electroluminescent wall hangings supplemented the downward light with their blue-white glow.

The space was high, and a circular balcony had been built to take advantage of it, self-supporting so as not to damage the stonework.

People were working up there, if lying on couches with infoshades on counted as working.

"What are they doing?" asked Newcomen. He spoke in a whisper. Perhaps he thought they were sleeping.

"Data mining. Digging into raw statistics and turning them into something people can use. It's our biggest export. Coffee?"

Petrovitch stopped by a wooden table and touched the back of his hand to a jug on a warming plate. He nodded with satisfaction and took two mugs from the tray, filling them with a thick oil-black brew.

While Newcomen stirred and added milk, Petrovitch took his mug down to the centre of the reading room, where there was a round table surrounded by chairs. Marcus was already there, dark glasses lying on the polished wood in front of him.

When the city authorities had sold them the building, they'd left all the books inside. Maybe they thought they'd all be thrown out: not so. The Freezone had kept them exactly where they'd been shelved. The bookcases were arranged around them, the spines of the books facing outwards. Those and the coffee: it smelled right.

When Newcomen joined them, Marcus slid the infoshades across to him.

"Where do I sit?"

"Wherever you want, son," said Marcus.

He dithered, and chose a seat two away from Petrovitch. He seemed thrown by the fact there was no subordinate position to take on a circular table.

"Put them on," said Petrovitch. "I'll try and explain as I go. So that you understand, I'll do my best to make it simple enough, even for you."

"Should I be grateful?" Newcomen unfolded the arms on the shades and slipped them over his ears.

"I'd prefer to get technical. If you'd had any science in your background, I might have been able to spare you the baby version." Petrovitch picked up his mug and blew steam off the top of it. "As it is, you're going to have to rely on my ability to explain complex concepts to complete ignoramuses."

"I have a bachelor's degree."

"In American literature. You may as well have done media

studies for all the use it is. Now *past' zebej* and concentrate. I'm not going to do this twice."

Petrovitch ran a solar system simulator and patched Newcomen into it.

"Tell me you recognise this. Please."

"Uh, it's the Sun." Newcomen paused. "Isn't it?"

"Yeah, it is. Gold star for you."

The Sun burned bright and steady, but around its edges, the light flickered as if it were dancing to silent music. Petrovitch zoomed in on it until they could only see the corona.

"The Sun spits out all sorts of junk. As well as visible light, it glows all the way from radar frequencies to X-rays. It also ejects charged particles, bits of high-energy matter. This goes out in all directions, and is called the solar wind. When the Sun's atmosphere is quiet, there's less wind. When it's stormy, we get a lot. The Earth's magnetic field deflects the solar wind to the polar regions. When the charged particles enter our atmosphere, they excite molecules high up and make them glow. These are the aurora, or Northern and Southern Lights. Stop me if you know this."

"I, uh, might have done once."

"If I were you, I'd be ashamed." Petrovitch brought up the magnetic field lines, holding the Earth like a basket would an egg. "I get laughed at because I know the value of the gravitational constant, but somehow it's social suicide not to know who Odysseus's mother was."

"Anticlea."

"Shut up, Marcus. Anyway, this stuff is relevant for later." Petrovitch drank more coffee. "The study of the interaction between the solar wind and the Earth's magnetic field is a mix between geophysics and magnetohydrodynamics called auroral physics. Lucy has a PhD in auroral physics, and she was collaborating with the University of Alaska at Fairbanks, testing out new sensing equipment. New equipment that she'd designed and built herself. The Northern Slope is a good place to test as it's electromagnetically very quiet. I wanted her to go to Svalbard or Greenland instead, but Fairbanks got in first with their invitation."

Newcomen scratched at his eyelid behind his lenses. "She was invited?"

"Yeah. And unless this is one big conspiracy, I have to assume it was genuine. Auroral research is a small community. Everyone knows everyone else, and Lucy's one of the bright young things. They wouldn't play with her life like that." Petrovitch stopped and shifted in his seat. He had to be right about that aspect of the whole *pizdets*, because the alternative was unthinkable: he'd asked for, and received, assurances from everyone involved that his girl would be treated right. "Okay, this is where we get down to the detail."

He spun the Earth, and closed in on Alaska. "One more thing: remember I said the Sun gets stormy sometimes? That causes us problems, even one hundred and fifty million kilometres away. As all the Sun stuff hits us, it pinches the Earth's magnetic field. The flow of energy is enough to cause power lines to fail, compasses to scramble, and to trash satellites. If you're in a spaceship or a high-flying aircraft, you can get a year's dose of radiation in a matter of minutes. Got that? Okay. Some twenty kilometres east of Deadhorse, the oil company town at Prudhoe Bay, is a research station: seventy degrees ten minutes thirty-two seconds north, one hundred and forty-eight degrees five minutes and fifty-seven seconds west. That's where Lucy was, as of last Monday night."

The points on the map flashed as he said their names. They faded away, except for the location of the research post.

"At nine twenty-three Universal Time, twenty-three minutes past midnight local, we lost contact with her."

Newcomen sat forward and tilted his head to one side, as if to understand the information better. "So her computer fails, or is taken off her, or she takes it off herself. I know you don't want to discuss the possibility—"

"You're right. I don't," said Petrovitch. "She's alive. See if you can think of something that'll kill a Freezone-designed link without killing its wearer."

Newcomen pulled his glasses off and rubbed at his eyes with the ball of his hand. "I don't know. You've done nothing but talk about it, so: solar wind?"

"You'll have to do better than just stumble across the right answers when we're out in the field, Newcomen, but yeah. Same process we used to nuke your bugs and my visa. An intense electromagnetic pulse will melt the circuitry of a link. It's hardened against e-m radiation, but a strong enough burst will kill it stone dead. We can discount a solar storm, because there wasn't one. Someone emped her."

Newcomen held up his hand. "Wait a second. That doesn't make sense: someone dragged a piece of equipment the size of the thing you put me in all the way out into the middle of nowhere just to ruin her portable computer?"

"Put like that, it's clearly mad." Petrovitch waved Newcomen's infoshades back on his face. "So we did some checking. Turns out that the Alaskan pipeline went offline at the same time as computers all over the North Slope and parts of Canada, and after a bit of a struggle, we found out that a lot of the early-warning radar stations you've got out on the Dewline went belly-up too. All roughly at the same time as Lucy's link went down. What does that sound like to you?"

Newcomen rested his head on the table. "Uh, sir. I don't know about this stuff. I'm not an expert in whatever-it-is. Why don't you tell me?"

"Because I want you to think for yourself for the first fucking time in your life!" Petrovitch slammed his hand down hard on the polished woodwork. "You've been told what to think, what to say, what to see, what to do for twenty-eight long years. Aren't you sick of it yet?"

He was breathing hard, and he had to restrain himself from shaking the American by the throat. Restrain himself for certain, because no one else was going to be capable of holding him back.

Newcomen's eyes narrowed, and something resembling a spark showed behind them. "It sounds like a Sun storm. But you already said there wasn't one."

"Bingo."

"Bingo?"

"Bingo," said Petrovitch emphatically. "So: what caused the geomagnetic storm, considering it wasn't the Sun?"

"I don't know."

"And neither do I."

The revelation made Newcomen frown. "What?"

"I know, I know. I do omniscience too well. When I say I don't know, I can give you a list of things that might have the same effects. But each one is more unlikely than the next. And your government is telling us precisely nothing." Petrovitch pressed his fingertips to his temples and made small circular motions. "So we went back to check again. Did anything else happen in a ten-minute window around the time we lost contact,

81

anything at all? Surprisingly enough, we found something. An earthquake."

"And how is that connected?"

"It's not. Alaska accounts for eleven per cent of all the world's earthquakes. Eleven. That day alone there were seventy-three discrete events. An average of one every twenty minutes. And all of them only measurable with a seismograph. However, the one that we looked at was different from all the others: it happened a long way to the north of the usual belt, though that in itself doesn't mean anything. But its seismographic signature was all wrong. It wasn't an earthquake at all, it was an explosion. We can even estimate its energy. Take a look."

The satellite image Newcomen saw was of a scar in the snow, dark against the white.

"It's a crater, some four hundred metres across. Recent snowfall's obscured it, but this was taken while it was still fresh: you can just about make out the crater wall. But I don't think anything exploded on the ground. Looks like an airburst. It's well beyond the northern limit of the treeline, so all that was damaged was rock and ice, twenty-four kilometres south-west of the research station, and thirty-two k south of Prudhoe Bay. I find it a coincidence of astronomical proportions that the two events, crater and electromagnetic disturbance, aren't connected. Same time, same place."

Newcomen was silent for a long time. He scratched his chin, while Petrovitch rubbed the bridge of his nose.

"Does," started Newcomen, then stopped. He gave it another go. "Does Assistant Director Buchannan know any of this?"

"Why don't you ask him?" Petrovitch waited for Newcomen to take off the infoshades again and place them warily on the table. "Sure as hell we're not the first to work this out."

"And in the middle of all this going on, your adopted daughter disappears."

"Yeah. How does it sound to you now? Sound like she just walked into the wilderness and froze to death? Or did something else happen to her? What did she see that night? More importantly, what did she measure?"

"What did she . . . measure?"

"Keep up, Newcomen. The kit she had with her would have been able to spot someone using a light switch at a hundred k. She was recording at the time. Could be that she interpreted the results on the fly. If it was something out of the ordinary, and she had proof of it, there might be a good reason to make her disappear. Have you heard of Haarp?"

"Of what?"

"Haarp. Aitch-ay-ay-arr-pee. It's been kicking around for fifty years as a superweapon designed to harness the Earth's magnetic field and focus it like a laser. It's all *kon govno*. I hope. But something happened that night. A nuke designed for an emp effect. Some sort of space-based particle beam gun that can punch through the atmosphere." He blinked. "Now that would be scary."

Petrovitch drifted off into a reverie, and was only brought out of it by Newcomen sitting up sharply.

"There might be another explanation," said the agent. "You say she was alone in the research station."

"Yeah."

"Can you be certain of that?"

"She never mentioned anyone. And no one was scheduled to be there with her until two days later, on a supply run." Petrovitch sucked at his teeth. Michael, all-knowing, hadn't said anything either. Lucy was allowed to keep secrets from

Petrovitch, from Madeleine, but not from Michael. "What are you implying?"

"How attractive is she?"

"She's . . . I'm her legal father. I don't think I'm supposed to have an opinion on that. She's, you know," and he threw up his hands.

"Lucy's only four years younger than you are."

"She's only four years younger than you, too. You tell me, do you think she's pretty?"

"I'm engaged to be married." Newcomen huffed and stuck his finger in his collar. "You must know there's about ten guys for every girl in Alaska."

"And you must know that statistic's bollocks."

"Could someone have taken advantage of the fact that her link was down? Could they have decided to mount their own rescue mission because they're infatuated with her?" Newcomen was on a roll. "Could she have not wanted to be rescued, and then been kidnapped?"

Petrovitch's mind temporarily fused. "I . . . I hadn't thought of that."

"If this is a kidnapping, it's federal business. She may have even gone willingly, if she thought she was going to be taken back to Fairbanks or this Deadhorse place."

"Deadhorse," said Petrovitch. "That's closest by far."

"When did the rescue team get to the research station?"

"Sunday morning. There was a snowstorm. The university couldn't get a team out until then, and they borrowed an air force unit out of Eielson."

"Two, three days. How far can you go in three days?"

"Twice round the planet," said Petrovitch. "But not if the vehicle you're trying to use has no electrics. Lucy had a snowmobile. Magnetic field strong enough to fry her link would have destroyed the ignition."

"It should be relatively easy to check who she'd met, who might have braved a three-day-long blizzard to go and get her, and who had the means to do it. The list of suspects isn't going to be huge. And whoever it is is unlikely to hurt her. Keep her prisoner, yes. Hurt her, no."

"I wish I could share your confidence. If any of this is remotely accurate, they might decide that if they can't have her, no one else will."

"I'm sure Lucy's very smart. She'll know how to play for time. She must know that you're coming for her."

"Oh, she'll know." The corner of Petrovitch's eye twitched. "We've done this before."

Petrovitch sent Newcomen away into a corner with a screen and a copy of one of the many unauthorised biographies written about him, and sat down with a fresh brew.

"What do you think?"

Marcus brought out a long-toothed comb and started to tease his hair to even greater heights. "That the boy has had an uncharacteristic flash of brilliance, or he's delving deep into his own psyche and it's not a pleasant place." He found a knot and tugged at it. "It's a credible scenario. Lucy's quite a looker. And remember, Sam: you're here to try and get her back, not bring down another president."

"We could do that later, I suppose. Are we going to have to break her privacy seal and find out what she's really been up to?"

"I'm surprised you haven't asked for that before," said Marcus. "In fact, I'll take matters out of your hands: Michael will call an ad-hoc, and if they agree, a counsellor will pick over what information there is. Michael will tell you if anything relevant comes up."

Petrovitch hunched over. "We've a good relationship. I know it's not like a father–daughter thing really, but we both behave as if it is. Newcomen's right on one thing: she is smart, but she doesn't get that from me. Otherwise she'd have inherited my low cunning, too, rather than the naïve optimism she excels in despite everything that's happened to her."

"You're scared of what the counsellor might find."

"Yeah. If it helps to get her back, I can live with the embarrassment, and so can she. We won't be the same, though." He let out a long breath. "I used to be a hard bastard. Nothing could get through. Skin like a rhino."

"I blame that wife of yours." Marcus laid the comb down. "She's changed you. Honestly, I think I prefer this Samuil Petrovitch."

"Caring makes it so much more difficult to behave rationally. Even to think rationally."

"You want to blame this on the Americans. We probably all do. She was in their care, and the name Petrovitch carries a lot of baggage with it. What else were we to think?"

"Now it makes even less sense than it did beforehand. Something happened in the sky that night, independent of whether she had a secret admirer who rode to her rescue on a white charger. That had something to do with the Yankees: I feel it in what's left of my bones."

"Finding out what it was is secondary, Sam." Marcus put his hand over Petrovitch's. "I know what you're like."

"Yeah. Focus, focus." He tried a smile, but it came out all wrong. "It's going to drive me crazy. I hate not knowing stuff. I really hate not knowing stuff that other people do know and are trying to keep from me."

"Your travel bag's almost ready. Make sure no one looks inside it."

"I'll do my best." Petrovitch looked over to where Newcomen sat. The man looked as white as a ghost, his lips thin, pale lines drawn over his teeth. "I don't think he's enjoying his book."

"Even if half the things written in it were true, he'll be shocked to his little Reconstructionist core. Where's he up to?"

"He's just skipping through it, reading about a paragraph a page. He's up to the point where I apparently order the slaughter of two hundred thousand Outies, and just before the second Battle of Waterloo."

"Leave enough time to get to the airport," said Marcus.

"Plenty. Hour and a half, flying from Newark. Newcomen's taking his girl out for Valentine's Day, something I think he should do. Something vaguely normal. It'll be the last chance he gets."

"He's taking his predicament well, I think."

"He's blanking it out completely. Perhaps he hopes it'll disappear if he doesn't mention it. Don't worry, I'll remind him often enough."

"And you really think you can keep him in line? What if he suddenly gets brave?"

"Then it'll be for the first time in his adult life." Petrovitch ran his hand over his chest, where the turbine spun quietly. "I'll deal with that if it happens, but I'll subvert him before then. He already thinks his boss might be lying to him, or at least not telling him the whole truth. In his binary mind, that probably counts as the same thing. Authority has to be trusted completely, at all times. That's a basic tenet of Reconstruction."

"Unless he wants there to be a good reason why he hasn't been told about the electromagnetic storm."

"And the crater."

"That too." Marcus picked some stray hairs from out of

the teeth of his comb, then slipped it into his back pocket. "Some people's capacity for self-delusion is prodigious."

"What am I going to do if I can't find her?" Petrovitch drank some more coffee and looked pensive.

"Some self-delusions are more inspiring than others. We call that kind hope." Marcus got up from his seat and collected the carpet bag being offered to him by a pink-haired woman with stripy tights. It was heavy with promise, and when he dumped it on the table in front of Petrovitch, it fell with a solid thump.

"Is that everything?"

"It's what you ordered. If you've forgotten anything now, then it's a little late."

Petrovitch pulled the bag into his lap and unzipped it. A flimsy piece of paper shoved on top popped out: he unfolded it and saw his inventory printed out and each item checked as it was packed.

"Where's the . . .?"

"Here." Marcus passed him the tags that would mark the bag as a diplomatic pouch. "I don't like it, though."

"This is the first time we've ever done this, while everybody else does it all the time – and we can prove it. Anyway," said Petrovitch, tying the tags on to the handle, "it's for all the best reasons."

"Just make sure you don't, you know."

"What? Blow stuff up?"

"It'd be good if you at least tried to behave." He grew serious. "We all want Lucy back, but you need to remember that you're part of the Freezone collective now."

"Yeah, I know all this."

"It's my job to remind you."

"Thank you, Mr Ambassador."

"Don't get shirty with me, Sam. We have protocols. We vary

them only in exceptional circumstances, so don't think they don't apply to you."

"Marcus, this is Lucy we're talking about."

"I'm painfully aware of that. I don't want you going rogue, you hear me? I want you back as well as Lucy. Michael will keep a close eye on you to make sure you stick to the few rules we have."

"I'm sure he will." Petrovitch chewed at his lip and counted to ten. Slowly. "Marcus, I know it's your job. I'm not going to screw up, okay? No declaring war on anyone unless it's absolutely necessary."

"Or at all. If you want to go off the reservation, talk to Michael, and we'll have an ad-hoc. And you'll behave yourself if the decision goes against you."

"It was easier when I could do what I wanted."

"You mean when you were always a hair's breadth away from getting yourself killed." Marcus sat down next to him, favouring his old bones. "I know how impulsive you are. Hell, I've seen the way you play chess, all or nothing. You need to take it slowly. Your usual way of doing things isn't going to work."

Petrovitch screwed the inventory up and threw it into a bin, then zipped up the bag. He locked it with his thumbprint and put it on the floor beside him.

"I'll do my best," he finally said.

"The Freezone's bigger than you, Sam."

"It's always been bigger than me. If," said Petrovitch, struggling for the words, "if it's a choice between me following the rules and me getting Lucy back, you know which way it's going to go, don't you?"

"I know. Everybody knows. Which is why we're all holding our breath, waiting to see what happens."

"Yeah." Petrovitch laughed. "It'll be fine."

"Time you were off, Sam."

"I wonder how many NSA agents are going to be on our tail this time."

"I've already complained to the State Department, for all the good that'll do. You don't honestly think they trust the FBI to control you, do you?"

"It would just be brilliant if they left me alone like they said they would." Petrovitch nodded in Newcomen's direction. "I've got an escort . . ."

"Who you drugged and boobytrapped," interrupted Marcus.

". . . who, I was going to say, should be enough. It's now more in my interest to keep him with me than bury him in the nearest snowdrift. They should be thanking me." He levered himself upright, scooped up the bag and advanced on Newcomen. "Come on then, G-man. You've got a date with a real live woman, which in itself is an accomplishment of sorts. Let's get you there on time and looking vaguely presentable."

Newcomen looked up from his reading, trying to match the skinny, scruffy blond man carrying the alarmingly heavy bag with the monster of legend.

"Did you do all this?" He nodded at the screen.

Petrovitch snorted. "Don't believe everything you read."

"Then why did you get me to read it?"

"Because some of it is true."

Newcomen tossed the reader into the chair opposite him, and stood up, straightening his jacket. "Which bits, then?"

"You don't honestly think I'd waste a second with that *govno*? *Yobany stos*, I was there at the time: I know what went on." Petrovitch retrieved the reader and rolled it up into a tube. He pushed it into Newcomen's top pocket. "And in some respects, it's not what happened that's important. Not ten years on and an ocean away. It's why a tabloid journalist should spend six months of their lives digging through all the old news reports and web pages to write a book that's only partly right. Figure it out. But later: we need to go."

He led the way back out to the library foyer, and Newcomen was reunited with his luggage.

"Is it clean?"

"Yeah, it's clean. Even that old satellite phone you've been lugging around with you."

"You . . . know about the phone?"

"You were unconscious and I only had my hands in your chest for a little while. I thought I'd have a poke around and make sure that you weren't carrying any contraband." Petrovitch shrugged. "It's not like the locks were difficult to crack. I had to assume the ones who sent you wanted me to look inside."

"I've been . . ."

"Talking to Buchannan on it. I know. Good work on not telling him about the bomb, by the way. Because if you had, you'd be dead by now."

"And . . ." Newcomen was aghast.

"Christine. Likewise. Though you employed so much corn on your last conversation I thought I was going to have to break it up by puking all over you." Petrovitch put his hand out to the door lock, and the bolts pulled back with a clunk.

"My private conversations."

"Yeah. I warned you when you first woke up: everything you say, everything you do, I get to find out about. You had no reason to assume your box of tricks was immune from that. Not that it'll be a problem any more, because both your tie and your sat phone are slag."

Petrovitch heaved the door aside. There was another taxi

waiting on the kerbside, the driver just emerging into the cold New York air. No Artak this time – he was away over in Brooklyn on another fare – it was just another guy with a car and a meter, looking to make a few bucks carrying a couple of out-of-towners down the New Jersey Turnpike.

When he saw the two men with their bags, he moved to open his trunk. Only the tall guy wanted his squared away, though. The foreigner shook his head with such steady conviction that he felt compelled to back away and get into his cab as quickly as he could.

"What you got in there anyway?" the driver asked conversationally once they were on the road.

"It's a, uh, diplomatic thing," said Newcomen. "Best not go there."

"Courier job, eh? Where you going?"

"Seattle," said Newcomen. He was disturbed by the lack of response from Petrovitch, sat in the seat next to him, bag firmly on his lap. He glanced around to see him with his head turned to face the back window.

"Are we," and he struggled to look for himself, "being followed?"

"Yeah. At least three cars broadcasting encrypted burst transmissions on shortwave. There may be more than three, but at least they've the good sense to keep radio silence."

"What this you're saying? We're being tailed? Better call the cops." The driver reached to turn his phone on.

"He is the cops," murmured Petrovitch. "So are they. Don't sweat it. We were followed on the way from JFK, too, just more artfully."

The taxi man pulled his hand back. "As long as you're sure. You guys in some sort of trouble, then?"

"I didn't think so," said Petrovitch, "but now I'm not so sure."

They were over Nebraska, doing five hundred k and climbing to get over the Rockies.

Petrovitch had been sitting quietly, hands folded in his lap, seemingly asleep. Newcomen was next to him, watching the clock and growing increasingly fretful.

"There's plenty of time," said Petrovitch, his voice barely louder than the hum of the air scrubbers.

"I thought you were . . ."

"You were wrong. Again. I'm working." Only his lips moved.

"On what?"

"Who might have taken Lucy. Working my way through all her contacts, cross-referencing phone calls, debit payments, key uses, CCTV captures, computer logins, canteen swipe cards. It's a complicated four-dimensional map, but it's the easiest way to spot patterns."

Newcomen looked around the cabin, at the stewards and stewardesses moving quietly among the passengers. Different to the flight across the Atlantic: not one had called on them, even once.

There was a different pair of NSA agents with them, too, sitting apart from each other and at least making an attempt to blend in. Petrovitch had pointed them out as soon as they'd taken their seats. He'd identified the account used to pay for their seats as being the same as for the flight from Heathrow.

"Found anything?"

"Yeah." He opened his eyes and pushed himself up slightly using the arms of the chair. He reached out and pulled the screen from Newcomen's pocket. "This man: recognise him?"

Newcomen put his palm behind the screen and waited for the image to brighten. "No. Should I?" A tousle-haired, ruddy-faced youth with a lopsided grin stared out at him.

"Jason Fyfe. Canadian citizen, twenty-three years old, degree in meteorology, studying for a doctorate in ionospheric interactions at McGill. Should be at Fairbanks, whereabouts currently unknown. Last seen a week last Saturday."

"Last seen, as in, he's disappeared too?"

"No one's reported him missing, if that's what you mean. He hired an all-terrain vehicle and headed off into the wilderness. No communications with him since."

"But you can track the RV through its locator, right?"

"I would if I could. He's gone off the radar completely. I don't know what that means yet." Petrovitch looked down at the geometric patchwork of fields swept with blown snow, thousands of metres below. "The university has ATVs of its own, and he's not doing field work. The timing of this unscheduled trip is making my spidey senses tingle."

"Anyone else?" Newcomen rolled the screen back up.

"I can, with varying degrees of accuracy, place everyone in

the physics faculty. I'm widening the search across the whole of the university, and eventually, everyone in Fairbanks. But let's start with Fyfe."

"I'll talk to the Assistant Director. We've two agents in Fairbanks: they can interview his friends, see if he and Lucy were . . ." he paused. "Close."

"Don't be so *yebani* coy, Newcomen." Petrovitch turned and focused on him. "That'd be a really good idea, except Buchannan's withdrawn those agents. There's now no FBI presence in the whole of northern Alaska. Fancy that."

"Why would he do that?"

"Presumably because he's been ordered to do so by someone well above an Assistant Director's pay grade. Doesn't this sound at all suspicious to you yet? Ignore the fact that it's me – I'm never going to be invited to the White House for a kaffeeklatsch – and concentrate on Lucy. A foreign national with diplomatic credentials goes missing in a remote area of Alaska in what turns out to be less-than-straightforward circumstances, and the FBI pull the only two agents they have on the ground? If you can make sense of that scenario, you're smarter than you look."

"Gee. Thanks."

"Seriously. Is this standard Bureau operating procedure?"

"I'm sure the AD has his reasons."

"Yeah, he's being leant on by someone further up the food chain." Petrovitch clenched his teeth. "When we finally see him, I've a mind to tell him that if my presence here is standing between him and being able to deploy the people he needs to, then I'll take the first plane out of here."

"But you don't think it is."

"No. No, I don't. I have to be certain, though. I don't think you appreciate just how much your security services hate me. I tricked the National Security Council into giving me your nuclear launch codes and forced the resignation of President Mackensie. They're never going to forgive me, and they're certainly never going to forget."

"I'm sorry," said Newcomen. "You did what?"

"That's the subject of chapter eighteen in *Samuil Petrovitch: an unlife*. I don't think you've got to it yet, and what's there is pretty much all wrong. What actually happened was that I faked an attack and stole the gold codes. Mackensie didn't really have anywhere to go after that."

"That's not what I remember."

"Of course it's not: your news is little more than wholly transparent propaganda, and has been for over three decades – but you swallow up every last lie because the guy in the suit tells you to."

Newcomen was breathing hard. "That is not true."

"Yeah, it is. Your generation knows less about the world than even your parents did, and most of them knew jack. Ignorance offends me, Newcomen. As a nation you've bought into a massive consensual hallucination: that you're the chosen people, that your country has a God-given right to stride the globe like a demented colossus, and anything, anything at all that you do is justifiable because it's you doing it. When Mackensie was president, he authorised assassinations, drone strikes, blackmail, the wholesale slaughter of a civilian popula-tion and the use of a nuclear weapon in the middle of a city – all of that aimed against me and the world's only artificial intelligence, who just happened to be my friend." Petrovitch leaned closer and growled. "And he never even apologised. Why would he? He still doesn't think he did anything wrong."

He became aware that the rest of the cabin was listening,

that they couldn't help but listen, because he wasn't exactly trying to keep it down.

He took a deep breath. The NSA men, one to his left, one behind, seemed to be resting their hands on their pistols, ready to fire aircraft-safe plastic rounds if necessary.

"You know what?" Petrovitch said, easing himself back into his seat. "I think I ought to stop there." He raised his hand to attract the attention of one of the stewards – not difficult since they were all looking at him anyway.

"Sir?"

"Can we have a couple of Jack Daniel's, please? I think they'll settle the nerves."

"Yessir. Coming right up, sir." The steward almost fell over in his hurry to complete the order.

"Is that okay with you, Newcomen? I know it's what you drink on the few occasions you do break your wholly unnecessary temperance."

"I think, in the circumstances, that liquor might be justified."

"It's pretty much mandatory where I come from. I am right, though."

"Are you? I don't hear many of these good people agreeing with you."

"I don't need them to: my rightness is entirely independent of their opinion. Information wants to be free, to be known by as many minds as possible and achieve meaning. It's a revolution – the emancipation of data."

The steward brought them their whiskey in two tiny bottles, set on a tray with paper coasters and glasses pre-filled with ice. A bigger bottle of still water sat between the glasses. The man's hands were shaking.

"*Yobany stos.*" Petrovitch looked up at the terrified steward. "Just leave it with us. We're big boys and we can sort ourselves out."

Newcomen folded his table out and unscrewed the water bottle. When he tried to add some to Petrovitch's glass, Petrovitch kicked him.

"Ow."

"That's not how I drink it." He grabbed his whiskey to prevent any further attempt at adulteration. "It's not how any decent human being should drink it, either."

He twisted the lid off and sucked the contents out in one go. He held it in his mouth for a moment, then swallowed. Then he puffed out his cheeks and blew.

Newcomen blinked. He broke the seal on his own bottle and dribbled a little into the near-frozen water at the bottom of his glass.

"When did you become such a," Petrovitch searched for the word, came up with several highly inappropriate ones in an online thesaurus, and finally selected, "such a milquetoast?"

"I am not," said Newcomen, shuddering, "one of those."

"I think I know. Your accident. I've seen it: it was enough to make the strongest man risk-averse. It was the last time you ever took a chance." Petrovitch played it in his head, the banners, the roar of the crowd, the cheerleaders all so pretty in their black and gold. "The State University coach was on the touch-line, and he was ready to hand you a scholarship. All you had to do was shine."

"I did. I did shine."

"For an hour and a half, under a hot autumn sun. Calling all those plays, throwing that pigskin. You were good, Newcomen. I can't say for sure, as it's always looked like a monumental waste of time and energy, but you were rated by those who cared."

"Petrovitch. I don't want you to mock me."

"I know you don't. I'm not. I'm trying to understand you: that's important to me, important to Lucy too. Start of the third quarter, you're well in the lead, and it's mainly due to you. Maybe that's when someone on the Xavier High team decides the only way they're going to stand a chance is to put you out of the game." He scratched at his nose. "A tackle like that? I can tell the moment your shoulder dislocates. And still you're trying to get that loose ball back, still taking a chance."

Newcomen poured the rest of his whiskey into his glass. His hand was trembling as he held it to his lips, the ice cubes chattering against each other to signal his discomfort.

"Do you know what it's like to have everything you've ever worked for taken away from you in one single second?" the American asked.

Petrovitch nodded slowly. "Yeah. I know. I even know what it's like to have my arm shattered like crazy paving. This," and he held up his left arm, "the skin's real. The blood pumping through it is real. The skeleton underneath? I could punch a hole in the fuselage with it and still have enough watts to rip the wing off."

"I couldn't go back. I just couldn't." Newcomen shrugged, his big shoulders slumping in defeat. "Even after they'd grown new bone and grafted it in, and I'd been told I'd be as strong as ever. So I took myself away. I went to Pennsylvania and hid."

"I don't blame you. I don't blame you at all." He waved the steward back over. "We're good to go again, right?"

"Are you sure, sir?"

"I have a robotic liver. I can pretty much metabolise alcohol as fast as I pour it into myself."

The steward recoiled. That cyborg thing again.

"All the same, I like the taste of it, and I got put on to rye whiskey by the head of the Papal Inquisition, who just happened to be a Yank." Petrovitch remembered. Cold stone steps, a bottle, two glasses. It'd been a while since he'd spoken to Carillo. "You haven't got any Stagg, have you?"

"Get him the whiskey," said Newcomen. "I'll pass."

"Sir."

"Is that true?" asked Newcomen when the steward had hurried off again.

"Which one? The liver or the cardinal?"

"Either, I guess."

"Both. Maddy always used to joke about my robotic spleen, since I vent it so often, but it turned out it was my liver that packed in first: too much cheap vodka destroying what was left of a radiation-damaged organ. And yeah, I get on well enough with Cardinal Carillo. He might even make pope one day. I don't pretend to know how that works – I know smoke's involved – but for a God-botherer he's okay."

Newcomen sat slightly hunched over, nursing his drink. The steward brought Petrovitch another bottle, thankfully without all the extras this time.

"*Za zhenshhin!*" he said, and again emptied the entire measure in one go. He smacked his lips. "There is a way back, you know. You don't have to live the rest of your life like . . ."

"Like a milquetoast, you mean."

"I should know. I've run before. I ran from St Petersburg. I abandoned my family and everyone who ever knew me. It got me into the habit of running from everything. Then, even before the whole New Machine Jihad thing kicked off, I decided I was in so much trouble, I was going to have to run again: I ripped up my Samuil Petrovitch persona, said goodbye to everyone important – though that took precious little time. I'd even booked plane tickets to Auckland under yet another false name."

"None of that was in the book."

The corner of Petrovitch's mouth twitched. "It wouldn't be."

"So what made you change your mind?" Newcomen frowned. He was becoming interested, despite himself.

"That is a mystery known only to, well, whatever God you believe in. The man threatening me with death was an even bigger bastard than I was, and I realised no one was going to be able to stop him. And right there and then I decided I was going to be the one to take him down. I stopped running and started fighting. It wasn't the wisest of decisions, and I can't even pretend it was anything but entirely self-serving." Petrovitch chewed at his lip. "But at least I can look at myself in the mirror without shuddering with disgust. That, as it turns out, is quite important when it comes to being a fully signed-up member of the human race."

Newcomen faced forward, and watched the back of the seat in front for a while. His face held a series of expressions, but Petrovitch couldn't read any of them. Something was starting to change. For better or worse.

12

The first thing Petrovitch did when he got into his hotel room was sweep it for bugs; he found five on the first pass, and another three on the second. Those he could dispose of out of the seventh-storey window, he did: those he couldn't, he zapped in situ.

Still not satisfied, he opened his carpet bag and placed a portable jammer on the table.

Newcomen was already looking at his watch. "I don't see why any of this is necessary."

"It's necessary because your side thinks it's necessary. Now, what I'm going to do, because I'm reasonably convinced that the rooms either side of this one, and above and below, are filled with personnel and listening devices, is check the hotel's occupancy list, and pick another room a long way away from this one. Then I'm going to reprogram my key card to open that door and tell the computer that, I don't know, Hyram T. Wallace from New Mexico has checked in, redeeming his reservation from three weeks ago."

He did that, and seconds later, the jammer was back in his bag. He headed out into the corridor and strode towards the lifts, Newcomen and his luggage trailing after him again. He walked straight by the metal doors and through into the stairwell. When the door had swooshed shut behind them both, he started down.

"Petrovitch, you can't do this."

"You say that like you have some authority to stop me." He paused on the next landing, and fixed Newcomen with a steady gaze. "You don't."

"I mean, I need to go. Now, or I'm going to be late. And it's that particular room number that my replacements are going to be asking for. If you're not there, if we're both not there, then what are they supposed to do? More importantly, what am *I* supposed to do?"

Petrovitch raised an eyebrow. "Okay. What you're saying is that because you're going on your date, and I have to have someone with me at all times, your colleagues will turn up to the wrong room and then just go away again because they can't find me? *Yobany stos*, your lot couldn't find your arse with both hands."

"I cannot leave you," said Newcomen. "It's my duty to stay with you."

"Then stay."

"I am supposed to be picking Christine up in fifty minutes. I have not showered or changed, or collected the presents I have for her because I have not been home because you kept me two whole hours extra in New York." Newcomen's words came in a deliberate, measured tone that indicated he was ready to burst with impotent rage.

"I'm not going anywhere. I'll wander down to the restaurant, have something to eat, do some work, then go to bed. I'll see you in the morning." Petrovitch made to carry on.

"If I leave you, I will be dismissed from the Bureau. Instantly. Someone else will be accompanying you north, someone you can't control."

Petrovitch stopped again, mid-step. "You know, you actually make a good point."

"If," said Newcomen, swallowing hard, "if you do this for me, I will help you willingly."

Petrovitch gave him a sceptical look, and the agent revised his rash offer.

"Less grudgingly, then."

"So I spend the night being watched over by a couple of guys – with a few dozen others behind the walls – you get to show your fiancée a good time at a fancy restaurant, and in return, you'll stop behaving like a spoilt teenager and man up just a little. Is that right?"

"I wouldn't put it like that." Newcomen looked at his watch again. "But yes."

Petrovitch sighed and turned around. "I hate being spied on." He tramped back up the stairs, reconfiguring his key card as he went, then shouldered his way into the corridor again.

"Thank you," said Newcomen breathlessly.

"You're welcome. See this?" Petrovitch held up his left hand and waggled his ring finger. "It is worth it, if you marry the right person."

"I know."

"What I'm trying to tell you is, don't fuck it up. For either you or her."

"I'm not going to do that."

Petrovitch swiped his card and threw his bag on to the king-sized bed. "When are these goons supposed be here?"

"Twenty minutes ago."

After pulling the curtains closed against the northern night, he turned the television on and cycled through the channels, all without touching the remote. "They're cutting it fine."

"I know." Newcomen ground his teeth.

"Go and chase them up."

"You nuked my phone."

"There's a landline on the table."

The agent made a series of quick, futile calls, his voice rising through each one until he was ultimately both shouting and pleading simultaneously.

In lieu of anything hard to break, he dragged his tie off, screwed it into a ball and drop-kicked it into the waste bin. Then he sat on the bed, holding his head in his hands.

The channels kept changing, one every half-second, until Newcomen snapped. "Either pick a programme or turn it off."

With an exaggerated blink, Petrovitch turned the screen off. "Sounds like you've been let down."

"Gowan and Baxter are nowhere to be found. Buchannan is in a security briefing and can't be disturbed. There's no one else. No one with the required clearance to relieve me." He scrubbed at his cheeks. "I'm . . ."

"Screwed?" Petrovitch nodded. "Pretty much. You going to call Christine and tell her?"

"I, uh." The agent didn't seem able to believe his predicament. "I, uh. What am I going to say?"

"She's not going to leave you just because you can't take her out on Valentine's Day." Petrovitch started to unlace his boots. "Not if she really loves you."

"I don't think you understand. This is a big deal. Like a really big deal to her."

"And to you." He forced first one boot off, then the other. He wiggled his toes and inspected his socks for holes. "You want to do this, don't you? More than anything. You can just go. I am probably the most watched person in the continental United States at the moment. Isn't that right, guys?"

Petrovitch picked up a boot and threw it against the wall. He imagined an operator clutching his bruised ears and howling in pain.

"I can't just go. I can't."

"Just go next door and sort it out."

"They won't answer: they're not supposed to be there."

Petrovitch flipped his key card at Newcomen. "They don't have to answer. You can walk straight in."

"I cannot take on the entire NSA."

"You ought to try it sometime. It's fun."

Both men stared at each other, one with despair, the other with detached amusement. Petrovitch broke first.

"Come with me." He pulled the jammer out of the bag and walked into the en-suite bathroom. He turned on the taps in both the shower and the sink, and, for good measure, flushed the toilet.

Newcomen closed the door behind them. "What is it?"

"Okay, it's like this. Your two friends, Gowan and Baxter? They're propping up a bar in First Hill. Buchannan's been at home for an hour. If you ask any or all of them why they're not returning your calls, they'll swear blind and pass a polygraph test that they never had a single message. You're not meant to meet Christine tonight, or any other night."

"But who would do such a thing? Why would they do it?"

"You *mozgoyob*. You've been left swinging in the wind, and you can't work out who's done this to you? First of all you get assigned, quite out of the blue, to go to one of the most dangerous cities in the world – for an American – to meet one of the most dangerous people in the world – me – and you have the temerity to come back home alive. Since that hasn't worked, you're now put in a situation where either you leave me here, go on your date and get sacked for it, or stay with me and your girlfriend dumps you. If that doesn't work, there are a thousand and one different accidents you can have on the North Slope, one of which is bound to kill you." Petrovitch pushed the toilet seat down and sat on the lid. He flushed again for good measure. "You're the detective. Work it out."

"No. Not getting this."

"Edward Logan. Christine's father. Honorary treasurer of the Washington State Reconstruction Party." When he got a blank look, he asked, "You have heard of him, right?"

"Christine's father?" Newcomen shook his head violently, as if to dislodge an angry bee. "You're kidding, right?"

"You don't have to believe me. It's not compulsory in any way. But I am right. Logan doesn't want you to marry his daughter. Status and money are everything to him. I bet he's got a line of eligible suitors ready to go: right after a suitable mourning period, of course."

"Mr Logan wants me dead?"

"No. If only because he'll have to spring for a funeral wreath. He just wants you, a lowly government employee, gone, and he doesn't care how that happens."

"But I'm a federal agent. He can't just . . ."

Petrovitch pinched the bridge of his nose. "You know what? You are too stupid to live. Of course he shouldn't, but he does, and because he's a big Reconstruction cheese, he's going to get away with it. No one is going to investigate him. No one is going to rat him out. No one is even going to look in his direction. This is how your country works now."

The sound of spouting water filled the deep silence. Newcomen worked his jaw and Petrovitch watched the patterns the steam made as it fogged the mirror. The extractor fan busied itself, venting the air to the freezing weather outside.

"Want to get even?"

Newcomen, sitting on the edge of the bath, looked up to see Petrovitch smiling at him.

"How am I going to do that?"

"You have exactly forty-one minutes before you're supposed to be picking Christine up. We'll be right down to the wire, but I have a plan. It takes about twenty-five minutes to get from here to Logan's place, depending on traffic. I can do something about that, so let's call it twenty. Ten minutes in the shower, ten getting ready. Yeah, we can do this."

"But what about—"

"*Past' zebej*. Shower, now." Petrovitch took the jammer with him back into the bedroom and pulled the door shut. He could hear Newcomen's shoes hit the floor, and the soft rustle of clothing as it fell away.

Time to test the epigram: money talks. He could shout louder than most; not just the personal wealth he'd signed away to the Freezone, but the collective's entire resources. Even Teddy Logan would be grudgingly impressed.

He didn't care about that as much as he did about wiping the condescending smile from Logan's face, the one he used on all his publicity material.

So Petrovitch made a list of things he needed, and sent virtual agents out across the network to find them. They came scurrying back with their results even as he was talking to the hotel's concierge.

"Yeah. This is going to be a tall order, but I'm prepared to shovel an obscene amount of cash your way if you can make these things happen. Your foyer is about to be besieged by couriers, and I need the stuff they're carrying bringing straight up to my room. Also, I need a hamper full of buffet-style snacks – you know, finger-food things – and some desserts that won't fall apart in the back of a limo. And a limo. A bottle of pre-Armageddon champagne, some soft drinks, glasses. Look, you know how to do this better than I do. A picnic for lovers, okay? And I need it in fifteen minutes."

There was a knock at the door, and Petrovitch opened it. Two men in hotel uniform stood outside.

"Wait there."

He kicked the bathroom door open, grabbed Newcomen's suit and shoes, and thrust the bundle into the men's waiting arms. "*Chyort*. One more thing." He delved into the waste bin for the tie, and handed it over. "I need this all back in ten minutes. Do what you can."

Then came the steady stream of people bearing all the things he thought were essential – that Madeleine thought were essential, because she was telling him exactly what he needed and what would impress.

By the time Newcomen emerged, wrapped in a towel, Petrovitch was dressed in a pale jacket with matching trousers, brown shoes and a white Nehru shirt.

"Not a *yebani* word, got that?" He held out a new shirt sealed in a plastic bag and a pair of cufflinks in a box. "That's your size. Get it on."

"Uh, shorts?"

Petrovitch threw another sealed bag at him. "Socks, too."

The door rattled again, and he took delivery of Newcomen's freshly pressed suit and shined shoes.

"You have four minutes."

Newcomen hurried, and it turned out that he scrubbed up quite well. Petrovitch adjusted the knot on his tie and shook the lapels of his jacket out.

"How did you do all this?"

"By being married to someone who knows what a woman wants, and who is continually frustrated by her husband's singular inability to provide any of it." Petrovitch checked the time. "Out."

He paused only to throw the jammer in on top of the open carpet bag and grab the handles. Newcomen found himself shoved through the barely open door and towards the lifts. One car was waiting for them, because Petrovitch had fixed it that way.

Thirty seconds later, they were in the foyer, being shown through the evening throng by the concierge. "Everything's ready, Dr Petrovitch."

"Everything except me. I'll settle up with you later, but yeah. Not bad for a Yank."

The concierge tipped his hat and opened the door for them.

A white stretch limo was idling outside, the driver in a dark blue uniform standing beside it.

"Is that ours?" asked Newcomen.

"*Yobany stos*, man. It's a wonder you can find your way to the office in the morning. It's ours, for the evening at least. Now, we're late, and I'm going to have to do some real-time traffic control in order to get us to the Logans' on time."

The chauffeur opened the door to the cavernous interior, and Newcomen climbed in. Petrovitch followed, the cold nipping at his ankles. The clothes he was in felt alien, uncomfortable, stiff. His usual stuff was his by right of conquest, but the jacket felt like it was wearing him, and his shoes were hard and unyielding.

He'd had to put up with worse. It was going to be fine.

13

It seemed to take an age for the chauffeur to walk around the front of the car to the driver's seat. Finally the engine note changed and the limo pulled away.

"This is all very . . ." Newcomen huffed. "Kind. But I don't see how it's going to get me out of the pickle of having to babysit you all evening when I'm supposed to be alone with Christine. Even if I get her to the restaurant on time, you're going to have to . . ." He huffed again.

"What? Sit between you and play gooseberry? Yeah, the ladies love that sort of thing." Petrovitch watched the lights of Seattle go by as they pulled out on to the interstate. "You can't go to the restaurant. It's just impractical. Sorry. I've cancelled your reservation, and we're going with plan B."

"I'm clutching at straws now anyway."

"Newcomen, listen. I'd barely turned eighteen when I had to execute a war against two hundred thousand crazed fanatics. And I won. If you think you can come up with something better than I have, then be my guest. As it is, all you've done is run around in circles, pulling at your hair. Take what I give you and be grateful."

"And what is it exactly that you're giving me?"

"What could be your last ever evening with your fiancée," said Petrovitch. "Some people don't get the chance of knowing. You kiss the wife goodbye, you step out of the door, and wham. Someone, something takes you out, and you've missed the chance to invest those few moments with meaning."

"I'm supposed to be grateful?" Newcomen's voice rose in pitch and volume.

Petrovitch's reply was matter-of-fact. "Yeah. You were never meant to meet her tonight, if ever. Now you can."

Newcomen stared and ground his jaw.

"You look like a cow when you do that." Petrovitch leaned forward, and realised the other bench seat facing him was too far away to reach. "Over there's a hamper filled with all sorts of goodies. There's champagne on ice, and I don't even want to think about how much that's cost us. There's two bouquets of flowers: tiger lilies for Mrs Logan and red roses for Christine. You've been to Logan's place: you know the summer house down by the lake. You and her can take the hamper down there and do whatever it is you two want to do, entirely undisturbed. When you're done, we go back to the hotel. *Vrubatsa?*"

"But what are you going to be doing in the meantime?"

"I'll be in the house with Christine's parents – I've checked they're not going out anywhere – and that should satisfy both you, and the pickiest of tribunals, if it ever comes to it. You'll be on the same property as me. If I need you, I'll call for you: barring disasters, I promise I won't call you." Petrovitch grimaced. "That's right. I'm going to spend the whole evening making pleasantries with the man who doesn't care whether his daughter's boyfriend lives or dies, and sees me as an aberration before God. I'd rather lie in a bath of broken glass, but there you go."

Newcomen threw himself back against his seat, and sat upright again as the chair began to massage him. He looked around at it with distaste. "Are you sure about Logan?"

"What? Whether he's going out or not?"

"No, not that."

"The other thing? Yeah. There won't be a paper trail I can follow, he's far too careful for that: but you know he hates you. You know his wife doesn't dare say anything to him. The only reason you've lasted this long is because Christine genuinely does love you. Then it got serious. You proposed and she accepted. You dared to pick a date and a venue. That was when he started to look for ways to get rid of you."

"This is still the father of my fiancée you're talking about." Newcomen slid across the car to inspect the hamper.

"*Yobany stos*, man. He's trying to have you killed, and you worry about good manners? *Chyort*, the only reason you're polite to him is because Christine is his chattel and he can do what he wants with her." Petrovitch laid a proprietorial hand over his carpet bag. "This sort of situation would never happen in the Freezone. It just couldn't. If Lucy had ever shown any interest in men, there'd have been no question of me interfering. Or even threatening to cut their *yajtza* off with a cleaver."

"She's your daughter, though." Newcomen opened the lid of the hamper, and his eyes grew wide. He was disarmed enough that his train of thought derailed and fell down an embankment.

"She doesn't belong to me. I belong to her. After she lost her parents, I was all she had. I might have been piss-poor as a dad, but even I knew I had to protect her, teach her, and try and turn her into a rounded human being. I pretty much failed on every count, but that doesn't mean I don't love her. What it does mean is that I don't own her."

The lights outside dimmed. They were crossing the Murrow Bridge. In the dark, Newcomen asked quietly: "You've not had children of your own?"

"There's a good chance that both me and Maddy are sterile. She's a mutant, I'm radiation-damaged." Petrovitch stared at the glint of his wedding ring. "We've not done any tests, not gone for any treatment. Yeah, a gestation tank would be the simple answer, but we're still young. And you know, we still enjoy trying at every available opportunity."

Newcomen pulled a face. "Oh, stop. Now."

"Bearing in mind this could be it," continued Petrovitch, "you might consider doing the same. Going out in a blaze of glory. Spawn and die."

"I am not an animal. And Christine . . ."

"It's often when faced by imminent death that you feel the biological urge the most."

"Shut up, Petrovitch." Newcomen balled his fists, but didn't do anything with them. "Just, shut up."

"Okay."

The limo cruised off the bridge and into a tunnel.

"We're still being followed," said Petrovitch. "Wish I could do something about that."

"Maybe they're wondering where we're going." Newcomen sounded relieved at the change of subject.

"They're not wondering at all. They made the plates on the car and checked the destination with the hire company. They're just doing it to piss me off. Did you know they've diverted a satellite so that it can track me better? Polar orbit, so it's only overhead for a short time each day, but they're bringing in another one tomorrow. All that expense, all that effort, just to see where I'm going." Petrovitch looked up from his lap at Newcomen. "Do you suppose they have a good reason why they're doing that, and not using those same resources to find Lucy?"

"If it's true . . ."

"Which it is. I don't think I've lied to you yet."

"Which itself is probably a lie," said Newcomen. "If it's true, perhaps they are using it to look for Lucy."

"Wrong footprint on the ground." Petrovitch gave a half-smile. "And we've intercepted the datafeed. We know exactly when it's live, and where it's pointing. You've got plenty of resources, you're just not using them right."

The car turned off the freeway and slowed to the new speed limit. It became obvious who was on their tail, as first one, then two sets of headlights peeled off from the main road but kept a respectful distance.

"Nearly there," remarked Newcomen. "Will you be listening in, when I'm alone with her?"

"It's not the way it works. Michael monitors you. If you say anything you shouldn't, he'll let me know. I can honestly say that you won't be overheard by another human being."

"So you're definitely bugging me?" He checked the inside of his jacket, as if he was going to find something obvious within the folds of his clothes.

"Yeah. We get to keep some secrets. Neither was I born yesterday, so let's change the subject." Petrovitch reached into the carpet bag for the jammer. "I will leave this for you, though. That should be enough insurance against your own side. I'll take my chances."

Closed high gates presented themselves in the limo's lights, and the chauffeur buzzed the intercom to speak to his passengers.

"There's no call button, sir. Can you contact the house, get them to open up?"

Newcomen lifted up his tie to access the keypad, while Petrovitch eyed the gates.

"I can open them for you. Security's good, but I'm way better." He realised what Newcomen was doing, and pressed his hand against the American's. "Fried, remember? I'll call."

Newcomen's face clouded over. "At least try and keep things civil."

Petrovitch spoke to one of Logan's staff, and despite their visit being prearranged, permission from the man himself suddenly became necessary.

"Logan knew I was here too." Petrovitch raised his eyebrows. "He's got someone on the inside. Fancy that."

"Everything you say is deliberately designed to reinforce the idea that you're right."

"Maybe so. Or perhaps I'm trying to get into your thick skull the fact that I am right. All the time."

The gates started to swing apart, and the driver nosed the car forward. The drive was gravelled, and stones crunched beneath the wheels as they pulled up outside the mock-Georgian frontage.

Lights blazed from every window, and a silhouetted figure was visible in one of the first-floor rooms, hands on hips, staring down at them. Petrovitch ran a pattern match, and found it was Logan. He was probably looking forward to this encounter as much as his guest was.

The chauffeur opened Petrovitch's door for him, when he felt he should really have done it for himself. "No need for that," he said.

"All part of the service, sir."

"Yeah. You should go back to college and graduate. Your grades were more than good enough." He jerked his head at Newcomen. "Better than his."

"I needed the work, sir." That Petrovitch knew didn't seem to surprise him. "And I guess after that, I just got out of the learning habit."

"Try it again. You might find you can pick up where you left off." His breath curled in the air, a coil of fog. "Come on, Newcomen. You're keeping the lady waiting."

The agent eased himself out. "Cold."

"Nothing aches like metal: trust me." Petrovitch frowned. "Flowers?"

Newcomen dived back in and re-emerged with the two shivering bunches.

"Give me the lilies. It's not like I can feel any more stupid than I do already."

Together they advanced on the front door, which appeared to be made of wood but was in fact a laminated sandwich of composite materials that even Valentina would have trouble blowing her way through. The place was a fortress, designed to seal and lock at the touch of a button. Either Logan was paranoid, or he genuinely had made some powerful enemies during his struggle to the top of the tree.

Newcomen rapped the heavy brass knocker, an entirely redundant gesture as there were cameras, pressure pads and laser nets covering their every move.

The door opened a crack. Logan had sent his wife ahead of him.

"Hello?"

"Hi, Mrs Logan," said Newcomen. "I'm here to pick Christine up, as arranged."

"Yes, yes, of course." She opened the door fully. "And you've brought someone with you."

"I'm afraid Bureau business has got a little out of hand, ma'am. Can I present Dr Samuil Petrovitch, the internationally renowned scientist and accredited diplomat of the Irish Freezone?"

Petrovitch stifled the urge to snort with laughter, and gave a short, formal bow. "Mrs Logan. These are for you." He brandished the bouquet, and she reacted as if they were a weapon. "They're just flowers. Honest."

"Th-thank you," she answered, and took them from him. She was terrified. Of Petrovitch, of the whole situation.

"If Christine is half as beautiful as you, Joseph is a very lucky man." Petrovitch used his yellowed teeth to flash her a suggestive grin. "Isn't that right, Joseph?"

"Joseph?" Newcomen seemed to have forgotten his first name. "Oh, yes. Absolutely. The apple hasn't fallen far from the tree."

It was pure corn, but Mrs Logan had spent a lifetime starved of compliments. Her neck flushed pink behind her string of pearls, and she allowed the perfume from the lilies to reach her nose.

"They're lovely, Dr Petrovitch."

"And I must apologise for the intrusion. Joseph's been badly let down by a series of administrative errors entirely beyond his control, and rather than see him break his promise to Christine, I suggested I throw myself on your mercy for the duration of their date."

They were still standing on the doorstep. While their faces

were being warmed by the air spilling out from the hall, their backs were collecting frost.

"Boys," said Mrs Logan. "You should come in. I know Christine has spent for ever getting ready."

The carpet was deep enough to drown in and so clean it shone. Petrovitch didn't feel comfortable walking in it, but since his shoes were so new, they hadn't had time to get dirty.

"I'm afraid we've had to change our plans to accommodate Dr Petrovitch's status," said Newcomen. "It's a condition of his visa that he's accompanied at all times by a federal officer, which means I can't take Christine to a restaurant as I'd wanted. So on, uh, Dr Petrovitch's recommendation, I brought some of the restaurant with me. If it's okay, I can take the hamper down to the summer house, and maybe he can wait up at the main house with the staff."

"It's an imposition," said Petrovitch, "but as a married man, I'm all for encouraging young love."

"You're married, Dr Petrovitch?" She seemed genuinely surprised. Perhaps monsters didn't get married.

"To the only woman who would have me, Mrs Logan." His eyes were drawn to the staircase behind her. Logan was walking slowly down towards them, his skin dark and his face set.

"Heating's off in the summer house," he declared. "Christine'll freeze out there, so forget it."

"Oh, Teddy," said Mrs Logan, then stopped abruptly. Whatever helpful suggestion she'd been about to make died on her lips. One look from her husband was all it took.

Petrovitch leaned towards Newcomen. "Leave the scum-sucking pond life to me," he murmured. "I've got previous on this."

Newcomen's face, already pale, turned white. "Mr Logan, can I introduce . . ."

"I know who he is." Logan reached the bottom of the stairs and advanced on Petrovitch. "You've got a nerve bringing this . . . man here. We're decent, God-fearing people, Joseph Newcomen, and I won't have him under my roof."

Logan was a big man: solid, round even. Taller than Petrovitch, he had presence and confidence, and he was on home ground. He took another step closer.

"I hope you don't mind your wife hearing this," said Petrovitch, "because husbands shouldn't have secrets from wives – I learnt that the hard way – but if you don't let Joseph and Christine spend the evening together in the limousine I've parked outside, which can't go anywhere because he has to stay near me, because of the restrictions your government has placed on my movements while I'm here, even though I've a diplomatic passport, I will personally see to it that I ruin you financially and politically by publishing your unaudited accounts for the last twenty years, which will reveal tax evasion and the payment of kickbacks on a frankly industrial scale. I am very aware of how quickly Reconstruction will turn on you and tear your bloodied carcass apart, leaving only scraps for the crows to chew messily on, because it happened to a friend of mine who ended up having to flee the country and become a penniless refugee in the Freezone. So, your call. What's it going to be?"

He took a deep breath and smiled again. This time, he meant it.

"Joseph!" Christine swept down the stairs, a cloud of green silk and emeralds. She tottered to a halt on her high heels, staring down at the strange tableau below, starring her parents and this white-haired foreigner she'd heard so many appalling things about. She tried to make sense of it, of the conflicting body language exhibited by her father and the stranger.

One thing was clear, though: Newcomen seemed to grow in her presence. He stood straighter and looked stronger. "Hello, Christine. You look amazing."

Logan almost said something. The corner of Petrovitch's eye twitched. They were so close, there was no way the man could miss its meaning.

Christine smiled, and her whole face lit up like a flashbulb. Newcomen held the dozen red roses out in front of him, offering them and himself up to her.

She came to collect them, and chastely offered her cheek to be kissed. He did so, trembling.

"They're lovely, Joseph. Now come on, or we'll be late, and that would be disrespectful." She had blonde hair, the colour of a lion's mane, which bobbed with every one of her precise, positive gestures.

Newcomen collected her coat from the closet — he'd been there often enough to know where it was and which of her many coats she'd need — and draped it around her shoulders.

"Actually, my dear, we're doing something slightly different tonight. I'll explain on the way to the car." He opened the door, and Christine caught sight of the long white limousine.

"Oh," she breathed. "Joseph."

With the carelessness of youth, she didn't look back at her terrified mother and furious father, just strode out into the night as if wolves only existed in fairy tales.

"Half eleven's late enough for you two, I think," said Petrovitch. "Be back by then. I need my beauty sleep."

Newcomen mouthed his suddenly heartfelt thank-you, and Christine's excited voice was suddenly muffled by the click of the latch, leaving Petrovitch alone with the Logans.

He grunted, halfway between satisfaction and displeasure.

Logan was in his personal space, and he didn't like that. He pressed the fingertips of his left hand into the man's expensively covered chest and pushed him slowly away. "Why don't you just relax and make the best of it. There are a million places I'd rather be, and yeah, I blame you for your part in this charade. Despite what you think, your daughter could do worse: much worse. So *past' zebej*: I don't want to hear another word from you this evening or I'll hand the IRS your *zhopu* on a plate."

Logan was used to being undisputed master in his own home. If he'd hated Petrovitch in the abstract before, he now loathed the reality with a passion bordering on obsession. But he was beaten, and knew there was nothing he could do about that. For now.

He turned and stalked away. "Margaret?"

He expected her to follow, to listen to his invective behind a closed door, perhaps even be the target of his ill-temper.

Time, thought Petrovitch, to twist the knife.

"Mrs Logan? I understand you're quite the artist. If you'd allow me, I'd like to take a closer look at some of those landscapes you've done. I've only seen pictures of them – the ones from the country club show – and I'm sure they didn't do them justice."

He linked his arm through hers so that she could guide him, even though he knew where she displayed them already. He saw her hesitate for the longest time.

Then a spark of defiance. Petrovitch knew how to kindle that into a flame. It would be a better revenge than paupering them all.

"Of course, Dr Petrovitch. My studio is just through here."

14

"Come on, G-man," said Petrovitch, kicking the bed. "It's time to get up."

Newcomen groaned and put the pillow over his head.

"Yeah, yeah. Even on a good day I could drink half a bottle of vodka before breakfast. A few glasses of fizzy French wine shouldn't give you a headache."

"What time is it?"

"Oh six hundred. What does the oh stand for?"

"I don't know," mumbled Newcomen.

Petrovitch peeled the pillow away and bellowed: "Oh my God, it's early! Now, up. We've got a full day ahead of us, and another flight to catch."

There was a thump as Newcomen fell out on to the floor. After a moment of lying as stranded as a beached whale, he started to crawl towards the bathroom.

"No pyjamas, then."

"No." Newcomen's legs disappeared into the bathroom. The door closed and the shower started up.

"I'll be back in five minutes." Petrovitch stepped back out into the hallway in time to see his own room door click: the green light on the lock was just winking off. He flipped his key card into his fingers and ran it through the reader. The light came on again, and the bolt whirred free.

He felt a surge from his heart as it responded to the chemicals in his blood. He checked his power levels, which were good enough, and twisted the handle.

The man inside was already pushing past him, trying to surprise him with his speed and agility. Petrovitch slammed him with his shoulder against the unyielding wall, lifted him off the floor by his right armpit, then pitched him across the full length of the bedroom.

The intruder hit the window with his back. His head cracked hard against the glass, adding a separate star to the blossoming spiderweb of cracks. The pane held – just – and he bounced on to the floor face first.

Three strides, and Petrovitch was on him again, grabbing the material of his jacket at his neck. He threw him again, and the man hit the wall upside down, denting it with his heels. Where his head had hit, there was a smear of blood.

He fell between the bed and the bathroom. Petrovitch took a second to scan the room: his carpet bag was on the floor next to the now-crazed window. He'd left it locked and it still was, but the outer material was now slashed. The inner flexible metal mesh seemed to have held. A sharp-bladed scalpel had been kicked half under the bed base.

"*Mudak*," said Petrovitch. He was about to step around the

bed to drag the unconscious man upright when he noticed the first of three laser dots dancing on his chest.

He looked down, then up at the three hooded figures crowded in the doorway, guns trained unerringly on him.

"You've heard of the Vienna Convention, right? What makes you think it doesn't apply to you?" He bent down slowly and lifted up his damaged bag. "I know you don't care, but I'm filing these images with the news wires as I speak. Upload, download, ready for anyone to use. US government interfering with diplomatic bags. Diplomat held at gunpoint. Breaking and entering. It's all good stuff."

One of them lowered his gun and started to edge in.

"Where are you going?"

The masked man didn't say anything. Perhaps he thought his voiceprint could be taken down and used to identify him, and he'd be right. Instead, he pointed at his fallen colleague.

"No. He's going to be arrested, processed and charged by the FBI officer in the room opposite, and there is absolutely nothing you can do about it, *suki*."

They disagreed, and kept on edging forward. Petrovitch calmly unlocked his bag and pulled out a fist-sized sphere. It had a safety guard over its trigger, which he flipped out of the way with his thumb.

The men froze. Petrovitch smiled.

"Yeah, you know what this is, don't you? You've got them yourselves by the planeload, ready to level whole cities at a moment's notice. Still, it's not comfortable being in the same room as one, is it? Especially when it's held by the guy who invented it." Petrovitch dropped the bag and held up the sphere. It was very black. "How many storeys are we up right now?

Reckon they'd find much of you by the time you're compressed to a point and dropped a hundred metres to the ground in amongst the debris?"

One of the men started to sight down his arm.

"Think you can kill me before I press this button? I don't. My reaction speed is simply faster than yours. You don't even know where to aim." He tapped his chest. "Kevlar under the skin."

There was a commotion behind them, and Newcomen found himself with the barrel of an automatic pistol jammed under his chin. He was only wearing a towel, and as his hands came up, the knot loosened.

"Yeah, you're now holding a gun to the head of a naked federal agent. That makes everything better."

Newcomen reached up and pushed the gun away, then retrieved his towel. "What's going on?"

"We're having our very own Watergate. You know about Watergate, right? Just in case that fell into one of the massive black holes that litter your education."

"I know it." Newcomen tried to muster as much dignity as he could. "Gentlemen, you're going to have to leave now. This man is a guest of the United States government. I don't know who it is you're working for, and I'd rather not find out. If you go, then we can say the matter's ended."

"Not that simple, Newcomen. They've got a man down, and I don't want them to take him with them."

"Petrovitch. Let them have him. He won't do you any good at all."

"I'm not planning on barbecuing him. I'm planning on you throwing the book at him. That's how it works, right? Due process, Miranda, all that jazz?"

"If these people are who we think they are, that's not going to happen. Ever."

"Why not? They're above the law? How the *huy* did that happen? You've got a constitution, and I don't remember seeing any amendments that said the Man can do what he wants and the citizens have to suck it up like a *shlyuha vokzal'naja*."

"Petrovitch, shut the hell up and let them all go. I'm wearing a towel and someone from the Secret Service has a gun pointing at my junk. You might have won last night, but you're not going to win this, so just give it up."

Petrovitch considered matters. "Yeah, okay. Take him and go." He took his thumb off the red button, and the two men targeting him lowered their guns. When they'd holstered them, he clicked the safety guard back down.

The closest one helped drag the still form from the room, and finally the door closed, with Newcomen on the right side of it.

"You said a rude word," said Petrovitch. He tossed the bomb back into his bag and resealed the lock. "Twenty bucks in the honesty box."

"You could have got yourself killed, you, you idiot."

"I'm not the one with their blood halfway up the wall. Or," he said, turning, "smeared on what's left of the window. No, I'm fine. Getting that out of the wallpaper's going to be tough, though."

Newcomen clenched his fists to disguise the fact he was shaking like a leaf. "You cannot die."

"I have no intention of dying, either now or at all. That it might come anyway is an occupational hazard I have to put up with. You're angry and you're scared, and so you should be. But this is what it means, Newcomen. This – all this *govno*

— this is what Reconstruction does to those who don't fit inside its comfortable little shell. And it's always been like this. I could tell you a thousand stories about ordinary people who've been crushed by your holy juggernaut: the only thing that's different is that it's happening to you now. You pledged to uphold this system. Regretting it yet?"

"How? How can you live like this?"

"I could say the same to you. I live like this because people like you let people like them get away with stuff like that. Someone has to stand up, give them the finger and tell them no fucking way." He flashed a grin, on and off. "Remind me to tell you about Lebanon when we have a spare moment."

Petrovitch looked around the room again. There was nothing he needed to come back for. Newcomen was resting his head against the wall, eyes closed. His world was disintegrating around him just at the moment when it held the most promise.

"I can't do this."

"I'm sorry. You don't have a choice. Or you do," amended Petrovitch, "but you won't take it."

He almost felt sorry for him. There was Lucy to think about, though, and his reservoir of compassion was never particularly full at the best of times. And the circumstances weren't exactly ideal right now.

"Shit," said Newcomen.

"Forty bucks." Petrovitch jerked his head towards the next room. "They're still listening. I wonder what would happen if we walked in next door? Would they fight us? Or would they watch while we trashed their equipment? Why are they even there? Who authorised this level of surveillance? What do they hope to get from it?" He scratched at the bridge of his nose. The scar there felt hard and strange today, and he remembered how it felt for the knife to cut him open and ruin his eyes.

Newcomen's shoulders sagged. "I should get dressed."

"Yeah. Trust me, the only one who should get to see your junk, as you so quaintly put it, is Christine."

There was silence between them: nothing to stop the sound of the traffic below, the hum of the aircon, the distant rumble of jets powering up.

"It's going to be okay, Newcomen."

"How can you possibly know that?"

"Because you can trust me."

"No, I can't."

"Good point, well made." Petrovitch shrugged. "My daughter's still missing, and this isn't finding her. I reckon we can make it back to your room without getting rolled. Go."

He was right, and while Newcomen put his clothes on, Petrovitch stared out of the window at central Seattle. They were in the area hit by the 2012 tsunami, and all the buildings were less than twenty years old, supposedly built with new technology to resist earthquakes, save power, use natural light as much as possible. He didn't rate them.

"Did Edward Logan cheat on his taxes?"

"I have absolutely no idea at all," said Petrovitch. The traffic was building up on University Street, far too early. It was still dark, and the Sun wouldn't be up for another three quarters of an hour. "I thought it was highly likely, given a quick perusal of his public filings over time and trying to match them to his holdings. So I just went for it."

"You bluffed him?"

"He could have defended himself. He could have denied it. He did neither. I have such a bad-ass hacker rep. Go me. Yay."

Petrovitch could see Newcomen's reflection in the glass. It was safe to turn around. "Maybe I will take him down after all."

Newcomen was half in his jacket. "Don't."

"Even though you know you're never going to marry Christine?"

"Especially because of that."

"How did it go last night? Everything okay?"

Newcomen sat on the edge of the bed to lace his shoes. "We had a good time – no, an excellent time. I'll remember yesterday for the rest of my life, however long that might be. I was gallant to the end. And you? You were good. Moral, even." He looked over his shoulder at Petrovitch, and held his gaze.

"Except I'm a complete bastard really, aren't I?"

The other man nodded sadly.

"When you flew to the Metrozone, did you care about what had happened to Lucy? Did you care about finding her?"

"No. All I cared about was the idea I'd been chosen for something special. That it would impress Christine. That it would impress her father. That my career was taking off, higher clearance, more money, me telling people what to do rather than the other way round. I didn't care about Lucy at all. I thought you were a stupid, careless parent for letting her go, and she was as good as dead, so why bother?" Newcomen went back to his lacing. "So I imagine I'm just as big a bastard as you are."

"Sixty bucks," murmured Petrovitch. "Does stack up, doesn't it?"

Newcomen stood up and started to throw things into his open case. After a while, he slowed down, and eventually stopped.

"I'm not going to need any of this, am I? Not where we're going."

"No, not really. I've ordered a whole stack of cold-weather gear that'll be waiting for us when we go north. Stuff that genuinely works, not the tourist kit." Petrovitch stood up and looked into Newcomen's case with him. "You never really needed much of it anyway. A toothbrush. That's about it, really."

"I could just leave it here. Someone will make good use of it." Newcomen reached in and pulled out the hefty brick that was the sat phone. "Should really return this, though."

"Doesn't work any more. Nuked that, too."

Newcomen threw it back in on top of his clothes and dropped the lid.

"Your office is what, a couple of blocks away? Why don't we go and have a talk with your Assistant Director while we're here?" Petrovitch turned from the window. "I do need breakfast first, though. Mrs Logan made me an omelette, which she didn't need to, but that wasn't really enough to keep the wolf from the door."

Newcomen grabbed the free pen and scribbled on the top sheet of the pad of paper that was next to it.

Help yourself, he wrote, and laid the note on top of his case. He stared at it, the little square of white against the grey of the plastic.

"Is this what it comes down to?" He chewed at his lip.

"Yeah. Pretty much." Petrovitch jammed his hands in his pockets. "Welcome to my world."

15

They walked in together, side by side, no thought that Petrovitch really ought to be a step ahead where he could be seen, guided, stopped if he got out of line.

There were agents and support staff in the foyer, doing whatever it was they were supposed to do: talking about the game, discussing a case or arranging to meet up, going home, clocking on. There were plenty of them, too: no shortage of manpower. Certainly no shortage of people to break off their conversations and watch Petrovitch pause briefly before he walked through the security screen.

The absence of alarms was deafening.

The two uniformed guards on duty pointed to the X-ray machine.

"You'll have to put your bag through," said the Moustache.

"I disagree," said Petrovitch. "Neither do I have to submit to any search, physical or electromagnetic, whichever frequency you choose, including visible light."

"Then the bag stays here. Since we don't allow unaccompanied luggage in the building, you'll have to stay too."

"Don't tell me, you've been reading Joseph Heller. Agent Newcomen knows all about Heller's satirical work, *Catch-22*, because he studied American literature at the University of Pennsylvania. Right, Agent?"

"Uh, Petrovitch, this isn't helping."

"Oh come on. All the time is learning time. We can't go in because of me, but we have to go in, because of me."

The senior man rested his hand on his colleague's shoulder. It was just like customs at JFK. A word from a higher authority, and the rules could be not just bent, but stamped on and broken into little pieces.

"You can carry on," said the guard. The corners of his mouth turned down.

"Of course we can," said Petrovitch cheerily. "There was never any doubt of that."

The pair of them made their way to the front desk.

"Just keep walking," said Newcomen, leaning in. "Don't let them intimidate you."

"Yeah, you really don't know me at all, do you?"

"Well enough to know a lot of you is just hot air." He reached into his pocket for his badge, and flipped it open.

Petrovitch squinted at it, then moved Newcomen's arm for a better look.

"Pfft."

"What?"

"I thought *I* looked like *govno* on my ID." He rummaged around in half a dozen pockets before he found his visa.

"Just let me do this, okay?" Newcomen eyeballed a receptionist. "I need my pass, and one for my guest."

She was so dazzled, she automatically started to reach into a drawer. Her supervisor, an older woman with formidable hair, interrupted with a touch on her arm.

"I'll deal with these gentlemen, Lenora."

"Oof. And you thought it was cold outside," said Petrovitch. He rested his carpet bag, now inexpertly repaired with ragged strips of wide silver tape, on the desk. The woman gave it a hard stare, as if she could make it disappear by willpower alone.

"Agent Newcomen. This is yours." She gave him a lanyard attached to a holographic card. "And this, Dr Petrovitch, is yours. You have to wear it visibly at all times, and return it to me when you leave. Do you understand?"

She dangled a visitor's pass towards him, with its bright red text face out.

"Well," said Petrovitch, and Newcomen kicked him.

"Yes. He understands, and I'll make sure he complies." He took the tag and hung it over Petrovitch's head. "Isn't that right, Doctor?"

"Yeah, okay. I'll behave."

Newcomen led them to the lifts, where Petrovitch had the novelty of waiting. Making sure there was a car ready for them would have been a little too obvious. Even as he tapped his toe, he could see out of the corner of his eye one of the security guys passing a variety of objects through the screen to see if it was still working.

The lift door opened, and two men were inside, talking animatedly. They stepped out together, and suddenly noticed who was standing in their way.

"Newcomen."

"Baxter. Gowan."

"How was, er, how was Europe?" said Baxter. Maybe it was something about deliberately engineering for tall, muscular, blond-haired men, but the Bureau had more than its fair share of them.

"Big," said Newcomen, and showed no sign of moving. "Noisy. Where were you last night?"

"I'm a suspect in one of your cases?" Baxter pressed his palm to his chest in mock surprise.

"You know exactly what I mean. The pair of you should have been at the Hilton with him," and he pointed at Petrovitch with a rigid, trembling finger, "last night."

"Him?" said Gowan. "This the cyborg?"

He leaned in for a closer look, checking Petrovitch's face for an access hatch or a data port. Petrovitch considered his options, the chief of which, and the one he personally favoured, was bringing his forehead smartly into contact with the bridge of Gowan's nose. Instead, he made his eyes glow a charnel red, and blinked slowly.

Gowan recoiled.

Petrovitch looked up at Gowan and his partner. They were so far down the food chain as to be the equivalent of krill. Even Newcomen was more important. They certainly weren't worth having an international incident over.

"Real people have work to do," said Petrovitch, "so why don't you two just fuck off? That would be brilliant."

Baxter stiffened. "That's . . ."

"And we're keeping the Assistant Director waiting," said Newcomen. "I'll be happy to tell him why we're late."

He held his hand up and turned it vertically so he could slice his way between the men, pushing first one then the other aside to make a gap big enough for him to fit through. He walked between them into the lift car and put his foot against the door to prevent it from closing.

Petrovitch joined him, and faced outwards. He extended his middle finger in the direction of travel and kept it there as the doors shushed shut.

"They have no idea what's going on, do they?" said Petrovitch.

"None. None at all. To be fair, neither do we."

"Let's hope your Buchannan can be a bit more forthcoming, then. I want some answers." He tapped his visitor's pass so that it bounced against his chest. "Is there anything you don't bug?"

Newcomen glanced down. "Doesn't look that way. Can you deal with it?"

"Sure."

They travelled up to executive country, where the important people were. The staff they met in the corridor moved aside for them. Perhaps they could smell the frustration and anger. Perhaps they didn't want to touch the eldritch foreigner, and perhaps they knew that Newcomen was a dead man walking, and there was no reason to catch that infection.

They passed a kitchen area. Someone was inside, making coffee, and Petrovitch heard the sound of the clinking spoon.

"Hang on a second." He stuck his head around the corner and spied the microwave. "Yeah, that'll do."

The woman in the pencil skirt busied herself with putting cups on a tray, and only turned around when she heard the beep of the cooker's timer.

"What? What are you doing?"

Petrovitch looked up from peering at his FBI tag going around on the revolving plate inside.

"Just, you know. Fixing stuff." He gave it thirty seconds and sprung the door. The tag was warm, and had a couple of burn marks where the electronics inside had arced. He dropped the lanyard over his head again.

Newcomen, propping up the door frame, shrugged uselessly, before standing aside for Petrovitch, who marched past and carried on down the corridor like he hadn't just destroyed federal property.

They reached the door marked with Buchannan's nameplate. Newcomen knocked, and a breezy voice told them to enter.

In days past, Buchannan would have been half invisible through air hazy blue with cigarette smoke, while the two of them were invited to sit in the slanting light coming through the nearly closed blinds on the window. They would have all worn hats – a trilby, a fedora: something dangerous – and they'd have talked over glasses of whiskey poured from a bottle hidden in the back of a filing cabinet. There'd have been trench coats hanging from the bentwood stand by the frosted-glass door, and the shadows of people walking by would have made them drop their voices and speak in short, clipped sentences.

As it was, Petrovitch missed the trappings. They would have reminded him of what was at stake, and made the whole proceedings less clinical and anodyne. At least the glass walls of the Assistant Director's office could be dialled opaque. There were bookshelves, with real books; photographs of friends and family; mementoes gained from thirty-five years of faithful service. Buchannan's first day as an FBI agent was the day before Armageddon. All his working life had been spent working against, and yet fearing, the actinic flash of a nuclear bomb.

Petrovitch had best remember that. He took the leftmost seat and placed his bag on his lap. Newcomen waited for Buchannan to indicate he could sit, which he did with an open gesture at the chair to Petrovitch's right.

"Dr Petrovitch? Welcome to America."

"No thanks, I've had enough already." He pressed the lock on his bag and unzipped it. "Do you mind if I check for bugs?"

"The whole building is regularly swept, Doctor."

"But not by me." He picked out a variety of devices and dumped the bag on the floor.

It was inevitable that he found five different radio transmitters within the confines of the four walls, and in trying to trace a sixth, he tabbed the motor on the window blinds to reveal a palm-sized mosquito drone hovering just outside, eight floors up.

Buchannan had the decency to look embarrassed. "Such matters seem to be out of my control, Dr Petrovitch."

"Maybe we should go for a walk," suggested Newcomen.

It wasn't a bad idea, but Petrovitch had a better one. "Your boss isn't going to tell us anything in private that he's not going to in public. Firstly, he's part of the machine; he's not going off-message for us, for you, or he would already have done so. Secondly, he knows I'm one big recording device, and he's probably already seen footage of our little incident back at the hotel. Let's save ourselves the biting cold and let him make his carefully rehearsed speech here, where at least it's warm and there's the possibility of a decent cup of coffee."

"I guess so."

They waited in silence for a secretary to bring them drinks. Buchannan, too old to have been gengineered, too squeamish to stand the smell of his own corneas cooking by going under a laser, wore small, round glasses. Like Petrovitch used to have. He took them off and polished them with a cloth handkerchief.

Newcomen fidgeted incessantly, playing with his fingers,

pulling faces, scratching. Petrovitch just sat and closed his eyes, feeling for the electronic equipment secreted around the room, for the operator of the drone, who was two floors down in a cupboard marked on the floor plan as janitorial supplies.

The delay meant that when the secretary and her tray arrived, he had a good idea of how to disable them all.

"Do you take milk, Doctor?" asked Buchannan.

Petrovitch shook his head. "Just sugar."

"How much?"

"About four of those little sachets will be fine. Defenestrating spooks before breakfast always takes it out of me."

"And Joseph?"

"Milk, please."

"Can we stop being polite to each other? None of us really mean it." Petrovitch watched while the Assistant Director ripped open the paper sachets and emptied their contents into a cup of black brew. "We're all grown-ups."

"Quite so, Doctor." Buchannan stirred the coffee with a metal spoon and slid the saucer towards Petrovitch. "Why don't you start?"

"Yeah, you don't want me to start. But I'll ask the first question: why are you going along with this charade? It must offend every instinct you have as a law-enforcement officer."

"I would deny that there is a charade I'm going along with."

"Meaning either there isn't a charade, or you're not going along with it? You look pretty well neck-deep in things from where I'm sitting."

"That's a matter of interpretation. Things look different depending where you stand." Buchannan slipped on his glasses and blinked in the bright light.

"I was never much one for moral relativism." Petrovitch got

a raised eyebrow from across the desk. "Well, if I'm being a shit, even for a good reason, I'll always put my hand up to it: I don't hide behind the national interest or the greater good. Call it what it is."

"And what do you think it is, Dr Petrovitch?"

"Difficult to tell. Something has happened, but we can't tell what. Pretty certain that Lucy saw it. Equally certain that she shouldn't have done. After that? We might have a lead: one I don't think I'll share with you."

"But you've already shared it with Joseph." The Assistant Director steepled his fingers and stared across the desk at Newcomen.

"Yes, sir."

"Are you going to tell me what this new lead is?"

Newcomen chewed at his lip, and eventually looked down at the floor. "No, sir."

"Interesting."

Newcomen's head came up again. "Why me, sir? You told me that I was the right man for this assignment. In a good way. I . . . is it true that Edward Logan pushed for me to get it so that he could split me and Christine up?"

"The whole idea is ridiculous, Joseph. Mr Logan is entirely separate from the Bureau, and has no influence over which cases get given to my agents."

"Except," said Petrovitch, "he's very high up in Reconstruction."

"All the same, Doctor, there is no possible link . . ."

"That photograph there." Petrovitch pointed at the bookshelf, then went to retrieve the photo frame. He inspected the buttons, and scrolled through the images until he found the one he was looking for. "Fund-raiser for the Party. Charity dinner, seats going for a thousand dollars a pop. I didn't realise you could afford that sort of thing, even on an AD's salary. Unless you're really enthusiastic about Reconstruction, of course."

"I was given the tickets, so I could be there in my professional capacity."

"You and your wife. Remind me who the keynote speaker was?"

Buchannan's lips went tight, so Petrovitch reminded him.

"Director of the Federal Bureau of Investigation. That's a big deal, right? And as honorary treasurer of the Washington State Reconstruction Party, Logan would have been on the top table. But they know each other anyway, don't they? Same Greek-letter fraternity at Yale? Logan grouses about his beautiful daughter being in danger of losing her virginity to some hick from Iowa. Two weeks later, this lands on his desk, and they need a fall guy in a hurry. Someone expendable." Petrovitch shrugged. "The dots join up. Can't prove it, but you were clearly told by someone to make Newcomen the patsy. I mean, why not someone from Anchorage? It's their patch. Except none of them is going out with the daughter of a mean *sooksin* like Logan."

He put the frame back on the shelf, and set it cycling through its stored scenes again.

Newcomen straightened up. "I think I deserve an answer, sir. I think we both do."

Buchannan touched his teeth with the tip of his tongue. "I have no answer to give you, Joseph."

"What about Dr Petrovitch?"

"I have no answer for him either. However regrettable that might be."

Petrovitch narrowed his eyes. Every word had taken on a significance beyond itself: it was all code, all meaningful, if only he could decipher it.

"I think we're done here," he said, and grabbed his bag.

The power went off: lights, computers, everything died at once. Then the emergency lighting flickered.

"You have thirty seconds to say whatever it is you have to say to each other without anyone overhearing. I'll be outside, and at the end of that thirty seconds, you'd better be standing outside too, Newcomen. Got that? Twenty-five seconds left."

He stepped into the corridor and pulled at the lapels of his jacket, as if adjusting himself for the outside. Heads had appeared from other offices, wondering what was happening, and what the cause was.

If they saw Petrovitch standing alone, it wasn't for long. Newcomen was there behind him, and then the power came back. The overhead fluorescents clicked and hummed, bathing everything in their cold blue light.

"Okay?" asked Petrovitch.

Newcomen was strapping on his wrist holster, the gun it usually held dangling from its tensioning cable below his arm.

"Yes," he said, keeping his voice entirely neutral.

"Good," said Petrovitch. "Why don't we go somewhere quiet and talk about what we're going to do next?"

16

Petrovitch leaned over the ferry's railings while Newcomen huddled down inside his jacket, pitifully thin against the subarctic air.

"I have a thermal jacket at home," said Newcomen. "It goes down to my ankles and has its own fuel cell."

"I have the ability to ignore the cold. Though I do have to watch out for frostbite." Petrovitch inspected his fingers, which were pleasantly pink, then looked out over the sea to the Seattle skyline.

The two men who'd followed them on foot down the quayside were just a fraction of a second too late to board the water taxi. Men like that didn't carry ID with them, because they never wanted to be identified. But it also meant that Newcomen could flash his badge and jump the turnstile, and leave them behind.

"You realise this trip isn't going to last very long."

"Ten minutes across the bay is fine. Even if someone makes a call and gets us turned around, we've still got time to play with."

"Why do we have to sit out on deck anyway? Won't they be watching us?"

"Of course they will. They may even get some lip-readers in to try and see what we're saying. All we have to do is turn our back on them. Besides, I've been cooped up for too long. Planes, hotels, offices. I spend a lot of my time outside now, just walking and talking, thinking and planning."

"What do you mean, too long? It's been, what? Two days?"

"I was never very patient. You should see me play chess." Petrovitch faced Newcomen, the wind whipping at his spiky hair, Mount Ranier pale and uncertain behind him. "What else did Buchannan give you? Apart from your gun?"

"How did you know?"

"Because I'm a genius. And you've been touching your suit just here," and he tapped where the internal pocket would be, "every couple of minutes since we left the Bureau, just to check you've still got it."

Newcomen dug his frozen fingers into his jacket and held up a standard data card, its golden electrical contacts glittering in the low winter sun.

"What did he say was on it?"

"Everything I'd need." Newcomen turned it around to show its ordinariness, then slipped it back inside.

"That's magnificently ambiguous. Anything else?"

"No. Just that. And that he was really very sorry." Newcomen shivered violently. "There's only so much you can say in that short a time."

"I'm sure I could have thought of something." Petrovitch noticed that Newcomen's nose had turned white. "For what it's worth, I'm sorry too. Though I haven't changed my mind about our arrangement. That's the problem with being a bastard: you get used to it."

"Would it make any difference if I just jumped into the bay?"

"Yeah. I don't float so well. Fishing you out again might be a problem."

Newcomen looked genuinely surprised. "You can kill me in a eyeblink. Why would it bother you?"

"Because I'm the patron saint of lost causes. I have the stigmata to prove it. And I reckon you're getting interested, despite yourself. Part of you is still absolutely terrified about the prospect of going north with me, trailing around while I ask my stupid, useless questions, and wondering if today's the day I snap and blow your heart out through your chest. Part of you is angry, because you know what I ought to do is wait for spring and see if Lucy's body turns up, and all this running around is a monumental waste of time. But part of you is intrigued. Part of you wants to know. Part of you, the detective part, the bit that loves justice and honour: you want to find her, or at least find out what happened to her."

Newcomen neither agreed nor disagreed. "It doesn't make any difference."

"It does to me."

The ferry puttered on, and the dock in West Seattle was visible across the tops of the waves.

"So what do you say?" said Petrovitch. "We'll be back ashore soon enough. There'll be fresh tails waiting for us. We'll get to the airport, and they'll board the plane with us. We'll be watched every single step of the way to Fairbanks and beyond. I'd like some time alone, not just to plot and plan, but to be invisible for a while. Fed up of living in this *yebani* goldfish bowl."

"What is it you want to do? And how illegal is it?"

"How many laws do you think they've broken? Do you imagine they even care? They think laws and statutes are for little people, Newcomen. That bad smell under your nose is a laminated copy of your constitution being burnt to ashes. What I have in mind is barely worth bothering about."

Newcomen shifted uncomfortably. Every time he moved, he exposed a new piece of skin to the cold, wet wind. "I promised to uphold the law. Just because someone else won't doesn't mean I was wrong."

Petrovitch sat down beside him. "Do you realise just how much trouble you're in?"

"I've a reasonably good idea."

"You've no idea at all. You've been betrayed and abandoned by the people you swore your oath to. You'll be effectively stateless: even if you survive whatever it is they have waiting for us, you'll never be able to go back. You'll be off the grid, a feral, living between the cracks of your society."

"Respect for my badge and what it represents is about all I have left, Petrovitch."

"You're a sheep, Newcomen. A *yebani* sheep. I can't stop you from being devoured by the wolves, and I was stupid to ever try." He got up and rested his hands on the freezing railings. "Yeah, go on then. Throw yourself in the sea. Temperature it is, you'll be in shock in seconds. Quick. Relatively painless too, unless you count the fleeting moment of regret at being a *mudak*. Leave the data card behind on your seat. I'll need to take a look at that."

The engine beneath them revved harder, making the deck shudder.

"You know I'm not going overboard," said Newcomen. "I'm too scared."

"Yeah, I know. This is just the last gasp of your ego before it collapses completely." Petrovitch seized the handles of his battered carpet bag. The boat bumped up against the quay. "What will you do when I say jump?"

"I'll ask how high."

"You know, we might actually be able to pull this off. Be ready."

There was a rattle of chains from the far side of the deck as the gantry was lowered. The few passengers emerging from below made their way to the exit, and trooped up the metal ramp.

Petrovitch and Newcomen were last off. Two men – different to the ones they'd shaken off downtown – were waiting for them in the terminal building. They watched them pass, then fell into step a few metres behind.

Outside, there was a taxi rank, a car park, a bus stop. Petrovitch ignored them all, concentrating really hard on the pavement in front of him.

"What are you doing?"

"Just keep walking. This is temporarily difficult."

They had the bay on their left, the rise of West Seattle on their right with its trees and houses. The tsunami damage was only partly repaired here, and there were still vacant lots scattered through the white new-build apartments.

The two spooks were almost on their heels. Maybe they figured something was up, but didn't know what. Their targets were due at SeaTac airport in an hour, and here they were, miles away, just strolling along, Newcomen without his luggage, Petrovitch seemingly without a care in the world.

"Ooh, seafood," said Petrovitch. They were coming up to the first of several restaurants.

"You had breakfast two hours ago." Newcomen shivered again, bending over against the wind. "Though I could do with a coffee."

"Come on then. I'll buy." Petrovitch turned and walked backwards for a moment. "How about you guys? Coffee?"

They looked at each other and then back at Petrovitch. They said nothing.

"Suit yourselves." He took a left and headed for the entrance, holding the door for Newcomen and letting it swing shut behind him.

The restaurant was just opening. A woman with a mop was busy swabbing the floor, and a couple of men joked in Spanish at the counter.

"Any table you want is fine," said the woman as Petrovitch wandered in. She made a figure of eight with the mophead on the chequered lino floor, right next to the "please wait here to be seated" sign.

"I'm really sorry about this," said Petrovitch. "None of this is your fault and you're in no way to blame."

He took the mop from her unresisting fingers and deftly threaded it through the handles of the double doors. The men outside suddenly realised what he was doing: their hands made the draw sign and the guns flipped out of their wrist holsters.

"Run," said Petrovitch. He took a moment to kick the wheeled bucket over, sending soapy water spilling across the floor in a wave, before heading to the back of the restaurant as fast as he could.

Newcomen was just ahead of him, shouldering the kitchen swing door aside. The glass in the front doors shattered, taken out with gunfire. It'd take the spooks another few moments to wrestle the mop handle free.

"There's nowhere to go," said Newcomen.

"Fire exit." Petrovitch darted in front, rushing past the stainless-steel counters and the big fridges. He planted the sole of his boot on the push bar: the door banged back against the outside wall, letting the cold north air spill in.

The view of Seattle was obscured by the flank of a gull-grey sports plane, the smooth curves of its aerodynamic outriggers hovering barely a metre above the waves and its high engine cowlings humming with potential.

"How did that . . ."

"*Past' zebej.*"

The fuselage door was open, and a narrow target to hit at speed. The wooden quay hammered like a hollow drum as they kept on running. Petrovitch launched himself off the end of the pier, over the lapping waves, and crashed against the far bulkhead inside the plane. He rolled out of the way just before Newcomen landed like a sack of Iowa potatoes in the same spot.

"Hang on to something." Petrovitch levered himself to his elbows. The plane was already moving, the big turbofans pushing them away from the shoreline and turning them to face the bay at the same time.

The engines roared: twin blasts of salt spray battered the quay just as the first of the following spooks made it to the fire exit. Before the agent could see again, the plane was a high-speed blur flying low enough to create its own wake.

Petrovitch dragged himself into the cockpit and concerned himself with making sure they didn't hit any other shipping, islands, buoys or broaching whales. He ordered the external door to close, and when it had fought its way back against the gale caused by their speed, the interior of the plane was suddenly quiet enough to permit coherent thought.

Newcomen appeared behind him, still crawling on the floor. "Whoever the pilot is must be mad." The agent clung to the back of the co-pilot's seat, and found only Petrovitch. "Oh."

"Yeah, yeah. Do you know how hard this is? Everything comes at you really, really quickly."

Newcomen looked down at the display, and turned even whiter when he spotted the right dial.

"You need to slow down."

"You need to shut up, but I can't see either of those things happening soon."

An ocean-going yacht, single mast high and in full sail, appeared in the gap between Kingston and Edmonds. Newcomen stiffened, but Petrovitch howled by at God's own speed, missing it easily.

"You're not even touching the controls!"

"Because hacking the autopilot is a hell of lot easier, especially if I have real-time satellite data to warn me what's coming up. A human couldn't do this, and that's what I'm counting on." The throttle stick automatically eased further forward.

"Did we steal this? Don't tell me we stole this."

"Newcomen, sit down, there or in the back. Just stop talking. When we're in Canada, we'll have all the time we need."

The aircraft slewed to put Hansville on its left and Whidbey Island to the right.

[Air traffic control has just shut down the airspace over the whole of Washington State.]

The corner of Petrovitch's mouth twitched.

"Does that mean they have no idea where I am?"

[Western Air Defence Sector is mobilised and operational. National Guard interceptors are being scrambled from both McChord and Fairchild.]

152

"Forget Fairchild, too far away. Tell me about McChord."

[Three F-15s are held in combat readiness at McChord, and whilst almost museum pieces, they have look-down radar and air-to-air all-aspect missiles. They are more than capable of destroying this craft, and will be airborne in ten minutes.]

"Okay. That puts me just short of Canada. If I go straight, they can't catch up before I cross the border. Doesn't mean they won't chance their arm, though."

[I have already informed the Canadians that a possible incursion is imminent. They are making pre-emptive representations to the Pentagon.]

"I can't get any lower without turning this thing into a submarine, and if those F-15s are the only thing I have to worry about, I'll take her up another twenty metres and crank the engines up to eleven. Anything else?"

[The Naval Airbase on Whidbey is on alert, though it will take them longer to mobilise.]

"If I had the time, I'd give them a fly-by."

He rounded the last headland. The foundations of the houses long since swept away flashed by at incredible speed. Vancouver Island was in sight, and there was nothing but clear sky behind him.

He blinked, and became aware of Newcomen sitting next to him, rigid with fear, barely daring to look.

"It's all information hitting the back of your eyeball. It's just a question of how fast it happens." Petrovitch leaned back and flexed his fingers, ready to take the controls when he switched to manual. "We'll get this executive penis-extension down safely somewhere, and we can take a look at what Buchannan gave you."

17

Petrovitch set the plane down in a clearing, dropping from treetop to forest floor quickly as they were no longer under power: he had as much control over the vessel as he would a hot air balloon, and he'd rather not scrape the paintwork – or one of the antigravity outriggers – on a trunk.

He folded the undercarriage out, and it made uneven contact with the ground. They were listing slightly to port, but he was satisfied he could correct for that on take-off.

The instrument panel glowed with a soft pink electroluminescence for a moment after landing. Then it winked out.

Petrovitch blew out a thin stream of air between his pursed lips. "We seem to be still in one piece. Good."

Newcomen peeled himself off the co-pilot's chair. His armpits were dark with sweat. "That was terrifying."

"You thought so? I quite enjoyed it. I lived mainly on adrenalin when I was younger, though, so maybe that has something to do with it."

154

"Did we steal this?"

"No. I hired it. Technically, someone else hired it, because if I'd hired it under my own name, the computer would have flagged it up to the authorities. But it amounts to the same thing. I hired it, got it fuelled, filed an entirely bogus flight plan – which is a low-grade federal offence – and then took remote control of it after knocking out its automatic locator beacon, which is another one."

Petrovitch looked around the cockpit and frowned.

"What?" asked Newcomen.

"It's always worried me how wildly complicated these things are, when they should grow simpler the more advanced they get. All the pilot does is choose the direction, altitude and speed. That's it, really. You might be interested in how fast the engines are turning and how much fuel you've got, but if you're running hot or going to be out of juice before you reach your destination, the computer should tell you first."

"Do you actually have a pilot's licence?" asked Newcomen, "Or are you insane?"

"The two aren't mutually exclusive. And in the Freezone, we don't do the licence thing. We concentrate on whether the man or woman at the controls is competent to make the flight." Petrovitch slipped from his seat and started towards the small cabin. "Rely on a piece of paper to tell us if someone can fly? No thanks."

Newcomen unbuckled his harness. Having struggled into it mid-flight, he now had to wrestle his way out. Petrovitch moved up the passageway, collected his carpet bag, and opened up the external door.

The scent of cold and pine burst in, and he breathed deeply, ridding his nose of the smell of his passenger's fear. The forest

155

seemed quiet enough: snow slipped off branches and birds called to each other through the dense green foliage. Apart from that, the most sound came from the cooling engines, ticking and clicking as the cowlings contracted.

A ladder unwound from underneath the opening in the fuselage. Petrovitch dumped his bag on the top step and collected it again when he was one foot from the ground.

He jumped. The undisturbed snow crunched and the leaf mould underneath gave. After their frantic escape, such stillness was welcome.

Newcomen appeared, blinking in the white reflected light. "Why are we going outside?"

"Because it's nice out, and trees are opaque to infrared. Come on."

Petrovitch tramped across the clearing and under the canopy of green. The forest was mature, and the trunks far apart, although they had to manhandle the overlapping branches in order to push through. When they were thoroughly embedded, and as far as Newcomen was concerned, completely lost, Petrovitch stopped and settled down on a mossy rock protruding from the carpet of soft brown needles.

Newcomen realised he wouldn't be able to sit anywhere he wasn't going to get his suit stained. So he stood instead, trying to shake the melting snow out of his shoes.

"Why did we run? I mean, we both know we're going to end up in Deadhorse sooner or later. They'll be waiting for us, despite this."

Petrovitch opened his bag and started to sort through the equipment inside. "I hate being watched. I hate being controlled. Most of all, I hate being at the end of such unmitigated spite and obstruction. My girl is still out there, and I'm having to deal with all this *govno*."

He found what he was looking for: a slim box with several slots in each side. He powered it up and gestured for Buchannan's data card.

Newcomen reluctantly handed it over, and Petrovitch peered at it, checking it for spyware. It was clean, literally a dime-a-dozen standard data card that could be bought from any electronics chop-shop across America.

Petrovitch located the right hole in his card reader. A yellow light winked away on the box to show it was busy. While they were waiting for the data to upload, he closed his eyes and tilted his head back.

When Newcomen cleared his throat, Petrovitch tutted. "Shush."

The yellow light was replaced by green.

"It's done."

Without opening his eyes, Petrovitch said: "There can be terabytes of data on each card. It all needs to be sorted and checked."

"By you?"

"By a committee. It's private information. If I need to know any of it, they'll pass the relevant files to me." He sighed and put the card reader next to him on the rock. "We value privacy much more than you do."

"You have an all-seeing artificial intelligence monitoring everything you do and everywhere you go."

"That's because Michael is an infovore. That's what he does. It doesn't follow that he passes that information on to everybody else. Or even anyone at all."

"So you're happy that this machine knows everything about you?"

"Are you happy that your God knows everything about you?" Newcomen took a sharp breath in. "That's not . . ."

"Not the same?" Petrovitch smiled. "No. Michael can't send me to Hell if he thinks I've been bad."

"Doesn't mean that God won't."

"You'd like that, wouldn't you? Yeah, I'm an arrogant little shit, but I pay for it. Who on your side is going to pay for abandoning a twenty-four-year-old to the Alaskan winter? You going to go home and hand out the indictments?" He mimed the scene. "One for you, Mr Director. Here's yours, General. Don't worry, Mr Secretary of State, I haven't forgotten you."

"You're just mocking me now."

"I would much rather see justice done in this life than wait until the next. Mainly because I think the idea's a pile of *govno*, but also because justice delayed is justice denied. Waiting till some of these wily old bastards die is just plain wrong." The light on the reader flicked back to yellow. "Interesting."

[The Secrets committee has met. There are files on the data card that would be detrimental to the personal security of several individuals should they be read by agents of the United States government. They have therefore requested that those files are deleted locally, while I retain secure copies.]

"What's going on?"

"Hang on." Petrovitch held up his hand and addressed Michael. "So what do we have?"

[Access codes to FBI funds and assets within the state of Alaska, along with contact details of personnel. Chiefly, though, we have been given the encrypted v-log of Assistant Director Leopold Buchannan, detailing his personal thoughts over the last week. His words are occasionally banal, but sometimes enlightening. One entry in particular is most revealing, and the committee wishes to share this information with Joseph Newcomen as well as you, since it most directly affects him.]

"Right," said Petrovitch to Newcomen. "Buchannan gave us his diary. You still got that screen I gave you?"

Newcomen patted his pockets, then searched through them, eventually coming up with the flat sheet of plastic. "I've got it."

"But you'll have no sound." Petrovitch thought about matters for a moment, then delved back in his bag. "So let's do this properly."

He came back out with a sealed plastic bag containing three pieces of equipment: an earpiece, a screen-reader, and a slim, curved rectangle in white. He tore the plastic with his teeth and sorted out the components on his lap.

"This is a Freezone thing, and you're the first person not in the collective to ever be offered one." He glanced up at Newcomen's sceptical expression. "It's not because you're special or anything. This is a purely practical decision. Now pull your shirt up."

"Like I'm not cold enough already."

"Stop being a baby and do it." Petrovitch lifted up the white rectangle and pulled a sheet of backing material off one side. "Turn around a bit."

Newcomen did as he was told, and felt faintly ridiculous. Petrovitch positioned the device over the left kidney region and got Newcomen to breathe in. Then he slapped the rectangle against cold white skin and held it there.

"Breathe out."

Newcomen did so, and Petrovitch took his hands away. The thing was stuck on.

"Fine. Tuck yourself back in. You'll notice it's there to start with, then not at all. When it warms up, it'll get to work. You'll need this too." Petrovitch turned Newcomen's palm upwards and pressed the earpiece on him. "Choose an ear and shove it in."

Newcomen tentatively offered the grey capsule to his right ear, but it kept on falling out.

Petrovitch took it from him and rammed it home. Tiny clamps bit into Newcomen's ear canal and held it firm.

"Ow." He shook his head to try and dislodge the thing, but it wasn't coming out. "It hurts."

"You really are a *balvan*, aren't you?" Petrovitch gestured to Newcomen, who bent over, proffering his ear. "Tap the end twice with your fingernail. Like this."

The clamps pulled back and the device dropped out into his hand.

"I suppose I have to put it back now."

"If you want to know what Buchannan said, yes."

Reluctantly, Newcomen did as he was told. He winced when the clamps deployed, but at least he kept his mouth shut. He frowned after a moment, listening to a voice only he could hear.

Michael was talking to him, running him through the protocols that he needed to know about being connected through the Freezone. He didn't have full access to the power of the system, but for someone unused to the always-on, augmented reality it provided, even partial exposure could be surreal.

Newcomen spoke to confirm his name, date of birth, and address. He seemed bewildered by the experience: there was something strapped to his side, another thing planted in his ear, but combined, they formed a presence that was both distant and immediate at the same time.

And the Freezone had been raising kids with this technology for almost a decade now, a whole generation coming through who'd known nothing else but their own personal mentor, guardian, friend being no more than a breath away.

"It says – he says – for you to give me the screen."

Petrovitch held it out and Newcomen took it. The plastic bloomed into life, fuzzy moving images blurred by being shot on a cheap camera flickering inside its translucent surface.

"It's Buchannan."

"I know. I can see it too."

Newcomen pointed to his screen. "But you're not . . ."

"I'm a *yebani* cyborg." Petrovitch reached up and tapped his skull. "It's happening in here."

It was, too. The Assistant Director was sitting on a park bench, swaddled up against the cold. Snow was drifting down around him, settling on his shoulders and melting on the lenses of his glasses. There was a lot of shake: he was videoing himself at arm's length.

"My name," said Buchannan, "is Assistant Director Leo Buchannan, FBI. The time is," and he glanced at his wrist, "ten forty a.m. on Friday February tenth, twenty thirty-four. I have just been approached by two men who declined to identify themselves but who knew the correct access codes for both the FBI building and my office. I shall call them Ben and Jerry, for want of anything better to call them."

Buchannan looked around him before continuing. "I have been asked to obstruct a federal investigation for the good of national security. A foreigner called Lucy Petrovitch is missing in northern Alaska. For reasons that are on a need-to-know basis – and I'm told I don't need to know – Miss Petrovitch must not be found, and no search for her should be made. I have to keep up the appearance of looking for her without actually doing so.

"To this end, I have been told to assign an agent to the case who is totally unsuited for the task. Agent Joseph Newcomen will escort the girl's father wherever he goes, but since this is not his area of expertise, any help he might render will be incidental rather than directed. I am also to withdraw any other agents from the investigation.

"I am very angry about the position I have been put in, and angrier about placing Agent Newcomen at risk from Samuil Petrovitch, who is known to display psychopathic tendencies and is a violent American-hating recidivist. However, my hands appear to be tied, and my orders come with the very highest clearance.

"This is the most distasteful episode in my professional life to date. I am making this recording and keeping it with my personal papers in case of internal investigation or audit."

The media stream finished.

Petrovitch cleared his vision. Newcomen seemed to have forgotten how to breathe.

"Why don't we go back to the plane," he said, "and see if it comes with a drinks cabinet?"

18

It did.

There were full bottles of bourbon and vodka and rum, with mixers, all crammed into a little cupboard in the bulkhead. Petrovitch unwound the cap on the vodka, grabbed two glasses and splashed generous portions in each.

He banged the bottle down on the table between the seats and gripped his glass.

"*Na pobedy!*"

"Uh, that." They both drank deep, but only Newcomen tried to spit his out again. Most of it had evaporated before it left his mouth. He tried to speak, but his vocal cords refused to work.

Petrovitch eyed the bottle and considered another finger or two. Or three.

"Maybe not." He resisted the urge to hurl the glass, and tossed it into the seat next to him. "No one likes to hear themselves called useless. Least of all by their boss. But do you get it now? Me sticking my fingers in your chest isn't what sealed your fate. You were shafted before you were even offered the job."

"What do I do now?" croaked Newcomen.

"Nothing's changed. Lucy's still missing, and we're going to find her."

"You heard what Buchannan said. They think she's dead."

"He didn't say that. He said that she mustn't be found."

"But . . ."

"I remember a time not so long ago when I told you that if you said that again, I'd kill you." Petrovitch bared his teeth. "She is alive. Do you understand? You've been pretty much wrong about everything so far, so I'm not going to listen to you. You don't know. You can't know."

"These Ben and Jerry characters: they told Buchannan he had to stop looking for her."

"Yeah. What's a better way of doing that than leaning on the head of the Seattle field office? Let me think." Petrovitch pondered for a moment, then delivered his verdict. "How about by turning up with the body? That they haven't is how I know she's still alive, and she's waiting for me to come and get her."

"What if there's no body left? What if they've disintegrated her or irradiated her or burnt her to a crisp?" Newcomen gagged. Petrovitch had him by the throat again. "Someone has to tell you these things."

"Just one more word."

"I've nothing left to lose, Petrovitch. You're absolutely right on that. They've taken my career, my girl, my country, and they've left me with nothing. Those were my life, everything I lived for. The reason for getting up in the morning. All that was important to me has gone. This is it now. Just me. Do whatever the hell you want."

Petrovitch let go, and forced himself back. They stared at each other.

"I just want Lucy to come home."

"I know you do. I know you want it more than anything else in the world, and that if I was a father, I'd feel the exact same way. And," Newcomen paused to scrub at his chin and look out of the cabin window at the freezing cold forest, "I'm sorry that my government has decided that it's okay to bury a twenty-four-year-old woman without a trace. I think I need to make that up to you."

"You'll come north with me?"

"I'll come north. I need to know what happened to her almost as much as you do."

"Okay." Petrovitch smiled ruefully. "I was going to offer you the option to bail. I could take you to Vancouver. You could claim asylum there – you wouldn't be the first American to make that journey by a long stretch. We have an understanding with the Canadians, so I'm pretty certain it would be fine."

"That's not going to be necessary." Newcomen pulled a face. "If there's a later? Perhaps."

"I thought, when we started all this, that it wouldn't be this bad. That they were just being obstructive because of her surname. Seriously, what the *huy* is going on? What have they done that requires all this sneaking around?" He gave in, and snagged the vodka bottle once more. He poured himself a small measure and, after offering it to Newcomen, screwed the lid back on and put it away. "It's like they've put a massive neon sign over the North Slope and told us, 'Look away. Nothing to see here.' It doesn't make any sense."

Petrovitch tilted his wrist and drank.

"That doesn't sound like a stupid idea," said Newcomen. "Not any more."

"No. No, it doesn't. Which theory of history do you subscribe to?"

"Sorry?"

"Cock-up or conspiracy?"

"Most events aren't planned." Newcomen laced his fingers together and leaned forward on to his knees. "Some junior guy at the front, no specific orders to do one thing or another, uses his initiative. War breaks out and people write books about all the careful preparation that went on months, years beforehand. It's rarely as neat as that."

"So. If all they're doing is reacting to events as fast as they can, we need to work out the order in which they happened. For that, we need evidence."

"We can get evidence. I'm still an FBI agent." He looked up at Petrovitch. "For the moment."

"You're still listed as active. Buchannan might suspect you've gone feral, but I don't think, given his confession, he's going to be telling anyone soon. And what they'll be counting on is your loyalty: in a crunch, they know which way you'll turn."

"Do they?"

"They think they do. I wouldn't count on them being wrong, either."

"What do you mean?"

"That your sudden change of heart is conditional, depending on the stakes. If it's just a few security officers going off the reservation, you'll stick with it. If it means destroying everything you've ever known? No way. Somewhere in the middle is where you draw the line, but you have no idea where that line is.

What's more, it'll keep shifting." Petrovitch shrugged. "I can live with the uncertainty, not because I have insurance that if you turn against me, it'll be the last thing you ever do, but because I'm more comfortable with moral ambiguity than I am with laser-like certainty."

He stood up and stretched, pressing his hands against the low roof of the cabin.

"It's a long way, and it's not getting any shorter by us waiting," he announced, and shuffled back to the cockpit.

Newcomen followed, and slumped into the co-pilot's seat. The display lit up, and lights started winking into life. The engines started to turn, breaking the naturalistic calm with their crude modernity.

"Last chance to get off the Futility Express," said Petrovitch.

"I'll stick around. See what happens. As long as you hold off on choking me to death."

"I'll do my best. I'm a man of sudden impulses." He returned his gaze to the forest outside. "We'll take off hard. The wind's getting up, and I don't want to ram a tree."

Newcomen took the hint and buckled up.

Petrovitch overlaid his vision with all the head-up displays he'd need. What was more important was that he could feel the aircraft. There was pent-up energy in the batteries; there was fuel sloshing in the tanks. The jets were warming up, and the antigravity pods on their streamlined outriggers were waiting to fulfil their destiny. The skin of the fuselage was his skin, the throttle his legs: he could taste its well-being with his tongue.

All he had to do was jump and run.

He poised: the aircraft came level, hovered for a moment, then rose straight up to treetop height. The engines flared, and steady pressure pushed his meat body back into his seat. Outside of it, he was leaning forward, angling his flight up and over the rise of the island, spilling down the other side. He could spread his arms wide and the whole sky was his.

It was his drug, his joy and his peace.

He aimed north-north-east, heading deeper into Canada and avoiding the finger of land that was Alaska on the Pacific coast. Let the Americans play their games: he had some surprises of his own ready and waiting in the high Arctic.

Trees and snow, rock and ice: pretty much all there was, all the way to the seasonally frozen pole. That, and a few scattered townships that were mostly no more than a collection of huts and an airstrip. These days, now a plane didn't need a runway for anything more than to stop itself from sinking into the melting permafrost, even those were falling into disuse. All these communities needed was a concrete slab and a tank of methanol.

Which suited Petrovitch just fine. The plane he was flying was modern, fast, and drank like a fish, the airborne equivalent of a Ferrari. He was more used to clunky cargo carriers, slow and steady, and parsimonious with the fuel. His range was little more than nine hundred k, and he had to go a lot further than that.

He hit the first stop dead on. With satellites to guide him and a map in his head, there was no guesswork. One moment there was nothing to see but white-capped trees; the next there were grey roofs laid out in a grid pattern and streams of woodsmoke rising into the sky.

He circled once, taking a good look at all the aerials, dishes and wires strung from chimneys and eaves, then sat the plane down on the pad in a blizzard of loose snow.

Petrovitch blinked, and he was back in the cockpit. Newcomen was beside him, eyes closed and head back, snoring slightly. They'd been flying for an hour and a half.

"Hey, Newcomen. Wake up."

The man started violently: the only thing to stop him falling to the floor was the fact that he was strapped in.

"What? What's wrong?" He gripped the arms of his seat. "Why've we landed?"

"Because I don't want to run out of gas in the middle of nowhere. And if you thought parts of Iowa were empty, we're flying over places that have probably never known a human footprint." Petrovitch unbuckled and headed for the door. "I need to find someone to take payment for the fuel and help me hook up the hoses."

"I can do that last thing."

"Sure you can." He started to open the cabin door, and the cold didn't so much steal in as conduct a full-frontal assault with tanks. "It's minus twenty outside: combined with the wind chill, it gives a figure of minus twenty-eight, which is more than enough to freeze flesh to metal. Which you'd know if you'd asked your link."

To illustrate the point, he pulled his sleeves down over his hands before he climbed down into the hard-packed snow. The door started to close again.

"It's there to be used, Newcomen. Freezone people know that."

Petrovitch stamped his way to the nearest hut. Nothing to mark it as anything different, but before he'd landed, he'd tagged a map of the town with all the information he needed. It was so instinctive, he didn't really need to think about it any more: it was just there.

The door was stiff, and he had to kick it. Inside was yellow light and brown shelves.

"Hey," said the grizzled proprietor, looking up from his screen reader. He watched Petrovitch knock the snow off his boots. He knew everyone for a hundred k in every direction, but not this guy. Then he took a second look.

"Hey," said Petrovitch. "Great beard."

"I'm . . ." He almost said *honoured*, then figured that wasn't the thing to say. "What can I get you?"

"I've hired some fancy pimped-up executive jet that's currently parked out on the pan. Good for outrunning the USAF, but not so hot for economic driving. So I guess it's fill 'er up."

"Sure." He levered himself up, and reached for his long caribou-skin coat, his furry hat and massive gloves. "Anything else?"

Petrovitch looked around the shelves. "I don't want to seem pushy, but does anyone do hot food here? I've been through all kinds of hell today and I'm still in a hurry, but I'm as much in need of refuelling as the plane."

The shopkeeper narrowed his dark eyes. "I'll make a call. Ten minutes good for you?"

"Yeah. That would be brilliant. There are two of us."

Petrovitch kicked his heels and looked at the stock. There was pretty much everything anyone could possibly want and couldn't kill or cut for themselves. The shelves kept on going back, and there was barely any room to walk between them.

He was admiring the wood axes when the door opened again, and the temperature inside dropped like a stone.

"Archie?"

"He's out fuelling the plane," called Petrovitch. He stepped out from between the shelves and saw a tiny Inuit woman with a foil-lined cardboard box.

"Then this will be for you." She held out the box and he walked over to claim it.

"Bacon," he said.

"And cheese." She looked up at him from her wrinkled brown face. "Hope you find your daughter, Dr Petrovitch."

"Thanks."

"When you get to where you're going, tell them Mary wants them to look after you."

She left the same way she'd come in, with the minimum of fuss and no expectation of payment. Petrovitch put the box on the counter and patted his pockets, looking for his cards.

Shuffling through them, he found his Canadian dollars, checked the local meths prices, added ten per cent, then went back for the axe. It was a beautiful piece of work, easy to swing and effortlessly sharp. He added it to the bill and pressed it to the reader.

He gathered up the box and the axe haft, and stepped out into the cold again. The man – Archie, he had to assume – was swaddled up well against the weather, with barely any flesh visible. He raised his hand and unhooked the fuel hose as Petrovitch approached.

"You're good for a few hundred more."

"I've paid already. If it's not enough, tell the Freezone."

"We make most of the stuff ourselves in a digester. It's not free, but it's cheap."

"You probably overcharged me then. Keep the change." Petrovitch told the plane to open the door, then reached up to slide the box of food inside, and followed it with the axe. "I thought I might just need one."

"You never know." Archie took off his glove to shake hands. "Good luck."

"Yeah. That and the axe, we're sorted." He climbed up, and shut out the night.

Newcomen was still in the cockpit, staring out through the windscreen. He looked around idly, and Petrovitch raised his eyebrows.

"That smells good," said Newcomen.

"One of the old girls fixed us some food." He pushed the box ahead of him and indicated that the man help himself. "The gun's for bears."

"Sorry?" Newcomen tried to speak around a plate-sized bread bun filled with rashers of bacon and melting squares of processed cheese.

"In my bag. I know you've been looking. The gun has explosive bullets and will reduce a polar bear to chunks of husky meat. It's important where we're going."

Eventually Newcomen started chewing again. When he'd swallowed, he said: "You know it's illegal to smuggle a gun into Canada."

"Yeah, I know. That's why, unlike you, I have a permit for mine. Don't worry," said Petrovitch. "I won't turn you in."

19

"I want to say goodbye to Christine," said Newcomen.

"You sure?"

The plane was making a loop over another collection of huts and a disused landing strip, this time in the dark. Lights burned pockets out of the shadows: the rest was featureless void.

"I think it's pretty clear I can't go back, and I owe her an explanation as to why."

Petrovitch puffed his cheeks out. "So you're going to tell Christine that her dad hates you so much he got the Director of the FBI to send you on a suicide mission. And you think she's going to believe you?"

"But I've got evidence – AD Buchannan's recording."

"Ooh, I can see a few problems with this already." Petrovitch lined up the plane over the landing pad and started the descent. He nudged the nose around so that it pointed upwind. "Just give me a moment. This is easier than it used to be, and still there are a half-dozen ways to screw up."

The radar altimeter told him his height, and he lined up the virtual crosshairs beneath him. The plane sank lower, and a telltale went *ping* when the wheels touched the ground.

"Fine." He started through the power-down procedure. "Where were we? That was it: you making a series of crashing mistakes. Why did you want to talk to Christine again?"

"To say goodbye."

"Not to try and explain what's been going on to make yourself look heroic, or tell her what a monster her father is?"

Newcomen started to answer, then shut his mouth.

Petrovitch turned off the flight instruments. The cockpit was as dark as the outside, except for the two points of red light behind his eyes. "It's perfectly human of you. I'm not blaming you for wanting to do this, but it can't happen the way you want. You can't tell her about the bomb. You can't tell her about her father. You can't tell her about Buchannan. You can't tell her where you are . . ."

"Which is?"

"Watson Lake, Yukon Territory. You can just ask your link, you know." Petrovitch shook his head, then remembered where he was on his list. "And you can't tell her where we're going. That really doesn't leave much to hang a story on."

Newcomen straightened up. "Why can't I tell her those things?"

"Mainly because it'll get you, or her, or someone else, killed. And even if you don't care about yourself, I'd have thought Christine would have been somewhere in your thoughts."

"She's never out of them. No one would kill her, that's just," he threw his hands in the air, "stupid."

"It would probably be the same people who'd kill Buchannan. And Logan. And his wife." Petrovitch saw the confusion on Newcomen's face. "You don't get it, do you?"

"No."

"How were you going to talk to Christine?"

"Not on my phone, since you destroyed it. On this link, I guess."

"Has Christine got a link?"

"You know she hasn't."

"So? Come on, join the dots."

"You're saying her phone's bugged?"

"At last. Bearing in mind we've just endured two days of constant and intrusive surveillance, did you think any conversation you could possibly have over an unsecured network would stay private?" Petrovitch pressed his fingers into his temples. "I'm surrounded by *yebani* idiots."

"So I can't even say goodbye." Newcomen slumped back in his seat. "That's just . . . dandy."

"No. Saying goodbye is pretty much all you can do. No reasons, no excuses, no evidence. Just: 'Hey. I won't be seeing you ever again. I love you very much. I hope you have a nice life.' Any more than that, and you'll be signing her death warrant."

Petrovitch unbuckled his harness and peered at the condensation freezing on the windscreen. It was minus twenty-three outside; a real cold snap, even for February, though Michael informed him the record there was minus sixty.

[Be grateful.]

"I am. Keep a close eye on Farm Boy, will you? If he wants to call Christine, he should, but put him on a delay and censor him hard, because I'm still not sure he gets it."

[It is regrettable that full information disclosure cannot be practised at this time.]

"Yeah. First law stuff. Hard lines."

[Information wants to be free, Sasha.]

"You could reasonably argue that Buchannan could have stood up to Ben and Jerry and told them to swivel on it. But he has kids, and a wife, so he didn't, and we're left with this mess. It'll still be difficult to make parts of this public when we write the history."

[The Secrets committee?]

"Best let them know now. See if they think some lockdown on the more sensitive bits is needed." Petrovitch went to see about refuelling, both the plane and him.

If it had been cold before, it was now like stepping into an industrial freezer.

"*Yobany stos.* I hope that outdoor gear's ready."

[It is en route, currently in a box at Fairbanks airport. It will be delivered to the address tomorrow morning.]

"Good. It's cold enough to freeze my *yajtza* off." He stamped his way across the snow to rustle up some help. "Any sign of movement from the Yanks?"

[Your evasion of them this morning has not been reported at all in the public media. Since you are only guilty of filing an incorrect flight plan, and one count of violating local air restrictions, it has been reasonably simple for them to just ignore the incident. The scrambled planes were stood down, and Washington air traffic control resumed operations within the hour. The delay was blamed on computer error.]

"Newcomen still on the active list?"

[He has not been officially withdrawn, although there is a great deal of activity surrounding his file: it has been accessed no fewer than one thousand and fifty-nine times since midnight last night.]

"Any redaction or alteration to it?"

[Some minor editing regarding his medical history. New MRI scans have been substituted for the originals, and they now indicate that Joseph Newcomen has an undetected aneurysm.]

"Head or heart?"

[Head. It is clear that if they wish to kill him at an appropriate moment, they have a ready-made cover story.]

"I ought to let him know. Though I very much doubt if even they can pretend that a bullet through the brain is a pre-existing medical condition."

He found the right hut, and the man asleep in his chair reluctantly left the warmth of his two-bar fire to do the deed.

Petrovitch took his place, just for a moment. He closed his eyes and dreamed.

It was dark, but not the dark of night, or of a closed room. This darkness was vast, unending, holy. It called to him to stare deep into it, because it held everything that ever was and ever would be. He looked, and was lost in wonder.

[Sasha? There has been a . . .] Michael paused.

He was instantly awake.

[Development.]

"The last time you said that, my world fell apart."

[It is not your world this time, Sasha. It is Joseph's.]

"I thought it had fallen apart already. You mean he's got further to go?"

The door to the fuel hut banged open. Newcomen staggered in, suffering from the cold and the extreme anxiety that had gripped him.

"You'll need to close that," said Petrovitch.

"We have to go back," slurred Newcomen. "We have to go back now."

177

Petrovitch reached past him and kicked the door closed. He grabbed the unresisting man and pushed him in front of the fire so his face could defrost.

"It's Christine. She's in terrible danger." Newcomen tried to wrestle Petrovitch out of the way.

"I don't care if she's fallen down the old well, Lassie: we're nearly fifteen hundred k north of Seattle and there are easier ways of helping than presenting ourselves back there with massive targets painted on us."

Newcomen hit him. Not hard enough to really hurt, but it was a surprise all the same. He only managed it once. Petrovitch closed his fist around Newcomen's own and squeezed.

Newcomen gasped and slipped off the chair on to his knees, shaking uncontrollably.

"Don't ever do that again. Do you understand?"

"Yes."

"Michael, what the *huy* is going on?"

[Joseph Newcomen wished to communicate with Christine Logan. I initiated the call and secured it from the repeated attempts to trace our location. I was even able to provide him with a visual feed from spyware located throughout the Logan residence.]

Petrovitch let go, and left Newcomen clutching his bruised fingers. "When you say throughout, you mean that in your precise, unambiguous way, right?"

[Areas that would normally be considered private for humans such as bedrooms and bathrooms are being actively surveilled. I have discussed the implications of this discovery with Joseph Newcomen.]

"Which is why he's crying at my feet and demanding I take him back to Seattle." He looked down. "You know, I could do without this."

[It is highly likely that Joseph Newcomen will make repeated attempts to return to Christine Logan alone, no matter how forcefully you prevent him. In addition, his psychological state will render him ineffectual.]

"More ineffectual? He's positively a black hole of effectiveness as it is. So what you're saying is we have to do something, or I'm going to end up kicking him out of a moving plane flying at five hundred k over the Canadian tundra just to get some peace and quiet."

[Essentially, yes.]

"It's not illegal to put surveillance cameras up in your own property, is it?"

[One of the fundamental tenets of Reconstruction is that a family is free to order itself within its own dwelling space, with no government interference.]

"Newcomen? I might be able to turn my ears off so I don't hear your whining, but I still know you're doing it. Sit in the chair and shut up. The grown-ups are trying to work out what to do." Petrovitch scratched at the stubble on his chin. "Could never grow a proper beard. Now, Archie's? That was serious beardage. Right, Michael: call an ad-hoc. I want to go after the house computer."

Half a world away, a committee was formed, told of the reason, and asked to come to a decision.

They did. It wasn't quite what he expected.

"Newcomen. I can make you an offer."

Newcomen looked up for the first time in a while. He regarded Petrovitch suspiciously. "Go on."

"Michael can attack Logan's house computer: wipe its memory, erase its programs. The security system's such that it'll go into fail-safe mode, and Christine's going to have to be rescued by the fire department cutting through the front door. That'll get her out of the house for a couple of days."

"But won't Logan just load everything back up again?"

"Yeah, course he will. Trashing his computer is conditional on you telling Christine what we've done and why." Petrovitch shrugged. "The ad-hoc says she has a right to know. Difficult to argue with that. And if you don't do it, I will; I imagine she's more likely to believe you without me having to get technical on her about where the spy-eyes and mics are hidden."

"I . . ."

"Five minutes ago you wanted us to turn around and appear on her doorstep. What, precisely, were you going to say to her then?"

"I hadn't really thought it through," admitted Newcomen.

"No. Let's try the brains before the balls, okay?"

Newcomen nodded. "Okay. I'll tell her."

"Good. Michael? Time to go to work."

The AI bore down on the Logan house computer and inserted itself like a crowbar between its external face and its internal functions. It systematically deleted reams of data, all the while telling the program that was supposed to watch for that sort of thing that everything was just fine.

Once it had erased pretty much everything, it started on the security system itself. Doors locked, shutters fell, alarms sounded. No more than a shell running a few lines of code, the computer turned itself off. Phones, lights, power. Everything gone. Christine and her mother were left with their mobiles to call for help.

"Done," said Petrovitch. "We need to get back in the air."

"That's it?"

"What did you expect? A really big explosion?"

"I don't know. Can I check on her?" asked Newcomen.

"Michael's monitoring the police: the dispatcher has just sent a squad car, and Mrs Logan's called her husband. They'll be out within the hour, even if they have to use a shaped charge." Petrovitch rested his hand on the doorknob. "This is just a distraction. Saving your ex-fiancée from her pig of a father is not why I'm here. It's not why you're here, either. I'm glad you're happier, but we did this so you could concentrate on finding Lucy."

"I'm still grateful."

"Good. Hold that thought."

20

Petrovitch kept on heading north, and again he immersed himself in the being of the plane. He'd turned from a kid who'd die if he ran too far into a man-machine hybrid who believed he could fly. It wouldn't stop there, either. Not if he had his way.

At some point, Newcomen excused himself and went to sit back in the cabin to talk to Christine: it wouldn't have made any difference whether he stayed or not. Petrovitch was entirely content to leave the matter to Michael, and was mostly unaware of anything that was happening in the cockpit.

A long time later, Newcomen came back. Petrovitch emerged from his fugue long enough to see that the man was red-eyed and occasionally shuddering with an escaping sob.

It must have been like a funeral, to finally see all your hopes and dreams piled up in one heap, then have someone hand you the match to light the cordwood that would turn them all to ashes.

Petrovitch retreated.

[He has told her.]

"Yeah."

[The conversation went as expected. Joseph Newcomen will be emotionally fragile for some time: we must factor that into our future treatment of him.]

"A broken heart is the least of his worries."

[As far as he is concerned, it is his only worry at the moment. He asked for music afterwards: Kenny Rogers, specifically.]

"It's worse than I thought. All this sitting around is giving him too much time to think: it'll be different when we get to Fairbanks. Whatever it is they've got waiting for us won't be bread and salt, at any rate."

[There is further analysis of the events of February third. Do you wish to review it now, or wait until you land?]

"It's fifteen minutes till Dawson City. It'll keep."

He dropped down into the Yukon Valley, the high mountains rising up either side. He turned hard to starboard, then to port, and suddenly there were lights on the ground in an unnatural geometric grid, burning bright against the snow. They illuminated the streets, and beyond: the glow carried out over the river ice. This was where he had to throttle down, and head up the Klondike to the airport. The residents wouldn't appreciate yet another jet roaring in overhead.

Beyond the strange wormy landscape of mine tailings, he spotted the airport squeezed in between the valley sides. He cut the power further and drifted in over the runway. There was a collection of half a dozen small cargo planes clustered around the main terminal, and he slotted his craft down behind them. Compared with the bulky outlines of the next nearest plane, his own looked fragile.

"Last stop before Fairbanks. Time to stretch your legs, Newcomen."

"I can stay here. I'll just get in the way otherwise."

Petrovitch pursed his lips. "You can mope all you like. But you're not doing it on my time. Now, out of your seat, and come with me."

"And how cold is it outside?"

"Why don't you talk to your link and find out? It's there: use it."

When Newcomen discovered it was minus thirty-five, he rebelled. "No way."

Petrovitch pointed through the windscreen at the next plane. A slit of orange light showed its cargo bay door was ajar. "We're going as far as there, that's all."

"So whose plane is that?"

"This is the way it works: Freezone people don't ask stupid questions because they're not lazy and they can find out the answers for themselves. It means that conversations can be direct, to the point, and mercifully short." He left it there, and made his way to the cabin door.

The ladder dropped its feet into the snow. Petrovitch trotted down and headed straight for the sliver of light. Minus thirty-five was genuinely awful without the proper gear, enough to turn his skin waxy and freeze the liquid lubricating his eyes. As he approached the other plane, the door opened wider, and more light spilled out. A preternaturally tall figure stood inside, waiting.

Petrovitch turned sideways through the gap, making sure he didn't touch any of the metal, and found himself enveloped in strong arms and a warm coat.

"Hey," he said.

"Hey yourself," she replied. "You made good time."

"It's fast, even if it does look like it'll break if you drop it."

Madeleine squinted through the door. "It will break if you drop it. You haven't dropped it, have you?"

"Not a scratch on it. We might even be able to return it in one piece."

"Something tells me that's not going to happen." She looked over his head. "Newcomen."

"Mrs Petrovitch." He stood in the doorway, looking uncertain.

"If you come in, I can close the door." She let go of Petrovitch and thumbed the mechanism. The door cranked shut with a bang, and Newcomen shivered.

Madeleine threw another coat at him, and he caught it and put it on quickly. He noticed that beneath her own coat, she had an armoury hanging from her wide belt.

"Those don't look like they're for bears."

"Is that what he told you?" She snorted. "And you believed him?"

Newcomen looked across at Petrovitch, who was sealing his coat at the front and lifting the fur-lined hood over his head.

"Doesn't mean there aren't bears, all the same."

"Of course, if we'd done this my way . . ."

"And you were voted down." Petrovitch's face was framed by the hood. "There's still plenty of time for this to turn into a hot war."

It was then that Newcomen realised just what was in the cargo hold with him. Long metal crates, with serial numbers and scripts in different languages. "These boxes. You can't be serious."

Petrovitch looked around him. He knew what was inside each one, and it still surprised him. "Maddy figures that turning up to a fight with nothing more than good intentions is a quick way to get yourself killed. But we're not looking to start the fight."

"They are," said Madeleine. "They've been moving assets north for the past week."

"Assets?" asked Newcomen. "What sort of assets?"

"We can't see through the tops of the trucks hauling north on the Dalton Highway, but we've a pretty good idea of what they're carrying. We thought we might need something to level the odds." She rested a foot on top of a steel case that looked like it might contain a surface-to-air missile launcher.

"You can't start a war. Up here. That's . . . ridiculous. There's two of you." Newcomen saw that both Petrovitchs wore identical expressions. "All these planes are yours, aren't they?"

"They might be." Madeleine jerked her head at her husband. "And he's never needed any help starting a war. The rest of us are only here to make sure it's done right."

"You're all insane."

"You think so?" Petrovitch tapped Newcomen's top pocket. "Get your reader out. Michael has something to show us."

Newcomen fumbled with his cold fingers for the plastic rectangle. Petrovitch didn't need one, hadn't needed one for a decade. He called up his sandbox and sat down beside it with Michael.

"Hey. What's the news?"

[We believe SkyShield targeted a satellite of currently unknown origin. If our theory, which currently enjoys some seventy per cent confidence, is correct, it has serious implications for global communications in general, and the integrity of the Freezone in particular.]

Ten years on from the lanky Japanese kid who'd guided him though the Outie war, Michael's preferred form was disturbingly like a young Hamano Oshicora. He could be literally anything he wanted, but this was his settled identity. It did no harm, and Petrovitch wondered if the AI had done this consciously: he never asked, and Michael never offered an answer of his own.

"No one's complained about any missing hardware."

[Which indicates that there are two secrets here: firstly, why the satellite's owners wish to remain anonymous, and secondly, what reason the Americans had for shooting it down,] said Michael.

"Unless the Yanks are testing out a new anti-satellite system on a bird they've put up themselves, in preparation for blanking out the sky for the rest of us."

[This is a possibility that falls within the thirty per cent uncertainty. Other options include a malfunction of SkyShield, the accidental targeting of a bolide, or indeed the deliberate targeting of a piece of debris that might have posed a threat to people on the ground.]

"But most of the analysts don't buy any of that." Petrovitch leaned over his sandbox, which transformed itself into a map of the northern hemisphere, pole uppermost. "Show me."

Michael started to draw his explanation. Red lines representing the orbits of objects in space, blue to mean the objects themselves.

[The raw data has been extrapolated to a best-fit scenario, but some things we can be certain of: a SkyShield interceptor in Low Earth Orbit fires a kinetic energy weapon at zero nine thirteen, Universal Time. Eight seconds later, a flash is observed one hundred and twenty kilometres away from the interceptor by a Freezone micro-satellite. The images captured are compromised by the low angle at which they were acquired, taken through the outer reaches of the atmosphere.]

"The originals look like *govno*, right?"

[A considerable amount of processing was required to extract useable data, yes. The object re-entered the Earth's atmosphere and, at zero nine twenty-three Universal Time, caused a seismic event measuring three point seven Richter. This equates to a yield of approximately one half to one third of a megatonne ten kilometres above the epicentre, south of Prudhoe Bay, Alaska.]

"That's way too much for a satellite." Petrovitch frowned and looked at the blue line described in the air in front of him, which arced down from space and terminated above the North Slope. "Or way too much for a regular satellite. What the hell did they have in there?"

[Barring a matter–antimatter collision, the conclusion is that only a nuclear explosion could provide such prompt energy.]

"A nuclear power plant won't blow up just because you hit it."

[Again, it is more likely that the explosion was a deliberate fail-safe against the re-entry and recovery of identifiable debris.]

"So, to summarise: someone put a satellite into orbit, carrying something so secret that they put a nuclear bomb on board too. The Americans got wind of it and took it out. The satellite starts to drop from the sky, and the bomb goes off before it hits the ground. Is that about right?"

[With the usual caveats, yes.]

"Then why the *huy* haven't we heard anything about this before now? We're supposed to be the planet's most sophisticated information-gathering system, working every minute of every day, yet we miss something like this? *Yobany stos*, this is not just *pizdets*, this is a whole new category of *pizdets*."

[We now know where to look and what to look for. This situation may yet yield results. We are checking the orbits of all known satellites, and attempting to locate visually those no longer in contact with their base stations, to confirm we have not missed a single one. This will take time.]

"And recent launches." Petrovitch swung the map around until he was looking up from underneath it, as if he was in Lucy's position, in a series of snow-covered huts under the dark sky. "Do you think it's the Chinese?"

[That possibility has been raised. They possess both the lift capacity and the required level of secrecy. It is also known that the Americans have active agents within the Chinese National Space Administration: perhaps one of them has leaked information about this project.]

"There aren't supposed to be nukes in space."

[No. China have signed but not ratified the Comprehensive Test Ban Treaty of 1996, putting them in the same position as the United States of America. What this means in practice is, I believe, moot.]

Petrovitch played the simulation again. The SkyShield component blazed away with its rail gun, sending a cloud of tungsten flechettes into the path of the oncoming satellite. The object deorbited rapidly, and as it came down, exploded.

"Everything is wrong."

[Please explain.]

"We're trying to fit the facts to the scenario: it should be the other way around. There's a whole stack of things that don't wash. The chief of which is why they left it so late to press the self-destruct button. Surely, once you know you're hit and out of control, that's when you do it – not when it's about to crash into the ground. And how did it get so far without breaking up? It had to have a re-entry shield. But why? What was in it?"

[We will have answers, Sasha. Soon.]

"If you can work out what this has to do with Lucy while you're at it, I'd be grateful."

Michael loved Lucy. She was the second person he'd ever talked to. He was her big brother, and her absence caused him something akin to pain.

[Do not be ill-tempered,] he said. [We are working – all of us – at our capacity. The resources of almost the entire Freezone are being dedicated to this.]

"Okay, sorry. We're missing something, though. Something big. Something *yebani* enormous."

[Your wife and the FBI agent wish to speak to you. They have seen the same simulation, with commentaries suitable to their level of comprehension. Joseph Newcomen has very little grasp of the technicalities of orbital mechanics, and therefore I cannot say how much he understood.]

"For once, it really is rocket science. Keep going. Let me know as soon as anything significant turns up." He smiled ruefully. "And thanks."

He kicked himself out of the virtual world and was once again sitting in the cargo hold of a small aircraft, with his wife and Newcomen. He looked at their faces to judge their reactions: Madeleine was watching him for the same reason, while Newcomen was sitting on a crate with his mouth open.

"The Chinese?" he said. "Nobody said anything about the Chinese being involved."

"We don't know that for certain." Madeleine put her reader away inside her coat. "There's a lot we don't know for certain."

"But what if the Chinese want what's left of their satellite back?"

"Now you're just being ridiculous," said Madeleine. She extended herself to her full height and stretched. Her hands pressed against the cargo hold's roof. "After an explosion of that size?"

"There's one way to find out," said Petrovitch, "and that's ask them."

Newcomen baulked. "What? Dear Comrade President, have you lost some space hardware that just happened to contain an atomic bomb?"

"Something like that, except you address him as Chairman. You might not know how Chinese bureaucracy works, but I do. You find some low-level functionary that'll take your call. They clearly don't have the authority to deal with such a question, but they'll issue a blank denial as a matter of course. Meanwhile, the note gets passed up the food chain until someone decides that someone below them should look into the matter." He shrugged. "It takes time. I'll get a call from a middle-ranking civil servant, who will ask me obliquely what I know. I'll tell him what I think he needs to know. It can go on like that for weeks."

"And you're happy with that?" Newcomen seemed both outraged and relieved.

"My happiness or otherwise doesn't make them move any faster. But they might tell me something useful I can't find out any other way. If it helps, I'll take it." Petrovitch looked up at Madeleine, and she down at him. "Newcomen?"

"Yes."

"For reasons that should be self-explanatory, even to a naïf like you, I'd like some time alone with my wife." He raised his eyebrows and waited.

"Oh. Yes. Okay. I'll just go back to our plane."

"Thank you."

Madeleine opened the door for him, and closed it again after.

"Hey," said Petrovitch again.

21

It was four hundred kilometres to Fairbanks, and Petrovitch flew them at zero altitude all the way. The terrain was a maze of valleys and hills, with the occasional mountain to worry about, and all of it, except for the snow-capped peaks, forest. In the dark.

He had to continually change either height or direction, and sometimes both at the same time. It was a technical challenge to keep between the high ground, so as not to expose the aircraft to radar, and still not crash. Newcomen went first white, then green, then ran to the cabin to find something to puke his guts up in.

They crossed the border into Alaska. They weren't shot down.

Newcomen eventually came back to the co-pilot's seat, pale and shaking.

"Can you talk?" he asked.

"As long as you don't ask me anything that requires more than a moment's thought. This isn't a car, and it doesn't fly itself." The whole brief for the plane's design was fast and straight. Petrovitch was making it do things it was never intended to.

"I've been thinking," said Newcomen.

"Careful now."

"Will you just listen?"

"Yeah, okay."

"They don't want you to find out what happened to Lucy, right?"

"Let's just say they don't want me to find Lucy, and leave it at that."

"Sure. But they're also gearing up for a fight. With the Chinese."

"Maybe."

"Can't we just tell them what we know? That everything Lucy could have found out we've worked out for ourselves, so there's no point in us not finding her. It'll make no difference. We could even promise them we wouldn't say anything in return for her."

"I'm sure someone, somewhere, has already suggested that. I'll check, but so could you. You've got a link. Use it. But look, you've already heard me cursing Chinese bureaucracy: your political mindset is such that you cover up first, then ask why later. By which time, too many important people have got too much to lose by coming clean. Some junior functionary on the ground orders evidence to be conveniently lost, he tells his boss, his boss makes up a story and tells his boss. So then he makes a couple of decisions based on layers of lies and misinformation, and when he finds out, he's not going to go public with the fact he's a *mudak*." He stopped talking long enough to hurl the plane around one valley spur and through a col. "So tell me what happens when we let Washington know that we've spotted SkyShield is taking potshots at foreign satellites?"

Newcomen shifted uneasily in his seat as their acceleration surged. "They try to get rid of us too?"

"There reaches a point where even the most dedicated conspiracy theorist has to admit defeat. We are nowhere near that point. My life, your life, Lucy's life are not as important as some guy's career advancement in military intelligence. You remember that."

"Oh."

"Nice try, though."

The plane's tail swung around and the jets roared for a second, then dropped to idling speed. There were bright lights in the distance, and the ground they had to cover was more or less flat.

"Fairbanks?"

"We'll take the last twenty k dead slow. No one should hear us, let alone see us."

Petrovitch nudged them forward at a speed that didn't generate too much wind noise – no more than the gusted, snow-laden branches made – and eventually cut the power altogether.

They drifted over a part of the forest that had been clear cut long ago, and was now an undisturbed sheet of shining white. The plane dropped swiftly, then hovered just above the surface of the snow. The ice on top cracked as it was pierced by the undercarriage, then crunched as it was pushed aside.

They were at rest. No sound of dogs, of voices, no sign of swinging flashlights or armed militias.

"The nearest houses are two hundred metres away, so once we're outside, you can't talk. I can speak to you through your link, but all you can do is shut up and follow me. Get your coat on."

Standing at the bottom of the ladder, Petrovitch closed the door and powered the plane down. It became no more than a dark shadow against the trees behind it. If someone was looking for it, they'd see it: that couldn't be helped. But it was out of the way, and wouldn't be there long.

It would have to do. There was a risk in everything he did.

He set off across the snow, guided by the map in his head and the light from his eyes. Every step, he sank in up to his knees. Back in St Petersburg, they had days like this, before the traffic and the soot turned the ice black and churned it up into semi-solid sculptures: days when the kids would pour out of their blank-faced apartment blocks and play. Some of them wouldn't be properly dressed, and they'd get wet and cold, they'd get a fever and for the want of a few roubles' worth of medicine, they'd die.

The snow would last for months, all through to spring, and it'd be all everyone could do just to make it through to the first warm sun of the year.

But for one day, one perfect day, everything that was horrible about living in a basket case of a city with a corrupt government, crooked police, hyperinflationary prices and radioactive death from the sky was all blanketed under a layer of bright white snow.

The lights of the houses shone through the gaps in the trees, and in the dark, a chain-link fence reared up. He followed it, and the shape of a roof formed against the clouds.

He unlatched the gate, silently waved Newcomen through, and closed it behind him, then stepped up to the wooden porch. He rested his hand on the door handle and pressed down. It opened, and before entering, he kicked the snow off his boots.

Both inside, Petrovitch shut the door again.

"If you move, you'll trip over everything. I'll get the lights working, and we can sort ourselves out."

"Whose house is this?"

"Mine, temporarily." Petrovitch found the cupboard hiding the power switch, and flicked it on, remembering to close his eyes and adjust his vision back to normal.

A single dim bulb flickered into life above Newcomen's head. It was enough to temporarily blind him to the several large boxes that lined the hallway.

"Yours?"

"Yeah. It's not in my name, obviously – that would be stupid. I needed a drop-off point for these." He kicked the cardboard side of one of the boxes.

Newcomen read the shipping label of the one closest to him, but it gave him no clues. "So, what's in them?"

Petrovitch used a fingernail to break the tape seal, and ripped it away. He dug deep and came out with a pair of heavy-soled boots. "Twelve and a half. They're yours. And these socks. And these. The thin pair go on first, the thick pair afterwards, in case there's any confusion. And don't buckle up too tight: you'll restrict the blood supply and be more likely to get frostbite."

Newcomen glanced down at his soaked shoes, soaked socks, wet trousers. He looked very sorry.

The other boxes contained thermal underwear, comfy-looking jumpers, thin gloves and thick mittens, hats, goggles, scarves – none of it with a single heating circuit or thermostat, all of it old-school Arctic survival gear.

"Meet you back here in five." Petrovitch gathered up his kit and headed to one of the bedrooms.

"What do I do with my suit?"

"I could make some suggestions, but none of them would be constructive. Now get a move on. It'll be closing time soon, and I need to find a bar."

"What? You're serious."

"I never joke about drinking. Four minutes forty."

Petrovitch stripped off, then dressed again. He spent the last thirty seconds transferring equipment from his trouser pockets into his coat, and one last delve into his carpet bag.

He kicked the bag under the bed and stepped out into the hall.

Newcomen was already there, buttoned up and ready to go. Petrovitch raised an eyebrow and turned the man around, checking he'd done everything properly. He was almost impressed.

"Not bad. Not good, either: you still look like a G-man masquerading as a trapper, but we don't have the time to do anything about that." Petrovitch stomped to the front door in his heavy boots and let some of the night air in. "We're running out of time, so let's go."

They tramped out on to the main street: the road was separated from the pavement by a waist-high ridge of ploughed snow and ice.

"Are we meeting someone?" asked Newcomen, looking faintly ridiculous in his fur-lined hat.

"After a fashion. I know where they are, but they don't know we're coming. Hopefully, they'll stay put for the ten minutes it'll take us to get there."

The walk into town was accompanied by blown snow drifting close to the ground, and the occasional rattle of snow chains as a car passed. The traffic lights cast pools of colour on the ground, and the street signs shone in white, blue and green.

Petrovitch stopped outside one particular bar, after passing several without a second look. A marlin, marked out in blue holographic neon, hung over the door.

He dug his hand into his pocket, and came out with a fluid-filled container. He gave it a shake to make sure the contents hadn't frozen.

"You'll need to put these on." He corrected himself. "In. You'll need to put these in."

Newcomen held the cylinder up to the nearest light. "I don't know where it goes."

"In your eyes. The bar's optical scanner will spot you coming, and I don't want people to know we're here until long after we've gone."

Newcomen swallowed. "I don't think I can. I've never had to wear contacts before."

Petrovitch pulled the gloves off one hand and stuffed them in a pocket. He unscrewed the lid and fished out a curved silvered disc. "Look up."

Their size difference was such that Petrovitch had to climb up the ice ridge.

"Okay, look up again. And don't blink." He held out the lens on his index finger, and Newcomen tried to look past it. His eye watered uncontrollably, and when he was properly blind, Petrovitch let the layer of moisture suck the lens on to the eyeball. Then he went back for the other one.

"That feels so weird." Newcomen batted his lashes. "Why's it so dark?"

"So the lasers bounce off your eyes and don't read the retinas. You'll need this too." He pressed one of his plastic eyeballs into

Newcomen's palm. "When you pass under the scanner, hold this up next to your head. Pretend you're scratching your ear, or something."

"Petrovitch, I did go to Quantico."

"Yeah. That's why I'm having to fill in the gaps in your education as I go along. A couple of ground rules: don't get drunk."

"That's not going to be a problem."

"And don't try and pay for anything. My cards only." He took off his own furry hat, and looked slightly less like a Hollywood comedy Russian than before. "In fact, try not to say anything at all."

"Thanks."

"Unless I kick you. Then feel free." He pushed at the bar's door, and held up his own eye. A red light flicked out and scanned him, then Newcomen. As far as the computer log was concerned, Hyram T. Wallace and Bertram K. Bendix from New Mexico had just entered. Both identities were over twenty-one and came with clean bills of health. No alarms tripped, and they were in through the second set of doors into the warm fug of the bar.

Petrovitch started to undo his coat, and scanned the patrons, running their faces through the US database. He spotted his target over in a darkened corner, well away from the jazz band doing their thing on the cramped stage.

"Ready?"

"I don't know what for, but okay."

Petrovitch ignored the several empty booths and chose one already occupied by a young man, only the top of his head visible above the seat back. He slid along the seat opposite him, while Newcomen found himself facing a startled dark-haired girl with a hint of an epicanthic fold about her upper eyelids.

"Don't try and get up," said Petrovitch. "We only want to talk."

The man – a slimmer, younger version of Newcomen – was pale already.

"Did my parents send you?" His voice quavered.

"We're not private investigators, and we're not here to enforce the injunction. Relax." Petrovitch threw his hat on to the table and shrugged his coat off. "You're not in trouble with me."

"Then what do you want?"

Petrovitch leaned forward and beckoned him closer. "My name is Dr Samuil Petrovitch."

The man blinked. "Oh my g . . . word. You are. You are him. How did you . . .?" He stopped and started again. "You just walked in here?"

"Yeah, pretty much. This is Joseph Newcomen, FBI."

"FBI? Oh."

"It's fine. He's with me, and he really hasn't got time to worry about you two." He looked at Newcomen. "Isn't that right?"

"I have no idea what you're talking about," said Newcomen.

"Excellent." Petrovitch turned back to the couple.

"I'm Alan," volunteered the man. "This is Jessica."

"I know who you are. I know all about you." Petrovitch smiled. "Let me buy you both a drink and you can tell me all about my daughter and Jason Fyfe."

22

Petrovitch caught the waitress's attention with a raise of his hand. She had epic breasts and a slightly too-tight blouse: not quite enough to get her hauled up on a public lewdness charge, but more than sufficient for Newcomen to blush pink and make a poor attempt at looking away.

"Whatever my friends had last time – unless you'd like something different – and whiskey for me and Joe Friday. Stagg if you've got it. Better still, just bring the bottle and some glasses."

"Sure thing, hon," she said. She collected an empty bottle of lite and went back to the bar. Her skirt was on the tight side, too, and Newcomen's gaze was drawn away from the table.

Petrovitch turned Newcomen's head back around and scraped his finger at the corner of the man's mouth. "Let's just wipe the drool away, shall we?"

"But she's barely wearing anything," said Newcomen, his forehead damp.

"*Yobany stos*, she can wear what she likes. Unless you're going to arrest her, leave her alone." He returned his attention to Alan. "So. Jason's a postgrad in your department, right? And you know him pretty well."

"He's my lab supervisor. He's pretty cool." He kept on glancing at Jessica, almost as if he was checking everything he was saying with her.

She wrapped her fingers around her soda and made the ice rattle. "He lets me hang out in the lab. I'm an arts major, and so I've got plenty of time spare. It made it easier for me and Alan, you know, to . . ." She watched the bubbles rise in her glass. "Spend time together."

"Yeah, look," said Petrovitch. "Anything that's going to help me find either Jason or Lucy is good. I need to know it all, no matter how uncomfortable it might make either you or me. Okay?"

Alan nodded. "Okay. Jason. Nice guy. Smart, but he had a talent for explaining hard stuff so that even a freshman could understand. He could be kind of intense at times, talking about his subject, or his music: this stuff, jazz. I liked him."

"How well did he know my daughter?"

"Pretty well, I guess. They hung out together: them both being foreigners was maybe a reason."

Jessica cleared her throat. "I think he wanted to know her a whole lot better." Alan raised his eyebrows at her, and she scowled back. "It's a girl thing to notice the vibes. He acted differently around her to when he was around me. I was a friend; she was someone he wanted to be more than a friend."

She stopped as the waitress reappeared with bottles and glasses and a pitcher of water balanced on her tray. She dealt out the coasters like a card sharp and got everyone's drinks right without prompting. Somehow she guessed that Petrovitch drank his whiskey straight up, and it was Newcomen who needed the water.

Newcomen winced once when she bent forward to push Alan's bottle of beer over to him, and again when she placed the shot glass in front of Petrovitch. When she'd gone, he glared.

"You kicked me."

"You were staring at her chest." Petrovitch cracked the seal on the whiskey and poured himself a generous measure, then slid the bottle down to Newcomen.

The agent splashed a little spirit out, barely enough to wet the bottom of the glass, and topped it up with water.

Petrovitch shook his head and raised his glass. "*Na bufera!*"

Without knowing what they were saying, the others joined in the toast. He hid his smile behind his glass.

"Where were we? Jessica?"

"Jason would look at her, at Lucy, when she was busy with something. You know, like when she had her head in something electronicky, or when she was doing the math at the whiteboard, or when she was halfway up a ladder fixing an aerial thing. He'd look at her that way you look at someone when you don't want them to know how much they mean to you."

"She didn't notice, did she? She broke his heart and she never realised." Petrovitch poured himself another finger of whiskey. "That's my girl."

"I'm pretty sure he wasn't the only one. But I think he had it the worst." Jessica stirred her half-melted ice cubes with her straw. "I guess she didn't know the effect she had. Some girls do that innocent act, in order to attract the guys. Your Lucy didn't act."

"Considering some of the stuff she's done, it's a wonder she turned out sane, let alone innocent. What did Jason do when he found out she was missing?"

"We were junking burnt-out circuits," said Alan, "and someone, can't remember who, stuck their head around the door. Said Lucy was out of contact. The next thing I knew, he'd gone, and had left a note with the Dean saying he'd taken some days off."

Newcomen hunched over, deep in thought. "There was a snowstorm. Lucy wasn't actually reported missing until three days later, when the plane from Eielson made it out there."

"We found out about that on the Monday, but Jason was long gone by then. I thought at the time he'd be interested in the news, but I had no way of reaching him. I didn't realise that he had a thing for Lucy."

Jessica put on her "stupid men" face and poked Alan in the ribs.

Petrovitch brooded, while the others looked on. Eventually he asked: "Anyone else been asking questions?"

Alan shrugged. "Not of me, or Jessie. Maybe some of the tenured staff, but none of the students. We talk about it sometimes, but when we ask the faculty, they say Jason'll come back when he's ready. They don't say anything at all about Lucy."

"I'm really sorry, Dr Petrovitch," said Jessica. "I got to know Lucy a bit: not many girls in a physics department, I guess. I asked her once if she minded all the things that they said about you."

Petrovitch drained his glass. "What did she say?"

She fixed him with her dark eyes. "She said you were the best dad a daughter could wish for. I know you adopted her and everything, and that you're only a few years older than she is: that was a really cool thing you did for her. I really hope you find her soon."

"Yeah. So do I." He sighed. "Thanks for talking to me, and I hope everything works out for you two. Keep your grades up: smart kids with qualifications go places that other kids can't. And if things get rough, the pair of you might want to give the Freezone a call. We're always hiring."

Alan and Jessica looked at each other, wearing expressions of surprise and fear.

"Even if being together is what you want most of all in the whole world," continued Petrovitch, "you still have to be useful to somebody else. *Vrubatsa?*"

Alan nodded nervously. Below the table he was holding Jessica's hand.

"Right, Newcomen. Time to go." Petrovitch grabbed his hat and set it on his head, then dragged the bottle of whiskey towards him and hid it inside his open coat.

While Newcomen laboriously dressed for the outside, Petrovitch paid the tab.

When he came back over, he pulled his gloves on, then the mittens over the top. "Remember not to look up or around as we pass through the door," he said, and led the way into the below-freezing night air.

Out on the pavement, Petrovitch stamped off into the night, leaving Newcomen to skitter along behind. His half-silvered contacts made it almost impossible for him to see where he was going, and he kept on running into street furniture.

"Wait up," he called, but Petrovitch was in no mood to slow down. He was angry and sad in equal measure.

Eventually Newcomen drew level and peered blindly at the shorter man. "What? What have I done wrong?"

"You've singularly failed – again – to understand what it is about your country that I hate the most." Petrovitch stopped to fume. "Take those lenses out. You look ridiculous."

"I don't know how."

"Then suffer. I don't care." He turned to go. "You really are the most useless sack of *govno* I've ever had the displeasure of meeting. Do something for yourself for a change. Anything. You're a grown-up. When I think of all the things I've done, then look at you . . ."

"No one ever asked me to do the things you did."

"But you never even did the things you were asked to do."

Newcomen pulled off his mitten and stuck his gloved finger in his eye. The contact peeled off and dropped to the hard, rutted ground. He did the same with the other. "I've done everything I've been asked to do."

"*Otlez' gnida.* I had to put a bomb in your chest just to make you care about finding Lucy." Petrovitch jabbed his mitten hard against Newcomen. "Everything good that you do is dragged from you while you complain."

Newcomen took the risk of batting Petrovitch's hand away. "I'm not to blame that the world doesn't work the way you want it to."

"Yeah, well. It should do." He started to walk again, dipping down and grabbing a handful of snow. He squeezed out a snowball and launched it against a left-turn sign. The sign bent, and shards of ice whipped through the air with the speed of ricocheting bullets.

"You're foul-tempered at the best of times, but what's got into you? Is it what those kids said about Lucy?"

"Or is it the fact that they hadn't had the opportunity to say it before? Maybe you don't think that Jason Fyfe's parents deserve some answers about what's happened to their son. They're sitting at home, worried sick that their boy's not coming back, and they don't even know why. Are you going to tell them? Would you even know, if we hadn't sneaked in here under the radar to ask the questions that no one else has either the wit or the inclination to ask? No, no, you're not going to tell them." He shrugged his shoulders at Newcomen. "I'm going to have to do it because no one on your side gives a shit. Thanks for that. Terrific."

"You think he's dead, don't you?"

"I know he's dead. He went after Lucy, and because Lucy mustn't be found, he was disappeared. And no way am I saying that until I'm absolutely certain it's true. *Pizdets*. This whole thing is drowning in a sea of *pizdets*."

Newcomen caught up with Petrovitch again, putting his head down against the wind. "You're going to tell me what was up with those kids too, aren't you?"

"They're not kids. He's twenty-two, she's twenty-one. I'd saved the world twice by that age, and that's not a job for kids, is it?" They were back on the road out of town, heading towards the house and the hidden plane. "How are you on Huxley?"

"T. H. or Aldous?"

"*Brave New World*. The genetic underclasses, as represented by little Jessica, don't really have much of a future in the society you help maintain." Petrovitch dug his hands into his pockets. It was getting colder by the minute. "Jessica's parents didn't get her assayed. They didn't grow her in a tank. They managed – as humans have for tens of thousands of years – to produce a bright, good-looking girl. Bright enough to make it to university on a scholarship. Alan's parents, however, like your parents, selected him, tweaked his genes and grew him in a vat of carefully monitored nutrients. Imagine how they feel, spending all that money only to face the prospect of their grandchildren being just plain normal."

"It's a shame, for sure. But they've invested a lot in their son. You can't say that his parents shouldn't know about the company he's keeping. It's their right."

"His genetic inheritance is not their property."

Newcomen pulled the collar of his coat down and knocked off a shower of ice. "It is. That's basic commercial law. If the boy's parents have forbidden him to marry her, they're committing a crime if they, you know . . ."

"Fuck, you mean." Petrovitch spat the word out.

"Have children."

"You don't need to get married for that to happen."

"You do in this country."

"Yeah, because if you do otherwise, your foetus is a copyright violation." Petrovitch's hands came out of his pockets again, and he started to wave them around. "*Yobany stos*, you don't even pretend you're created in God's image any more. You're made in some recombinant technician's idea of *Homo superior*. Short-term advantage over long-term gain."

"Sorry?" Newcomen was utterly baffled.

"What makes us strong is our genetic diversity. While you're busy making yourself practically perfect in every way, you've forgotten that's how evolutionary dead ends occur. It's not who fits their niche best. It's who fits most niches best. Adaptability, not specialisation."

"I don't see you doing much to ensure the survival of humanity."

"I'm making sure your gonads freeze and fall off before you get to spawn, aren't I? The future will thank me." Petrovitch growled and kicked at a lump of snow that had fallen off the roadside levee. "And I'm building a star drive, so *past' zebej*. I'm doing what I can."

"Uh-huh," said Newcomen.

Petrovitch rounded on him. "I'm this close." He showed Newcomen the narrow gap between his thumb and fingers, showed it to him right up against his nose. "The maths is simple. It's the engineering that's ludicrously complicated, but it's only just out of reach. When I get there, I'll give it to the world. Free. Except your lot: we'll ban you from going anywhere. The rest of us will travel to the stars and it'll take days, not centuries. We'll spread out, carrying the virus of life with us, and we'll have seeded the universe with the possibility of consciousness for as long as there is space and time."

"And how long is that?"

"Maybe another ten billion years. Depends on whose model you buy into." The cold was getting to him: he could feel it in his metal and his bones. It was time he stopped arguing, no matter how much fun it was. It was time they both went inside and got some sleep. "Alan and Jessica? They can come with us. They can have as many children as they like and they'll be light years away from anyone who says they can't."

He turned away, towards the house that promised shelter. Then he turned back to Newcomen. He grabbed the front of his coat and pulled him down until they were face to face.

"You know something? You used to be brilliant. The whole country from sea to shining sea. You did some really shitty things, but you also gave us miracles. You built rockets that went to the *yebani* Moon. There are spaceships you launched that are out of contact with the Earth because they're simply too far away. You cured diseases, you made movies, you invented and thought and created your way to most of the Nobel Prizes ever awarded. You were giants. You made our music and you wrote our books. You had Lincoln and King and Feynman. The world lived and breathed you, whether they liked it or not.

"Then along came Reconstruction, and you started going backwards. Pif and me beating you to the Grand Unified Theory, two kids with nothing more sophisticated than pen and paper, was just a symptom. You were ruined long before that. Reconstruction meant you gave up being daring. That's what I resent the most: that you let me down before I was even born."

He released Newcomen, and batted out the creases on his chest. "The Freezone are here now. We're going to do what you don't have the *yajtza* to do any more. I just want my Lucy to be part of it too. I promised her. I promised her, and I'm not going to let her down."

23

Petrovitch kicked the bedstead. "Come on. Breakfast."

Newcomen's face emerged from inside his sleeping bag, lying on the bare mattress. "What?" He blinked and squinted as the single naked bulb above his bed grew in luminescence.

"Breakfast, I said. Recommended calorie intake is around ten thousand for an Arctic environment, so unless you like snacking on bars of butter, I'd shift your arse into the kitchen."

"What time is it?"

"What am I? Your wristwatch?" Petrovitch kicked the bed again. "Use your link. That's what someone who belongs to the Freezone does."

Newcomen rolled around in his bag, wriggling like a great grey maggot. Eventually a hand appeared at the neckline and worried the zip down a fraction.

"I don't belong, though. Do I?"

"And yet you have a link. There's a riddle to start the day with." Petrovitch left him there and went back to the stove.

His frying pans were heating up nicely, and one advantage of seeing in the infrared was that he could tell precisely how hot they were.

He retrieved a cardboard box from the fridge – a massive American thing that looked like a chrome coffin – and opened it up. If the store had got his order wrong, he was going to look a complete *mudak*.

But here were strips of bacon and minute steaks, a tray of a dozen eggs, a block of lard, a loop of blood pudding, hash browns, links of pink sausages, and at the bottom, a tin of corned beef with its own key.

He became absorbed in the ritual of making, banging a battered enamel coffee pot on to a spare ring and feeding more wood to the ever-hungry furnace. Soon, things were frying, and the smell drifted out into the hall and down the corridor.

Newcomen staggered through and slumped at the kitchen table. "So what time is it?"

"Six thirteen. We have a lot to eat and a long way to go. Six hundred k. North." Petrovitch opened enough cupboards to track down two plates and some cutlery, which he dealt out on to the work surface. "And a full day's work ahead of us."

"We don't even know what we're going to find when we get to wherever it is."

"Deadhorse. Of course we don't. That's why we're going. We can do only so much remotely. We can look from the sky, we can listen and measure and track and record. But we have to be there, too. Do you think Alan and Jessica would have responded to a couple of messages left on their usual dropboxes? Considering his parents are desperate for them to stop bumping uglies?"

"Oh please. I haven't even got a cup of coffee yet."

"Yeah, sorry about the poor service. We don't have a woman in the house to do the cooking for us."

"Just, just." Newcomen rested his forehead on the warm pine tabletop. "Don't start."

"Hah," said Petrovitch triumphantly. He started banging the heavy iron skillets around to free the food within them. "Make yourself useful and find some mugs."

Newcomen dragged himself from his chair and started opening doors. "I don't suppose you've got any milk."

"I don't have any sugar, more to the point. I'll cope, and so will you."

Using a metal slice, he started to divide the food more or less equally between them. Newcomen found two china mugs and reached for the coffee pot. Petrovitch slapped his outstretched hand with the slice.

"Ow."

"The coffee inside is boiling. Any reason why the handle is going to be any colder?" He threw an oven mitt at him and carried on lifting and turning.

By the time he'd finished, the plates were piled high and it was barely possible to carry them the short distance to the table.

Newcomen drew his knife and fork towards him. "Am I going to be allowed to eat this without a lecture about the decadence of my country or a list of my own personal faults?"

"Yeah, okay. Though 'my own personal' is tautologous." Petrovitch twirled his fork through his fingers and back again to his grip. "Dig in while it's hot."

"I hate you," said Newcomen.

"I don't care." He stabbed a sausage and held it on the tines while he ate first one end, then the other.

"And there's no oh-jay."

"Yeah, I never heard Armstrong or Aldrin refusing to take that one small step because they didn't have juice for breakfast." Petrovitch picked up a hash brown, and regretted not ordering mushrooms. "You've fallen so far, so fast."

Newcomen jabbed across the table with his knife. "I thought you said you weren't going to lecture me."

"So I did. *Prijatnovo appetita.*"

Petrovitch worked his way through his food methodically, one ear to the news reports from around the world that his agents had selected. Each one came with a commentary from Freezone analysts, whether they could confirm or debunk it, and if the Freezone collective was involved in any way. They had virtual fingers in lots of the pies, from co-ordinating food distribution in Mindoro to transparent accounting in Namibia. The naked newswires poured into his head, with a slew of additional information: blogs, pictures, biographies, historical background and future trends.

He felt compelled to keep himself informed, especially at a time like this. It was a truism that the one connecting fact that linked together everything he was doing could appear half a world away. He wasn't the only one watching, reading, collating and sifting, but he was a link in the chain: too much information was being generated for any one man to know, but he wanted to try.

Nothing from China yet. The US press was silent on his whereabouts, and the FBI's Most Wanted list didn't feature either him or Newcomen. Amsterdam spot prices for crude were up: he dug a little further and found a supply problem. The Alaskan pipeline hadn't restarted pumping yet. Maybe another week, while the technicians and mechanics replaced circuits and reprogrammed computers.

So there was something to look into. Hardly anyone worried about the price of crude oil any more, since most people didn't burn it in their cars. But as a chemical precursor, it was vital. He passed a message back to the data miners and stuck a priority flag on it.

He looked down: his stomach was as full as his head.

"Okay. I'll go and turn the turbines over, and you see to the washing-up."

Newcomen was halfway through his food and slowing. "Where's the dishwasher?"

"I'm looking at him." Petrovitch wiped his mouth on his sleeve, to Newcomen's obvious disgust. "Plenty of hot water in the tank. Leave it to air-dry, and I'll see you back at the plane."

"It was dark last night . . ."

"It's dark now. Use your link. Michael knows where you are, where I am, and has maps of the bits between." He pushed himself away from the table, and carried his plate to the sink, making a show of rinsing it off and placing it in the bottom of the bowl. "Don't be long. But don't make a half-arsed job of it either. We leave stuff as we find it."

"Unless it's breaking windows and walls with people's heads."

"Yeah. There are exceptions to the rule." He leaned back against the work surface. "When others cause the mess, I let them clean up after themselves."

Newcomen kept on chewing. "I thought you were going to start the engines."

"I have already. I'll just get my bag and I'll go." He levered himself upright. "Don't bother locking the door. Just make sure it's shut."

Petrovitch went to delve under his bed for the carpet bag.

He looked around to see if he'd left anything: just the sleeping bag, and he didn't need that again.

Ready, except for the five minutes it took him to dress for the outside.

The cold snap was stretching itself, but was due to break tomorrow. Warm, wet air from the Pacific was pushing up the coast. It meant rain in Seattle, but if anything was left when it reached them, it'd be snow.

He could hear Newcomen in the kitchen, banging plates and rattling the pans, muttering all the while under his breath. With a little enhancement, he could tell what he was saying – not at all what a good little Reconstructionista ought to be vocalising, whether or not they were thinking it.

"Oh, Christine. I don't know who's had the narrower escape: you or Farm Boy."

[It is highly likely that Christine Logan's trust fund, once invested, would have paid for domestic help. It is also probable that while Joseph Newcomen's mother would have made him do chores when he was younger, he has not washed up after a meal for several years. Christine, never.] Michael stopped, then started again. [A meat question: if competence in a wide range of skills is desirable, why do people not take every opportunity to display those skills? Especially if those people were desiring a mate – appearing both knowledgeable and competent across a diverse set of normal human tasks would surely increase that person's chances of attracting a life partner.]

Petrovitch pulled the front door closed behind him and set off across the snowy ground.

"You mean, like I do?"

[You fit the pattern of competency I have outlined, yes.]

"Because being able to do or fix something can be seen as a

commercial transaction. We're used to that: poor people often see it as drudge work, rich people as beneath them. Working with your hands is something you either get paid to do, or pay others to do for you. There's also learned helplessness and deliberate incompetence, too, but they're passive-aggressive strategies and anyone who uses them needs a kick up the *zhopu*."

Away from the front of the house, it was properly dark. He turned his eyes on and blinked away the visual world.

"But you're going somewhere with this, right?"

[Joseph Newcomen managed to attract a rich, beautiful woman without displaying any of the characteristics you believe to be important. How, then, did he achieve this feat?]

"Yeah. Some things are just mysteries."

[Or it could be that your theory does not cover the totality of their relationship.]

"People don't behave rationally when they believe they're in love."

[I have more than sufficient evidence of that. Neither am I immune, Sasha. But your opinion is that Joseph Newcomen and Christine Logan would have been an ill-matched pair: I challenge that view. They share a culture, political leanings, religion and life goals. They would have been happy.]

Petrovitch ducked under a tree branch laden with snow. "He's changing. He's putting up a lot of resistance, but his faith in Reconstruction is in tatters. He wouldn't go back now, even if he could."

[And I maintain that even if it required massive cognitive dissonance on his part, he would return to his relationship with Christine Logan should circumstances permit. Sasha, you cannot look on transforming Joseph Newcomen's world view as a priority.]

"I don't," he said.

[You are beginning to. It was noted that his assistance would be vital, but not his conversion.]

"Conversion? He already has religion."

[You are attempting something equally fundamental. It is distracting you from your main task. I would not be your friend if I did not point this out to you. You are with Joseph Newcomen every waking moment, and it is natural for you, since he is both a citizen of the United States of America and an adherent of Reconstructionist philosophy, to seek to influence him.]

"Did Maddy put you up to this?"

[Madeleine Petrovitch shares my concerns, but they are my concerns nevertheless. Joseph Newcomen is not the man who ordered the infiltration of the Metrozone. He is not the man who planned the Outie invasion. He is not the man who ordered my destruction and yours. Convincing him that Reconstruction is a self-contradictory and self-destructive quasi-fascistic nationalist movement that ought to be rejected is not going to change the policies of the United States government. And since he is not the man who is responsible for Lucy's disappearance, it will not bring her back either.]

"I know this, okay? I really do."

[Then remember that he is neither your enemy nor your friend. He is a victim for whom you may rightly have compassion, but he is still a special agent of the Federal Bureau of Intelligence. Unless you intend to suggest he becomes part of the Freezone collective, by converting him you will be denying him any possibility of reintegrating into his society after this affair is over. They even have a word for it.]

"Feral." Petrovitch stamped through the snow to the frost-rimed outline of the plane. His and Newcomen's were the only footprints to approach it – human footprints at least. A moose had wandered past, leaving only a pile of scat and its tracks. "Off the grid."

[And unlike the collective's laissez-faire attitude to our own remainers, the ferals are despised and live as an actively persecuted underclass throughout the United States. Would you have Joseph Newcomen live like that, assuming he lives?]

The turbines were turning over, blasting hot exhaust out across the clearing and causing an early spring thaw to the trees directly in their path. He sent the command to open the door, and it popped free. Inside, the lights flickered on.

Petrovitch knocked the snow off his boots and stepped up and in.

"Yeah, okay. I'll take your advice. If I start banging on again, let me know." He dropped his bag on one of the cabin seats and started to warm up both the cockpit and the instruments. He had enough fuel to get to Deadhorse, maybe with a teaspoon or so spare, and everything else working more-or-less fine. Nothing was going to drop off just yet.

He wondered if he actually needed Newcomen at all; whether the kindest thing would be to abandon him here, where there was civilisation and some way of getting back – because he was certain he was flying straight into a trap. He just didn't know who the trap was intended for.

But he'd already offered him an out, and the agent had refused. That meant something. Or other.

"Yeah, Michael. Is there any possibility that Newcomen is a plant? That he's the best agent they have, trained in all sorts of black-ops stuff, and has been reprogrammed like Tabletop was so he doesn't remember any of it – until the critical moment when he knifes me in the back."

[We have done a thorough background check on Joseph Newcomen. As far as we can tell, his life can be completely accounted for and verified by external sources.]

"And you're absolutely certain the guy who's walking towards me right now is the same one who broke his arm in a football game, and that Joseph Newcomen isn't holding up a bridge somewhere."

[We have a confidence of almost one hundred per cent on that being the case.]

Petrovitch looked out of the windscreen at the figure dragging its feet through the snow.

"You know what? I'm regretting this more and more." He got out of his seat and went to get his polar bear gun from his bag. Then he decided that the rest of the bag ought to be in easy reach too.

He was sitting back in the pilot's seat when the plane rocked and Newcomen appeared.

"Is everything, uh, ready?"

"Yeah." Petrovitch told the ladder to retract and the door to close. "We're ready now."

24

There were several roads that led out of Fairbanks. Route Eleven headed north towards the Arctic Ocean and Prudhoe Bay. Sometimes it made seemingly random turns, swinging to the left or right to navigate a hidden obstacle or difficult terrain, but what it did do was follow the pipeline wherever it went. The two were never far apart, and in winter, when snow and ice covered the landscape, it was often the only indication of where the road was: somewhere parallel to the fat grey tube held clear of the ground on pylons.

The pipeline ended where Petrovitch's search started, six hundred kilometres away on the shore of a mostly frozen sea, inhabited only by oil men and natives – some of whom were also oil men.

He was flying low, out of necessity, out of habit, bare metres above the trees where there was forest, and the folds in the ground where there wasn't, following the road north because that was the way Jason Fyfe would have gone. Cross-country wasn't an option in anything but a tracked vehicle: the RV that Fyfe had borrowed had fat balloon tyres with studs for gripping the frozen surface of the snow, but if it had left the hard substrate of the road surface, it would have foundered.

He knew — Michael had told him — that most of the oil companies moved their personnel by plane, and most of their equipment by landship around the coast to avoid the mountain range between south and north.

That was what had made the trucks heading towards Deadhorse stand out so. Anonymous, white, big. Taking the road was the quicker option, and a series of massive transport planes dropping in on a runway at the edge of the world would have been simply blatant.

Even if the Freezone hadn't been watching for it, someone else — the Chinese, perhaps — would have seen them from space.

Something was going on, and it infuriated him that he didn't know what. Yet. He would, eventually. And he'd find Lucy, too, and bring her home.

There was a lot to concentrate on: the act of flying, the minute course corrections even when the road was straight, the slew of other data flooding in, his own thoughts, the gun burning heavy and hard against his chest. They flew on, and the trees petered out. Nothing now but rock and ice until the sea — not a featureless landscape, but muted; its vastness muffled and softened by the deep drifts of snow.

He almost missed the figure raising his hand to the plane as it roared overhead in the half-light, dragging a snowstorm in its wake.

"Did you . . .?" asked Newcomen, twisting around in his seat, as if he could see behind him through the opaque fuselage of the plane.

"Barely." Petrovitch pulled back on the throttle and executed a long looping turn that took them wide over the tundra. As they turned, they could see the man again as a dark shape against the white ice. A snowmobile stood a little way off, and behind that, a towed sled.

The man had his arms outstretched, angled up. He held them there, turning to face the plane as it came back around.

"What does he want?"

"There's only one way to find out," said Petrovitch. "And that's talk to him."

He lined up with the road and lessened the power to the gravity pods. They sank towards the ground and started to drift laterally. He gave the control surfaces a nudge: the plane turned, and he came to a halt with the nose diagonally to the direction of travel.

The man lowered his arms. Petrovitch could just make out button-bright eyes hiding beneath the fur-rimmed hood, and the outline of a rifle slung across his back.

"Muffle up. It's even colder outside than it was in Fairbanks." Petrovitch slid from his seat and made his way back to the cabin. He cracked the door open, dislodging a thin layer of ice that had formed there.

The ladder extended reluctantly, and he jumped the last step down on to the iron-hard surface. His coat steamed with stored moisture, and a white crust formed on its skin. Newcomen followed him into the freezing air, shuddering at its touch.

"Hey," said Petrovitch, when he was close enough. "We almost missed you." He could feel the hairs in his nostrils bristle and grow hard.

The man pulled his collar down to expose his sallow, tanned face. "Hey. Where're you from?"

Petrovitch looked around, flicking from visible light to infrared and back. The skidoo was just about warmer than its surroundings, meaning it had been there a while without having been parked overnight.

"Out of Fairbanks," he said. "You?"

"Allakaket."

The man was an Inuk, then. Petrovitch could cobble together some Inupiaq, but he wasn't confident he'd be at all intelligible. He stuck to English.

"Hunting?"

"Got me some wolf." He nodded over at the sled, and the lumpy tarpaulin covering its contents. "I heard you coming from the south. A vehicle's come off the road: I was going to report it next place I came to, but seeing as you're here . . ."

Petrovitch's eyes narrowed. "RV?"

"Big one. It's in a river just over there. I wouldn't have seen it, but I went over its rear fender."

"Plates?" asked Newcomen.

The Inuk turned his attention to the tall American, dressed in traditional clothing but on a vastly different scale. His face sneered for a second in a way it hadn't when talking to Petrovitch.

"Alaskan. I wasn't going to dig it out any further than that: it's nose down on the ice, and the snow's covering it all."

"We'll have a look," said Petrovitch. There was a shovel strapped to the side of the skidoo, and he pointed to it. "Okay if we take that?"

"No reason why not." He freed it, deftly manipulating the clips despite his thick mittens, and led the way below the underside of the plane to a spot that looked almost exactly like every other, except for the small mound of freshly turned snow.

Petrovitch walked towards it, off the road surface, and started to wade. His feet sank in to his knees, and there was much further to go if he wanted. He bent his head to the hole, and could see the yellow and blue of the registration plate, almost flat to the ground. Part of the rear bumper and some of the black paintwork framed it.

He read the number. "Yeah, this isn't good."

Newcomen scrambled over and peered down. "Fyfe?"

"The number matches. Only one way to find out. Ask our friend for the shovel."

As Newcomen straightened to speak to the Inuk, Petrovitch undid his parka and pulled off his mitten. He dipped his hand inside, and came out with his gun. He flicked the safety to off.

The man's eyes widened, and he thought about going for his rifle.

"Yeah, I wouldn't," said Petrovitch. "You're a hunter: a crack shot, patient and careful. I'm a complete bastard who doesn't need an excuse to put a bullet in your head. And these are explosive bullets. You'll be lucky if you're left with anything above your belly button."

Newcomen twisted around. "What are you doing?"

"Trying to work out why he's lying to us. I'd rather do that without him having a rifle over his shoulder." His aim didn't waver.

"And how do you know he's lying?"

"Because there aren't any snowmobile tracks anywhere near this wreck. He no more ran over it than I used to wear a mini-dress and go by the name of Brenda. Which means we're being set up."

Maybe the man thought Petrovitch was distracted for a moment. His hand strayed towards the strap of his rifle.

Petrovitch shook his head. "Whatever they're paying you

225

isn't enough. Newcomen, go and get his gun before he has an attack of the heroics."

Taking care not to come between Petrovitch and the man, Newcomen waded back to the road and circled the Inuk until he was behind him. He lifted the rifle up and over the man's head. The shovel lay at the man's feet, and he went to kick that away too.

Petrovitch stopped him. "Okay, let's get this out of the way. Two sorts of people in the world, aren't there? Those with guns, and those who dig." He pointed at the shovel, then at the Inuk. "You dig."

The man bent down for the shovel, and stood up again holding it. Newcomen was at his back, rifle pointing nowhere in particular, and Petrovitch was at his front, the barrel of the pistol not even wavering with a tremulous heartbeat.

"I didn't mean to cause trouble," the Inuk said. "Just doing a job."

Petrovitch waved him over. "What job was that?"

"Two guys told me to point out this crashed RV to another couple of guys who needed to see it. That's all."

"How long have you been here?"

"A day. Two. They told me you'd be in some fancy executive plane, and I was to flag you down."

"What if we'd kept on going?"

"Just to radio back to them that I'd seen you." The man put the shovel blade in the snow and took out a chunk of the RV's paintwork. "They said I'd get paid a bonus if you stopped."

The corner of Petrovitch's mouth twitched. "Worth the money?"

"Not really."

Petrovitch carved himself a seat and sat down while he watched the rear of the vehicle slowly emerge from the drift.

"What's your name?" he asked, just to see if he'd lie about that, too.

"Josie. George Josie."

He hadn't lied. "That's Newcomen. I'm Petrovitch."

The man stumbled and paused, then dug with renewed energy.

"If they'd told you, would you have thought twice about taking the job?"

"Maybe more than twice," said Josie. "The rear windshield's all busted up. Snow's inside."

Petrovitch crawled up the bank made by Josie's digging. The snow had crusted over what remained of the back window, and the shovel blade had gone straight through into the dark pit beneath.

Ice crystals dribbled into the hole and out of sight.

"I'll put my gun away if you promise not to hit me with the spade," said Petrovitch. "It won't do you any good, and I'll kill you straight after with my bare hands. Deal?"

"Guess so," said Josie warily.

"Good decision." Petrovitch put the safety back on and slipped the gun back into a pocket. "Now, let's get this hole cleared. Newcomen, over here."

"What do I do with the rifle?"

"That's another of those leading questions you ought not to be asking. I don't really care: George here isn't going to shoot anyone. Are you?"

Josie moved another handful of snow away from the granulated glass. "Are you going to shoot me?"

"I'm kneeling next to you, digging. That should tell you all you need to know."

The three of them cleared the rectangle of snow from around the window, and it grew clear that the interior of the RV was charred black. There should have been a smell, but it was cold, so very cold.

"You still got that torch, Newcomen?"

"It's back on the plane. I can get it if you want." He made to go, but Petrovitch shook his head.

"We can do without. But there's little variation in temperature: everything's *yebani* freezing." He knocked away the remaining glass that clung to the rubber seal. It fell away, twinkling in the dark. "Lower me down. I'll take a look."

Josie was slowly working things out. "Is there someone still in there? They must be . . . you know."

Petrovitch ran his mitten across the scarred interior roof of the vehicle, and showed a black hand to the Inuk. "He was dead long before he came off the road."

"Soot?"

"I'm guessing an air-to-ground missile or a few depleted uranium rounds. Incinerated the contents in an instant." He swung his legs around and dangled them through the hole. "And when I say contents, I mean Jason Fyfe."

There was a fitted cupboard within reach. Petrovitch pressed against it with his toe, and though it creaked, it held. Everything loose had catapulted down to the front, and there was a jumble of soft furnishings and equipment piled around where the driver should have been.

It didn't smell burnt. But he could taste it, a catch in the back of his throat. He slid inside and crouched. He could climb down using the wall of what was probably the toilet, and then to the bench seats in the kitchen area. That would put him just above the mess of debris.

It wasn't like he didn't know what he was going to find. He just needed to be certain.

He looked up at the impossibly bright sky. "I won't be long."

Petrovitch turned and lowered himself to his next perch. The wood bent under his weight, and the door popped open with a click. It waved at an angle for a moment, then one of the hinges gave, leaving it dangling.

"Everything okay?" asked Newcomen.

"It's fine." He looked down. "I hope."

He shuffled so that he was standing on the part of the wall that was fixed to the floor, then eased himself across to the back of the first row of seats. Then again to the ones facing them: the table that should have been between them had fallen forward.

He was above the driver's seat. The seat belt still seemed to be attached to the door pillar, the webbing strained forward and locked into position. The seat itself, seared and burnt, was lost under some singed cushions, which he scooped out of the way.

Kneeling down, Petrovitch reached forward to shift the table, which he'd just exposed. He heaved with his left hand, and it moved enough to see under it.

It was the back of a head, cracked with deep red lines between the black. No hair – the mass of brown curls had burnt off. The arms were clenched around the steering wheel, and the elbows locked in place.

"Is it him?"

"Unless you've got his gene sequence and a portable DNA tester, I'm going to have to do this old-school. I can pull his dental records, but yeah . . ." He adjusted himself on his perch. "No rings, no jewellery that I know of. Even his mother'd have trouble recognising him."

Petrovitch looked to see if he could get any closer. Snow had forced its way through the shattered glass of the windscreen and side doors. He stamped some of it down and moved on to it.

He looked up into the rictus grin. He had Fyfe's picture in his databanks, and used some software to overlay it on the too-tight skin.

"Yes, no? What do you reckon?"

[The low light levels and the damage to the gross facial features introduce error, but we can confirm with a high degree of confidence that this was Jason Fyfe.]

"I remember once before being shown a body and I leapt to all sorts of conclusions that weren't helpful. Or even right."

[Then a full investigation must be carried out by the relevant authorities before the identity of the body can be established for certain. However, as a working hypothesis, it would be reasonable to assume that it is Fyfe.]

"Yeah." He huffed. Moisture from his breath collected on the frost-rimed burns. "If things had worked out differently, this poor bastard could have been my son-in-law."

He straightened and judged his journey back.

"I'm coming up."

25

Petrovitch held his arms up: his weight proved difficult for the wiry Josie and the athletic Newcomen to manage, but they struggled on and got enough of his torso through the window that he was able to drag himself clear.

"How heavy are you?" asked Josie.

"Couple of hundred kilos. Titanium's dense compared with bone." Petrovitch sat down on the snow and used handfuls of it to scrub as much of the soot off his parka as he could. "So, George. Any idea what you've got yourself mixed up in?"

"No one said anything about dead guys. Just the RV."

"This was Jason Fyfe, a Canadian citizen. He worked with my daughter. He was going to rescue her, because she's missing up on the North Slope. Seems she saw something she shouldn't, and some people are desperate that she doesn't pass that on. Desperate enough to kill this good man."

Josie hunched over and looked sourly at the black hole of the RV's back window.

Newcomen cleared his throat, and pulled his collar away from his mouth. "Did you, uh, see anything? In the sky, on the ground?"

"Might have done. Depends how much more trouble it gets me into."

"We know a lot about it," said Petrovitch, "except we don't know what it actually looked like. So we'd appreciate it if you just said what you saw."

The Inuk carried on thinking about it, so Petrovitch tried again.

"Yeah, we're trying to stop World War Three here, amongst other things. No pressure, though."

"War?" Josie looked up sharply. "Who said anything about war?"

"We're not the only ones interested in what happened that night. The Chinese, for one."

"The Chinese?" Josie looked down again. "This is crazy."

"You Yanks and the Chinese knocking the crap out of each other might be amusing to watch, but I'm very aware that fallout doesn't respect national boundaries."

Josie glanced at Newcomen, almost as if he were asking permission. Newcomen shrugged in his dense coat.

"It doesn't look good," he said. "Anything you can tell us might help."

"It was after midnight. Bright light in the sky, going from east to west. Brighter than any shooting star, sharp enough to make shadows, almost like you couldn't look at it. It seemed to flicker, then there was one big burst of light before it went out. We lost our TV signal, some of our computers stopped working. Radio still isn't fixed." Josie jerked his head towards his sled. "They gave me a new one."

"And you saw this yourself?" said Newcomen.

"The dogs started barking, so I went to the window: couldn't see it from there, but I could see something. I went out, and there it was. Lasted maybe twenty, thirty seconds." Josie shrugged. "Could have been less, but it seemed that way. I was standing out in the street with some of the others, and we were talking after the flash. There was this sound, like thunder. That went on and on. Bouncing off the mountains, I guess. It must have been a real big bang."

Petrovitch looked away to the north. "You were this side of the Brooks, right?"

Josie nodded. "Something fell from space, didn't it?"

"Yeah."

"Something Chinese?"

"We're trying to work that out." Petrovitch straightened up and patted away the snow still clinging to him. "Looks likely, though."

"So why is it just you two out looking? Why isn't everyone working on it?"

"I'm sure they are, but not only is no one telling me anything, they seem determined to make it as difficult they can. Like this." Petrovitch pointed at the RV. "What was the point in killing Fyfe? They could have slashed his tyres in the night and had done with it. There was no need. No need at all." He reached down for Josie's arm, and pulled him upright with seemingly no effort at all. "That's the sort of person you're working for, George. I'm not impressed."

"They never said anything about dead Canadians. Just stopped me in the middle of nowhere, up where Bettles used to be, told me where to wait during the day." Josie looked grim. "I don't get what I'm supposed to do now, though."

"You do what you've been told to do. Tell your handler that we were here, and we've seen Fyfe's body – you might want to add that you didn't enjoy that little surprise – then forget you ever saw us."

"Hold on," said Newcomen. "You want to give our position away?"

"If George doesn't tell Ben and Jerry we were here, how can we go on to report the location of Fyfe to the Canadians?"

"Why do we have to tell them? Can't we just . . .?"

"No. I'm thinking about Fyfe's parents. Not about us." Petrovitch realised he was still holding on to Josie's arm. He let go with a murmured apology.

"I'm sorry too," said Josie. He nodded at Newcomen. "He's right: this isn't good."

"There's still a chance to redeem yourself," said Petrovitch. "You could tell your friends – your real friends, not the ones that give you expensive toys and lie to you – that we're on our way. We need help finding Lucy, and they've been on the ground throughout: ask them to let me know what they've seen and heard."

"Will they get into trouble if they do?"

"I can't promise that they won't. But I can promise it won't be me giving them grief. I'm not a bad man, George, no matter what you've heard."

Josie didn't say what he'd heard. Up in Alaska, Reconstruction hadn't bitten quite as deep, and for men like him, the border with Canada didn't have the same iconic status as it did for most Americans.

Petrovitch was counting on swaying the man, turning him to his cause.

"Bear in mind what I've said, George. It's just me and

Newcomen searching for my girl, and frankly, he's not much use. Some say she's dead already, but I'm certain she's not. The faster we find her, the better, and the more eyes and ears we have, the happier I'll be."

"I can't promise you anything useful will happen, but," Josie nodded slowly, "I'll do what I can."

"Give him his rifle back," Petrovitch said to Newcomen.

"Are you . . .?"

"Yeah. I'm sure."

Newcomen wasn't, but he lifted the strap over his head and passed the gun into Josie's waiting hands. He kept hold of the breech. "Do you know how lucky you are?"

"What d'you mean?" Josie jerked his head at Petrovitch. "Him?"

"Him. He's supposed to put a bullet in your head about now, or one through your engine block so you'll freeze to death, slowly." Newcomen frowned. "Instead, he's being nice to you."

Petrovitch looked on, amused. "I shoot everybody in the head, apparently. That's what it says in the bumper book of Petrovitch, right?"

"Something like that," said Newcomen.

"I just want to be left alone. You wouldn't think it'd be too difficult to manage, but no: *govno* like this happens, and suddenly we're in a whole world of *pizdets*." He took one last look around. "Just let go of the rifle and get back on the plane. We've been shown what they wanted us to see, and now it's time to leave."

Newcomen released his grip, and Josie drew the gun close to him.

Petrovitch started away from the RV, ploughing through the loose snow to the road, where it was more compact. He could hear Newcomen dragging after him, then catching him up.

"He could still kill us," said the agent.

"In your binary world, people are either full-square behind you and can be trusted completely, or they're criminals who'd sooner slit your throat than look at you. The truth, as ever, lies somewhere in between." Petrovitch shifted his shoulders. "He won't shoot. Well, he won't shoot me, at least."

"Thanks."

"You're welcome."

The plane's door popped open, and Petrovitch scaled the ladder. He glanced around at the top: Josie was still standing there by the pile of snow he'd dug, wondering what had just happened.

He'd call his handlers for certain. Whether he'd pass on the message to his North Slope friends and family remained to be seen.

Petrovitch climbed inside and threw his furry hat on to one of the seats. He started to take his parka off, and remembered to grab the gun perched uncertainly inside. He laid that on the seat next to his hat.

Newcomen stamped snow off on the top step and stood at the door, looking out.

"He's just watching us."

"That was his job. It probably still is."

"So they know we're coming. Or will do before we get there."

"They always knew that." The frost that had collected at his collar had turned to beads of moisture that was starting to soak in. Petrovitch gave the parka a shake, and tossed it aside to dry. He picked up the gun, and headed for the cockpit, starting the turbines spinning as he slid into the pilot's chair. "The only variable was when we got there."

"They could always have stopped you," said Newcomen from

behind him, still trying to squeeze the toggles of his coat through the loops with cold-heavy fingers.

"That was never going to happen." Petrovitch engaged the antigravity, and the plane pulled itself free of the road in a shower of ice crystals that tumbled away in white streamers. He let the direction change freely, the nose taking in a full circle of Alaskan vista before he applied any throttle.

"They could have." Newcomen finished wrestling with his coat fastenings and sat in the seat next to him. "Stopped you, I mean."

"Of course they could. Killing someone is easy. As they proved with Fyfe. If they'd really, really wanted me dead, they'd have put a bomb on the plane from the Metrozone, and you, me, and a couple of hundred other people would be propping up the Mid-Atlantic Ridge by now. Problem solved."

"Then . . . hang on. What are you saying?" Newcomen blinked, staring out through the windscreen. They were starting to climb over the mountain range ahead, the peaks shrouded in low cloud that wasn't low at all. The pipeline was a grey snake off to the left, and the road a white line underneath.

"I've been – we've all been – working on the assumption that the US government doesn't want me sticking my nose into this, that they want to keep me as far away as possible from the North Slope, and absolutely, definitely don't want me to find Lucy." The corner of Petrovitch's mouth twitched. "What if I'm wrong?"

Newcomen shifted uneasily in his seat. "I thought you were never wrong."

"Let's pretend for a moment, then, that we live in a universe where such things are possible. The first people to look for Lucy were the university, who had to rely on the military to get to the research station. They didn't find Lucy because she wasn't there any more. They didn't have the resources to search for her themselves, so they called in the FBI. You started slowly, stupidly slowly, like you weren't that bothered – an act guaranteed to enrage me. You put a couple of field agents into Fairbanks when we complained, but you were warned off: the agents were recalled and Buchannan was told to look the other way.

"But what about Jason Fyfe? He's a wild card. He's not a US citizen, and he wasn't going to take kindly to anyone telling him not to rescue Lucy, not when she clearly needed rescuing. So he was killed: quickly, cleanly, and with a minimum of fuss. Then the body displayed to us like a hunting trophy."

"But they haven't killed you," said Newcomen. "They haven't even tried to kill you."

"No. Not yet. Why do you think that is?"

"Because you're too important?"

"I'd like to think so, but that'd just be the ego talking. Come on, time to work that atrophied walnut you call a brain. Why haven't they killed me?"

"Because they need you alive?"

"Yeah. They do." Petrovitch looked Newcomen square in the face. "Why do they need me, Samuil Petrovitch, the Antichrist, the tyrant of the Freezone, the slaughterer of thousands, the humiliator of the holy United States of America, continual thorn in the flesh, alive?"

"Because they want you to find Lucy," said Newcomen, mounting horror in his voice. "Because only you can find her."

"That's right. That's absolutely right. They can't find Lucy on their own, and not just because they'd draw attention both to the search and to whatever it is they're trying to hide. They can't find her because she's deliberately and actively hiding from them. They don't want the FBI looking for her, and they certainly didn't want Fyfe blundering around up there. So they make it difficult enough for me to think they don't want her found, but not so difficult that they'll actually stop me from finding her."

"She knows you're coming, surely?"

"She knows it. She believes it in her soul. And don't call me Shirley."

Newcomen growled his annoyance. "What do they do when you find her?"

"I imagine that our first hello will be our last goodbye."

"That's . . . awful. If that's what's going to happen, you can't carry on."

"Of course I can. I'm going to find my daughter."

"But you'll kill her!"

"No. Your side will kill her. It's not an insignificant difference."

"There's no difference at all. She'll still wind up dead." Newcomen slapped the console in front of him. "And so will you. You're going to have to turn around and find another way to do this."

"I can't." Petrovitch's voice was calm, his mind clear. "If I stop now, Lucy's going to die anyway: time's their luxury, not ours. Every day that passes is a day closer to when she has to break cover. If I ever want to see her again, then I'm going to have to give away where she's hiding." He shrugged. "They understand me much better than you do. They know that even if I managed to unravel it this far, I'd still press on, though it means both our deaths."

"But she's your daughter. You can't do this to her."

"Your lot could have saved a lot of fucking around by

explaining all this to me right at the start. I'd still be here, doing exactly what I'm doing now."

"You make it sound like it's already been decided. It hasn't. You have to fight. You have to think of something." Newcomen grew agitated, desperate even. "You can't die."

"I'm not going to sell myself cheap. I'll make it as messy and uncomfortable as I can. But I know how much firepower you've got stacking up on the North Slope. It looks like there's something out there worth starting a war for, and Lucy knows what it is."

"No. You have to listen, you, you selfish pig. You're going to live. And so am I."

Petrovitch raised his eyebrows. "You make it sound like either of us has another option."

"I haven't come this far to fail now. If you die, I die, and you're not going to throw my life away in your grand gesture. I don't care how much you hate America. I don't care how much you love your Lucy. I want to live. I want to live, Dr Samuil bloody Petrovitch of the Freezone collective, and if that means hauling your metal ass across a freaking ice flow, I will do it. We will find your daughter and we will get her to safety and you will take out this bomb in my chest and I will live happily ever after and for God's sake pull up!"

The cloud that had enveloped them cleared for a moment. In that moment, the ground came rushing towards them. Either side of the cockpit were towering black splinters of rock. The saddle of land between reared upwards like the crest of a breaking wave, intent on smashing them to pieces.

The turbines howled and the plane pitched nose up.

Certain they were going to hit, were hitting, had already hit and had lost the rear half of the fuselage, Newcomen clutched at his head and pulled his feet clear of the floor.

When he opened his eyes again, they were still flying. The ground was receding below the plane, and was losing its solidity in the mountain fog.

"Oh, dear Lord, oh, my sweet Jesus. Oh thank you."

"The antigravity would have pushed us over," said Petrovitch, less convincingly than he would have liked. "Perhaps you ought not to distract me, at least until we get on the ground again."

Newcomen put his head between his knees and prayed so hard the tears squeezed out.

26

[Sasha?]

"Yeah. I'm paying attention."

[No mountains?]

"Not at the moment. Not until the Urals at least, and they're an ocean away."

[Do you have the time to talk to the First Vice Premier of the State Council of the People's Republic of China?]

Petrovitch sat bolt upright in his seat. "*Yobany stos.*"

[They asked specifically for you.]

"Me? Why me?"

[Most likely they are wedded to outmoded models of governmental organisation, and still have great difficulty believing that the Freezone does not have a vertical power structure where a single individual has ultimate authority.]

"So they pick the guy they've actually heard of and pretend?"

[Essentially, yes. They are waiting for you.]

"And are we happy with that? I'm not a good spokesman for

anyone but myself, and even then I'm not so sure." He resisted the urge to flatten his hair and scrub the soot from his cheeks. He swallowed hard. "Okay. We're secure, right?"

[Secure from our end, yes. Everything you say will be as closely scrutinised by their analysts as it will be by ours.]

"Hang on." He blinked. "Newcomen?"

"Uh-huh."

"I've got the Chinese on the line. Tell Michael if we lose an engine or the plane cracks in two. He'll kick me out: otherwise, you won't get a response from me for a bit."

Newcomen stopped worrying at his nails. "Are they going to admit it's one of theirs?"

"They'll never say it straight. They'll hint at it obliquely, and expect me to be just as oblique back." The corner of his mouth twitched. "Yeah. Like that's going to happen."

[First Vice Premier Zhao Zhenwang is still waiting, Sasha.]

"Okay, let's do it."

Petrovitch saw an office: it could have been anywhere, but the feed was geolocating to Beijing. The only splash of colour to the bland decor was the furled red flag attached to the wall behind the desk. Everything else was monochrome, even the skin of the man in the centre of the screen.

Zhao had short cropped black hair – maybe he dyed it to cover the grey – and wore a black suit. He had his hands clasped on the desk in front of him, and his outsized glasses framed his too-large eyes. Michael helpfully popped his short-form biography up beside the man.

Petrovitch scanned it: a scientist by trade, electronics degree followed by a successful business career and a swift rise through the party ranks. He was an interesting choice of representative for the Chinese to make.

"Dr Petrovitch." Zhao bowed slightly.

Petrovitch's image – the one he chose to project – was on a big screen facing the vice premier. He kept it simple: photo-realistically him, set against a neutral background. In the labyrinthine government that ruled the People's Republic, Zhao weighed in somewhere between the seventh and eighth most powerful official in the land, depending on whose analysis could be believed.

Plenty power enough, Petrovitch reckoned. "First Vice Premier Zhao, a pleasure to talk to you."

"You are too kind, Dr Petrovitch. How are you today?"

"How . . . I'm surprisingly fine, considering the circumstances."

[He will expect you to enquire about his health in return.]

Petrovitch gave a little nod. "And First Vice Premier, how are you?"

Zhao took a moment before responding. "I am very well, thank you for asking. My sincerest condolences on your missing daughter. I hope she will be returned to you soon."

"I appreciate your concern, First Vice Premier. The Freezone collective is anxious to have her back."

[Zhao Zhenwang is wearing an earpiece. I can attempt to access the datafeed if you wish.]

"Give it a miss for now," Petrovitch said to Michael. "We don't want to piss them off."

Zhao stared at Petrovitch's feet across the room, across the thousands of kilometres that separated them. Petrovitch stared back.

"You wish to discuss something with me?" he finally asked when his patience ran out. It had only taken a few seconds.

"There is a situation we might examine further." Zhao

indicated his willingness to continue with a tilt of his head. "I would like to hear your thoughts on the matter."

"And would that situation involve a certain American anti-ballistic missile system?" Having his teeth pulled without anaesthetic would be kinder.

"It might well do so, Doctor. There have been recent activities that have concerned the People's Republic, and we are seeking reassurance that these activities are not detrimental to us."

Petrovitch imagined Michael standing next to him, just off screen. "He's a wordy bastard and no mistaking. His English is probably better than mine, but he doesn't have to show it."

[Expect these circumlocutions to continue for a while, Sasha.]

"Yeah, well. I hate it already. He'd be better off talking to Marcus: he loves this diplomatic *kon govno*." Petrovitch forced his image to affect a concerned nod, and made sure his hands were well under control. "First Vice Premier, the Freezone also has much to lose if SkyShield has begun to malfunction."

Zhao pursed his lips. "Your previous experience with the system would be useful in our deliberations."

"You mean, when I hijacked it and forced Mackensie to quit over giving me the nuclear launch codes? In which case, yes: I've got experience of SkyShield."

"Indeed, Doctor. In your opinion, is it likely that the government of the United States of America is fully in control of all the SkyShield assets?"

[Careful.]

"I'm there already." He posed his best slightly hurt expression on his face and looked at the floor. "I can assure the President that neither myself nor anyone belonging to the Freezone collective has attempted to interfere with any part of SkyShield."

Then he gave up. "Look, bluntly put, it's not us. You probably know as much as we do: a SkyShield platform opened fire on something in orbit, brought it down over Alaska, where it exploded about ten k from the ground. Beyond that, we're pretty much in the dark."

The vice premier made a non-committal noise in his throat like a grunt. "And you do not know what it was that fell?"

"Our best assumption was that it was one of your birds. Which you may or may not have fitted with a nuclear fail-safe."

"Putting nuclear weapons in orbit would violate several treaties to which the People's Republic is party."

"Yeah. It would, wouldn't it?" Petrovitch unclasped his hands from in front of his body, and reclasped them behind him. It was only an avatar: it would do what he told it to do, but he was desperate to start waving his arms around like a demented windmill.

[Face, Sasha. Do not make him lose face.]

"I don't care about his face."

[But you do care about Lucy.]

"It might be better to assume," continued Zhao, "that we would therefore not walk that path."

Petrovitch looked at the flag, the desk, the shaded window. "If we were to make such an assumption, it leaves the Freezone with an interesting problem."

"How so, Doctor?"

"There are only a few countries or blocs with the required lifting capacity to get that sort of mass into orbit. We've done a lot of analysis in the past couple of days, and we're pretty certain we can account for most, if not all, of the existing satellites. Yours, we're not so sure about." He shrugged his shoulders.

"It's a compliment. You've got the knowledge to put a hundred metric tonnes into space, and the means to do it reliably and regularly. You've got a Moon mission planned for next year. Even I'm excited about that."

Zhao permitted himself a brief smile. "I am eagerly anticipating the event myself. But to return to the matter in hand: China is not in the habit of putting nuclear weapons on board peaceful space missions."

"So does that mean you've broken the habit, or this wasn't a peaceful mission? Because the Yanks were really keen to take out whatever it was."

[Oh, Sasha.]

"What? What did I say?"

Michael's own avatar shook his head sadly, and Petrovitch was left to make his apologies.

"Apparently I've spoken out of turn, Vice Premier. I regret that."

Zhao was listening to the voice in his ear: Petrovitch recognised the gesture, the slight faraway look, the angle of the head. Whatever it said seemed to have an immediate effect. His face softened from an impassive mask and he leaned forward slightly: the height of informality.

"Dr Petrovitch, the satellite in question was not ours. We would very much like to learn whose it was."

"That's . . . interesting," said Petrovitch. "Do you think it was American, and they used it for target practice?"

"It is possible. It is worrying enough that SkyShield has the capacity to target and then destroy satellites. It is more of a concern that they feel the need to demonstrate this now, in plain sight."

"There's an awful lot that scenario doesn't explain, though. Like why they're trying to find my daughter without actually looking like they're trying to find her. Why she ran in the first place. Why they've moved enough military hardware on to the North Slope to conquer a small nation. As an explanation, the US testing an anti-satellite weapon blue-on-blue just doesn't cut it."

"Do you have an alternative explanation?"

"No. There's something big we're all missing. Something big enough that they're prepared to move heaven and earth to cover it up."

"The People's Republic would be suitably grateful for any information the Freezone might provide."

Petrovitch unconsciously scratched at his chin. Somewhere in the distance, he could feel his stubble. "You wouldn't be jerking my chain, would you?"

Zhao frowned briefly, and listened again to the voice in his ear.

"Dr Petrovitch, I appreciate that the People's Republic natural desire to protect its national interests has been interpreted less than favourably by some in the past. However, in this matter, I am being completely candid. The satellite was not ours. We do not know who it belonged to, or who launched it. We do not know the significance of the attack. We are concerned, but our private enquiries have met a wall of obfuscation and denial from Washington."

"Yeah, I know the EU has just had a meeting – nothing public, but the head honchos descended on Brussels a couple of hours ago. The Canadians? They know roughly what we know, but they're not going to mobilise against the US now or ever. Brazil and India and South Africa are aware of the problem." Petrovitch stopped, then started again. "This isn't sounding good, is it?"

"The whole world has grown to rely on satellites, Doctor: for communication, navigation, surveying, surveillance. Consequently, it is vital that the Americans do not gain a monopoly in space. It is regrettable, but we would be willing to insist on our rights using all and every means at our disposal."

"You're not going to invade California any more than I am, Vice Premier Zhao."

Zhao's lips disappeared as he drew them tight. "Yet that option remains. Since there are many more of us than there are of you, I believe our chances of success would be higher."

"*Chyort.* Can I ask what sort of timescale you're thinking of?"

"We require answers, Doctor. We are willing to wait for those answers – providing there are no further attacks."

"And if there are?"

"Our response will be proportionate."

"And immediate?"

"As you say," said Zhao. "We have given this message to the American ambassador, who accepted it without a word of comment. In the circumstances, I felt that you should be told of this also."

"That's something you didn't have to do. Part of me knows you're only doing it because it suits your interests, but thanks all the same. It's better to know stuff than not."

"As ever, Dr Petrovitch, you are wise beyond your years."

"Wise? I've been accused of a lot of things in my time, but not that. Normally, I do stupid things impulsively, then try and pretend that's what I was going to do all along."

"It has worked in the past. It may yet work again."

"Yeah. You'll be saying we live in interesting times next."

"We are, Doctor. We are." Zhao stood and bowed. "Perhaps we will speak again before long. Until then, I wish that your search is both short and successful. My regards to your wife."

Petrovitch's avatar bowed at the waist. "And to yours."

The connection closed. He found himself back in the cockpit, staring out over the fields of ice and snow below him. Beside him, Newcomen saw him shift.

"What did they say?"

"Too much. Too little. Who knows?" Petrovitch scrubbed at his cheeks. "They're swearing blind the satellite wasn't theirs. But that if it happens again, they're going to retaliate. They called your ambassador in to tell him as much."

"We don't like being threatened."

"Again, the automatic reversion to 'my country right or wrong'. It's just a bit wearing and not a little strange, considering what your country has done to you."

"Someone will make it right," said Newcomen. "Someone has to."

Petrovitch closed his eyes and shook his head. "This isn't a mistake. This isn't some rogue FBI cabal going off the reservation. This is meant. You're holding your opinion despite the evidence, not because of it."

"I know it looks bad . . ."

"*Yobany stos*, man. When this started off, I thought you couldn't be bothered to look for Lucy because of her surname. Now I'm attempting to stop the first war to be fought in Low Earth Orbit. And believe me, it may start there, but it won't end there." He opened his eyes again. There were lights in the far distance, red signals high off the ground, white ones beneath them. Almost there. "We need to do this, and do it quickly. It's not just about her any more."

27

They flew in low over Deadhorse. It was a town there for one reason only, and that reason was becoming increasingly irrelevant. It was kept going because it was important that it wasn't abandoned. That was all.

"Ten years ago I gave you the means to produce all the energy you wanted, simply and cheaply. The world's awash with oil, and yet you're still up here, doing it the hard way." Petrovitch circled one of the drill rigs, hidden inside its insulating tower. There was another half a k away, and another beyond that. The whole landscape was punctuated with these strange monoliths, grey and glowing in their arc lights.

"It's commerce," said Newcomen. "Part of the strategic reserve, too."

"It's not commerce. Do you know how much of a subsidy ARCO get for simply being here?"

"No, I . . ."

"Ask your link. The guys down at Dawson have their own

fermenter that knocks out methanol at cost." Petrovitch turned the nose of the plane back towards the airport. "It's stupid to keep on doing the old thing when the new thing is so much better."

"Don't you think you lose something when you reject the past?"

"You mean like retrofitting DNA and growing babies in artificial wombs?"

Newcomen was silent, and Petrovitch snorted.

"Compared with you, I'm virtually normal."

"Just . . . just land, will you? I'm not in the mood." Newcomen turned his head away. "I assume there's things like hot showers and hot food down there?"

"There's a hotel. The Caribou. It even has cable."

"And they're expecting us?"

"We've had reservations for days." The runway lights lined up in two lines, pointing to the horizon. "We've a show to put on, and I hate disappointing my public."

Other airports of comparable size would have had a drift of light aircraft on the apron, but in the far north, the weather was hard on airframes. Instead, there was a row of hangars, each one big enough to hold a wide-bodied jet.

He contacted the tower for permission to land. It was a formality: they weren't going to say no, and he wasn't going to take no for an answer. Everything was converging on this point: none of them had any room for manoeuvre. He almost felt sorry for the spooks, consigned to the near-perpetual darkness. He was guessing that most of them had no idea why they were up in the frozen north. The more of them that knew, the more likely there'd be a leak that'd get picked up by the Freezone's data miners.

The required permission came, nevertheless, along with a hangar assignment. Petrovitch dropped the plane on to its wheels and steered it towards the opening doors. Inside the hangar, it was bright and full. There were only a couple of bays that were still vacant, all the others taken by functional light transports bearing the ARCO livery.

He applied the brakes when he was within the yellow lines, and cut the power. As the turbines wound down, the heavy gears that closed the external doors cranked into life.

Still Petrovitch sat there, staring at the blank wall in front of him.

Newcomen unbuckled his harness, but Petrovitch wanted to wait for a moment, to savour the tension in the air.

"Can you feel it?" he asked. "It's here. Everything's just fallen into place – us, them, Lucy. The game's ready to begin."

"This isn't a game."

"Yeah, yeah, it is. Just because we're all going to die doesn't mean that we're not playing. Your lot have the advantage: you hold all the cards bar one. But I've gambled more on less."

"At least I'll die clean and fed, then. But not warm."

"Don't be petulant. Perhaps it does suit you, but I don't have to listen to it." Petrovitch hit his own buckle and shrugged the straps away. "Believe it or not, it's actually warmer outside than when we were in Canada. Snow's due in the next twenty-four hours."

He called for the door to open and the steps to lower. On the way, he scooped up his bag. He was half expecting a welcoming committee: cold-hearted killers, bright-eyed analysts, pipe-wielding heavies. Waiting to impress on him the importance of his mission, the urgency of it all. Find her, they'd say, you know you want to.

And he did.

But there was no one. They were alone in the hangar, with nothing but cold still air to greet them.

"Isn't it about now someone says that it's too quiet?" asked Newcomen. He was fastening his parka unbidden, and Petrovitch thought that there might be some hope for the man.

"Only if they're in a bad detective movie."

"And we're not?"

"Different kind of movie altogether." Petrovitch's mouth twitched. "We have to check in, then we'll do a tour of the sights." He reached out and patted the fuselage. "Need some more fuel for the bird."

He trotted to the bottom of the steps, and strode out across the hangar, looking back briefly. His borrowed plane was like a swan compared with the bulky ARCO service models. It was going to be a shame to lose it.

There was a human-sized door inset into the main motor-operated door. He opened it up and stepped outside. It might have been a few degrees warmer, but it was still double-digit cold.

Newcomen closed the door behind him, and they walked together towards the distant buildings. Somewhere under the ice were roads, and maybe they could have arranged a transfer to the hotel, but Petrovitch wanted the time to talk.

"This place will be wired, completely. Anything you say or do will be recorded in half a dozen different ways, right down to the volume, velocity and composition of your farts. Almost everyone you meet – who's not an Inuit – will be a plant, and then some of them, too. There's been a wholesale rerostering of ARCO employees: ringers with fake resumés straight out of central casting are in, regular Arctic workers out."

"Won't the company's profits suffer for that?"

"The chairman of ARCO is so thoroughly Reconstructionist, I doubt he'd think twice about making the whole outfit a CIA front."

"So, what? The whole town's populated by secret agents?"

"I wouldn't call it a town, but yeah. That gives us a surprising degree of latitude."

"How so?"

"Ever seen *Westworld*?"

Newcomen frowned. "Don't think so."

"Made in the seventies. It's about a special theme park, populated by robots, that rich people can visit to fulfil all their wanton, hedonistic desires. Fight, kill, have orgies, the lot. End of the day, the staff just clean the robots up and get them ready for the next bunch of tourists."

"That sounds horrible! Gross, perverted."

"And it is. The story does have a happy ending: the robots rise up and slaughter the humans."

"That's just as bad."

"This is not a pointless anecdote," said Petrovitch. "We're in our own personal Westworld. We can do, more or less, anything we like, and it's all consequence-free. They might decide to take our guns away if we kill too many of them, but that's about it. As long as we find Lucy for them, they don't care."

Newcomen stared at him from underneath the fringe of his hood. He was aghast.

"We're not going to do that, though. Right?"

"No one's going to stop us. If I want to shoot someone in the head, then that's okay by whoever's in charge." Petrovitch shrugged inside his heavy coat. "You're not the only expendable agent here. Take a look at the eyes of everyone we meet: see if you can spot the fear in them. But us? We're in a state of grace. We can commit no sin."

They walked down the middle of what passed for a main street. The buildings – far apart, all raised clear of the permafrost by stilts – were functional and nothing else, and often little more than prefab sheds surrounded by discarded and part-cannibalised equipment.

As the darkness drew about them, the day shorter still, he spotted the blinking neon sign for the Caribou.

"Take the receptionist at the hotel," said Petrovitch. "He's not the regular guy. He's not even one of the occasionals. I'm guessing that last week he was working out of an office in DC, or New York. They've dragged him up north, no experience of Arctic conditions, little idea of why he's here: he's got a script, like they all do, all the ringers and replacements."

He was at the bottom of the steps up to the hotel's front door. He blinked away some ice crystals and wondered about adding antifreeze, or at least extra salt, to his tears.

"You're going to try and make him go off-message, aren't you?" said Newcomen.

"*Chyort*, yeah." Petrovitch tramped up the steps and shouldered his way into the foyer.

It was simple enough: a desk, a chair behind it, and a slightly pudgy, slightly balding man rubbing his sweaty palms nervously on his trousers. He cleared his throat, once, then again, because the first time hadn't quite got rid of the dry, prickling hoarseness he felt.

"Good afternoon, gentlemen," he said.

"*Dobre outro*," said Petrovitch. "We have reservations. Lots of them, but we've also got a couple of rooms booked. Petrovitch and Newcomen."

"I've got your keys here." The faux-receptionist slid two plastic cards across the desk at them. "I'll need to, ah, see some ID."

Petrovitch eyed the sign behind the desk, telling him he wasn't allowed either firearms or alcohol in his room. The corner of his mouth twitched. "ID? Sure." His hand dipped into his pocket and retrieved a plastic eyeball, which he buffed against his sleeve.

When it was shiny, he rolled it towards the man, who stopped it with his fingertips and looked up at Petrovitch, then Newcomen, and back to Petrovitch again.

"Maybe we should waive the formalities this once." He held out the eye and dropped it into Petrovitch's waiting palm. "Your rooms are through that door, second and third on the left."

"Aren't you supposed to ask whether we want bugged or unbugged?"

They looked at each other again, and the receptionist's tongue attempted to moisten his lips. "I'm afraid I don't know what you mean, sir."

Petrovitch dumped his bag on the desk, and made an ostentatious show of thumbing the lock, unzipping it, and rummaging around inside, his brows rising and falling as he felt each object in turn.

He pulled out a small wand, with a series of lights running up to the tip. He pressed a button on its base, and the lights pulsed once, settled down, then started rising again.

"Ooh, what do we have here?" Petrovitch held the wand up and traced arcane lines in the air. "The place is alive, Newcomen. We'll have to mind our language, and everything else."

He suddenly stabbed the wand at the chest of the receptionist, who jerked back, but only as far as the wall behind him. He was still within easy reach of Petrovitch.

The stubby wand crawled up his neck, his chin, his nose, and hovered, poised, over one eye. The man swallowed and watched the lights flicker near to their maximum.

"You're wired," said Petrovitch. "This whole place is wired."

"I . . ."

"That was a statement of fact, not a request for information. I'd just like to take this opportunity, now that I know your controllers are listening for sure: you think you've got me. You couldn't be more wrong."

He pulled back the wand and dropped it in his bag. He passed Newcomen one of the keys and threw the other in the face of the receptionist, who flinched and tried to duck.

"Like I ever needed one of those. Come on, Newcomen." Petrovitch grabbed his bag and took a step back towards the door outside. "Let's go and put more fuel in the tank and take that tour."

Back out in the snow and the dark and the cold, Newcomen rounded on him. "Is that it?"

"Yeah, pretty much. Just letting them know we've arrived, and we're not scared."

"You mean, *you're* not scared."

"Sorry, projecting. I assumed you'd grown a backbone, but I managed to be wrong, yet again." Petrovitch frowned. "That better not become a habit. A lot depends on me being right."

Newcomen ground his teeth. "Can you manage to be a little less rude next time?"

"What? You mean the desk jockey back there?" Petrovitch stopped in the middle of the street. "*Yobany stos*, man. He's got orders to kill me. Why the *huy* should I be polite to him?"

"And you're a prophet now?"

"That man has been sent here to see you, me and Lucy in an

early grave. They all have. They're the teeth in the trap. Just because you share an employer doesn't mean you're going to escape what they've got planned for you." He started walking again. "It hasn't so far, has it?"

"In the end, they'll not do that. If I can convince them I've done my duty . . ."

"Okay, let's try something." Petrovitch put his bag on the ground and pulled out his pistol. He tugged his mitten off with his teeth, and pressed the barrel of the gun against Newcomen's forehead.

Newcomen was very, very still. "Doctor?"

"Right," called out Petrovitch. "You can see me, right? You going to stop me? Here's an FBI agent. He's one of yours. Come and save him from the big bad Russian."

There were figures in the shadows: he could see them in infrared, the bright colours of their faces, muted greens and lighter blues where their clothing shielded them from the cold. But no one asked him to lower his weapon, no one came out to press his gun hand down.

"What are you waiting for? Don't you care?"

Newcomen closed his eyes.

"No one? No one at all?" Petrovitch shrugged, and tossed the weapon back into the open bag. "Guess not, then."

He pulled his mitten back on and grabbed the bag's handles, but didn't move from the spot.

Newcomen opened one eye, then the other. He shuddered. "You, you . . ."

"Wouldn't have shot you? No. You won't get the same offer anywhere else in this town, though. You'd better remember that."

28

Newcomen had reverted to sullen silence. Perhaps his capacity for self-delusion had finally reached its limit, and he was contemplating just how much of a *pizdets* his situation looked. Or he could have been sulking because Petrovitch had drawn a gun on him.

From the pilot's seat, Petrovitch glanced across. He shrugged. Any hope he'd had of turning the agent looked increasingly unlikely. Fine. They'd do it the hard way.

The plane coasted slowly across the North Slope plain: the research station was out of town, but not so far that it required any great speed. Five minutes and they were there, back in the full dark of the Arctic winter.

Petrovitch used satellite maps and night vision to guide the plane down somewhere safe. There were no lights, no power – not since the instant of Lucy's disconnection. He felt his way, and the moment the wheels touched down on the snow crust was a moment of obscure relief.

Skids would have been better, but there was hard substrate beneath. He was able to cut the power to the suspensors after allowing the undercarriage to settle properly.

"Here we are: seventy degrees ten minutes thirty-two seconds north, one hundred and forty-eight degrees five minutes fifty-seven seconds west."

Newcomen huffed. "This place will have been picked clean: all your daughter's effects are in a locker in Seattle, and anything useful will have gone."

"So: you don't know why you're here." Petrovitch punched his buckle through. "You'd much rather be chowing down on steak or standing under a shower until it runs cold."

"It's all I have left. If you don't kill me, someone else will." Newcomen made no effort to get ready to face the outside.

"Not quite. The deal still stands. Do your job: help me find Lucy."

"But you say even my own countrymen won't let me live."

"Surprised as I am to find myself saying this: I'll try to stop them from killing both you and me. I can't honestly say how much that promise is worth, but, hey." Petrovitch lowered the steps into the snow and popped the door. He stood up and began to fasten his parka. "I want to take a look around. There are questions your lot haven't even thought to ask. I'm guessing the answers might still be lying around."

His bag yielded two tiny, intensely bright torches. He pocketed the gun, too, then stepped outside into the freezing wind.

The biggest building was a prefab whose main doors had been sealed with binding strips of yellow and black tape: police line, do not cross. The tape riffled and fluttered.

Petrovitch stared at it, and considered what it meant.

Eventually Newcomen joined him and shone his torch beam around him.

"It's not much, is it?" He illuminated each of the weather-beaten huts, then searched further out. There was nothing but snow and ice.

"In summer, it's home to forty ecologists, botanists and biologists, plus field trips from the university. In winter, it's closed, except for the auroral physics people." Petrovitch dragged at the tape until it snapped. "What were you expecting? Some kind of great white-faced facility with a chain-link fence and patrolling security guards? It's not Stanford, you know. It's as much as they can do to keep this place from falling down."

He pushed the handle on the door, and it creaked open. Inside, it was cold and still. He turned his own torch on and swept it down the corridor, across the notice boards, over the recessed doors that led to dormitories and labs. Everything glittered with frost.

Newcomen walked a little way down the bare boards and, out of habit, tried a light switch. It clicked hollowly.

"So this is where Lucy was when she lost contact."

"Not exactly. There's a winter lab a hundred metres off, closer to the aerial farm. All her datafeeds were routed there." Petrovitch looked around again, but didn't enter. As if he didn't want to break the spell, as if looking at her empty room would send her spinning off into oblivion, never to return. "She had all her winter gear on her. Sleeping bag. Food and a stove. Rifle."

"Rifle?"

"Yeah." He clicked his torch off and let the red light behind his eyes be his guide. "You're probably wondering how we got that through customs."

"Her coat, though. We've got that. And boots and—"

"Tourist gear," said Petrovitch. "I ordered her the same sort of stuff we're wearing. It's missing, so I assume she's still got it all."

"You knew. You knew all along. Why didn't you tell me?"

"Because you'd have told Buchannan, and he'd have told Ben and Jerry."

"You didn't trust me with the information."

"I still don't. Get over it. I'm going to see the physics hut. You can poke about here, see if there's anything left."

There was no path as such – probably one would emerge once the snow had melted – but Petrovitch could see the squat shape in the distance, lit from above by a tenuous apple-green curtain that swung lazily in the sky.

It would have been a good night for an experiment. Lucy would be crouching down over her instruments, watching the real-time data stream across the screen, and she'd read the peaks and troughs like a composer looking at a stave and hearing the music. She'd have a cup of builder's tea in her hands, and she'd reach forward to a panel every so often, to change the amplification of a signal or correct a drift in the driving voltage.

When he tore the police tape away and opened the door, she wasn't there.

Her equipment was, though. Hand-crafted labels in her tiny, spidery handwriting identified each switch and knob. Inside the grey cases, her signature soldering would be plain.

A bare cable was draped over the desk. The computer it had been attached to had gone. That was something that was in the inventory of things taken to Seattle, yet Petrovitch knew it had never arrived.

He settled into the wheeled chair and turned on his torch.

She would have sat right there, rolling from place to place rather than getting up and walking the two steps to where she needed to be. Just like a kid.

"Michael?"

[Sasha.]

"Talk to me. Tell me something I want to hear."

[You were right.]

"Good. I was beginning to think I was losing my touch." He shone his torch at the clocks on the wall: old-school analogue clocks, each face as big as a dinner plate. Four of them, each marked with a plaque: GMT, Alaska Time, Pacific Time, Local Time. The last one read twenty-three minutes and a few seconds past twelve.

[We have made a further analysis of the electrical and electronic disruption experienced in the Deadhorse area. While all the events are essentially simultaneous, within a margin of error, it appears that by ignoring the error and relying on the raw timings alone, a pattern emerges from the data.]

Petrovitch leaned back. "Let me guess. Things get fried earlier in the east than the west."

[It is a matter of tenths of seconds for some of the intervals. And the main explosion that registers on the seismographs destroys less sensitive electronics back up the range, confusing the data.]

"This is insane."

[The obvious conclusion is—]

"It's not obvious at all," he complained. "But it's the only conclusion left. *Svolochi*. Someone beat me to it."

[Just because we can explain the phenomenon does not mean we can then know everything about it.]

"We need to. Someone put a fusion reactor in space. The Americans shot it down."

[The Chinese have denied it was theirs.]

"So they say." He got up and started to pace the tiny room. "I'm still up on fusion. I know people in all the top facilities. How the *huy* could this have gone under the wire, and then ended up in *yebani* orbit? We're talking tonnes. Tens, probably hundreds of tonnes of wire, shielding, all sorts of crap."

[Yet analysis of Vice Premier Zhao's conversation with you did not reveal any unusual stress patterns. It is likely that he was telling you the truth. Is it possible that he is not party to this secret?]

"What's not possible is that the Americans knew and we didn't. But it has to be the Chinese." He threw himself back into the chair. "Doesn't it?"

[Their major facility is at Zhejiang. Analysis of their research yields no evidence of a single instance of a sustained fusion reaction.]

"Of course it doesn't. I'd know about it, along with the rest of the planet."

[And if they are not ready to reveal their success?]

"There's a world of difference between everybody knowing you've done it but you're denying it, and so secret that no one knows you're even capable of it. I mean, fusion. *Yobany stos.*"

[And sitting here, in this room, Lucy Petrovitch worked it out.]

They were both silent, man and machine.

"Why did she run?"

[I do not know.]

Petrovitch slammed his fist on the desk. It was his right hand. If he'd used his left, he'd have reduced the thing to matchwood. "Every time. Every time it looks like we're getting close, we find we're really moving further away."

[And now Joseph Newcomen is wondering what is delaying you.]

"Bring him down here. I want a second pair of eyes."

He met the American at the door of the hut. Newcomen's torch caused the snow to glow.

"Turn it off. I want to try something."

"Will it involve you putting a gun to my head again?"

"No. I haven't got an audience out here, and I don't do it for my own personal pleasure anyway."

Newcomen laboured at the switch until it clicked. Once again it was just the ground and the sky. The aurora flowed overhead, obscuring the stars as it washed across them.

"We have to think like her," said Petrovitch. "Do you think you can do that?"

"I can try," said Newcomen, even though his whole body seemed repelled at the idea of imagining himself a twenty-something foreign-born woman. "I don't know how good I'll be at it."

"You're sitting in that hut. No windows, no indication of what's going on outside except what's on your instruments. Then quickly, without warning, your readings go off the scale. Almost before you can react, everything dies. The lights go off, your computer stops, the screen goes blank. Most importantly, your link dies." Petrovitch knew what that would do to him. For Lucy it was less immediately catastrophic, but all the same, it would have been a surprising and bewildering experience. "What would you do?"

"The power's gone. I'd find a torch."

"Yeah, maybe. You try it, and you get nothing. Candle?

Storm lantern?" He couldn't remember seeing one, but he was forgetting something. "The next moment it sounds like God's knocking to come in."

"Then I go for the door. I open it and step outside."

"It's not dark any more. There's a fireball, up in the sky, towards the west. You watch it boil away. The light fades and you're left in the dark again." Petrovitch stared at the horizon. Deadhorse was invisible. "Why? Why spend time putting things in a rucksack and then leaving the obvious place of safety?"

"Did she think she was under attack? That a war had started?" Newcomen spun slowly around. "How would she know which way to go?"

"She knew the night sky like the back of her hand. With or without a compass, she'd be able to navigate just fine." Petrovitch grunted with frustration. "I thought coming here would make all the difference: that by seeing what she'd seen, I'd get some clue about where she's gone."

"And it hasn't?"

"No." He blew out the stale air from his lungs. "Let's close up here for now. Go and get some food and some rest. Start early tomorrow and see where that gets us."

Petrovitch turned his own torch on and trudged back to the main cluster of buildings, and the plane parked behind it.

"Did you find anything in the dormitory?" he asked Newcomen.

"Nothing. Stripped clean. They've taken the mattress she slept on. I . . . didn't expect that." He kicked at the snow. "It wasn't part of our investigation."

"Of course it wasn't. Your investigation isn't the important one." Petrovitch took one last look around. The wind was picking up further. Ice crystals were starting to blow across the snowscape, eroding the footprints they'd made, and there was a line deeper than black to the south-west. It would have been a night just like this, clear but with a storm coming, when Lucy had set out, alone and in the dark.

That was important. It would have limited her choices, told her how far she could go before she needed to seek shelter.

Except there was no shelter to find. No trees, no rocks, no buildings that weren't ARCO-owned and thoroughly searched by now. An igloo would have been all but impossible without a saw or shovel. Could she have found one? Did she take it with her?

"It's twenty k to Deadhorse from here," he said out loud.

"Sorry?"

"Twenty k. She knew that if she stayed where she was, she'd be trapped by the storm, for days. What if she walked back to Deadhorse?"

Newcomen shivered at the thought. "That's a long way."

"This is the girl who walked the entire length of the Shannon, source to sea, just because she could. The distance is nothing; it's whether she could have made it before the weather closed in."

"They must have turned Deadhorse upside down looking for her already."

"Doesn't mean they would have found her. It's a demonstrable fact that they haven't."

"Because she's not there."

"Where else could she be? Seriously, think about it. It's the only place to go for a hundred k. Even in a place that small, there has to be somewhere to hide."

"Look, Doctor . . ."

Petrovitch eyed Newcomen balefully.

"Petrovitch. This just won't wash. If she was in Deadhorse all this time, someone would have found her — noticed food going missing, stuff like that."

"So she has an accomplice." Petrovitch snorted. "She can be very persuasive. I should know."

Newcomen looked away. "I wouldn't know about that."

"This: this is the whole reason I'm here. To find her, because I can work out what she would have done. We're getting some-where, Newcomen. At last."

"And then we all die. Swell."

"Stop your complaining and get up those steps. Dinner's on me."

29

Petrovitch slotted the plane back into the same hangar bay they'd left, and it was like they'd never been away. Everything was as cold and still as before. The only difference was the creaking noises made by the building's superstructure as it flexed in the wind.

"I'm going to refuel now, save time in the morning. Besides," he said, peering through the windscreen, "you never know when a quick getaway might be needed."

"You really do think she's here, don't you?"

"Yeah. I do. Someone's hiding her. Sooner or later they'll find out I've arrived, and that'll be when the fun and games really start."

"It'll have to be someone they've not replaced. Can you get a list?"

"Sure, but so can you. We can't go around just interrogating people – they won't want to die – but we need to be alert for subtle signs."

"You. Subtle?" Newcomen raised his eyebrows.

"*Past' zebej*," said Petrovitch, but there was no force behind his words. "Whoever it is is risking their life to protect Lucy. They'll be terrified of discovery, of giving themselves away, of just breathing out of turn. Yet they'll have to maintain the pretence that nothing is wrong, every second of every day. That's bravery for you, Newcomen. *Yajtza* bigger than the Moon."

Newcomen was very still for a while, then he got up abruptly and went to the door, poking at the release mechanism until it responded.

[Be careful, Sasha.]

"Yeah, well. I've tried being nice, I've tried indoctrination, I've tried appealing to his better instincts. All I'm left with is shame."

[He is conflicted. He is torn between doing his duty to the country that is actively betraying him, and returning Lucy Petrovitch unharmed to the Freezone.]

"We both know which way he's going to jump. His instincts will make the *mudak* side with Uncle Sam, even though they're going to kill him with no more thought than they'd spend over swatting a fly."

[He may yet surprise you.]

"Which is the only thing keeping him alive. I don't need a bomb next to his heart any more. Up here, I could shoot him in what passes for daylight in front of a dozen witnesses, and all the response I'd get would be 'Where's the girl?'"

[As you have adequately demonstrated. Although the probabilities have shifted, my analysis indicates he is still a significantly positive factor when measuring possible outcomes.]

Petrovitch heard Newcomen's footsteps ping down the metallic steps, and the cold began to seep into the cockpit. "If you mean having him around is keeping me alert and angry, sure. I still reckon I can maintain the required level of rage all on my own."

[He raises your chances of success from zero to almost zero. That might be the best anyone can offer.]

"Then I'll suppose I'll have to take it." He roused himself. "This isn't getting fuel in the tank."

Petrovitch dressed for the outside again, and went in search of the bowser. Up here, in the high Arctic, no one was going to do it for him. Everyone was expected to be capable, or have someone with them who was. Winter was no place for tourists.

The electric cart that pulled the tank of fuel was stored away from the aircraft – of course it was, because anything else would have been stupid – so he had to trek to a separate building and wheel it back. He'd got there, nodded at Maintenance Guy, who wasn't on his roll call of genuine people, and was halfway back when Newcomen ran up to him, breathless and shaking.

He looked around for a fire. There wasn't one. Yet.

"Yeah, when you calm down, that sweat's going to freeze hard."

Newcomen gasped and blew. "Come and see." He leant down and braced his hands against his knees.

Petrovitch looked around at the several thousand litres of fuel he was towing. "It's going to have to wait."

"But . . . you have to come now."

"Yeah. Your priorities are not my priorities. I'm going to refuel the plane, then I'll come. It'll wait, right?"

Still shaking, Newcomen looked around at one of the other hangars. "You don't understand."

Petrovitch followed the direction of Newcomen's gaze. There

was nothing to differentiate that building from the ones either side. Something inside, then. He had a pretty good idea what.

"Seriously. I want to keep the plane topped up, for all sorts of reasons, and I won't be deflected from that by some wild goose chase they've dreamed up for me." He thumbed the button on the handle, and the bowser swayed and sloshed its way towards its destination.

Newcomen, agitated and upset, trailed along behind. He watched Petrovitch wheel the tanker into place, then wrestle with the hoses until he was satisfied with his connections.

"I could do this quicker if you helped."

"I wouldn't know how."

"And learning is against your religion?"

"That's not the point."

"Uh-huh." He got the fuel pumping, and watched for leaks.

"I'm going to be dead soon. Why do I need to know how to put aviation fuel in an aeroplane?"

"If not curiosity, what about necessity? It's the mother of invention." The mechanical counter clicked over – gallons and parts thereof – as the pump whirred. "So, what have you found? Scary?"

"I've seen them on the news, and at the movies. That one at the airport. They've always been on my side before."

"And now they're not. Maybe next time—"

"If there is a next time."

"Next time, you'll have a little more empathy with their victims." He checked the counter. He didn't want to overfill, but he needed enough for what he'd planned, and maybe a little more for emergencies. Not that the whole situation wasn't a big bag of *pizdets* anyway. "How many were there?"

"I don't know. The hangar door was closing as I walked past.

The guards with them stood in the way and made it difficult for me."

"More than one, though."

"Three, at least."

"Uplink stuff? Relay station? The jockeys themselves?"

"I, I don't think so."

Petrovitch glanced at the counter again. A little more. "Yeah, those guys will be in some warehouse in Nevada, getting hyped up on battle drugs and heavy rock. No one's going to put their meat on the line: way too valuable to lose."

His hand hovered over the cut-off switch. In the distance, a door slammed shut. Newcomen started, but it was just one of the Inuit workers taking a short cut. He had a bag heavy with tools and a metre-long adjustable wrench slung over one shoulder.

He nodded under his furred hood at Newcomen, and then at Petrovitch, as he passed by.

"Real," said Petrovitch, when the man had gone through the door at the front of the hangar. He flicked the pump off, then began the laborious task of unscrewing the hoses and coiling them back up, ready for the next user.

Newcomen was in an agony of impatience. "Tell me you don't have to take that back across the airfield."

"I ought. But I don't have to. No one's going to say anything to my face." He patted the side of the tank. "I'll leave it here."

"So you'll come now?"

"I'll get my things." He trooped back up the steps, gathered his bag from the cabin, and on a whim scooped up the axe he'd bought too. He met Newcomen back in the hangar. "Let's go and see what we're up against."

Once outside, Newcomen pointed to the next hangar but

one. It looked locked down, no lights showing, no one hanging around. Petrovitch searched for cameras, telltale signs of digital transmissions: they were there, and there, and there too, and those were just the nearest ones. As they walked, images were sent and commands were received, broadcasting from a building the other side of the runway.

He glanced up as a camera's housing turned slowly to face him. He wondered if Ben and Jerry were hunkered down over the monitor, maybe a coffee in hand, watching him back, wondering what he was doing.

They weren't going to have to wonder for long.

"This one?" Petrovitch rattled the door.

"They're not just going to let us in, are they?" Newcomen looked around nervously.

"You still don't get it, do you?" He dropped his bag in the snow and rolled the axe off his shoulder. The lock was just below the door handle. "We can do what the *huy* we want."

He kicked the lock with the heel of his boot. Not only did the door give, it bent. It shuddered back on its hinges and banged against its stops. The cold, dark space beyond beckoned.

Finally there was some activity behind him. He could hear motors starting up: two, three petrol engines. They weren't going to get to him before he'd had a good look around. He swung his bag through the opening, and held the axe loosely in his left hand.

He switched to infrared as he stepped over the threshold. There were the softly glowing shapes he was expecting, but what he was really looking for was the light switch.

There, the other side of the main doors: a big board, complete with fuses. "Wait here," he said to Newcomen, and navigated his way over to the still-warm switches.

He clicked them on, one by one. The lights in the high ceiling flickered on in banks, slowly illuminating the scene. When he'd done, he saw that they'd sent thirty-two fully armed and armoured teletroopers after him.

They sat in neat rows, crouched over and dormant. Their heads rested on their massive chests, and their gun arms pointed at the ground. Their reversed knees were bent slightly. Whip aerials extended over their backs, and cooling fins radiated like coral growths from their spines.

"Ugly bastards, aren't they?"

He walked up to one and looked into its stereoscopic imaging equipment. It looked disturbingly like huge black eyes.

"What are we going to do?" asked Newcomen.

"I thought we'd spray-paint them pink and give them each a girl's name." Petrovitch circled the one he was closest to. "Isn't that right, Svetlana?"

"There are so many of them. I didn't know."

"Yeah, I'll agree with you there. This is a lot of hardware for just us. Almost as if they're expecting a much bigger party than the one we might possibly throw." He reached out and laid his hand on Svetlana's thigh. Her hip was as high as his head, and the joint – every joint – was carefully recessed and protected with interlocking plates. Not enough room to even wriggle his fingers inside.

They were designed to be tough to kill, to take the bricks and the bottles, the bullets and buckshot, even the smaller anti-tank rounds. They could dish it out, too. Rotary cannon and assault shotgun, grenade launcher. Shoulder-mounted rockets, even.

A man, maybe a thousand k away, would sit in a virtual rig and control it all like it was one big video game. Boom. Head shot. Soldiers under fire would find cover, call in an air strike, scramble back to safety, and only rarely press on to their objective. A teletrooper would shrug off the small-arms fire and just keep going. The rattle of shells and shrapnel against its hull would be muted, less it was distracting.

The cavalry finally arrived. Engines roared outside, doors opened and boots clattered. Petrovitch carried on his circumnavigation of the teletrooper, ignoring the fact that he was being surrounded by men dressed in Arctic camouflage. They all had guns, and they all pointed them at Petrovitch.

He watched them watching him through their full-face masks, each of them printed to resemble the same skull that sat beneath their skin. Except the eye sockets were larger, and the grins more toothy. Ghouls. He was encircled by ghouls.

"Step away from the machine, Dr Petrovitch."

He looked around for the source of the voice. A figure, dressed in bulky, expensive top-of-the-range civilian kit, but still wearing the skeletal mask, stepped through the ring of soldiers. He had a shotgun held loosely in his hands.

"So which one are you? Ben or Jerry?" Petrovitch looked around for Newcomen. The American was being ignored by his countrymen as someone of no consequence, a mere bit-part player to the main act.

The question confused the man. His hidden face flexed the surface of the mask. "I said, step away from the machine."

"Or what? You'll shoot me?" Petrovitch's bag was by the door, but he was still carrying the axe. "I don't think that's going to happen."

"For the third and last time, step away from the machine." Even his voice was disguised, subtly filtered and modulated.

"Fuck you and the horse you rode in on." Petrovitch switched the axe into a two-handed grip. "Where's my girl?"

The man, Ben or Jerry, raised his shotgun and fired it without warning. The taser round caught Petrovitch in the fleshy part of his outstretched palm. The impact rocked him backwards. He kept his feet, but he couldn't prevent the discharge that followed.

No matter that he could block the pain: he had no control.

He swung the axe, but couldn't see where it hit. His arm thrashed, and the weight of it threw him to the floor.

Someone had modified the taser. The shock went on for far longer than it should. If he'd taken it to the chest, it would have stopped his heart.

It ended, eventually. Petrovitch looked up at the circle of gun barrels and fixed-grin faces. He gripped the plastic body of the shell and pulled the barbs out of his hand. Blood oozed out.

"Step away from the machine, Dr Petrovitch." The man in the skeleton mask chambered a fresh shell, indicating that he was more than prepared to keep shocking him until he complied. The used cartridge clattered on to the concrete.

The axe had embedded itself in Svetlana's leg. The blade was wedged in the shin, enabling Petrovitch to use the haft to lever himself up. "I want to know where Lucy is."

With a sound like a sigh, the man raised the butt of his shotgun to his shoulder.

"I can keep this up all night if I have to."

Petrovitch gripped the axe, tore it free. "It's the only thing you can keep up all night, dickless."

This time, the taser hit his side. He was just too slow, too disorientated, too full of interference and conflicting signals to parry it. The electrodes had to punch their way through his dense jacket, though, and only just grazed his skin. He was thrown to the floor again, but as he fell, the device shifted and lost contact.

It gave him a moment to recover. The man, with a hiss of annoyance, worked the pump for another shell.

"That's enough."

Petrovitch thought at first it might be his own voice. He blinked away the stars to see Newcomen, armed with his own FBI-issue pistol, aiming at his tormentor's back.

"Agent Newcomen," said the man. "What in God's merciful name are you doing?"

"I'm stopping you. This, this isn't right." Newcomen's voice was wavering, but his gun was steady.

"I think you're forgetting which side you're on."

"No," said Newcomen. "I know which side I'm on. I'm on the side of the law."

"Sometimes, Agent—" said the man, but Newcomen interrupted, his voice a roar.

"No State shall make or enforce any law which shall abridge the privileges or immunities of citizens of the United States; nor shall any State deprive any person of life, liberty, or property, without due process of law, nor deny to any person within its jurisdiction the equal protection of the laws. That's the four-teenth amendment to the constitution of the United States of America, you bastard, and you will obey it." He was gasping for breath by the time he'd finished. He also looked ready to pull the trigger.

Petrovitch hauled himself up again. He was sore, deep inside. He used the axe as a crutch and walked forward until the barrel of the shotgun taser was against his chest. "If it was me, I'd have killed you by now. I'd have put a bullet in your head, because, hey, it's what I do. And you'd deserve it. Newcomen here? You should be on your knees thanking him that he still plays by the rules. He's an idiot, because he thinks the rules haven't changed, but I'll take an honest idiot any day over a *niegadzai sooksin* like you."

Beneath the mask, muscles twitched and a decision was made. "Okay. Let's move out."

The soldiers snapped their guns upright and jogged to the door. The man in charge was in their midst, surrounded, safe. Then they were gone. Engine sounds faded away, and they were left with the creak of the hangar and the sympathetic swing of the lights.

Newcomen was locked rigid in his shooter's stance. Petrovitch hobbled over and rested a hand on the agent's wrist.

"We're done here."

Newcomen's expression turned from concentrated determination to startled bewilderment. "What just happened?"

"You rediscovered your spine." Petrovitch pushed the gun down until it was pointing at the floor. "And I'm grateful."

30

Dinner had been unsatisfying. Not because the food hadn't been good, or plentiful, but it had been like eating in an experiment, closely observed by the researchers. Newcomen had been in turn sullen and nervy, and Petrovitch's own emotional state had even now barely dropped below incandescent.

That they'd been served by Reception Guy, a known secret service plant, just added insult to injury. Petrovitch had gone to sleep with his gun in his hand.

[Do not move, Sasha, or show any sign you are awake.]

He lay perfectly still. Even the finger curled around the trigger guard didn't twitch.

"Problem?"

[Several men have entered Joseph Newcomen's room.]

"Are they going to kill him? I sort of promised him I'd try and stop them from doing that."

[If they were intent on an extra-judicial assassination, they would have done so already. His door was opened with a master key card: Newcomen had placed a chair against the door jamb, as per your instructions.]

"So he's awake. What's he doing?"

[I have built up a soundscape of his movements. Without visual confirmation, I am only ninety-eight per cent certain he is pointing a gun at the intruders.]

"Tell me he's wearing pyjamas this time."

[I am eighty-five per cent certain of that.]

Acutely aware that he should be hearing raised voices, and possibly a bit of gunplay, from the next room, Petrovitch flexed his ear.

"So. Spooks in Newcomen's room. What do they want?"

[There have been no spoken words as yet. It could be that they wish to take revenge for his act of defiance this evening.]

"Or?"

[They want to parley.]

"Maybe I should intervene."

[Perhaps I should make him aware that we know of his situation. If he was a member of the Freezone collective, it would be my duty to ask whether he needed assistance.]

But Petrovitch didn't stir, and Michael didn't speak.

"What's he doing now?"

[There is no change in the situation. His breathing and heart rate, initially elevated, are now slowing again. His arm will begin to tremble in another minute or so, and eventually he will lower his weapon. The men facing him are most likely unarmed.]

"He won't shoot."

[No. Despite all you have told him. Perhaps even because of it. He still possesses huge psychological barriers to killing.]

"Unlike me."

[Now is not the time to discuss this.]

"I want to get up and find out what's happening."

[We have a better chance of finding out if you do not.]

"They wouldn't be so stupid to try and cut Newcomen a deal while we're listening. They do know we're listening, right?]

[It seems likely that they do, since they have not uttered a word. The link earpiece is still visible when inserted, and there would have been ample opportunity to discover that Newcomen was linked while he was being observed in the restaurant.

"You want to find out whether Newcomen is going to betray me or not."

[We have told him we can punch a hole in his heart at a moment's notice. You held a gun to his head this morning. You nearly flew him into a mountain range earlier. He owes us no loyalty.]

"And yet he pulled his gun on the spooks in the teletrooper hangar."

[A perfectly sound psychological response to seeing a vulnerable person repeatedly hurt by larger, more aggressive people. Even you have that reaction, Sasha. When you are caught off guard.]

The shade of Sonja Oshicora drifted through the hotel room. It felt colder, and Petrovitch risked turning over and wrapping himself more tightly in the duvet.

"Yeah, okay. He doesn't owe them any loyalty either, though. They've pretty much taken everything he thought important away from him."

[And still he persists in entertaining the fantasy that there might be a way back.]

"It is just that, though. A fantasy. They're not interested in him at all."

[Yet it is his room they have entered. We must assume therefore that your analysis is flawed in some way.]

Petrovitch, face down in his pillow, worried at his lip. There was no sound at all.

"Give me the live feed."

He could hear Newcomen, his laboured breathing, the faint rustle of his clothes, the odd pop as he swallowed and forced air up his Eustachian tubes. Behind that, the hum of the hot-air ventilation system, and after a quick analysis of the waveforms, three other people.

There was a rustle and a sigh. Newcomen lowered his arm. The light switch clicked on, then came another noise that Petrovitch couldn't quite make out.

[Notebook.]

A pen rasped across the rough cellulose surface of a fresh white sheet of paper.

"I don't suppose you can . . ."

[My powers are limited to the possible, Sasha. Guessing the shape of words from the sounds they make when written?]

"They have cameras in every room."

[They are watching for any hint of intrusion. Naturally, when the time comes, I can hijack their entire system, but then they will know that I have. Theirs is not an insecure public network: it has been constructed with care as well as haste. They might not be able to keep me out − something they hope they can do but fortunately cannot − but they will know I am there.]

"Then we should have bugged Newcomen better."

[The threat of immediate death not being enough to keep him in line?]

"Funny how things turn out. We've turned a craven,

incompetent Reconstructionista into a decent human being, and he doesn't do what we want."

[I have several pertinent literary allusions ready to deploy at a moment's notice.]

The piece of paper used to write the note was scrumpled up, and – it sounded like – eaten. Then another page was turned, and another message made.

Newcomen's breathing and heart rate rose again.

[He is subvocalising. One moment.]

Petrovitch waited in the dark, aware of every point of contact between his bedclothes and his body.

[Incomplete. One word is most likely 'deal'.]

"We should stop this. Newcomen's *zhopu* is mine."

[Are you not interested in what he will do?]

"Will my knowing help me find Lucy?"

[I cannot say. Wondering whether he will betray you as opposed to knowing he already has? I suggest it is important to know what lies in his heart.]

"But they're shafting him all over again. They sold him up the river, and now they're promising him passage back. He has to realise that."

[And as you have already said: he will fall for it. They will tell him he is the most important part of their mission. That it will fail without him. That he will be a hero. That he can make contact with Christine again. That he will get a medal from the President. Newcomen will forgive them for what they have done because he is just waiting for someone to tell him all these things and make it better.]

"At least when I blackmail someone, my terms are clear and transparent. I'm honest about what I want."

[Yes, Sasha. But what if they are telling him the truth?]

Petrovitch almost sat up. His muscles tensed, and he caught his breath.

"Say that again?"

[It seems obvious now. We have been operating under the impression that Newcomen is entirely the wrong agent for the task. What if he is not? What if he is, in fact, exactly the person they required? Someone who, for example, they could abuse and treat appallingly, and who would still come back to them when they judged the time was right.]

"*Chyort*. That's . . ."

[Evil? We still do not know their reasons. What looks like evil to us may appear completely different to them. They could reasonably believe they are doing the right thing.]

The paper being shown to Newcomen was screwed up and consumed.

"What's he doing?"

[He is simply standing there. His breathing and heart rate are peaking, as if he is in a fight-or-flight scenario. I calculate he will decide what to do shortly.]

The pen nib scratched out a third note.

"So: they're standing in the doorway, scribbling stuff on scraps of paper and holding them up so he can read them."

[Yes.]

"They've actually thought this through."

[So you must be careful. You know the whole town is a trap designed to capture Lucy. That they have done it well should not surprise you.]

"Then why bring the teletroopers up here? Thirty-two of them? They have to realise that they're virtually gifting us an army."

[And yet there they are. Perhaps they have been modified in

an unexpected way. Perhaps they want us to think we could take them over, only for us to find we cannot when it is too late. Or—]

"Enough already. Give it to the analysts and tell me what's happening next door."

[Newcomen's vital signs are still running near maximum. His core temperature has increased, and he is becoming hypocapniac.]

"He's going to faint? Yeah, they'll want to avoid that. He's a big man."

[He is under great psychological stress. His unmitigated physiological responses to that stress are inadequate, as they are in all unmodified humans.]

The note with its hidden message was pressed inside the palm of a closing hand and destroyed in a mouth.

There was nothing for the longest time. Then someone stepped closer to the microphone embedded in the link. The sound of paper and pen was much closer, too. Newcomen was writing a reply.

That part was over quickly. Footsteps: one set out into the corridor, right outside Petrovitch's door. Then another, moving the other way. The third paused before following them. The light switch clicked clearly off, and the chair used to inexpertly block the doorway clipped the wall with a slight tock.

The third man's feet brushed against the door jamb, then the door itself was eased back. It closed almost – almost, but not quite – silently, the catch gently released until it engaged.

Another gap, and finally the sound of cloth against cloth as three pairs of trousered legs walked away up the corridor.

Next door, Newcomen let out a ragged gasp.

"They're more careful than he is."

[We know this. He is not secret-agent material. His one strength is his closeness to you.]

"So do I get rid of him, or do I keep him? What did he tell them? Who did he decide for? Me or Uncle Sam?"

[There is no way of knowing.]

Newcomen's gun slithered back into its wrist sheath. Then, with the greatest of care, the American tiptoed back into bed, slowly drawing up the covers as he lay down again.

The mattress sighed with weight.

"I could ask him, I suppose. I could ask him right now."

[You are disappointed in him.]

"He was good today. He actually cared. He empathised rather than thought about his own skin. It wasn't an act, he didn't do it to make himself look good or to win me over. He saved my *zhopu* from a beating."

[And, paradoxically, that action may have paved the way to his rejection of your threat to kill him. He is no longer scared of death. He has reached some degree of peace with its inevitability. The only thing he believes he can control is the manner of his going.]

"And you think he's going to do that in the service of his country."

[Yes.]

"But you can't be certain."

[No. I can, however, recalculate the percentages for your successfully retrieving Lucy and escaping the territory of the United States of America.]

"They've all just dropped to zero, haven't they?"

[Whether or not you keep Joseph Newcomen with you.]

In the darkness, the corner of Petrovitch's mouth twitched.

"Yeah, well. No one said this was going to be easy."

31

It was morning, as measured by the clock. The Sun wasn't due up for another three hours. Petrovitch sat on the edge of his bed, staring at the wall opposite, and wondered if this was going to be his last day.

[Good morning, Sasha.]

"Hey." He worked his mouth, and undid the nerve lock on his trigger finger. The gun slid out of his hand and on to the covers. "Anything new I need to know about?"

[There has been considerable diplomatic traffic overnight between Beijing and Washington. The ambassadors of both the US and the People's Republic have been required to attend meetings at the respective foreign ministries, for strongly worded messages. The contents of these are as yet unknown, but sources indicate that Space Command on both sides is at high alert.]

"How about the ICBMs? Fuelled or unfuelled?"

[That is also unknown. It would be safe to assume that no one has been standing down their missile teams. Also, the

Chinese cyberwarfare division is highly active at the moment. This may be something we can use to our advantage.]

"Yeah, okay. Go carefully. Anything else?"

[Yes,] said Michael.

Petrovitch waited. "Okay. Do go on."

[I am uncertain what to make of this data, and whether it is a processing artefact. It is certainly anomalous.]

"Are you going to tell me what it is, or are you going to leave me guessing?"

[Sasha, what is the orbital velocity of an object in Low Earth Orbit?]

"You know I know this. I know you know this. Why are you asking me?"

[The object that was shot by the SkyShield satellite was travelling at between seven and a half and eight kilometres a second.]

Petrovitch frowned. "That's wrong. And didn't we clock it going slower?"

[Post-encounter. Reanalysis of the admittedly poor images we have of the object suggest that its velocity was up to twice that before it was struck.]

"And you've checked everything at least ten times, right?"

[A group of analysts spent most of yesterday arguing about the results.]

Petrovitch pursed his lips. "So let's get this straight: you're suggesting that between being hit by SkyShield and entering the atmosphere, it lost half its orbital speed. And that it was going way too fast in the first place."

[Yes.]

"*Chyort.*"

[Indeed.]

"What the *huy* was it?"

[I still do not know.]

"Is Newcomen up?"

[No. He finally achieved sleep only a few hours ago. I will wake him if you wish.]

"I'll do it. I want you to keep crunching those numbers. See if you can work out where it might have come from, now we know its vector. Astronomical plates, reports from amateurs, sky-flash cameras: anything that might be useful." He looked at the door to the tiny en-suite bathroom, and shrugged. He reached for his clothes and patched himself through to the sleeping man in the next room. "Hey."

He could hear a slight sigh, then the snoring resumed. He ramped the volume up all the way to eleven.

"Hey! Newcomen! Get your fat Yankee *zhopu* out of bed. Breakfast in ten."

There was a thud that reverberated through the wall. "What? Who?"

"Me," said Petrovitch. "We've got work to do."

"I," said Newcomen, and hesitated. This would be an opportunity to confess. "I didn't sleep too good again."

So that was how he wanted to play it. Okay. "Tell Mister Sandman, because I don't give a shit. Nine minutes."

Petrovitch finished hitting his socks on the wall, and dragged the now-limp things on to his feet. He slipped his feet in his boots without lacing them, and looked around.

He picked up his gun and posted it in his waistband, laid the axe lengthways along his bag, then scooped up the handles in one hand. In the other went his bundle of outdoor clothes. That was it: everything he needed.

It was a short walk from his room to the dining room. He

slumped into the same seat he'd sat in yesterday – in the corner with a good view of all the doors. He dropped his stuff by his feet and laid his gun on his side plate.

Reception Guy, alerted one way or another to his presence, ambled in.

"Good morning, Dr Petrovitch."

"*Past' zebej*. If you insist on maintaining this *yebani* charade, the least you can do is bring me some coffee. Or I can just shoot you. I might do it anyway." Petrovitch looked pointedly at his crockery. "Don't push it."

The man's eyes narrowed, and his initial attempt at good humour wasn't repeated. He poured Petrovitch coffee – his guest's only response was a growled "Leave the pot" – and retreated to the kitchen to bang some pans around.

Petrovitch was left to brood, but despite being served by a trained killer, the coffee started to do its job.

"Michael, I've just thought of something."

[Which is?]

"If the object managed to decelerate from eight to four k a second between the time it was hit and the time it blew up, maybe it was going even faster before that."

[That would put it close to, if not above, escape velocity.]

"Who do we know has a Moon mission planned?"

[Sasha, have we been asking the wrong questions?]

"I think we have. Can we get some recent ultra-high-res pictures of the lunar surface?"

[I will search the databases.]

"And convene the Secrets committee. I want to keep this private for a day or two."

[They will consider your request. Any particular reason?]

"Yeah. Whether I'm right or wrong, we need the Chinese

on side for just a little bit longer." Petrovitch looked up and saw Newcomen appear at the entrance to the restaurant. "It's all about face, right? And especially about not losing it in front of a global audience."

Newcomen sat down opposite him, and Petrovitch dribbled a stream of black coffee into the proffered cup.

"You're looking pointy," said Newcomen. He wiped his hands on his thighs. Sweat.

"Yeah," said Petrovitch. "I am, aren't I?"

The agent noticed the handgun on the table. "Trouble?"

"Pretty much all the time." He changed the subject even while his mind was racing away down a new track. "Breakfast is on its way."

"I really don't know how you can be hungry." Newcomen shook his head. "Did they . . . damage you yesterday?"

"I've run the diagnostics a couple of times. Nothing burnt out. I'm fine."

"Seriously? You took it hard, especially the second shot."

"I didn't enjoy it, if that's what you mean." Petrovitch shrugged. "Next time I see him, I shove his shotgun up his *zhopu*. Then I pull the trigger: see how he likes it."

Newcomen added milk to his coffee, and Petrovitch poured himself a second cup.

"Do you dream?" asked Newcomen. "I mean, I don't know. I'm just asking if you do or not."

Petrovitch sat back in his chair, wondering whether or not to answer. "Michael does. Or did, at least. When he was trapped in a quantum computer under the Oshicora building, he had nothing to do but dream the days away. So he constructed this world – a universe, really – and dreamed about what it would be like."

"Doesn't that need imagination? It's . . ."

"Just a smart program? No. No, it's not. Michael can be creative in ways that are frankly scary. And he's a citizen of the Freezone, a person in his own right."

"I'm not comfortable with that."

"Yeah. Figures. Of course I dream, same as I always did. Being a cyborg doesn't take away your humanity; just adds to it."

Newcomen did that thing where he adjusted himself on his seat; the little sideways shuffle to the right, then the left, that showed he was emotionally disturbed.

"I was just interested." He looked around, up at the ceiling to see if there were any microphones dangling down, then towards the kitchen door, in case there were more obviously human ears listening in. "Does it – does Michael mind me talking about him like this?"

"He has feelings to hurt, if that's what you mean, even though his feelings are different from ours because they don't come with the same range of physiological responses. His emotions are very pure; no hormones to cloud his thinking. That has its good side and its bad side."

"How so?" He had Newcomen's full attention.

"Because if he's got a reason to be pissed at you, logic dictates he's going to stay pissed for ever, until he's taken his revenge. He can't calm down and forget about it, because he doesn't get angry in the same way. His fury is cold and hard, and eminently reasonable. Remember that." Petrovitch saw the kitchen door bang open, and Reception Guy came through bearing two plates. "Eat up."

When it had been set in front of him, Newcomen stared ruefully at the plate full of meat and carbs. His expression slowly slipped and he looked despondent for a moment.

"What?"

"Doesn't matter."

"Okay then." Petrovitch spun his fork between his fingers. "Get shovelling. Fuel, remember?"

He started to eat in his usual cram-it-in style. Reception Guy came back out of the kitchen to watch, until Petrovitch reached across his plate for his gun and without looking up, aimed it unerringly at the bridge of the man's nose.

He held it steady until he and Newcomen were again the only people in the dining room.

"I hate that," he mumbled between mouthfuls. "I'm not a freak show."

"They're still watching you. Us." Newcomen threw his cutlery down. "You. How come it's all about you?"

"Because I'm the one that's going to lead them to my daughter." Petrovitch slurped coffee. "Maybe they figure you'll have nothing to do with that."

Newcomen looked around again. "I can be useful," he said. "I was yesterday."

"We'll see," said Petrovitch.

His plate was empty, and he let out a mighty belch of appreciation. Newcomen started to recoil, then just shook his head.

"You've got the manners of a pig."

"Yeah. Some find it endearing." He threw his serviette into the centre of his plate and pushed his chair back. "Or at least, they've learned to live with it. Anything in your room you need?"

"My outdoor things." Newcomen looked at the bundle on the floor next to Petrovitch. "I left them there."

"Okay. I'll fire up the jet. Don't be long."

Petrovitch dressed there in the dining room, quickly and

efficiently, his hand never far from the butt of his gun. He put his boots in turn on the chair, tied them tight, then made his way through reception. The man was at his desk.

"You done?"

Petrovitch stopped. "If I was done, I'd have my daughter back."

"We're all just doing our jobs, Dr Petrovitch." The man leaned back and folded his arms.

"Yeah. But at least my job doesn't suck sweaty donkey balls." He thought about leaving his axe buried in the man's sternum, but on reflection, it wouldn't actually help. He shrugged and kicked the main doors open.

Cold. White ground. Dark sky.

"*Yobany stos*, you'd think I'd be used to this."

[The Moon is a significant area to search, and we have limited access to hi-res dark-side images. Where should we concentrate our efforts?]

"Putting two and two together to make several billion, I'd go for frosty craters around the poles. Somewhere where helium-three is known to be rich. And water. Remember they may have buried any permanent structures under the regolith."

[It is unlikely that we would be able to spot anything even at half-metre resolution.]

"But we have to try. I'm going to try something equally unlikely." He puffed out a snowstorm of air. "I'm looking for debris."

[Sasha, anything that was not consumed in the fireball will have been collected already. We have ascertained the Americans are not stupid. Nor blind.]

"And yet, if I don't look, I might not find what they missed."

He tripped down the stairs, and nearly slid on the small padded envelope lying on the ground.

There had been snowfall while he'd been inside. There was more forecast for later. He put his bag on the ground so that it covered the white paper, and knelt down to adjust his boots. All perfectly natural.

Two options: either it was insignificant, and there was nothing of importance inside – just discarded rubbish, blowing on the Arctic wind – or it had been deliberately dropped, right outside the hotel where he and Newcomen were the only guests.

The envelope was small enough to tuck in the top of one of his mukluks. He swapped the foot he was supposedly checking and knocked the axe off his bag, so that it fell in the snow. When he picked it up, he had both envelope and haft in his hand.

The axe went back on the bag, and the envelope was in his boot.

He stood up and straightened his clothing, then stooped again to pick up his bag.

There was a man a couple of hundred metres distant, by the corner of a building. He appeared not to be doing anything in particular, just dawdling on his way somewhere else. He was muffled up, and Petrovitch couldn't tell who it was. The man was short enough not to be genengineered, but he was wearing ARCO gear all the same.

Petrovitch gave him no more than a glance, but on his way to the airfield, he replayed that glance over and over again. The sharp corner of the envelope dug into his ankle with every step.

32

Obviously, he was being watched. That was a given. But he knew he'd been spotted picking up the package as he approached the hangar: maybe it had taken them that long to review the images from outside the hotel, compile a sequence of events from multiple angles, and come to the conclusion that there'd been a drop.

They'd missed it as it happened, but they weren't going to compound their error. Over at Ben and Jerry's not-so-secret base of operations, the whole anthill of operatives spilled out and into their vehicles.

Petrovitch had no wish to be tasered again. He had his gun and his axe: he'd make a fight of it this time, but depending on what was in the envelope, they might actually not need him any more. They could just shoot him and take what they wanted without having to go through the rigmarole of asking.

"Newcomen?"

"I'm coming, okay? Just the other side of the runway to you."

"Yeah. There've been some developments, not necessarily for the better." He opened the hangar door and slipped inside. He had a minute. If that. "Even if you run, you're not going to make it in time. Turn around, go back towards the hotel. Walk quickly."

"I'm coming anyway. You need me with you."

"No. Not now I don't."

Petrovitch looked around and assessed his assets. Even as his heart spun faster, he realised that he didn't just have one plane. He might have an airforce.

"*Yobany stos.* Michael?"

[Sasha.]

"We need to get as many of these up in the air as possible."

[The ARCO planes do not respond to my initial commands. They are not in a standby mode. They are completely shut down and require manual activation.]

"*Chyort.* Plan B."

[Is it a good plan, Sasha?]

"No. No, it's not," he said, even as he fired up his own plane and ran towards it. "But frankly, it's all I've got. Permission to go off the reservation?"

The plane's door opened and the ladder extended, but he ignored them for the moment. There was the fuel bowser he'd left parked the night before. He opened his bag, and started to rummage.

[I have an ad-hoc on standby. You have thirty seconds until contact.]

"Enough of the stopwatch already." His hand came up, clutching the appropriate munitions and a roll of tape.

Mittens, in bag. Bomb, on the tank. Tape, ripped between his clenched teeth. One piece and stick. Two pieces, because it

absolutely mustn't come off. A third piece of tape nipped off.
He thumbed the cold, cold switch and pulled the handle to
start the bowser moving, then quickly wrapped the tape around
the handle so that it stayed on.

It lurched out into the hangar, and Petrovitch pointed it
roughly in the direction of the doors.

[You have no guarantee that it will steer straight.]

"No shit, Sherlock. In the absence of a low-orbit ion cannon
I can use, it's what I'm left with."

[No one has a low-orbit ion cannon.]

"Only because I don't have time to do everything." Even with
the bowser rumbling towards the far end of the hangar, he made
no attempt to board the plane. "How's the ad-hoc doing?"

[It would help them if they knew what you were up to.
Sasha? The plan?]

His beautiful executive jet rose into the air, and the turbines
started to turn.

"Yeah. About that plan. It sucked anyway." He picked up
his bag and ran to the dangling ladder, latching on with his
free hand. Theatre, nothing more. Dangerous theatre, a stunt
that could get him killed. But he needed to be seen, just for
one last moment.

The bowser had wandered: rather than going straight, it had
curved gracefully to the left, but had managed to avoid the
front skids of one of the ARCO planes. It banged up against
the hangar door, and started to edge further leftwards.

"Tell me they're right outside." The plane rose further, and
him with it.

[They are right outside. Sasha, I think you should reconsider . . .]

"I don't. Go or no go?"

[Go.]

He triggered the bomb.

A white flash lit up the hangar. The pop of the explosive was lost beneath the hot roar of the plane's turbines as they cranked up. The tank of fuel ripped apart, and the liquid inside vaporised as the shock wave hit it.

"Cameras. Now."

The fireball lit with a dirty orange roar, and he let go of the ladder. Higher than he'd like, he fell to the concrete floor, and landed in a heap. The heat from the burning cloud of fuel washed over him, and he pressed himself against the ground.

[Hangar cameras are offline. Sasha?]

"Yeah, yeah." He looked up and the structure was ablaze. The external doors had blown out, with the remains of the steel shutters lying on several cars. Flames met falling snow in the dark pre-dawn, and inside, bright blue fire was running in rivers towards him. There was shouting and screaming, but none of that seemed to be coming from him.

Over his head, his plane was moving towards the newly exposed opening. Its white paintwork was black and bubbling at the nose, and both engines seemed to be labouring. Still, it didn't have to fly that far. He launched it forward.

Inevitably, all eyes still capable of seeing watched it leave, bursting from the bank of churning flame and trailing smoke. Barely aloft, it skimmed the runway as it limped across the airfield.

Using the distraction, Petrovitch picked himself and his bag up, and ran for the back door. His ankle turned. He blinked away the pain and kept going.

The explosion had weakened the hangar's structure. Fire had done the rest. It groaned and creaked, and started to fall. First the arch sagged, then the walls failed.

On the far side of the runway, Petrovitch's plane ploughed into Ben and Jerry's control centre. It tore through the building, breaking itself and whatever was inside the one-storey prefab. At some point before it came to rest, its fractured fuel tanks gave up their load, and a second fireball rose into the Arctic sky, red reflected against the underside of the clouds.

[They are completely blind.]

Hot metal was falling from above, peppering him and the other planes at the far end of the hangar. There was the door. He didn't stop, just aimed a two-footed kick on the lock.

He fell outside, in the swirling snow. It was dark, and no one knew he was there.

The hangar was still collapsing, and as the ARCO planes underneath cooked, they added more fuel to the fire. Something went bang, and shrapnel sang by. It was a singularly unhealthy place to be, but his ankle was giving him all kinds of trouble. The pain he could deal with – it was making sure he kept his foot pointing in the right direction that was the problem.

He hunched over and hobbled towards the next hangar, putting his shoulder to the falling snow. The light from the burning fuel was a bright glow: explosions sent meteors arcing through the air to land hissing in the drifts.

Petrovitch put his back against the metal wall of the hangar, even as it reverberated with a dull clang. "Newcomen?"

"What have you done?" He sounded aghast.

"No more Mr Nice Guy, Newcomen. The gloves are off." He looked down at his hands. "At least figuratively. Their surveillance network is down, and I'm a free agent. This is what I want you to do: grab a snowmobile and make sure it has enough fuel to get you to the research station."

[Sasha?]

"I know what I'm doing," said Petrovitch. "Watch and learn."

"How am I supposed to do that?" Newcomen was saying. His breathing was ragged, panicked.

"Just take one. No one's going to stop you. If you ever want to see some answers, you'll do as I tell you."

"You'll die here. And that'll kill me."

"Look, I'm not holding your hand any longer. Do it now or get caught in the crossfire. Your call." He was interrupted.

[The teletroopers awaken.]

Petrovitch swallowed hard. "Okay, Michael. Talk to me. Can we do this?"

[One moment.]

"*Chyort*, not again."

[It is not like jihading a commercial car. These are highly sophisticated weapons of war with entirely different protocols and encryption. Different again to the model you encountered at the airport.]

"You're just building your part up now, aren't you?"

[Yes. It seems absurd that they have not learnt the lessons of a decade ago, but there is no accounting for the stupidity of humans. They have brought these machines here for some reason or other: I am not inclined to pursue that avenue at the moment.]

"Good. Let's chase them off the streets, just like we did the Outies."

[Very well,] said Michael.

Petrovitch watched him do it, brutally ripping control of the teletroopers away from their virtual masters and slaving them to his will. One moment the jocks in Nevada were popping the next stimulant in the blister pack and preparing to hunt his scrawny Russian hide down; the next, every rig had flatlined, limp and unresponsive as a fresh cadaver.

"You did this once before," said Petrovitch. "You made monsters and marched them across the Metrozone."

[And now someone else builds the monsters. I merely make them march.]

The crackle of flames and the billows of smoke had started to die down. The creaks and groans of the collapsed hangar had calmed to the occasional settling moan. It was quiet enough to hear shouted instructions and the revving of engines. Quiet enough to hear the pressurised hiss of pistons as the first of the teletroopers unfolded from its resting position and straightened up to its full height.

Its cameras scanned the darkness. Through Petrovitch, Michael knew where the manual door mechanism was. The teletrooper stamped over and a retractable blade extended from the back of its hand, thin enough to be able to spear the on switch.

The chain started to rattle, and the snow flurried in through the widening gap. Petrovitch watched, piggybacking the images Michael was receiving, as the other thirty-one robots pulled themselves upright and levelled their weapons.

"*Yobany stos*. No wonder they win wars."

[Sasha? What of mercy?]

"What of it?"

[Do we show mercy?]

"Did they show us mercy? Did they tell us the truth? Did they help us?" He pulled on his mittens. "Did they look after Lucy for us, or did they try and feed us all to the wolves?"

[Is that your answer then? I should kill them all?]

Petrovitch tested his ankle on the ground. Weak. Unstable. He'd torn something. It didn't matter for now. "They would have killed us. They still will if they get the chance."

[Then permit me to deny them the opportunity.]

He started to limp away, further from the pyre. "All yours. I need to see what's so important about this envelope."

He dug it out of its hiding place, and gave it a shake. There was definitely something inside, but it was small, flat. He guessed at a data card, and for that, he needed the reader in his bag, and somewhere safe to use it, inside and out of the driving snow that was blinding him every time he looked up.

He trudged on, dragging his foot with every step. There was another hangar coming up: he'd try in there, even if it meant just sitting in a cockpit with the heater turned on.

The teletroopers lined up outside. Even though he'd destroyed their comms centre, Petrovitch assumed that Nevada had some other way of telling Ben or Jerry, or anyone else still on the ground, they'd lost control. It didn't look like it, though. No one was running for cover, breaking out the heavy weapons or calling for air support.

Michael was right. They'd learned nothing from their first encounter with the New Machine Jihad. Relying on remotely operated weapons? What were they thinking? Didn't they know who they were up against?

"For old times' sake, then." He patched himself through to the lead teletrooper, and activated the speakers. There was a spook not ten metres away, trying to peer through the dark and the snow, his eyes shielded with one hand while he lazily held an automatic in his other.

"Prepare," said the teletrooper.

The man turned sharply. "Not reading you." He tapped his hooded ear.

"Prepare."

"Did you just say . . . Oh. Shit."

"Yeah. Pretty much." The teletrooper took three quick strides forward, eating up the distance between them, and backhanded the spook with his cannon arm. The snow sprayed red, and he aimed a missile at the nearest car: hot target, engine running white under the red of the bonnet.

[You have more important tasks, Sasha. I have command.]

Petrovitch was eased off the virtual levers gently but firmly, and he was back outside the hangar, frost accumulating in his hood's fur.

The gunfire was abruptly intense. Michael picked off their vehicles first, then started to divide his forces: some walked off in the direction of town, while others chased the living away, into the blizzard, with no clear idea of where they were heading. A third group, numbering five, went back down the runway towards the control tower, spreading out into a line across the tarmac, illuminated by the bright lights meant for aircraft.

Petrovitch picked up his axe and hacked at the door. The lock gave, and he pushed the door in. The images were dark, confusing, but there seemed to be no one there. The lights were off, and there were no telltale splashes of body heat. He pushed the door back closed, and wedged it shut with a half-filled barrel of waste oil.

Parts. He was surrounded by parts. A repair shed, then. Where there were mechanics, there'd be a kettle, and something to put in a mug.

Aware of the incongruity, he weaved his way around the darkened benches and half-assembled skidoos in search of coffee, while outside, thirty-two robotic killers hunted for prey.

33

Petrovitch rattled the office door, and it swung open. It was little more than a ropy prefab hut dumped in one corner of the hangar, but it had lights and power, and in amongst the pieces of paper thumbtacked to the notice boards and oily bits brought into the warm were fingerprinted mugs and empty plates.

He dumped his bag on one of the debris-strewn tables and sorted through it. There was a replacement for Lucy's link: a little curved computer with its earpiece, all wrapped in plastic and ready to pass on. There was a singularity bomb, an anti-gravity sphere, a pencil-thick hi-def video camera, battery packs, more plastique, remote-control units.

And the card reader. He pulled it out and sat it on the table, but was distracted by the sight of a half-cup of cold coffee, its black surface trembling with distant explosions.

He had time enough for a brew.

He found an almost-clean cup on the draining board of the not-completely-plumbed-in sink, and over on a workbench, a bare heating element wired into the wall. It didn't look entirely safe, but he'd used worse. And there were biscuits in one of the drawers, along with a fistful of coffee sachets.

He poured two of those into the cup, topped it up with water and lowered the heater into it. There was a satisfying blue spark when he turned it on, and the slowly blackening water started to seethe.

The biscuit packet was new: he ripped at one end with his teeth, and extruded the first directly into his mouth. Thereafter he chain-ate them, swallowing one as he started chewing the next.

His coffee boiled. He turned off the element at the wall – another snap of electricity – and carried the mug to the table. He retrieved the envelope again, and this time eased his finger under the gummy flap, easing it open.

Turning it over, he tipped the contents out. A little black rectangle clicked on to the scarred formica. An old-school memory card from a camera: fifteen, maybe even twenty years out of date.

"You have got to be *yebani* kidding me."

[Is there a problem?]

Petrovitch held up the card so Michael could see.

[This is frustrating. Your reader does not take that format.]

"No. No, it doesn't." He pressed the card to his forehead. "Nothing. Nada."

[Either you find a suitable data port in your locale, or you will have to solder wires to the contacts and manually interrogate the data. It is likely the information on that card is critical to the success of your mission.]

"Haven't you got robots to command, rather than stating the *yebani* obvious?"

[Yes, but they do not require much oversight. A relatively simple iterative search program coupled with an executive order protocol that flags up possible targets for me to consider renders intensive management redundant. One trooper has been disabled by small-arms fire, and another by a mechanical defect. The environment is extreme, and I expect the rate of attrition to be high.]

Petrovitch was already on his feet, inspecting the workstation hiding in the corner. "Just the regular slots." He spun it around and inspected the back. *"Chyort vos'mi."*

He knelt down and systematically worked his way through all the cupboards, then started on the benches. Nothing. And no guarantee that if he found something, it would still work. He was about to break something gratuitously when he saw a couple of bags hanging from hooks behind the door.

He spilled the contents of the first one out on the floor, and sorted through them with his sweeping hands: small bronze coins, loose keys, bits of paper, a couple of pens, a hip flask, a slim notebook with dog-eared pages. The second was heavier; rather than just upending the bag, he plunged his hand between the jaws of the zip and struck figurative gold.

His fingers tightened around a dense cold lump, and he knew by its heft it was tech. He pulled it out: a compact video camera, paint worn out with use, silverwork scratched. It looked ancient, a museum piece. He checked its make and model. It had been new twenty-three years earlier. By rights, it should have been consigned to the bin ages ago.

But once he'd found the on switch, he discovered its battery was half charged up. And there was no memory card in the little slot. He had not just found a suitable bit of hardware to slot his card into, but the original camera it had come from.

Whoever owned it worked in that very hangar, repairing things for ARCO.

Petrovitch sent a virtual agent to work through the duty roster, trying to find suitable suspects: while he waited for it to report back, he fished out the memory card, turned it the right way around, and gently eased it into place.

The camera digested its new information, then displayed the updated results. The card was all but full. He found the preview button, checking with an online copy of the original documentation to make sure it was the preview button because he was paranoid about deleting something by accident, then pressed it.

Video had accumulated like coral: it looked like no one had bothered to either download or wipe any image they'd ever taken, and the time stamp on the earliest clips was from two decades ago. But Petrovitch wasn't bothered about personal memories from the mid twenty-tens, more about what had happened last week.

He scrolled back past the first image to the latest scene. There was something wrong with the file: it should have been a video – but it wouldn't play, despite his urging.

"I'm going to have to do this the hard way after all. Can you make sure I'm not disturbed?"

[The Americans have retreated to an ARCO drilling facility some two kilometres distant. I have set up a perimeter to keep them away from the settlement, but they appear content to stay where they are. I have lost seven teletroopers due to mechanical failure, another three to enemy action. Of the remaining twenty-two, only fifteen are fully operational. However, it is the sterilisation they have ordered that concerns me.]

Petrovitch stumbled into the table in front of him, spilling his coffee and dislodging one of the biscuits so that it rolled on to the floor. "St . . . what?"

[A flight of planes from Eielson has been delayed due to the weather. Delayed, but not postponed.]

"How long do I have?"

[Perhaps as much as twenty minutes.]

"*Yebat' kopat'.*" He went back to his bag. Right down at the bottom was a tube of conducting glue.

[Pin values for the data card.] An image hovered in front of him.

"Thanks."

[You will need to supply two point seven volts to pin four.]

"Yeah. I know."

[Pin three is ground. These two must be connected first.]

"Michael. Shut the *huy* up." He filleted his reader, extruding the wires in a fan. "I was doing this before you were born."

[I am only twelve.]

"Precisely my point." He stripped the sleeving off each wire with his teeth. "You don't even have opposable thumbs."

Petrovitch remotely accessed the reader's set-up screen, and assigned the correct values to the wires. He cleared a space on the workbench with a sweep of his arm and set out the reader, its bundle of wires and the card. Bending low, he cranked up the magnification on his eyes, and started to stick each wire to each metal contact in turn.

"Yes? No?"

[One moment.]

"I don't have a *yebani* moment. They're going to bomb the town flat in less than fifteen minutes and I need to know if this card tells me Lucy's in the line of fire."

311

The light on the reader flicked from steady green to blinking yellow.

[Interesting. The most recent file is incomplete: I will recreate the end-of-file data. Done. The file is ready to play. We have analysts standing by.]

Petrovitch blinked, and suddenly it was night.

Night, but not dark. A streamer of burning light tore through the sky, east to west, shedding pieces as it went. In the raw data, the camera jerked and shook, but he could correct for that, keeping the main incandescent mass in the centre of the frame, while bits calved off and flashed with their own energy.

It wasn't quiet. Two voices exchanged opinions on the meteor: one was the camera operator, distinct and loud. The other was quieter but more excitable, standing a little way off. They talked in Inupiat and English, swapping between the two when the vocabulary in one became stretched. Behind both men was the distant grumble of air being superheated and torn aside, and the yowl and yip of husky dogs.

The speed of the thing meant that the image sometimes went dark. Then the lens was hurriedly re-aimed and the white-orange glare would fill the little screen once more.

Twenty seconds in, the interference started. Another ten, and the information stopped being stored, the electronics over-whelmed by the intense magnetic field passing overhead. He was lucky the portion that remained wasn't corrupted beyond recognition. Old tech: the camera had simply ceased working, while a newer device would have tried to self-repair, and in failing, junked the file.

Thirty seconds of moving images at twenty-five frames a second. One of those hundreds of pictures was important.

He went through them in twos, flicking from frame to frame,

mapping the differences between each pair, building up a picture of what had happened to that thing that had fallen from space. Breaking up, for sure, with fragments of its skin peeling off and spinning away as it crashed towards the Bering Strait.

The shards burnt bright, briefly, until they were either consumed, or had slowed enough to turn invisible.

That was it. He backed up to the beginning, looking at the size of each piece as it spalled off the main mass. There: fifteen seconds in. With a flare that almost whited out the screen, a piece detached itself. In the next frame, it had gone.

He repeated the three frames, over and over again: before, during and after. Then he sat back and thought about it, clearing the images from his vision and realising that he was still sitting in a hangar, surrounded by broken machinery, and his coffee had gone cold.

[Have you spotted it?]

"Yeah. Anyone else?"

[One group has zeroed in on those particular frames. They are discussing the significance of them currently, and will inevitably reach the conclusion you have.]

"It was a re-entry capsule, under power." Petrovitch picked up his equipment and stuffed everything back in his bag. "Other bits, when they came off, you can see them for up to five, six frames. This thing? It's off and gone. That flare? Explosive bolts and rocket fuel.

[This scenario remains highly speculative.]

"Look, we've been circling around this idea for a while without actually coming out and saying it straight. This is a secret Chinese Moon mission, using some sort of prototype fusion drive. If it was manned, the astronauts may have had both the opportunity and the means to bail. Nothing else fits."

[Except there is no evidence of the Chinese having developed a fusion drive.]

"You're wrong. There is evidence, and we're looking right at it."

[No external evidence, then. There is also the question of why. Why would the Americans shoot down a Chinese spaceship, and risk a confrontation that would be in no one's interest?]

"I don't know why. Maybe they're just stupid. Maybe it was an accident." He thumbed the lock on his bag and swung up his axe. "But seriously. It has to be the Chinese. Who the *huy* else could it be?"

Michael, always ready with an opinion, was silent.

Petrovitch blinked and stared at the wall. "*Huy tebe v'zhopu zamesto ukropu!*"

[Have you worked it out, Sasha?]

"You're serious. Of course you're serious. *Chyort. Chyort vos'mi.*" He disconnected the data card from his jerry-rigged reader and held it up to his face. "How long have you known, and when were you going to tell me?"

[The possibility – at an admittedly tiny probability – has been one of the options since the beginning, as have many other extremely unlikely causes, including an evaporating black hole and antimatter collisions. However, the more we learned, the more accurately I could assign probabilities to the various scenarios. Now that we have the final piece of information required to finally choose between them, there is only one that has anything approaching my full confidence.]

"But . . ." Petrovitch stared at his cold coffee. He didn't want it any more. He wanted something a lot stronger. There was that hip flask in the first bag he'd emptied, and there'd definitely been something in it. "*Yobany stos.* Zhao said 'that satellite'.

That satellite was not ours. But wasn't a satellite. It was aliens."

[The First Vice Premier was not lying,] said Michael. [He did not know what it was, he still does not know. We do. It is the only possible answer to all the questions we have been asking.]

Petrovitch reeled into a chair, knocking it over. "The re-entry pod?"

[The strewn field of debris would easily encompass the research station. The object moved almost directly overhead. Once ejected, the descent module could have achieved either a controlled landing, or an uncontrolled impact, depending on the mechanical state of its components, its design limits, and whether any automatic systems were functioning at the time. If their technology relied on electrical impulses to transmit information, it would have been unlikely to withstand such intense electromagnetic fields at such short range, no matter how well shielded.]

"It came down near Lucy. She either saw it fall, or heard it, or felt it." He struggled past the fallen chair to the table with the emptied bags. "She would have gone out to take a look."

[Again, this is likely. It is the explanation why she subsequently disappeared. It is the explanation why the Americans want to find her before she can say what she saw.]

"What did she find when she got there? Did it look like something we'd make, or something else? Was there a door, or a hatch? Did she force it open, or did they come out?" Petrovitch's hand trembled as he unscrewed the top of the hip flask. The fumes were sharp, almost without flavour. Vodka, then: how appropriate.

[I do not know, Sasha. They may not have survived the descent.]

"What did they look like? Like us, or . . . not at all?" He tilted his wrist and drank deep. He needed it, needed it badly. "*Yobany stos*, Michael. We have to find Lucy."

[That is why you are in Deadhorse.]

"Yeah." The clock ticked over another second, then another. "Whose camera is this anyway?"

[This repair centre is run by an engineer called Paul Avaiq. It is most likely to be his.]

"Tell me you haven't killed him."

[Not purposely, no. I have made every effort only to target those personnel who have been swapped in recently. I have even erred on the side of caution, which has contributed to a loss of our assets.]

"But we've just torn the town apart. What if he's run with the other Yanks?"

[I will search for him. Meanwhile, we have sufficient information to at least find out where Avaiq was when he took the video, to within a manageable margin of error, by comparing it with the known behaviour of the craft.]

"Dog team," said Petrovitch.

[Explain.]

"*Balvan! Mudak!* Ship crosses the sky, explodes, trashes electrical and electronic systems at will. Starter coils for skidoos and four-wheel drives, the ARCO planes? They're not turned off: they're all dead. Everything they have has either been brought in since or repaired. So how do you cross the snow if everything mechanical is fried?"

[By using a dog-pulled sled.]

"There was the sound of dogs on the clip. We should've been looking from the very start for someone who runs a dog team." Petrovitch gulped the last of the vodka, and threw the flask on the floor. He picked up his bag and limped through the hangar and out into the pre-dawn light.

34

The sky was invisible behind a storm of snow. Petrovitch spat out a mouthful and turned his head out of the wind.

"I can't see a *yebani* thing."

[You must hurry. Only with Paul Avaiq will you stand a chance of finding Lucy in time.]

"Give me a map and find me some transport."

A wire-frame model of Deadhorse popped up in his vision. Buildings, teletroopers, roads, all marked out in the overlay, even if everything was lost in the whiteout. His path was shown by a thick yellow line on the ground. Eyes down, he started to follow it.

It led off to his left, towards the faint burning mass of Ben and Jerry's ruined control centre. "We can't make too many more mistakes." Petrovitch turned into the wind, and was all but blind. "What are they going to drop?"

[Fuel-air explosives to destroy the solid structures. The second wave will use napalm and phosphorus. Conventional explosives will be more or less undetectable to the global seismology network, and there will be no telltale fission products on the wind.]

Petrovitch kept on walking, head down, following the line at his feet. Just ahead was a building on fire, the snow hissing as it touched the flames, and before it, a skidoo.

Petrovitch reached out and heaved the white-coated body off the seat and on to the ground. The single shot had punctured the man's back, and he'd slumped over at the controls. He'd bled out over the left-hand side of the cowling, and it had mostly frozen already. Mostly.

[Does it disturb you?]

Petrovitch bungeed his bag to the carry-rack and sat astride the vehicle. "What? That he's dead, or that the seat's a little sticky?"

[Human disgust responses seem to be abnormally absent from your psyche.]

"Hardly news." The magnetic key was missing, and he spent a few extra moments he didn't have dismounting, rolling the body over, and patting down its pockets. "It's meat. Nothing more."

He came up with a key ring and a coded plastic card. He got back on, and pressed it to the ignition. The lights came on, and the fuel cell started pushing power to the turbines. The path changed direction, pointing towards where Michael hoped Avaiq would be.

[I can try and stop the planes. They will be more difficult to interfere with than missiles, but I can attempt to hack the GPS signals: they will be flying on instruments and I should be able to fool them into missing Deadhorse completely.]

"Maybe. But we don't know where Lucy is. Tearing up a random piece of tundra might be exactly the wrong choice."

[Then you have less than ten minutes to find Avaiq and Lucy and get to a safe distance.] Michael paused. [That is not long.]

Petrovitch glanced at the controls, worked out what they all did, and dragged on the accelerator. The tracks at the back bit into the soft surface and dug in until they reached the hard, compacted ice below. The machine lurched forward, and he had to hang on.

"I'm going as fast as I can."

The snow shovelled itself at his face at twice the speed now, so it became a freezing, stinging blizzard. He drove flat out until his route indicated a hard left; he throttled back in order to take the turn, then opened it up again. He was the only vehicle moving. Even the teletroopers, the ones that couldn't make it to the edge of town, were still.

"Who's left here?"

[Those who have not fled with the security forces will probably be hiding. The buildings are well insulated. The teletroopers' infrared capabilities cannot see through the walls.]

Petrovitch turned right on to the road that would take him past the hotel. He glanced up to see it properly on fire, orange flames pulled ragged by the wind. "I think we should warn them to get out. Can we do that?"

[Door-to-door searches for survivors are time-consuming. I can announce the impending air strike like this:]

Every teletrooper blared out: "Warning. Warning. Warning. Residents and workers of Deadhorse. An air attack on your settlement is imminent. Evacuate immediately. The Freezone guarantees the teletroopers will not harm you. You have nine minutes."

[The cellphone network has been disabled, although I am detecting several satellite phone signals. I will contact them personally and assure them of our good intentions.]

The glowing yellow road lurched abruptly right again, and terminated at the foot of a two-storey building that loomed out of the snow so fast Petrovitch thought he might not be able to stop in time.

He hung the back out, and slid around in an almost perfect circle, ending up nose on to the wall. "Yeah. I bet you I couldn't do that twice."

The teletrooper at the crossroads lumbered around. One leg was stiff, immovable. "Warning. Warning. Warning."

Petrovitch pitched himself off the snowmobile, picked up the bag and his gun, and dragged his foot all the way to the door.

"You have eight minutes," called the teletrooper.

"I know I've got *yebani* eight minutes." He rattled the handle, found it locked, and kicked out at the wooden frame. It splintered. He went back for another go. The lock gave and the door slapped back on its hinges.

He was in a corridor which went left and right. There were stairs at either end, and in between door after door. If he had to check each one, he was going to be incinerated along with everyone else.

He filled his lungs with cold air. "Avaiq! Paul Avaiq! It's Petrovitch."

The sound of his voice trailed away, to no response.

"*Pizdets*. Why is nothing ever simple? Which room is he supposed to be in?"

[First floor, two-one-two. Go left.]

He was halfway down the corridor when a figure appeared at the far end. "Dr Petrovitch?"

"Yeah. Paul Avaiq?"

Petrovitch stopped, because he was tired, and behind his tiredness, everything hurt.

Avaiq was dressed for the outside, parka already fastened, hood down to reveal his sallow face and short black hair. He hurried towards Petrovitch. "You took your time."

"*Yobany stos*, man, I think I was pretty smart considering how little I had to go on." They were nose to nose. Avaiq was fractionally smaller.

"Those things out there are saying—"

"I know what they're saying. I got them to say it. The Yanks are going to bomb the crap out of Deadhorse, then cremate what's left. Where's Lucy?"

"She's not here."

"Then where the *huy* is she? And how about the other . . . others?"

"What? No." Avaiq was agitated, almost vibrating with tension. "It's not—"

"Explain on the way." With both gun and bag, Petrovitch had no free hand to grab hold of Avaiq's collar and propel him to the door.

"Where are we going?"

Petrovitch growled. "Do you know where Lucy is?"

Avaiq steadied his nerve. "Yes."

"Then what are we waiting for? In seven minutes' time, this place will be matchwood."

[It is now six.]

"Thanks for that." Petrovitch heard a noise behind him, a door opening. The hinges squeaked, giving him a moment's warning.

A man leapt out, already firing an automatic pistol. Maybe if he'd taken the trouble to sight it, rather than just pulling at the trigger while falling, he might have hit one or other of his intended targets rather than blowing holes in the plasterboard.

He managed three shots before he collided with the opposite wall, throwing his gun hand high.

Petrovitch aimed for his head and left a neat hole above the left eyebrow. "Yeah, and you can fuck right off." He swept the corridor front and back for anyone else. Avaiq was crouched on the floor, arms wrapped around his head. "Michael? You didn't get them all."

[Inevitable. Can I suggest you leave the locale immediately?]

"Gladly. Avaiq? Up." He kicked the man for want of anything else he could do. "You are the only person on the planet who can tell me where my daughter is, and you are coming with me."

"He could have killed us," Avaiq pointed out.

"Could have, but didn't. Get up, man!" Petrovitch dropped his bag, dragged the Inuit on to his feet, and grabbed the handles again. "You've shown yourself to be an exceptionally brave and resourceful man. You've protected Lucy against every threat for the past week. You only have to keep going for a little longer, and then you can stop. Promise."

It seemed to be the right thing to say. Avaiq only flinched once when he had to step over the legs and the blood welling out of the shooter. There was a spatter mark on the skirting board, and he looked away sharply.

Then they were back out in the driving wind and snow, the sky luminous with both celestial and earthly fire.

"Can we find our way in this?" Avaiq shouted to Petrovitch.

"Yeah. We can. Hopefully they'll have more trouble." Petrovitch stood astride the snowmobile. "Got your own?"

"It's still in the shop."

"Then get on, you mad bastard. We have less than six

minutes." He nodded to the back of the seat and pressed his bag on the man. "Put this between us: there's nothing in there that'll break. Sit down and hang on."

[Less than five. The planes are lining up for their first run.]

"Really hang on," said Petrovitch. He backed up for a metre, then started to accelerate forward, heading between the accommodation block and the next building. Beyond that was the river, frozen hard, snow blowing in sheets across its surface.

There was a small windshield, barely enough to deflect the freezing wind around his body, and certainly not tall enough to hide his face behind. He was blind: but for the overlay of wire shapes and coloured lines, he'd have driven into one of the supply lines that ran to the pipeline proper.

The path he had to follow directed him around the end of the pipe. It meant another minute within Deadhorse.

[The first of the bombs has been released. They are parachute-dropped, and will take about ninety seconds to descend to detonation height. Due to the adverse weather conditions, the bomb yield and blast radius will be degraded, but still considerable.]

"Will we make it?" He was going so fast, every rut and crack in the underlying ground felt like a chasm.

[One moment.] The yellow line abruptly changed direction, no longer trying to guide him south-east. Due east now.

"*Chyort.*"

He was on the river ice. The valley was so shallow as to provide him and his passenger with no protection at all. Somewhere on the other side was a service road that would be brilliant if he could hit it, because it felt like what was left of his internal organs were being jolted out of what was left of his body.

He kept going, his teeth clenched, his eyes screwed tight shut, relying solely on what Michael could show him.

[Right. Go right.]

He did, and felt, rather than saw, the light. The ground trembled, and a second later came the sound of God clapping his hands: low, sonorous waves of noise that felt like a punch in the gut and just as churning.

It was all but impossible to control the snowmobile at the speed he was going. He wasn't dead yet, so he cut the speed and glided it to an almost-halt. They were the other side of the river, lost in the snow.

Flashbulbs were going off over the scattered structures of Deadhorse, and the air was stiffening with every explosion of orange-white.

Petrovitch waited for a lull, then asked, "You okay?"

"I guess so." Avaiq relaxed his death grip for a moment. "Why? Why are they doing this?"

"Because they're scared. That's why."

There was nothing to see but the changing brightness of a wall of snow. Time to finally get the answers he craved.

35

By the time Petrovitch steered the snowmobile next to Newcomen's, he was so cold he could barely let go of the handlebars. His fingers had set into claws, and he wondered if he'd lose some to frostbite.

It was only meat, he told himself. Just flesh and bone. Replaceable. Upgradable.

He forced his mouth to work. "Off."

The snow had eased, temporarily: enough so that he could see the black buildings of the research station against the white of the ground and the grey of the sky.

Behind him, Avaiq backed off the pillion seat and stumbled in an uncompacted drift. He muttered as he tried to regain his balance, failed, and sat down in the powdery snow.

Petrovitch rubbed his mittens against his jawline, turning the hard crust of frost inside his hood into flakes of ice he could inexpertly scoop out.

Avaiq stayed where he was, slumped, defeated.

"I can't go back, can I?"

"There's nothing left to go back to. The town's gone: the pumping stations, the company facilities, the hospital, the airport. There's nothing left, and by the time the Yanks have shot all the survivors, there'll be no one to say what happened either. They'll put it down to a series of massive gas explosions – which, in a way, it was – and rebuild the place a kilometre or two down the coast."

"I know that," said Avaiq, looking up at Petrovitch. "What I meant was, I can't go back."

"No. You can't. Sorry. And neither can Newcomen, because I'm probably about to shoot him in the head." He threw a handful of frost to the ground. "Unless I think it's too much like hard work. You can claim asylum in Canada. If you don't think that's far enough away, you can come and work for the Freezone. We're always hiring."

"So. It's all over." When Avaiq breathed out, his whole body sagged. "I suppose I shouldn't regret what I did. But I do."

"Well, I'm grateful. The whole of the Freezone is. And if it's any consolation, your fate was sealed the moment you and your friend with the dogs decided to see if the strange European girl needed help." Petrovitch tried to stand, and ended up in a heap next to Avaiq. "*Chyort*. That was what happened, wasn't it? You were, where? Down by the edge of the sea ice, about ten k north of here? You saw the light in the sky, and you had your camera. Then everything electrical you had stopped working. While you were trying to work out what happened, you saw it fall. The capsule. Where did it land?"

Avaiq frowned. "What d'you mean?" He turned over on to his hands and knees and pointed to the frozen river below the slight rise on which the research station was positioned. The broad, flat valley was pocked with shallow lakes, and the river meandered around and through them on the way to the Arctic Ocean. "Right there. That's where it came down. I thought you knew."

One of the lakes had a circular ring of ice on its surface: great jagged plates thrown up by whatever had impacted its centre. In the daylight, it was obvious. It may as well have had a kiosk next to it, selling postcards.

"*Yebat' kopat.*" Petrovitch stood and stared. "How the *huy* did that get past us?"

[You came here in the dark, and we have no centimetre-resolution satellite imaging capacity ourselves.]

"That has got to change."

Then Newcomen came out of the main doors of the research station. "Petrovitch? I thought . . ."

"What exactly did you think, Newcomen?" Petrovitch batted the snow away from his chest and dipped inside for his gun. He pulled his mitten off with his teeth and spat it in the direction of his skidoo. "This is Paul Avaiq, by the way. ARCO engineer. Avaiq, meet – albeit briefly – Joseph Newcomen, FBI."

Petrovitch straightened his arm. Newcomen looked like he might make the draw sign. Slowly and deliberately, he put his hands down by his side.

"Can I ask what I've done?"

"What did you tell them? Last night in your room, you had visitors. Didn't exchange a single word, but they wrote stuff down and held it up to you, and you, in turn, gave them an answer."

Newcomen closed his eyes and clenched his fists.

"Fucking look at me, you bastard. What did you tell them?"

"Why don't you just kill me now? One command. Boom. You don't even have to pull the trigger."

Petrovitch took a step closer. The barrel of his gun was a bare breath away from the bridge of Newcomen's nose. "You told them I thought Lucy was in Deadhorse, didn't you?"

He opened his eyes. "Yes. I told them."

"What did they promise you in return?"

"Nothing. They told me I was a loyal American, and that the President thanked me for my continuing service."

"That was all it took?" Petrovitch's breath condensed in clouds in front of him. "Pet the dog once and everything's all right again. Have you forgotten that even your own boss dry-fucked you and left you swinging in the wind?"

"Oh, I haven't forgotten that," said Newcomen. "I remember it all, every last thing they did to me. What I do know now is that there was a reason for it. I understand they did what they did for reasons of overwhelming national security. That was why Buchannan sacrificed me. Why the Director ordered it. I signed up to protect and defend the United States of America and that's exactly what I ended up doing. Part of me wishes they'd told me first, but you'd have got that out of me one way or another. Considering what you did to me, I'm glad they didn't tell me."

"What I did to you?" Petrovitch shifted the weight off his ankle. It hurt. A lot. In unguarded moments, it felt like it was on fire.

"You put a bomb in my heart."

"Oh. That." His eyelid twitched. "I lied."

"You what?"

"I lied. While you were unconscious, I just put a strip of skin on your chest, then lied my *zhopu* off." Petrovitch frowned.

"Is that worse that actually cutting you open and placing explosives in your chest? I don't know."

"You bastard."

"I can say that: you can't. Twenty dollars. Look, everyone expected it of me. Those watching us certainly did. They didn't care as long as I led them to Lucy. But with your new-found enlightenment, you agree with that. Everything that was done to you, every last little indignity they heaped on you. I'm a lot less sanguine about it than you are. Then again, I'm not serving the ravenous god of national interest."

"I served my country. They were a better judge of my character than I was. They used me like a weapon, and yes, I submit to their authority." Newcomen's hand had lost its mitten, and now he made the draw sign. His automatic slapped into the palm of his hand and his stance mirrored Petrovitch's. "Lucy's dead, and you're under arrest."

Petrovitch squinted into the shadow inside Newcomen's gun. "You do realise your gun hasn't even got a firing pin."

Newcomen had to try. He managed to move his finger the small distance required to pull the trigger. He was expecting the gun to kick, an empty shell to spin out, and the recoil to load another bullet. All he got was a click.

He tried again, and again. He pressed the gun against Petrovitch's forehead, twitching his index finger as fast as he could.

"I didn't want you shooting me by accident. Or design." Petrovitch knocked Newcomen's arm aside, hopped forward and brought his knee up hard. All the bombast flew out of the American in one explosive gasp. "Looks like a smart move now."

Newcomen roared in pain, and, to his credit, tried to stand, his gun dangling from its tether. Petrovitch simply put a foot in his chest and heaved him on to his back.

"Come on, you must have had worse playing football. On your feet, soldier. I want you to regret you've only one life to give for your country." Petrovitch felt a hand rest hesitantly on his shoulder, and he shook it off. "I thought you'd woken up! Turns out you think just like them. It's not just the planet that belongs to you. It's the whole of space, too. I just hope we don't find out that you've committed the biggest fuck-up in recorded history."

Again the hand, and again the angry brush-off.

"We had one shot at this. One chance to get it right. It fell to you, and what did you do? You blew them up! *Huy tebe v'zhopu!*" Petrovitch went to kick the prone Newcomen, and this time the hand clamped tight.

"What are you doing?" Avaiq pulled him around, and Petrovitch finally remembered it wasn't just him and Newcomen. "He's down. Beaten."

"I want to make him realise what he's done."

Grabbing a handful of Newcomen's parka, Petrovitch lifted the man bodily off the ground and threw him in the direction of the frozen river. He landed heavily, slid a little, dug in through the crust of surface snow to the soft powder beneath.

"Petrovitch, you have to stop." Avaiq stood between them.

"He needs to know."

Newcomen, shaking snow from his head, half sat, half lay on the ground. "What? What do I need to know?"

"Look behind you."

"Do you really think I'm going to—"

"Just look. There. Right there. That's where it came down. Part of it. It fell from the sky and came down right there."

Newcomen finally looked over his shoulder, and saw the ice ring. "What are you saying? What is that?"

"It's an impact crater. It's an impact crater made by the re-entry vehicle from an alien spaceship that the United States of America shot down using SkyShield. A spaceship that had a working fusion drive, a spaceship that exploded in the atmosphere some twenty k south of Deadhorse, a spaceship that started its journey around another *yebani* star and made it all the way here across light years of nothing, only to get blown up as it arrives — by you!"

Newcomen was looking alternately at the crash site and Petrovitch. "You're ragging on me."

"Ragging on you, Farm Boy? Does it look like we're ragging on you?" Spinning around, Petrovitch held his arms out wide. "Didn't your handlers explain this to you? This is what it's all been about. From start to finish. My little girl found an alien spaceship in her back yard." He pointed to Avaiq. "This man saw it. He was here when they opened it."

Newcomen's eyes were suddenly bright with fever. "Opened it?"

"Yeah. Opened it." Petrovitch glanced at Avaiq. "You did open it, right?"

"Of course we opened it. What were we supposed to do? We thought there might be someone inside. Someone who needed our help."

Now Newcomen was slithering backwards, pushing with his hands, trying to distance himself from Petrovitch and Avaiq. "Get away from me." His voice started off normal and ended in a low moan. "Get away! You said it was the Chinese. You said!"

"I was wrong," called Petrovitch. "It wasn't the Chinese after all. I should have worked it out a long time ago, but your lot have known ever since the beginning. They've got what's left of it after they hit it with a cloud of tungsten flechettes and forced it to break up in our atmosphere. They came here and took everything, hoping to make it look like nothing ever happened."

"Nothing did happen here," screamed Newcomen. "Nothing. Nothing at all. No aliens. No spaceships. Nothing."

Avaiq, listening, called out: "That's not true." Petrovitch turned to stare, and he added quietly: "About them taking everything."

The final piece of the jigsaw slotted home, and Petrovitch shivered with anticipation.

"What was it?"

Avaiq shrugged, his parka rising and falling. "I don't know. A thing. She's got it with her. She might have even figured out what it is by now." He nodded at Newcomen. "Why is he acting like this?"

"I don't think it's an act," said Petrovitch. "I think he's genuinely lost it."

"I want to take you to your daughter, and we're just wasting time here." The Inuit regarded the sky. "You need to do something about him – either leave him, or . . . whatever."

"Tempting, but no."

Petrovitch advanced on Newcomen, and the struggle was brief and to the point. Newcomen tried to keep the smaller man away, using the still-tethered pistol as a club. Petrovitch grabbed it, ripped it free, threw it away and slapped him on the side of his head with his left hand. It was like being hit with a bag of bolts.

"It could have been different. It should have been different.

Yobany stos, I was actually starting to like you. I was even ashamed of lying to you." Petrovitch went through Newcomen's pockets for the snowmobile key. "It was Tabletop who suggested the bomb: the others agreed, and I fought it all the way. I beat them down to faking it. I still went along with it, though, so yeah. I was ashamed."

He found the key, a silver bar with a plastic fob, and straightened up.

"We were meant," Newcomen slurred, "we were meant to be alone."

"I hate to break it to you, but it doesn't look that way."

"You're wrong. They're wrong. It's all a mistake."

"It's too late for that, Newcomen. You can't pretend. We're going to get Lucy. Good luck with whatever it is you decide to do now. I'm sure someone will come for you at some point. Maybe even before you freeze to death." As he limped away, he told Michael: "Terminate his link. He won't be needing it again."

36

The closer they drew to the coast, the foggier it grew, until they were driving in a bubble caused by their own existence. Beyond, there was nothing, and the rest of the world could have ceased to be. Almost.

[Sasha. What do you propose we do?]

"I don't know. Someone must have come up with a good idea." Petrovitch followed Avaiq down the frozen river towards the sea, behind but not directly so because of the snow that the tracks kicked up.

[There are plenty of suggestions. Some are mutually exclusive. Others could be joined together to form a more-or-less coherent strategy. But there is no unanimity. On a decision as momentous as this, we should reach a broad consensus rather than a simple majority.]

"So give me a rundown of the factions. Not the personalities, just the proposals."

[The first faction is centred around the idea that we should keep this discovery secret.]

"We don't keep secrets. In fact, we're in this *pizdets* because the Yanks wanted to keep it secret."

[A point that is not lost on the plan's advocates. However, they suggest that the secrecy only lasts as long as you and Lucy are within the borders of the United States. Once you have been successfully extracted, along with whatever artefacts Lucy has been able to retrieve, we will make an announcement. By maintaining our silence, they believe the Americans will be fooled into thinking you have died.]

"That has its merits. Next."

[Another faction believes we should use distraction to cover your escape, most likely by launching a massive information war on key US infrastructure targets, perhaps aided by the Chinese, in the hope that they will be too busy firefighting those to track you down. I have pointed out that not only is the result in doubt, but the methods used in the Jihad attack on SkyShield depended on careful planning, an unsuspecting target and the preplanting of code. Still, people remember the success while not appreciating the level of difficulty.]

"It also gives the game away that Lucy's still around. We're smarter than that. Who else?"

[The third faction supports full and total disclosure of all the data we have gathered so far, and the release of more as and when we are in a position to disseminate it. They believe that by neutralising the secrecy element, we disarm the Americans' need to silence either you or Lucy – your deaths would become counterproductive to their cause.]

"That's hardly a comfort to me if they do it out of spite. I die, Lucy dies, and all the evidence ends up locked in a crate in Area Fifty-One." Petrovitch considered all the plans. Each one held out the promise of escape, but none of them were foolproof. The variables, the uncertainty involved: none of them were brilliant.

[So the Silence faction and the Open faction are in conflict. Each is attempting to enlist supporters of the Attack faction, but the Open faction hold the ultimate veto. While I can block their Freezone-based discussions from entering the infosphere at large, I cannot prevent any of them from simply talking to another human being. Not all of the Freezone is on the island of Ireland. It is only a matter of time before the news leaks, in a haphazard, partial, and uncontrolled way.]

Petrovitch drove on. He guessed where Avaiq was taking him: to the spot where the video had been made. There had been some sort of camp there. Which begged the question, why hadn't it been found?

[Sasha?]

"I'm thinking. I'm cold, I'm hungry, bits of me are dropping off, I've been blown up and shot at, I'm pissed off and I have to help decide the fate of the planet and everyone on it. I'd like a few moments."

He realised he was still totally at the mercy of the Americans. If they could find him, they could finish him. Newcomen was right: there'd be no evidence, just a lot of dismissible crazy talk.

So what was important was the evidence. Get that out, whatever it was, and they'd be over the worst. Yes, they could all still die, but that was the point of the Open faction's argument. Death wouldn't matter if the story lived on.

Petrovitch nearly fell off the snowmobile. He slowed down to stop his uncontrolled wobble, and ended up sideways to the river. Avaiq, swaddled up against the freezing wind and with the noise of the engine in his ears, failed to notice. He disappeared into the fog, though the sound of him was clear enough.

"*Yobany stos*," said Petrovitch. "I need to talk to First Vice Premier Zhao."

[He is still at home.]

"I don't care if he's hang-gliding off Everest. He's my go-to man."

[Sasha, you are not authorised to do any deals with the Chinese. There will have to be, at the very least, an ad-hoc. Possibly more.]

"We don't have the time."

[We have to make the time.]

"You know what the Chinese are like! They'll take for ever to come to a decision if we do this through the usual channels. I want to talk to Zhao and make an offer in person. They can change. They can be flexible – remember, Zhao called me."

[The choice is not yours.]

"Well, it should be."

[Every time you rail against having to consult someone else about a course of action that affects the Freezone as a whole and not just you, I have to remind you that you designed the decision-making process, you consciously and deliberately eschewed any special exception for yourself, and you told me that if you were to ever change your mind, I was to have you shot.]

Petrovitch hit the handlebars with both fists. "Bastard."

[Me? Or you?]

"Both of us."

[Shall I convene an ad-hoc while you explain your idea?]

"Yeah. Okay." He reluctantly returned to the business of guiding his snowmobile over the ruts and runnels of the river

SIMON MORDEN

ice. "All three factions have something, but on their own, it's not enough. And you're right, we have to make a decision now, or simply by default a decision will be made for us."

[Your proposal, Sasha. The ad-hoc is waiting.]

"We'll skip the introductions, if that's okay." He could see them, though. Moltzman was one of them, which was both good and bad, because he wouldn't give Petrovitch an easy ride. "The problem is getting out of Alaska, alive, with the artefact that Lucy has. It's two hundred and eighty kilometres to the Canadian border, and the Americans will stop at nothing to prevent us from getting there. What I want to do is sell a share of the artefact. To the Chinese. For a dollar. Are you with me so far?"

[Sight unseen.]

"Yeah, that. Look, we're flogging half of an alien doohickey for less than a six-pack of cheap beer. The price isn't important. What it actually is isn't important either. We could end up with a wiring loom with none of the stuff it attaches to. We could have the equivalent of the entire ship's memory. What is important is that we get it out of the country."

Moltzman leaned in close to his camera. "How far away are you from Lucy? Because you'll have pictures soon enough. Why not wait?"

"Because then we'll know what it is we're selling, and they'll know what it is they're buying. I don't want to run the risk of having to ask Zhao if he wants to buy a pile of melted crap that could have come from anywhere. He commits his government to the purchase now, while neither of us have a clue what it is."

Then O'Malley, a repatriated Irishman, extended his forefinger from his big fist and shook it at Petrovitch. "We don't actually

338

own this whatever-it-is, do we now? So how can we be selling it?"

[Technically, Lucy Petrovitch has a claim of ownership, since she found the material abandoned. There is no immediate prospect of finding the original owner.]

"Isn't there some law about things that fall from space?"

[I have made a brief overview of Alaskan state law within title thirty-four, chapter forty-five, and I can see no reason why she does not have a valid claim. Certainly she must register her find, but not until the first of November of this year.]

"But," argued O'Malley, "won't the government just say it's theirs?"

[They indisputably will. But they have no basis in law to do so. The law of treasure trove does not apply, Alaska does not escheat abandoned vehicles, and she was not trespassing on the land where the artefact was found.]

"So it is the girl's?"

[Yes.]

"Just not the Freezone's."

[The concept of individual versus corporate ownership temporarily escaped me. Apologies.]

There was a deep and profound silence. After a while, the youngest member of the ad-hoc found the courage to speak up. "We shouldn't make a decision without Lucy." Her brown skin flushed darker with embarrassment, and she lowered her gaze. "I mean, I know you're Sam Petrovitch, and you know we all love you. But . . . you need to ask her. Sorry."

Moltzman gave a frown that threatened to obscure his eyes completely. "I'm sorry too, Doctor. I move we suspend this ad-hoc. Lucy Petrovitch needs to makes the request, not her father."

"*Pizdets*," hissed Petrovitch, and the ad-hoc voted to disband.

SIMON MORDEN

[I still maintain the capacity to be surprised by humans.]

"Surprised? *Yobany stos*, we needed to set this up now. We can't wait."

[And yet wait we must. Lucy's rights as finder cannot be violated simply because you find it expedient. The Freezone holds much in common for its members, yet we still maintain a separation between communal and personal property. She can gift the artefact to whoever she wishes; it is her choice.]

"Why the *huy* did she have to grow up?" Petrovitch gunned the motor on the snowmobile and started chasing Avaiq in earnest.

[I understand that is a common complaint that fathers have against their daughters. Sasha, you have brought her up well. She is intelligent, wise, fearless and kind.]

"Yeah, all those things despite me. She's going to do something stupid: I can feel it in what's left of my bones."

Avaiq's skidoo appeared out of the fog bank, parked up on the east side of the river. He was no longer on it. Petrovitch slowed down and coasted to a halt next to it. A single set of footprints led away.

Grabbing his bag, Petrovitch followed the trail across the snow. He felt his heart spin faster, his feet pick up pace in sympathy. Everything suddenly hurt less.

"Lucy? Lucy?"

Out of the fog came a single word.

"Sam?"

Then there she was. Whip-thin despite the swaddling of coats and blankets, her face translucent-pale, her eyes dark and heavy. But she seemed to have all her limbs, and her head.

He dropped his bag and they stumbled towards each other. Even though she was fractionally taller than him, he caught her up and crushed her to him.

340

"Hey, Dad," she said.

"Hey." She smelled of her, of short-term panic and week-long fear, unwashed and unkempt. "You'll never guess what."

"Part of an alien spaceship crash-landed close to the research station, while a decaying fusion drive knocked out electronics for tens of kilometres. You opened it up and took something vital. You then hid out here until either I came to get you or the Americans found you and killed you." He looked over her shoulder. "Where is here, exactly?"

She pushed him away. "How did you know? How could you have possibly known?"

"Some people think I'm quite smart." He kept on looking for some sort of shelter or structure, but couldn't see anything that might resemble one. Avaiq's dark shape appeared, and stood a way off. Petrovitch flipped to infrared: deep blue but for the people and the snowmobiles.

"I would have thought you'd have said it was the Chinese."

"Yeah, that was so this morning. You have to move fast to keep up." He reached out for her and gave her a rattling shake. Nothing fell off. "You okay?"

"If I have to eat another tin of lukewarm beans, I'm going to hurl. I'm tired, cold, stir-crazy, and I've spent the best part of two weeks wondering where the hell you were. What took you so long?"

"You hide pretty well, and Avaiq wasn't exactly advertising where you were," he said. "Where is it, then?"

"Back in the igloo. Come on." She walked towards where Avaiq was, stopping to look back at Petrovitch. "You're limping."

"I jumped from a plane. A flying, burning plane. Doesn't matter."

She took him at face value. "Okay."

"I blew stuff up, too. And we jihaded some teletroopers. That was fun."

"It doesn't sound like they made it easy for you."

"Quite the opposite. They did everything to make sure I could find you. But they were playing a different game, one that ended with you and me eaten by bears."

"And you decided not to go along with it?"

"I never liked rules, did I?"

There was a small hill, a flattish mound some two metres tall. It had a slit at its base, just wide enough to crawl through. It was impossible to see, even when right up close: someone could walk over it and never even notice it was there.

"There," said Lucy. "What d'you think?"

"Not too shabby. I take it you added the thermal blanket."

"Snow," she said. "It's called snow."

"Yeah. But you wanted to make yourself invisible to infrared."

"It took three of us half a day," said Avaiq. "At least it seems to have worked."

"Speaking of which, what happened to Dog-team Guy?"

"Inuuk. He's one of my uncles. He tries to live the old ways. Hunting, fishing. Works a sled team. He can't do it any more: it's the weather, the animals, the community – everything he knew is now wrong, so I help him out. That's what I was doing here, taking him supplies. He," and Avaiq looked away. "The weird shit doesn't scare him. He says he's seen all kinds of things out here alone, on the Slope, in the winter. Yet when we – him, me, your daughter – managed to get the hatch open and this clear Jell-O just pours out? It was all I could do to stop him from running off into the night."

"Like the gel inside impact armour," said Lucy. "It looked, you know . . ."

"Wrong?" offered Petrovitch.

"Very."

"So after we got back here and made her safe, he took off. Towards Barrow. He dragged me and the skidoo back to Deadhorse and didn't stop. I guess he didn't want to hang around any longer than he had to." Avaiq looked glum. "I don't know where he is. Alive, dead, I don't know. I haven't heard anything either way."

"No radio?"

"Broken. Worked before, didn't work after. He wouldn't have used it if he could. He knew we were in the shit." Avaiq looked at Lucy. "You told him yet?"

"I thought he should see for himself."

"Yeah, okay: if you're trying to get my attention, trust me, it's all I can do to hold myself back." Petrovitch eyed the entrance.

"Come on in, then. We've been out in the open long enough already." She lay belly-down in the snow and reached inside the tunnel, pulling herself inside in stages. First her shoulders, then to her waist, then everything down to her knees. Her heels disappeared, and Petrovitch and Avaiq both indicated the other should go next.

"You first," said the Inuit. "I've seen it. Creeps me out enough to know I'm not in a hurry to see it again."

Petrovitch lowered himself until his cheek was pressed against the cold whiteness of the ground. He pushed his bag ahead of him, and a hand reached out to grab the handles. Then, like Lucy, he dragged himself forward.

37

It was dark inside. The blanket of snow above their heads stopped the heat from escaping as well as it prevented the light from outside penetrating through the blocks of ice that formed the dome of the igloo.

The only illumination came from a single candle in a glass jar, tucked into an alcove carved into the wall. Even the stick-thin air hole had an angle in it, in case the glimmering telltale it made gave her away.

Her sleeping bag was on a snow ledge, on a blanket, and the floor was clear apart from two piles of tins and boxes, one for full, and the other for empties. She'd kept it as neat and clean as she could.

"Welcome, be it ever so humble, et cetera." Lucy untoggled her parka – the kit he'd ordered for himself came from the same place as hers did – and let it swing free. "Sam, how are we getting out of this?"

"Had enough?" He searched the shadows. There was a bundle, long and low and slim, wrapped in a sealskin pelt.

She nodded. "No magic bus this time, either."

"The cavalry are coming. This is one of the things we could actually plan for. Their air-defence radar shouldn't pick anything up, and while we can't do anything about the planes being eyeballed, they're coming in over the ocean, in a fog bank, maintaining total radio silence. There's an AWACS platform in the sky that's about to mysteriously develop a fault. We still might have to bust our way out of here the hard way." He took an involuntary step towards the sealskin. "Is that it?"

"Yes." Lucy was momentarily distracted by Avaiq pulling himself in. "When did our lifters leave?"

"About twenty minutes ago. Part of the protocol: I find you, they take off." His mouth twitched. "One of them will try and make it through, with the others lining up to sacrifice themselves to the missiles and guns they'll throw our way."

"Madeleine's on one of them, isn't she?"

"Yeah. So's Tabletop, against all common sense. And Tina." Petrovitch swallowed. Avaiq stood up next to him, his head almost at the ceiling. "Just discussing our escape plan. It's a bit crap, but it might just work."

"A bit crap?"

"Meh. We'll be fine." He got down on his knees and ran his gloved hand over the soft seal fur. He thought he should be able to feel something different, but he was disappointed. "May I?"

"You won't break it, if that's what you mean," said Lucy. She got down on the floor next to him and dug her hands under the pelt, pulling both the object and the skin towards them. She unwrapped it almost casually, as if she'd done it a hundred times.

She probably had. But it was Petrovitch's first.

It looked like a big oval serving dish, curved on both upper and lower surfaces. Its matt grey surface shone dully in the candlelight.

"No space jelly left?"

"It seemed to go from gel to liquid, then evaporate away. I think it was there just to protect this."

Petrovitch pulled his mittens off and laid them by his side. "By the way." He opened his bag and pulled out the components of a link. "Present for you."

"Thanks." She took it from him and unwrapped the curved computer. After she lifted up the polyester fleece she wore under her parka, there were two more layers after that, and only then her bare skin. "I so need a shower."

Petrovitch leaned in close enough for his breath to mist the object's surface. Droplets of water formed on its cold surface, and started to run off. "Low friction."

"It's as slippery as soap. I dropped it. Twice."

"No boom?" He pulled his thin gloves off and added them to the pile.

"No boom." Lucy readjusted her clothing and took up the earpiece.

Petrovitch ran his bare palm over the object. There was no join, or seal, or button or switch. It appeared completely feature-less. He turned it over, with difficulty because it was so hard to hold, and searched the other side. "So I don't spend time we don't have wondering, does it open?"

"It opens. Took me long enough to work it out, and then only by accident." She screwed up one eye as the earpiece clamped on inside her ear. "Hey, Michael."

She smiled at the response.

On a whim, Petrovitch flicked his eyes to see infrared. It was a completely uniform temperature. He pressed his hand against it, and the heat just leaked away. When he took his hand off again, the whole of it was very slightly warmer.

"Superconductor of heat," he said. On a whim, he tried ultraviolet. There was nothing. He flipped the object again – it was heavy, but not suspiciously so – and saw, in faintly glowing outlines, a block of symbols in between two largish circles.

"You can't see UV, can you?"

Lucy frowned. "Well, no. Being completely biological and all."

"You missed the writing."

"There's writing?" She went back into the bag for her screen. "Show me."

Michael fed her real-time images – barring the lag of transmitting the feed up to a satellite and beaming it back down again – so that she could see what Petrovitch saw.

"How was I supposed to know?" She moved her finger over the surface. It obscured some of the angular symbols. "I've been in the dark for eighteen hours a day."

Lucy held up the screen so Avaiq could see. He took the little rectangle in his hands and stared. "Doesn't look like any letters I've ever seen before."

"I think you'll find," said Lucy, "that's only to be expected, given where this is supposed to have come from."

"And those circles? That's where you put your hands."

"Which would have made it obvious from the start."

Petrovitch rubbed his palms on his trousers. "Do I say a magic word or something? Abracadabra?"

"What do you think?" said Lucy.

"Just checking." He put one palm on the glowing disc on

the left, then his other on the right. Nothing happened for long enough to allow him to raise an eyebrow and glance at Lucy.

Then the writing faded, and a crack appeared down the centre line of the object; simultaneously, another fissure ran around the whole circumference. The object started to split apart, two halves of the lid folding upwards.

Inside was . . .

"*Yobany stos.*"

"That's what we thought."

It looked exactly like an alien weapon should. It had a black barrel, surrounded by a split four-piece blued metal shield that ran its length. The grip was designed for something that didn't have an opposable thumb, and was embedded inside the device, so that the user would have the shield covering their forearm.

It was held in the case in a tightly fitting surround that was almost invisible. "Is that an aerogel?" asked Petrovitch, poking it.

"Only you could be more interested in the packing than the cargo." Lucy reached out and picked up the device. It resisted for a moment, then popped free.

She held it in both hands and presented it to him.

Petrovitch's mouth was suddenly dry. "This, this is stupid."

"When has that ever stopped you?" She proffered it again.

"It looks like a *yebani* ray gun!"

"We know. That's why we hid it."

"Why are aliens we've never met sending us hardware like this?"

Lucy finally forced the thing on him. "I've had nothing to do but think of possible answers to that question. Lying here in the dark, with it just there at my feet."

He hefted it, checking its weight. It didn't seem particularly dense, but it was strong and rigid. The material it was made from – he daren't call it metal, even though that was what it closely resembled – was cold to the touch.

He peered down the barrel. There was no hint of a mechanism inside.

"I take it you haven't . . ."

"We don't even know if it is a weapon. It could be anything at all. And if it is, using it could be a sign that we should all die."

"Or that if we don't, we're all doomed."

"Or it could perform some sort of ceremonial function, like giving gifts of whisky and rifles. What if it needs bullets, or a power pack, or a password, or we've accidentally left the second part of it in the pod, or there was a second pod that burnt up or fell out to sea?"

"Yeah, okay. I get the idea."

"I've got all these things floating around in my head, and I don't dare find out which one is true."

Petrovitch pointed the barrel downwards and looked at the other end. There was a bulb-like grip, with five thick grooves running down it. It looked like a lemon squeezer with fewer teeth. He could put it in the palm of his hand and close his fingers around it. Whether anyone who didn't have a cybernetic arm could then support the weight of it was just one question amongst many.

"I haven't tried to hold it in what looks like the proper way. There are metal surfaces at the far end of the grip. In the absence of anything else to press, those could be the controls." Lucy pointed out the smooth mirrored insets at the base of the grip, barely visible through the gap in the shield sections.

"I'm holding something from another planet. Another solar

system. Something that travelled trillions of kilometres to get here. Imagine the astrogation needed. All that information, all that technology, gone in a instant." Petrovitch looked up at Lucy. "A starship. And we shot it down."

"Shot it down?" Lucy's eyebrows rose.

"SkyShield." He was tempted just to reach into the device and wrap his fingers around the smooth ridges of the grip. "Railgunned it out of the sky. Even though it was the Americans who did it, do you honestly think that whoever sent this will notice the difference between all our squabbling little factions? We could be in deep shit here. Nova bombs, relativistic kill vehicles, von Neumann swarms. This thing."

[Do you still want to sell half of it to the Chinese?]

Petrovitch blew out a deep breath, and Lucy pulled a face.

"You wanted to do what?"

"It was an idea I had. We still might have to do it, if it means getting out of here alive."

Avaiq stamped his foot. "I want to be in on this conversation. If it concerns me, I want a say."

"Yeah. Sorry." Petrovitch stroked the smooth line of one of the shield panels. "There are people coming to rescue us. Whether or not they can is out of my hands, and is trusting a lot to luck. I wanted to make sure we had a bargaining chip if it came down to a stand-off, and one way would be to sell a share of this to someone with the clout to make the Yanks hold back."

"You can't," said Lucy.

"I know I can't. But apparently you can. It's yours. You found it. You get to decide what happens to it." He reluctantly held it out to her, and she took it from him, cradling it in her arms.

"Is that actually true?" asked Avaiq.

"Apparently. Our tame lawyer reckons that according to Alaskan state law, it's legally Lucy's. I don't think that'll bother the US government one bit, considering they just levelled Deadhorse."

Lucy blinked. "They did?"

"Yeah."

"Is there anything else I should know?" she asked, her voice rising.

He shifted guiltily. "Probably." He really hoped Michael wouldn't tell her about Jason Fyfe. Not just yet.

She gave him a hard stare, but thankfully didn't ask any more questions. "There's always the UN. That way the Chinese have an interest in it, and so does everyone else. Including the Americans."

"If you hand it over to UNESCO, you'll never see it again. I doubt if anyone else will, either. No one will be allowed to touch it because the arguing will go on for decades." Petrovitch flipped over so he could sit down and stretch his leg. "You've realised that this thing is what the aliens considered most important."

"Duh. Getting this to us was the whole point of the mission."

"I wonder if there was a pilot. Or pilots."

Lucy started to say something, then stopped. "I was about to say, we'll never know. But that's not actually true, is it?"

"No. No, it's not. One day I'll ask them."

Avaiq coughed. "Can you two keep your minds on how we're going to save our skins? I'm just a mechanic. I fix stuff. I'm not like you."

Petrovitch rubbed at his face. "Okay. Our lot are about thirty minutes away. We can be back in Canada, if we go in a straight line, in less than three quarters of an hour after that. We've got to cover our arses for an hour and a bit. Any suggestions?"

[There is always the Attack faction. My efforts would be partial, and the effect here would be limited. It would also serve to antagonise the Americans further.]

Both Petrovitch and Lucy shook their heads.

[I am also picking up satellite-bound transmissions from the research station. It is likely that Joseph Newcomen is now in the custody of other US agents.]

"Who?" mouthed Lucy.

"Later," said Petrovitch. "He doesn't know where we are."

[He knows which direction you were heading. They will follow your tracks along the river, and then they will find the vehicles. Then they will find you, no matter how well hidden Lucy's shelter is.]

Lucy kicked him. "I hide out in the middle of nowhere for over a week, and within minutes of you turning up . . ."

"I should have been more careful," said Petrovitch. "I should have shot him."

"What are you talking about?" Avaiq's temper was stirring.

"They've got Newcomen. That means we're going to have company." Petrovitch leaned forward and pressed his fingers into his damaged ankle, feeling for the muscles and ligaments. "About the same time as our lot turn up, so will they."

"Okay," said Lucy. She suddenly launched into a flurry of activity, pushing the weapon thing back into its case and slapping her hands on the two halves of the open lid. "The cold might have made you stupid, but not me. I suggest we run for it rather than wait for certain death. Less futile, slightly healthier."

The artefact's lid folded back down, and the join became a crack, a line, then vanished. She wrapped it up in the sealskin and slid it towards the entrance, then started buttoning up her parka.

"She's right, of course," said Petrovitch.

"Of course I'm right." She pulled on her mittens and gave herself a shake. Clearly, she was missing something. She lifted up her sleeping bag, swept her hand under it, and came out with a ceramic carbine. "Ready. Let's go."

38

Lucy sat behind Petrovitch. Sandwiched between them was the carpet bag: zipped inside it along with all his other kit was the sealskin-wrapped case. He could feel it pressing into his back.

[You are going to run out of land.]

"Yeah, where we're going, we don't need land. The sea ice'll be thick enough." He squinted down at the controls. "I'm more concerned about running out of fuel. These things burn meths like it's going out of fashion."

[Based on the vehicle's previous performance, you have sufficient for another forty-five kilometres. However, Lucy Petrovitch is an extra load on your engine. This will cut the range to around thirty kilometres unless you lower your speed.]

"How about the chasing pack?"

[There are too many unknowns. Judging from the position of the satellite phones some of them carry, they are travelling faster than you. This might mean they catch you up, or it might mean they empty their fuel tanks before they reach you.]

"And this will all happen in the next ten minutes. Those planes out of Eielson? How are they doing?"

[The ones that attacked Deadhorse are returning to base. They have scrambled two more that were not at combat readiness, but since Eielson is some six hundred and forty kilometres away, those aircraft will not be overhead for another half an hour at least.]

"This isn't inspiring me with confidence."

[I can all but guarantee their planes will not find our planes. My chief concern is that they are guided to their target by visual cues given by personnel on the ground.]

"Can you jihad the planes?"

[These are the Wild Weasel variant that are specifically hardened against electronic countermeasures. Sasha, again: just because they are Americans does not mean they are stupid.]

"I'll take that as a no." They were close to the sea. Ahead of them was the pressure ridge of ice that had been forced up on to the shore by the tides that still raised and lowered the water that lay beneath. "In fact, if I didn't know any better, they've got us pretty much where they want us."

[Considering all the resources expended to make sure you were never supposed to get this far, we are technically ahead.]

"Go on, make it worse, why don't you?"

[As you wish. If you cannot locate suitable access, you will need to carry the snowmobiles over the broken littoral zone to reach the flat pack ice.]

"*Yobany stos*, stop it."

Lucy interrupted, speaking over the link even though she had her head against his shoulder blades.

"What are we going to do?" She'd worked it out. Michael had been talking to her at the same time as Petrovitch.

"The obvious thing." Ahead of them, at the mouth of the river, Avaiq had already throttled down. Thick slabs of blue-white ice stood cracked and jumbled in front of him, as chaotic as a Victorian graveyard.

Petrovitch pulled up next to him. He tapped Lucy's hands so he could dismount.

"There's usually a way through along the sand spit that sticks out into the bay," said Avaiq, pointing north-east.

"Good," said Petrovitch. He laid his bag across his seat and unzipped it. He took out the sealskin, and tied it tightly on to the snowmobile's carry-rack.

"Sam? You can't," said Lucy, though she already knew that he could.

"Yeah. I'm doing that thing that fathers do at times like this." He unclipped the axe and threw it into the snow. "So let's assume we've had the argument, the tears, the rest of it, and it turned out that I was right all along. Go."

She unslung her carbine and gave it to him.

"Avaiq will see you safely on to the ice. Michael will guide Maddy to you. There is," and he popped up a map, "a massive iceberg grounded some five k offshore. Make for that."

Avaiq looked confused. "Aren't you . . .?"

"No. No, I'm not. You're going to drive behind to make absolutely certain that the alien doohickey doesn't fall off." Petrovitch threaded his arm through the gun's strap, picked up the bag and the axe, and started towards the ice ridge. Halfway there, he turned and shouted. "What are you waiting for? *Pascha?*"

"Sam?" said Lucy over the link.

"We're not discussing this. You and the artefact go. I stay."

"I just wanted to say that I love you very much and you're the best replacement dad a girl could hope for."

"If I cry, my targeting system won't work properly." He kept on walking. "You can say all this as you drive. Probably better that you don't, though. I don't need distracting."

She slid forward to take Petrovitch's place and opened the throttle. The engine roared, and she drove off, heading east along the coast. Avaiq stared at Petrovitch for a moment, then followed Lucy. The two of them vanished into the fog bank, and he watched the glow of them in infrared fade and wink out.

He looked around. It wasn't the best place to make a last stand, but he guessed that choosing somewhere appropriate wasn't a luxury that most people in his position could afford. He climbed up the ice barricade to the top. He could hear motors buzzing away, but the noise seemed to be coming from all around him. That couldn't be the case, so he slowly turned his head and ran the waveforms through an analyser.

He could discount the two sources behind him. The ones ahead were coming at him in a line, stretched out wide so they could cover the maximum area without losing sight of each other.

That would work to his advantage.

"Tell me as soon as they're picked up."

[Due to the nature of the aerial threat, the Freezone units are maintaining complete radio silence. I have instructed Lucy to do the same. Their links are switched off so they do not emit any radiation at all. Confirmation will come as an audiovisual signal, which you will have to confirm.]

"Distress flare, then. Okay." He checked his pistol, and sorted through his bag for the gifts from the Freezone's weaponsmiths.

A couple of quantum gravity devices: old school, but still terrible. Three pop-ups, which he would have planted already but he'd run out of time. He had a good arm on him to increase their range. A remote, too. He ought to get that going now.

He worked quickly: it came in almost unrecognisable parts that clipped together around a first-order antigravity sphere. The remote would hover at knee height, and move around with little electric fans. On the bottom was a hook, and on that hook he hung one of the gravity bombs.

He talked to the remote, and it hummed into life, rising from his lap and spinning around once. Then it headed off back towards the land, dipping and lifting as it crossed the ground. It would have probably been better if he'd got hold of some white paint from somewhere, but at the very least it'd be a distraction they'd waste bullets on.

He was set. He zipped up the bag and threw it on to the ice behind him, then got into position for sniping. The noise of motorised vehicles grew loud, and the first dark shapes appeared out of the fog. Three of them, thirty metres apart: not the end of the line, but not the middle of it either. Somewhere on the right flank.

Petrovitch pasted the three targets with crosshairs, and let his onboard computer take over. One, two, three. Explosive rounds, meant for protecting a young woman from predatory polar bears, hit the widely separated men within a second. Each projectile bored into a chest, then detonated. One of the skidoos caught fire as stray chemicals ignited leaking fuel. All three drove on, riderless. The snow-rimed shore was marked with stark red blood and ruined, steaming corpses.

The echo of the explosions and the sudden run-on of the snowmobiles before they crashed into the ice wall ahead of them was not as loud as the silence that followed.

Convention dictated that he change position. But he wasn't trying to avoid detection. He was actively courting it.

"How long now?"

[Unknown. I am . . . blind. The Freezone collective are my eyes and ears. To be cut off from any of them is unnatural and wrong.]

"I never thought I'd die this way," said Petrovitch. "*Chyort*, I never thought I'd die. The dreams I had. Kept having. I was old and I still didn't die."

The engine noises cut off, one by one.

"There should be two more to my left, the rest of them over there. They're not talking to each other."

[Because they would rightly surmise I could listen in.]

The flames from the burning snowmobile flickered prettily and started to die down.

"They'll have to overcome me quickly. They have to realise that Lucy is out on the ice, and I've stayed behind. So no subtlety."

He sent the remote rightwards, and picked up the first pop-up. He threw it hard, hard enough that it skittered to the ground only just within his vision, then slid away. That was it; that was all he had to do. Automatics would do the rest.

He launched the other two the other way, towards where he assumed the main force would be attacking from, then took control of the remote.

The image from the fish-eye camera was confusing until he deployed some software to deconvolute it, turning it from a distorted circle into a virtual bubble with him at the centre. He orientated it, and flew it north towards the ice barrier. Cracked ground, heavy with snow, passed underneath, and eventually he found a group of lines – made by two outer runners and a broad, teethed track — that meant someone had passed by.

He turned the remote again, and chased it up the tracks. He'd probably only get one shot at this, so he pushed the fans to their limit. The whine they'd make would be audible, but only if there wasn't other noise around.

The outline of a snowmobile appeared. And another. And a whole bunch more. They'd parked them together, decided on their tactics, and carried on on foot. They were on their way, and there was nothing Petrovitch could do about that.

He could do something about their transport, though. He flew the remote into the middle of the impromptu car park and activated the bomb.

The camera died instantly. He blinked, taking in the wide expanse of snow and ice, and heard the distinctive sharp crack of plastic and shriek of tortured metal. He was too far away to feel the abrupt change in the direction of down, but imagined it all the same: frozen ground breaking free and rushing up, loose snow and anything resting on it drawn in towards a momentary, vast mass.

The fog bank flickered with more burning fuel.

One of the pop-ups went off. Bright green laser light pulsed and died.

"This is it, then."

He stood up and snapped off three more rounds, aiming for the ground just beyond what he could see. The explosions turned the fog bright, and there were the shapes of men lit up inside it.

He tagged them, shot two figures on the shore side, and swung around to go for another on the sea side of the ridge.

The second pop-up blew, driving a chemically powered beam

of light through the quickly calculated centre of mass of another man. The third burnt another, behind him.

Petrovitch's muzzle flashes had given him away, and suddenly the air was full of soft lead and hard ice. Things zipped into his face and punched the surface of his parka. He was bleeding. His leg burned and the finger-sized hole in his trousers spread a dark, wicking stain all around it.

A lull. Maybe they thought they'd killed him. Again. He came up firing, but this time it was his thigh that refused to take his weight. Another two, three, four dead, and the effect of seeing another human being simply torn apart by the force of the burning gases inside them made the others falter, fall back.

Petrovitch crouched down in what little cover he could find, wedged between two blocks of sea ice. His face was pressed against one slab. He could see the tiny bubbles of air caught within it, frozen at the moment the water changed.

He looked up, to the north. Three diffuse stars were fading, sinking to the ocean's surface. He'd almost missed the signal. Almost, but not quite.

"She's been picked up."

[There is a problem . . .] Michael hesitated. [Sasha?]

They started shooting again. His torso was sort-of-hidden. His legs took another two hits, foot and calf. Different legs. The second struck bone and broke it before leaving his flesh. He clamped down on the pain, all his pains, and it left him cloud-high and floating.

"Yeah. Kind of busy."

He was lying on the last gravity bomb. He picked it up in his left hand, flicked the switch, and threw it in the direction of the North Pole.

It drew their fire as it rolled along, bouncing over the almost flat ice that covered the ocean. Why they shot at it was anyone's guess, but before they could destroy it, it destroyed itself.

The ice buckled and heaved. A fountain of glassy green water burst out and rose like a fountain, before losing shape and splashing back down, pushing shards of thick ice away from the hole. The sea continued to slop up and over for a moment, then retreated, quiet once more.

The sky darkened.

Petrovitch took his chance. He'd run out of ideas, time and hope. He was bleeding out. He was dying. Yet directly above him was a descending plane, and he knew his wife was on board, and that she was coming to save him.

First, he had to save himself.

The axe.

He dropped the carbine, wrapped his fingers around the wooden shaft, and threw himself off the ridge of broken ice.

Now they were shooting at the plane, and the people – his people – were at the doors of the plane shooting back. Not just guns: missiles. No one seemed to be looking in his direction as he crashed on to the solid surface of the sea.

No one except a lone, slight figure walking in off the sea, pulling the mist along behind her, her right arm clamped tight by complex alien machinery, her left hand supporting her elbow as she raised the device.

Petrovitch looked up at Lucy just as lightning started to play around her. "Ah, *chyort*." Stupidity did run in the family after all.

Then Newcomen came out of the fog at him, sprinting like he was trying to make a touchdown.

Petrovitch slammed the axe blade into the ice, and gave the mightiest pull on the haft that he could. He was sliding, sliding over the white ice and towards the hole he'd made, that cut through almost a metre of frozen sea to the cold, dark water below.

"Too *yebani* slow, Farm Boy."

They hadn't given Newcomen a gun. If they had, Petrovitch would never have made it. The American dived for his ankles, even as Petrovitch got his fingers into a crack at the edge of the abyss.

He pulled himself forward. The block of ice he was on bobbed, and started to tilt.

"Petrovitch! Don't you dare take the coward's way out." Newcomen lay sprawled on his belly, his hand ineffectually snapping at anything of Petrovitch that might still be in reach. "You've done the wrong thing. Exactly the wrong thing."

The sky above them was brightening, almost blinding, and Newcomen hadn't noticed.

"You have to bring Lucy back."

"She is back," said Petrovitch, and the tablet of ice he was clinging to turned over.

The water closed over his head, as thick as oil and cold as death.

He sank down, and watched the circle of light above him flash momentarily blue. His feet slowly struck the gritty sediment of the seabed, and his legs buckled beneath him. The water clouded with both clay and blood, though only a little of both. He found he was barely underwater at all, this close to the shore. He could reach up and touch the underside of the smooth, sculpted ice, if he wanted to.

He let his heart race. Near-frozen blood coursed through his constricting veins, from his skin to his core. Still conscious, still thinking, even though everything else was shutting down.

[Sasha.]

"My turn for the long sleep now."

[One moment. Help is coming.]

"If they get me out now, I'll die for sure. This way . . ."

[Sasha.]

He disabled the security locks on his heart, and readied himself. The pressure on his lungs was growing, and he bled the air out in a thin stream of bubbles that danced like quicksilver on their way up.

He was empty. He knew he had to breathe in, to make it right. He would, just not yet. He deliberately slowed his heart right down, to almost a stop. He was blacking out, embalmed by the Arctic water, lit by the unnatural sky.

[Sasha?]

39

He was patient, and he waited. He was aware of the waiting, and at the same time unaware of just how long that waiting was. One moment it was interminable, an eternity. The next, a blink, the moment between breaths. Both were the same.

He was nowhere, either. Or somewhere. It was dark – no, not dark, just not there. Then it was light, and he was in a white landscape with no features, no beginning, no end. Again, it was both.

There was nothing to do but wait. He'd chosen this path. He'd choose it again. No point in feeling anything like anger, denial, despair. He'd been right to do what he'd done. Time ran on like a *shinkansen* or crawled like a slug.

He couldn't feel or see or smell or hear. He thought to himself that it was very odd: when Michael had slept, he'd dreamed of a whole universe. Empires that spanned entire galaxies had been born within his imagination. Those same empires had withered and died there, too. Yet Petrovitch seemed to be stuck in this trance, where all moments met and collapsed into timelessness.

But now he could remember that thought. That put it in the past. Unless it had always been in the past, and he had only just remembered it now. Or he had forgotten it a million times, and was surprising himself anew with the memory.

Metaphysics had never been his strong point. If he had had a throat, and lungs, he would have growled.

A tear, a rip, a sharp dragging sensation that felt like half his head coming away. It faded, and it left a row of numbers behind. They clicked over in a steady progression. One was followed by two.

A chequered pattern appeared. Lines. Circles. Colours.

A reboot. That was what was happening. He was rebooting. That information was coming from his eyes.

He'd annoyed himself alive.

Everything was happening in a rush: he was being lifted, thrown up in the air, then falling and landing with such a crack that the abruptness shocked him.

He was in a room. A ward. In a hospital. There were other beds, other patients. There was a ceiling, and ceiling lights, and another really bright burning light that was being shone directly into his right eye.

He tried to jerk his head away. Not only could he not, the light travelled the short distance across his face to burn out some of the receptors in his left eye as well.

He wanted to tell the light to go away. He couldn't talk either. There was a snake in his mouth.

That would be stupid. Snakes didn't do that. It had to be a tube. A tube attached to a ventilator that was hissing away on a trolley next to him. He could just make out the shape of it, but as he couldn't move his eyes, he wasn't sure.

The light receded. It belong to a man in blue scrubs who put it away in his top pocket. He shook his head, walked out of view, and away.

Another figure appeared. As he bent down and peered at Petrovitch, his mop of black hair fell forward over his face.

[It worked, then.]

The voice echoed in his head. He answered the same way. "I don't know yet. Why can't I move? Or feel anything?"

Michael stood in the middle of the bed, his waist projecting above the sheets. He raised a speculative eyebrow. [Considering you have been dead for thirty-three hours, a lengthy recovery is to be expected.]

"Thirty-three? Okay. Best comeback since Lazarus."

Michael's avatar walked through the rest of the bed and affected to look at the equipment surrounding him. The heart monitor registered zero beats, as it ought, and no blood pressure, which it ought not. [Did you dream?] he asked.

"No. I thought I would. I just . . . was."

[Should I tell the others you are awake?]

"Give me a minute first." He tried to blink. It wasn't happening. The heart thing worried him, though. "Is that machine connected? Hang on. I think I need to spin up."

[Your core temperature is still below normal. In fully human patients, therapeutic hypothermia protocols suggest restarting the heart only when thawing is complete. Please go slowly: I am standing by to record the results of this experiment for posterity.]

"So I'm still clinically dead?"

[I believe the diagnosis is mostly dead. Which was the effect you were trying to achieve, after all.]

"I'll take it to a quarter-revolutions, then."

Michael peered down at Petrovitch again. [Welcome back.]

367

"Yeah. I haven't been dead for years. Can't say I miss it." He willed his heart controls into virtual being, and examined the interface carefully. "Here goes."

He slowly nudged the controls forward, and everything started tingling. All sorts of electronic alarms sounded around him, and he was suddenly surrounded by a flurry of medical personnel shouting obscure cant at each other.

On Petrovitch's part, he ignored them because it felt like he was being eaten alive by ants. Pain from one or other part of his body he could deal with. The whole of him? It was tempting just to slow his heart down again, but he wasn't quite done with the meat. Not yet. Not today.

He was cold, unspeakably, indescribably cold. He hadn't realised just how cool they'd kept him, how carefully they were defrosting him. But Michael hadn't gainsaid his course of action, and he trusted his friend wouldn't let him do something that might actually kill him, properly this time.

"Dr Petrovitch?" It was that madman with his torch again. This time, though, his irises closed to pinpoints when it was aimed at him. "Blink if you can hear me."

"Of course I can hear you, you *balvan*. Now get this *yebani* tube out of my gullet before I vomit into my lungs." That was what he wanted to say. Instead, he blinked, slowly and obviously.

"You've woken up early. We need to warm you up carefully, so bear with us." A nurse impaled the canula set in his forearm with a syringe, and squirted the contents into his sluggish bloodstream.

He immediately felt himself slipping away again. "Michael? Is this okay? Am I doing it right?"

Michael's avatar appeared behind the technician who was turning up the heating elements for the pads he was lying between. [You realise the reason they know what your core temperature is is because you've a probe in your anus?]

"Terrific. I have wires up my *zhopu*, and I feel like crap."

[You feel like crap because you are alive, Sasha. I have given the medical team all the information they need to effect your successful recovery and, unsurprisingly, they have previous experience of this procedure. Let them do their jobs.]

The pain continued to flay his skin, but at least he could move his eyes now, and he let his gaze wander. At the far end of the ward, behind the locked double doors, he could see a face pressed against the glass. Madeleine's.

"What happened after I went under the ice?"

[There was, inevitably, a firefight, in which one of our lifters crashed and Lucy used the alien weapon to disintegrate parts of Alaska.]

"Disintegrate?"

[Whilst we have not been able to conduct experiments under laboratory conditions, the device appears to produce a beam that disrupts matter at a molecular level. Energetically.]

"Is she . . .?"

[Lucy Petrovitch is well. The designers were thoughtful enough to include shielding to protect the user. She is currently in the local police station under armed guard. Tabletop is with her. She will come to no harm.]

"So how long was I under the ice for?"

[Twenty-nine minutes and seventeen seconds. You drifted, and they had to make a new hole in the ice. You floated past, eventually.]

Madeleine's expression was set firmly to neutral as she watched. Her arms were above her head, resting on the top of the door frame. Perhaps she'd run out of emotion after pulling her drowned husband out of the frozen sea, and the faint scowl she wore was the only remnant of her grief.

"She knew what I was trying to do, right? That I would have bled out otherwise?"

[Knowing that you had to and watching you do it are, I understand, two very different concepts. One is of the mind. The other is of the heart. She was distraught. She had to be stopped from diving in after you.] Michael walked through the techie to Petrovitch's bedside. [Another thing. Your leg.]

He remembered being shot. At least twice. One bullet had passed clean through his thigh, missing his femoral artery. Another had hit his lower leg, and the only thing holding his foot on had been the friction between his socks and his trousers.

"Is it off?"

[From the lower thigh. The surgeon wanted to try and save the knee, but I persuaded him it would be better for you not to have to undergo long-term and potentially unsuccessful reconstructive surgery.]

They looked at each other, man and machine. "I'm running out of body parts," said Petrovitch.

[If you want, I can show you a graph that predicts your complete replacement with cybernetics within thirty years.]

"Maybe later." At last the burning pain started to recede. "Why are my ears cold?"

[You are wearing a cap which circulates cold water. It is usually used so that chemotherapy patients keep their hair. I suggested it might be useful here.] The avatar shrugged in a very familiar way. [I became an expert in your condition; it was necessary in order to ensure your survival. I would, however, like to discuss my earlier offer of reconstituting your personality as a virtual construct at some point.]

"Earlier offer? That was a decade ago."

[You declined then. Perhaps recent events will cause you to reconsider.]

The doctor came back to Petrovitch's face. He got out his torch again.

"Can you tell him to stop that? I'll shove it up his nose and illuminate the inside of his skull in a minute."

[That would require voluntary movement on your part. Something you lack to a great extent.]

Petrovitch didn't need to move, though. The doctor's phone beeped. He ignored it and carried on with his examination. It chimed again, more insistently, and eventually he pulled back to answer it.

He looked at the screen, and the message on it. He looked at the bed, then back to the phone. He frowned and approached.

"Dr Petrovitch?"

"Yeah. Thanks," Petrovitch typed. "Can we lose the ventilator? It feels wrong. And don't shine your little light in my eyes again. It hurts. And while you're on, I'm fucking freezing and I can feel everything."

"I was warned about this," said the doctor. He told the rest of the intensive care team to stop for a moment, then put his mouth next to Petrovitch's ear. "You're my patient. You'll do as I say."

The phone buzzed with an incoming message. "You'll be saying next you preferred me dead."

"Or I could just let your wife in to see you, and you can sort out who's in charge here with her." He glanced at the door, and Madeleine's gaze flicked from Petrovitch to the phone, and back to Petrovitch. Her expression didn't change. The doctor's did, though. "As next of kin, she gave me written consent. And frankly, I don't want to be the one to piss her off, because she looks ready to take someone's – anyone's – head off with her bare hands. I'd rather that wasn't me."

"I surrender."

"Good. Because we're not set up for repairing decapitations. Now shut up and stop harassing me. You seem to be in control of your faculties, but not your body. That part is my job, and I'll do it the best I can." He muttered something about governments and guns, then put the phone back in his scrubs.

As he retreated, the rest of the staff moved back in to continue what they'd started.

"Michael, I thought she'd be happy."

[She was happy, Sasha. She was happy that for ten years no one was shooting at you or trying to blow you up. Now, as a result of what Lucy has done, everybody will be trying to shoot you and blow you up. And not just you, but her and Lucy, together with the rest of the Freezone. While you were dead, the President of the United States of America called us "the single most dangerous organisation in the history of civilisation". Even accounting for hyperbole, that puts us in a difficult position.]

"Yeah, that's good coming from him. *Mudak*." Petrovitch programmed his heart to spin a little faster. "I wasn't the one who shot down our First Contact."

[All Madeleine can see is a war without end and an immediate future without you. Sooner, rather than later, she believes you will die, and there will be nothing she can do about it. She is already in mourning for you.]

The doctor had gone to the door, and Madeleine had stepped away to let him out. Petrovitch could see them through the glass, her with her head down, listening, and him with his head up, explaining what was going on.

When they were done, she resumed her vigil.

Petrovitch checked to see what was happening outside. The hospital was surrounded by camera crews and reporters, and he dipped into their broadcasts to catch a flavour of what they were saying.

"*Yobany stos.*"

[Did you expect people to react differently?]

"To be honest, I didn't think about how they'd react at all. Who leaked it?"

[There was no leak. Marcus went to the UN, talked to the Secretary General, and addressed the Security Council even before you arrived at hospital.]

"And?"

[There is a very real risk of the United Nations expelling the United States. That pressure is likely to increase over the coming days as governments formulate their official response, rather than just preliminary reactions from their representatives in New York.] Michael's avatar raised his eyebrows. [There is no other news. Some people believe us. Others do not, either because they prefer the lies or they hold, like Joseph Newcomen, that we must be alone in the universe. I change my mind when the facts change. Why won't they?]

"No one said we were a wholly rational species." Petrovitch could move his index finger. Just a little. The sooner he was out of this bed – which was where? Whitehorse? – the sooner he could get to work. It was a good job he didn't need much sleep.

Valentina looked though into the intensive care ward, her thin face even more pinched and pale than usual. As she turned, he could see her *kalash* over her shoulder. This was what it had come to. All because of him.

No: all because of Lucy.

"Good girl," he said.

extras

orbit

meet the author

Dr. Simon Morden is a bona fide rocket scientist, having degrees in geology and planetary geophysics. He was born in Gateshead, England, and now resides in Worthing, England. Find out more about Simon Morden at www.simonmorden.com.

introducing

If you enjoyed
THE CURVE OF THE EARTH,
look out for

GERMLINE

by T. C. McCarthy

*Germline (n.) the genetic material contained in a
cellular lineage that can be passed to the next generation.
Also: secret military program to develop genetically
engineered super-soldiers (slang).*

*War is Oscar Wendell's ticket to greatness. A reporter for
The Stars and Stripes, he has the only one-way pass to the
front lines of a brutal war over natural resources buried
underneath the icy, mineral-rich mountains of Kazakhstan.*

*But war is nothing like he expected. Heavily armored
soldiers battle genetically engineered troops hundreds
of meters below the surface. The genetics—the
germline soldiers—are the key to winning this war,
but some inventions can't be undone. Some
technologies can't be put back in the box.*

extras

Kaz will change everything, not least Oscar himself.
Hooked on a dangerous cocktail of adrenaline and drugs,
Oscar doesn't find the war, the war finds him.

I'll never forget the smell: human waste, the dead, and rubbing alcohol—the smell of a Pulitzer.

The sergeant looked jumpy as he glanced at my ticket. "*Stars and Stripes?*" I couldn't place the accent. New York, maybe. "You'll be the first."

"First what?"

He laughed as if I had made a joke. "The first civilian reporter wiped on the front line. Nobody from the press has ever been allowed up here, not even you guys. We got plenty of armor, rube. Draw some on your way out and button up." He gestured to a pile of used suits, next to which lay a mountain of undersuits, and on my way over, the sergeant shouted to a corporal who had been relaxing against the wall. "Wake up, Chappy. We got a *reporter* needin' some."

Tired. Empty. I'd seen it before in Shymkent, in frontline troops rotating back for a week or two, barely able to walk, with dark circles under their eyes so they looked like nervous raccoons. Chappy had that look too.

He opened one eye. "Reporter?"

"Yep. *Stripes.*"

"Where's your camera?"

I shrugged. "Not allowed one. Security. It's gonna be an audio-only piece."

Chappy frowned, as if I couldn't be a *real* reporter, since I didn't have a holo unit, thought for a moment, and then stood. "If you're going to be the first reporter on the line, I guess we oughta give you something special. What size?"

I knew my size and told him. I'd been through Rube-Hack back in the States; all of us had. The Pentagon called it Basic Battlefield Training, but every grunt I'd met had just laughed at me, and not behind my back. Rube. Babe. Another civilian too stupid to realize that anything was better than Kaz because Kazakhstan was another world, purgatory for those who least deserved it, a vacation for the suicidal, and a novelty for those whose brain chemistry was messed up enough to make them think it would be a cool place to visit. To see firsthand. Only graduates of Rube-Hack thought that last way, actually *wanted* Kaz.

Only reporters.

"*Real* special," he said. Chappy lifted a suit from the pile and dropped it at my feet, then handed me a helmet. Across the back someone had scrawled *forget me not or I'll blow your punk-ass away.* "That guy doesn't need it anymore, got killed before he could suit up, so it's in decent shape."

I tried not to think about it and grabbed an undersuit. "Where's the APC hangar?"

He didn't answer. The man had already slumped against the wall again and didn't bother to open his eyes this time, not even the one.

It took me a few minutes to remember. Sardines. Lips and guts stuffed into a sausage casing. Getting into a suit was hard, like over-packing a suitcase and then trying to close it from the inside. First came the undersuit, a network of hoses and cables. There was one tube that ended in a stretchy latex hood, to be snapped over the end of your you-know-what, and one that ended in a hollow plug (they issued antibacterial lube for *that*), and the plug had a funny belt to keep it from coming out. The alternative was sloshing around in a suit filled with your own waste, and we had been told that on the line you lived in a suit for weeks at a time.

I laughed when it occurred to me that somewhere, you could almost bet on it, there was a certain class of people who didn't mind the plug at all.

Underground meant the jitters. A klick of rock hung overhead so that even though I couldn't see it, I felt its weight crushing down, making the hair on my neck stand straight. These guys *partied* subterrene, prayed for it. You'd recognize it in Shymkent, when you met up with other reporters at the hotel bar and saw Marines—fresh off the line—looking for booze and chicks. Grunts would come in and the waiter would move to seat them on the ground floor and they'd look at him like he was trying to get them killed. They didn't have armor on—it wasn't allowed in Shymkent—so the guys had no defense against heat sensors or motion tracking, and instinct kicked in, reminding them that nothing lived long aboveground. Suddenly they had eyes in the backs of their heads. Line Marines, who until that moment had thought R & R meant safety, began shaking and one or two of them would back against the wall to make sure they couldn't get it from that direction. *How about downstairs? Got anything underground? A basement?* The waiter would realize his mistake then and usher them into the back room to a spiral staircase, into the deep.

The Marines would smile and breathe easy as they pushed to be the first one underground. Not me, though. The underworld was where you buried corpses, and where tunnel collapses guaranteed you'd be dead, sometimes slowly, so I didn't think I could hack it, claustrophobia and all, but didn't have much choice. I wanted the line. Begged for a last chance to prove I could write despite my habit. I even threw a party at the hotel when I found out that I was the only reporter selected for the front, but there was one problem: at the line, everything was down—down and über-tight.

The APC bounced over something on the tunnel floor, and the vehicle's other passenger, a corpsman, grinned. "No shit?" he asked. "A reporter for real?"

I nodded.

"Hell yeah. Check it." I couldn't remember his name but for some reason the corpsman decided to unlock his suit and slip his arm out—what remained of it. Much of the flesh had been replaced by scar tissue so that it looked as though he had been partially eaten by a shark. "Fléchettes. You should do a story on *that*. Got a holo unit?"

"Nah. Not allowed." He gave me the same look as Chappy—*what kind of a reporter are you?*—and it annoyed me because I hadn't been lit lately and was starting to feel a kind of withdrawal, *rough*. I pointed to his arm. "Fléchettes did *that*? I thought they were like needles, porcupine stickers."

"Nah. Pops doesn't use regular fléchettes. Coats 'em with dog shit sometimes, and it's nasty. Hell, a guy can take a couple of fléchette hits and walk away. But not when they've got 'em coated in Baba-Yaga's magic grease. Pops almost cost me the whole thing."

"Pops?"

"Popov. Victor Popovich. The Russians."

He looked about nineteen, but he spoke like he was eighty. You couldn't get used to that, seeing kids half your age, speaking to them, and realizing that in one year, God and war had somehow crammed in decades. Always giving advice as if they knew. They *did* know. Anyone who survived at the line learned more about death than I had ever wanted to know, and as I sat there, the corpsman got that look on his face. *Let me give you some advice…*

"Don't get shot, rube," he said, "and if you do, there's only one option."

The whine of the APC's turbines swelled as it angled downward, and I had to shout. "Yeah? What?"

"Treat *yourself.*" He pointed his fingers like a pistol and placed them against his temple. The corpsman grinned, as if it was the funniest thing he had ever heard.

Marines in green armor rested against the curved walls of the tunnel and everything seemed slippery. Slick. Their ceramic armor was slick, and the tunnel walls had been melted by a fusion borer so that they shone like the inside of an empty soda can, slick, slick, and double slick. My helmet hung from a strap against my hip and banged with every step, so I felt as though it were a cowbell, calling everyone's attention.

First thing I noticed on the line? Everyone had a beard except me. The Marines stared as though I were a movie star, something out of place, and even though I wore the armor of a subterrener—one of Vulcan's apostles—mine didn't fit quite right, hadn't been scuffed in the right places or buckled just *so* because they all knew the best way, the way a veteran would have suited up. I asked once, in Shymkent, "Hey, Marine, how come you guys all wear beards?" He smiled and reached for his, his smile fading when he realized it had been shaved. The guy even looked around for it, like it fell off or something. "'Cause it keeps the chafing down," he said. "Ever try sleeping and eating with a bucket strapped around your face twenty-four seven?" I hadn't. Early in the war, the Third required their Marines to shave their heads and faces before going on leave—to keep lice from getting it on behind the lines—but here in the underworld the Marines' hair was theirs, a cushion between them and the vision hood that clung tightly but never fit quite right, leaving blisters on anyone bald.

Not having a beard made me unique.

A captain grabbed my arm. "Who the hell are you?"

"Wendell. *Stars and Stripes*, civilian DOD."

"No shit?" The captain looked surprised at first but then smiled. "Who are you hooking up with?"

"Second Battalion, Baker."

"That's us." He slapped me on the back and turned to his men. "Listen up. This here is Wendell, a reporter from the Western world. He'll be joining us on the line, so if you're nice, he might put you in the news vids."

I didn't have the heart to say it again, to tell them that I didn't have a camera and, oh, by the way, I spent most of my time so high that I could barely piece a story together.

"Captain," I said. "Where are we headed?"

"Straight into boredom. You came at the right time. Rumor is that Popov is too tired to push, and we're not going to push him. We'll be taking a siesta just west of Pavlodar, about three klicks north of here, Z minus four klicks. Plenty of rock between us and the plasma."

I had seen a collection of civilian mining equipment in the APC hangar, looking out of place, and wondered. Fusion borers, piping, and conveyors, all of it painted orange with black stripes. Someone had tried to hide it under layers of camouflage netting, like a teenager would hide his stash, just in case Mom didn't buy the *I-don't*-do-*drugs, you-don't*-need-*to-search-my-room* argument.

"What about the gear in the hangar—the mining rigs?" I asked.

A few of the closest Marines had been bantering and fell silent while the captain glared at me. "What rigs?"

"The stuff back in the hangar. Looked like civilian mining stuff."

385

He turned and headed toward the front of his column. "Keep up, rube. We're not coming back if you get lost."

Land mines. Words were land mines. I wasn't part of the family, wasn't even close to being one of them, and my exposure to the war had so far been limited to jerking off Marines when they stepped off the transport pad in Shymkent, hoping to get a money shot interview, the real deal. *Hey, Lieutenant, what's it like? Got anyone back home you wanna say hi to?* Their looks said it all. Total confusion, like, *Where am I?* We came from two different worlds, and in Shymkent they stepped into mine, where plasma artillery and autonomous ground attack drones were things to be talked about openly—irreverently and without fear so you could prove to the hot AP betty, just arrived in Kaz, that you knew more than she did, and if she let you in those cotton panties, you'd share *everything*. You would, too. But now I was in *their* world, land of the learn-or-get-out-of-the-way-or-die tribe, and didn't know the language.

A Marine corporal explained it to me, or I never would have figured it out.

"Hey, reporter-guy." He fell in beside me as we walked. "Don't ever mention that shit again."

"What'd I say?"

"Mining gear. They don't bring that crap in unless we're making another push, to try and retake the mines. If we recapture them, the engineers come in and dig as much ore as they can before the Russians hit us to grab it back. Back and forth, it's how the world churns."

There were mines of all kinds in Kaz, trace-metal mines *and* land mines. The trace mines were the worst, because they never blew up; they just spun in place like a buzz saw, chewing, and too tempting to let go. Metal. We'd get it from space someday, but bringing it in was still so expensive that whenever someone stumbled across an earth source, usually deep underground, everyone scrambled. Metal was worth fighting over, bartered for with blood and fléchettes. Kaz proved it. Metals, especially rhenium and all the traces, were all the rage, which was the whole reason for our being there in the first place.

I saw an old movie once, in one of those art houses. It was animated, a cartoon, but I can't remember what it was called. There was a song in it that I'll never forget and one line said it all. "Put your trust in Heavy Metal." Whoever wrote that song must have *seen* Kaz, must have looked far into the beyond.

VISIT THE ORBIT BLOG AT

www.orbitbooks.net

FEATURING

BREAKING NEWS
FORTHCOMING RELEASES
LINKS TO AUTHOR SITES
EXCLUSIVE INTERVIEWS
EARLY EXTRACTS

AND COMMENTARY FROM OUR EDITORS

WITH REGULAR UPDATES FROM OUR TEAM,
ORBITBOOKS.NET IS YOUR SOURCE
FOR ALL THINGS ORBITAL.

WHILE YOU'RE THERE, JOIN OUR E-MAIL LIST
TO RECEIVE INFORMATION ON SPECIAL OFFERS,
GIVEAWAYS, AND MORE.

imagine. explore. engage.